COMING OF AGE IN
YELLOWSTONE NATIONAL PARK

COMING OF AGE IN
YELLOWSTONE NATIONAL PARK

David M. Huffman

Waterside Productions

First Printing, 2022

ISBN-13: 978-1-958848-05-0 print edition
ISBN-13: 978-1-958848-06-7 e-book edition

Waterside Productions
2055 Oxford Ave
Cardiff, CA 92007
www.waterside.com

This book is dedicated to my Yellowstone family.

TABLE OF CONTENTS

Prologue xi

Chapter 1	The Adventure Begins	1
Chapter 2	Getting Acquainted With Old Faithful Inn	10
Chapter 3	Learning The Bells.	19
Chapter 4	Zipper Creek Float Trip	28
Chapter 5	The Gang's All Here	33
Chapter 6	A Night Hike to Observation Point	41
Chapter 7	Best Pick Up Method Ever	49
Chapter 8	Shoot Out At Old Faithful Lodge Rec Center	57
Chapter 9	Near Disaster On Yellowstone Lake	65
Chapter 10	Hotpotting At Norris Geyser Basin	74
Chapter 11	Hanging With Carnival	81
Chapter 12	Sojourn To Flat Mountain Arm	90
Chapter 13	Thank Tauck For The Beer.	102
Chapter 14	Raid On Bats Alley	110
Chapter 15	Grizzly Encounter In Hayden Valley	119
Chapter 16	Respecting Others' Culture and Customs	130
Chapter 17	Dancing In Yellowstone	138
Chapter 18	Fishy Business With One Of America's	
	Foremost Trial Attorneys	144
Chapter 19	Fire At Old Faithful Inn.	157
Chapter 20	Twenty-First Birthday Surprise.	164
Chapter 21	Less Than Respectful Activities?.	173
Chapter 22	Flirting With A Don't Rule	180
Chapter 23	The Shraner Cart	190
Chapter 24	Ms. Yellowstone Is A Sleeper	198

Chapter 25   Buffaloed On The Way To Fairy Falls. 208

Chapter 26   The Bellmen's Banquet. 215

Chapter 27   Farewell To Old Faithful Inn 226

Epilogue. 237

Appendix 241

Acknowledgements. 245

About the Author. 247

PROLOGUE

Almost everyone experiences a 'coming of age' moment in their life. For some, their coming of age moment occurs at a prescribed age when they are accorded rights, privileges and responsibilities of adulthood. But for most people, their coming of age moment doesn't necessarily come at a prescribed age. Rather, their moment arrives at a point in their life when they begin to re-examine and question the customs, practices and beliefs with which they have grown up. For these people, their coming of age experience may result in a totally different individual who lives life with a much larger, more fulfilling perspective.

This story is about one young man who experiences his coming of age moment while working in Yellowstone National Park during the twenty-first summer of his life.

CHAPTER ONE

THE ADVENTURE BEGINS

OFFICE CLOSED UNTIL 8:00 A.M. MONDAY

Dan Johnson reads the handwritten sign taped to the front door of the corporate offices for the Yellowstone Park Company located in Gardiner, Montana and sighs. It's Sunday morning and Dan's late reporting for work. He's almost never late for anything. In fact, Dan sets his wristwatch ten minutes early to avoid any inadvertent tardiness.

Dan knocks on the door repeatedly, but no one answers. He peers through the window of the building where he's supposed to report for his summer job, but sees no one inside. There are no lights on inside the building. Dan looks up and down the street for any signs of life. There are only a few buildings in the entire town of Gardiner, assuming Gardiner really is a town. Dan can see no one anywhere. Gardiner is as deserted as a proverbial ghost town.

Disturbed that he might not even have a job because he has arrived late, Dan notices a piece of gravel on the sidewalk in front of the office building and kicks it into the grass in frustration. He finally sits down on the concrete walkway in front of the building and props his legs up on the large suitcase which contains all of the clothing, jackets and shoes he's brought with him in anticipation of working the next three months in Yellowstone National Park.

Dan stretches out on his back on what little grass grows against the building. He stares vacantly at the late-May Montana morning sky which is a deep blue color dotted by large cumulus clouds of various shades of gray and white. As the sun warms his body, he takes off his high school letterman's jacket-sans the letter- and uses his jacket to pillow his head. Dan closes his eyes to avoid the sun's penetrating rays and begins recalling the events that have led him to this moment.

He recalls that his plan to work in Yellowstone National Park developed during one of his older brother Bill's weekly telephone calls to his parents in late February.

"Dan, your brother wants to speak with you." His father handed the telephone to Dan.

"Hi, Bill?"

Dan immediately recognized the voice that replied. "Hi, Dan. This is Bill."

"Of course it's you. I'd recognize your voice anywhere."

"Dan, I just shared my good news with Mom and Dad. I want to share it with you too."

"What news?"

"Have you heard or read anything about the military wanting to draw down the troops with the Vietnam war winding down?"

"Yes, I'm aware of the situation," said Dan.

"Well, the military asked for volunteers to resign their commissions. I submitted my request and it's been accepted. I'll be out of the military as of June 1st."

Dan's brother Bill had accepted a Naval commission to avoid being drafted several years earlier. As the Vietnam war wound down in the early 1970s and the public's sentiment toward the draft changed, Dan knew that the military was granting early discharges to servicemen.

"That's great," said Dan. "Are you still planning to attend law school after your discharge?"

"I've already been accepted at Indiana University Law School starting in September." Dan could imagine the grin on Bill's face at that moment.

"What do you plan to do in the interim?" asked Dan.

"I plan to work in Yellowstone this summer as a bellman at Old Faithful Inn." Bill had worked a couple of summers as a bellman at Old Faithful Inn in Yellowstone National Park before he'd accepted his Naval commission. Bill continued speaking. "And, I want you to come and work with me in Yellowstone this summer."

Dan paused for a moment. "Bill, I'd love to work with you in Yellowstone, but Mom and Dad are planning to take a trip to Europe this summer. Dad wants me to go with them."

"I know that you've never visited Europe before, but I think Yellowstone would change your life. I know a vice-president in the Yellowstone Park Company who I think would help you get hired as a bellman at Old Faithful Inn this summer. We'd be working together on the Bell Crew."

"Bill, I'm not sure about this."

"Dan, think about the opportunity. If you work as a bellman at Old Faithful Inn, you should save enough money to pay for most of your college expenses next year. You'd be working in the coolest building in our nation's most famous national park. You'd be working with college students from all over the United States. I can't begin to describe how incredible my friendships have been with some of the people who have worked with me in Yellowstone. And, best of all, you'd get to work with me."

"Ha, ha," said Dan. "Actually though, you make a lot of valid points. The thought of working together in Yellowstone does sound fantastic."

"Listen, Dan. I'm using a pay phone and I'm almost out of change so I will make this quick. Contact the Yellowstone Park Company immediately and get an application. The corporate offices are located in Gardiner, Montana. Fill the application out and return it as soon as possible. In the interim, I'll call my contact at YPCO and try to get you on the Bell Crew at Old Faithful Inn."

"Okay," said Dan. "And, Bill, thank you. I really would enjoy working with you this summer."

Dan recalls that he had filled out the application and returned it to the Yellowstone Park Company. With Bill's assistance, he was given a 90-day contract to work as a bellman at Old Faithful Inn starting on the last Saturday of May. Plans were made for him to fly from Chicago to Billings, Montana on the preceding Friday. However, his father hadn't given up on his plan for Dan to go to Europe with his parents that summer. Dan recalls another telephone call from Bill on that Friday.

"Dan, what do you mean? You missed your flight to Billings?" Bill was obviously flabbergasted when he told him the latest development.

"Bill, I'm really sorry, but Dad's been lobbying me to go to Yellowstone next year. He really wants me to go to Europe with him and Mom this summer."

"Is that what you really want to do?"

"Well, I'm not sure," said Dan. "Yellowstone sounds like a lot of fun, but I've never been to Europe and don't know when I will get the opportunity again."

"Dan, can I give you a little brotherly advice?"

"Sure." Dan felt that he needed all the advice he could get.

"I know that going to Europe with Mom and Dad would be fun and educational," said Bill. "But, remember that you chose a different path for college than me. I went away for college and ended up with a lot of debt as a result. You chose for financial reasons to live at home and attend the small college where Dad has been a professor for over 25 years. There's nothing wrong with your decision, but I believe as your brother that it's important for you to experience another way of life different from what you are accustomed. I really want you to reconsider and get on an airplane to Billings."

"Thanks for your advice, Bill. You're right. I probably need to experience something new and different."

Dan recalls his parents' disappointment after telling them that he needed to work in Yellowstone this summer, but his father drove him to Chicago on Saturday and got Dan on a flight that arrived in Billings at almost midnight. Dan took a Greyhound bus from Billings to Livingston, Montana which is located approximately 60 miles north of Yellowstone National Park.

Dan recalls that upon arriving in Livingston early on Sunday morning, he got off the bus with his large suitcase and walked outside the terminal intending to hitchhike to Gardiner. A cold, brisk wind blew off the mountains into his face. He'd worn a lightweight sport coat and tie for traveling which the wind easily pierced. Traffic on Livingston's main street was almost non-existent. So, Dan rubbed his hands together and blew his warm breath into them. He pulled the collar of his sport coat up against his neck and picked up his heavy suitcase by its handle. He then started to slowly walk out of town waiting for a vehicle to stop and give him a ride.

After an hour of walking with no luck hitching a ride, Dan found himself outside the city limits of Livingston. With no structures to block the wind, he'd grown colder and colder. He finally set his suitcase down beside the highway and opened the top to retrieve his letterman's jacket. He took off the sport coat and tie which didn't seem to have helped in attracting someone to stop, and put on his letterman's jacket.

Suddenly, an old dilapidated pickup-actually, it might better be described as an ancient dilapidated pickup-approached slowly and pulled over. An old, really old, cowboy dressed in a plaid flannel shirt with pearl buttons and a big black, crumpled cowboy hat reached over and rolled down the passenger side window.

"Son, do you need a ride?"

Dan was so cold that he could only nod his head up and down. The driver instructed him to toss his suitcase in the bed of the pickup beside the bales of hay and join him in the cab. When Dan sat down in the passenger's side of the bench seat, he rubbed his hands together and put them close to the heater vent. The driver turned up the heater fan, but the pickup was so old that little heat came out of the vent.

"Where are you headed?" asked the driver as he pulled back onto the highway.

"Gardiner," said Dan.

"I'm only going about twenty-five miles, but it may help you out. Why are you headed to Gardiner?"

"I have a summer job to work in Yellowstone National Park and am required to check in at the corporate office in Gardiner. At least I think I have a job. I was supposed to have reported yesterday but was delayed. To be honest, I'm worried about whether they'll still accept me or not."

"Son, I wouldn't worry about that," said the driver. "In this part of the world, good help is always hard to find. Where are you from?"

"I'm from a small town in Indiana. Muncie, Indiana. How about you, do you live around here?"

The driver rubbed the stubble on his weathered face. "Yeah. My Pa homesteaded some land in the late 1880s and the family's lived on the ranch ever since."

"What type of ranch—cattle, sheep, horses, hay, grains?" said Dan.

"Cattle ranch although we do have a lot of horses and grow a lot of grain."

"What type of cattle?"

"White faced mostly, but we've started breeding black angus too."

Dan turned in his seat to look at the cowboy. "Do you mind if I ask how many cattle you have on your ranch?"

"No, I don't mind. The cows are still birthing so we don't have an accurate count yet. But I guess it'll be around 2,000 head once the cows and calves are all counted."

Dan whistled in surprise. "Wow, we have farms in Indiana, but I don't know of anyone who has that many cattle."

As the miles passed, they became better acquainted. The cowboy took his hat off and placed it on the seat between the two of them. Dan noticed that his white hair was receding and the area of his head normally covered by his hat was stark white. The contrast of colors on the cowboy's head reminded him of a two-toned fudgesicle—brown on the bottom and cream colored on top.

"If I drop you off where I planned, you may have trouble catching another ride," said the cowboy. "I have some free time this morning and will take you to Gardiner."

The old pickup finally pulled up outside the corporate offices of the Yellowstone Park Company in Gardiner. Dan got out of the pickup and retrieved his suitcase from the pickup bed. He put the suitcase on the ground and leaned into the cab from the open door on the passenger's side. He took the old cowboy's outstretched hand and shook it warmly.

"I can't tell you how grateful I am for the lift all the way to Gardiner. Thank you," said Dan.

As he started to release his grip on the old cowboy's hand, the older man held onto his hand a moment longer.

"Good luck to you this summer. You'll be in God's country in Yellowstone. Son, if you ever need anything, just let me know. My name's Slim Duncan. Just ask anyone in the Valley for Slim and they'll know how to find me."

Dan watched the old pickup make a u-turn in the road and continued to watch until it faded from sight.

Dan lies on the walkway outside the corporate offices with his eyes closed as he remembers the kindness of the old cowboy. He feels his body cool slightly as if a passing cloud has blocked the sun's warm rays. Dan opens his eyes and sees four people with their bodies bent over peering at his face. All of their eyes are trained on him.

An older woman with a nice smile speaks first. "Are you alright?"

"I'm fine," Dan says.

"What're you doing here?" says an older man.

Dan sits up. "I'm waiting for the office to open so I can report for work."

"We're the Smiths from Ogden," says the woman. "We've brought our seventeen-year-old son Kyle to check in for work this summer in the Park."

As she says this, Mrs. Smith points to a young man who Dan assumes must be Kyle. Kyle wears a white tee shirt, tight jeans and a black leather jacket. He has long hair and a silver band on his left hand. Dan thinks that Kyle doesn't look like a farm kid from Indiana, but he probably is seventeen. Dan is then introduced to a young girl who's Kyle's sister.

The man who must be Mr. Smith says to no one in particular, "There doesn't seem to be anyone around." He turns to Dan. "When does the office open?"

Dan points to the handwritten sign. "I guess tomorrow morning."

Mr. Smith shrugs his shoulders. "Well then, I'm going to see if I can find anyone and figure out what to do."

Mr. Smith leaves everyone waiting there and returns a little later.

"I've arranged for Kyle to spend the night in a motel around the corner," says Mr. Smith. He turns to Dan. "You're welcome to stay there as well since there are two beds in the room. Both of you can check in here at the Yellowstone Park Company offices tomorrow morning."

"Thank you, Mr. Smith," says Dan. "This is very generous."

Dan and the rest of the Smith family follow Mr. Smith to a motel located nearby. Mr. Smith proceeds to check Dan and Kyle into a room.

"Well, I guess we're going to have to leave for home," says Mr. Smith as he extends his hand to shake Dan's hand. Everyone hugs Kyle. Mrs. Smith hugs Dan as well. Before leaving, Mr. Smith pulls his wallet out of his back trouser pocket and takes out a $20 bill. He hands it to Dan.

"This is for you to buy dinner and breakfast for Kyle and yourself."

Dan looks at him. "Thank you, Mr. Smith, for all your kindness."

As soon as Mr. and Mrs. Smith leave with their daughter, Kyle pulls out a pack of cigarettes hidden in his jeans and lights up. He blows smoke out of his nostrils and looks at Dan.

"Do know where I can buy some weed?"

At that moment, Dan laughs inside. He now realizes that Kyle's parents have been so kind to him because they expect him to be Kyle's adult babysitter.

The next morning, Dan wakes up early. He tries to waken his young roommate, but Kyle rolls over and tells him to go away. At precisely 8:00 a.m., Dan's waiting when the Yellowstone Park Company opens the main door to its corporate office in Gardiner, Montana. A gal about his age opens the door and takes the handwritten sign down.

"Are you here to check in for work?"

"Yes," says Dan. "I was supposed to report Saturday, but got delayed. I hope that it won't be a problem."

"No, that's not a problem," says the gal. Dan sighs with relief.

The gal goes behind a desk and pulls a drawer open. She takes a file out of the drawer and opens it. The gal takes several things from the file and hands them to Dan.

"Here's an instruction sheet and your identification card. Go to the back room and Mr. Green will take care of you." The gal points in the direction of the back room.

Dan can't suppress the smile on his face since he now knows for sure that he still has a job. He walks to the back room and is surprised that it appears to be a storage room filled with boxes and an old wooden chair. A man is standing in the room with his back to him.

"Are you Mr. Green?" says Dan.

The man turns to face Dan. "I am indeed. Please take a seat on the chair."

Mr. Green pulls the chair toward him and Dan sits down. He puts an apron over Dan and picks up a comb and scissors.

"Oh, you're a barber," says Dan. "Normally, I like to just take a little off the edges so my hair comes down to the bottom of my ear and slightly over the collar."

Mr. Green laughs. "You're the boss."

As is his normal practice, Dan closes his eyes to catch a little catnap while his hair's being cut. After a considerable amount of snipping, Mr. Green shakes his shoulder softly and hands Dan a mirror.

Dan looks in the mirror and gasps. Mr. Green has sheared off his long hair. Instead of long hair, he now has white sidewalls around both of his ears. Dan feels as naked as a newly shorn sheep.

"Sonny, please walk out to the front of the building and get on the yellow Yellowstone Park Company bus that's parked outside. When enough new employees are onboard, the driver will take all of you to your respective work locations."

An hour later, as the bus heads south along the Gibbon River, Dan presses his face to the window of the bus and watches the Gibbon River flowing through thick stands of lodgepole pine trees. As he watches the ripples and falls of the river, Dan thinks to himself, 'I did it. I made the right decision to work in Yellowstone National Park this summer.'

CHAPTER TWO

GETTING ACQUAINTED WITH OLD FAITHFUL INN

"Those of you working at Old Faithful Inn, this is where you get out," the bus driver announces.

The Yellowstone Park Company bus is parked beside the portico of Old Faithful Inn with the engine idling. Dan walks down the steps of the bus and looks around to acquaint himself with his new home. His eyes look to the right and then to the left. He sees the massive log structure of Old Faithful Inn with its huge red double doors leading into the building. When he looks up, he sees flags flapping in the breeze from flagpoles at the top of the Inn. Dan lets out an involuntary "wow" and slowly walks to the back of the bus to retrieve his suitcase. He enters the building through the huge red double doors, walks twenty feet inside and stops. He slowly lowers his suitcase to the floor as his head looks seven stories upward and seems to swivel as he measures the enormity of the Inn's lobby. His mouth flies open and he murmurs-again involuntarily- "double wow".

Dan feels an arm around his shoulder and notices a young man dressed in dark brown slacks, a tan shirt and a bolo tie with the Yellowstone Park Company emblem standing beside him. The young man's wearing brown laced hiking boots. He's slim but has a muscular build and reddish-sandy colored hair.

"Must be your first time in the Inn. Everyone has the same reaction. They just stop, raise their eyes upward and their mouths fly open at the spectacle," says the young man. "By the way, are you the new bellman?"

"I am. My name is Dan Johnson."

"Glad to meet you. I am Louis Chamborg, but my friends call me Lou." Lou extends his right hand and the two shake hands.

Lou's head slowly moves up and down as he inspects the new bellman. "Are you Bill's brother?"

"Yes, I am," says Dan. "But Bill doesn't arrive until next week."

"I'm new this summer too, but I've heard about Bill and look forward to meeting him when he arrives. C'mon, let me show you around and introduce you to the other bellmen." Lou reaches down and picks up Dan's bag.

"You may not know a lot about the Inn." Lou makes a sweeping motion with his arm and continues. "The Inn was built in 1903-1904 using local logs. The lobby is seven stories tall. The rock in the massive fireplace that you see reaching to the roof was quarried locally. Most of the staff live in dormitories behind the Inn, but the bellmen and a few bar staff live at the top of the Inn in a place called Bats Alley. That's Bats Alley up there."

Lou points up to a staircase and door located above the third-floor mezzanine. Dan follows the arc of Lou's finger to the door which is clearly a floor above the third-floor mezzanine. "The bellmen are like a small fraternity-they come back year after year to work at the Inn, although there are four of us new ones this summer."

As he talks, Lou starts walking toward the staircase across the lobby.

"Let me take my own bag," says Dan. "It's pretty heavy."

Lou shakes his head. "Don't worry about it. There are no elevators in the Inn. That includes the East Wing and the West Wing. Oh, did I mention that the East Wing was built in 1912 and the West Wing in 1928? Believe me, after a few days on the Bells, you won't have any problems carrying heavy bags up and down all these stairs."

Before they reach the foot of the staircase, they hear the voice of a young female with a definite Southern drawl coming from behind them.

"Lou, is this a new bellman?"

Dan and Lou turn to face a pretty young woman who Dan estimates is about the same age as them. She has long brown hair and is wearing red lipstick.

"Yeah, this is Dan Johnson. He just got off the bus," says Lou and turns to Dan. "I forgot to ask, where you are from?"

Dan blushes slightly. "A small town in Indiana."

"This is Mary Ann Betts from Mississippi. She works at the travel desk." Lou points across the lobby to a large counter area with posters taped to the walls which portray various natural features in Yellowstone.

Mary Ann bats her eyes at him. "Well, Dan, we all love the bellmen. I look forward to getting to know you." Mary Ann turns and heads toward the travel counter.

Lou starts walking up the first flight of stairs. As they walk up the stairs towards Bats Alley, Dan looks around and is fascinated by the Inn. Everything seems to be made of wood except the seven-story fireplace. The stairs look like large pine logs were sawed in half and nailed to a frame. The banister railings are made of contorted lodgepole pine and seem highly polished after decades of use. The balusters are gnarled lodgepole pine sticks. The wooden floors are covered in places with red carpet.

As they walk along the second-floor mezzanine to take the stairway up to the third-floor mezzanine, Dan notices that the wooden railing which circles the lobby has chairs and small tables for guests to sit and sip their drinks while watching people mill around the lobby. When they reach the third-floor mezzanine, Dan sees that it is similar to the second-floor mezzanine except there is another wooden stairway on the right side with a chain across its entrance and a sign that reads: "Closed to the public."

Dan points to the closed area and says, "Where does this stairway go?"

Lou points to what looks like a wooden cage at the top of the roofline. "That's the Crow's Nest. The bellmen access the Crow's Nest and then climb another shorter stairway to a door that opens onto the roof. We use this route to hang the flags on the flagpoles at the top of the Inn."

After climbing the final stairway located at the far side of the third mezzanine, Lou opens the door for Dan. "Welcome to Bats Alley."

Dan steps over the threshold and peers down the hallway. There are doors off the hallway on the left side and the hallway seems to make a slight jog left.

Lou shouts loudly enough so everyone can hear. "New bellman on deck." As he leads Dan down the hallway, faces begin to pop out of rooms like prairie dogs. Lou stops wherever a face appears to introduce Dan.

At the first door, Lou stops. "This is Room 1. Dan, meet Andy Capehart. We actually call him 'Eagle.'"

Dan steps forward and shakes Eagle's meaty hand. "Nice to meet you Eagle. How did you get your nickname?"

Eagle has a thick neck which rests on a well-muscled frame and short clipped brown hair. Eagle appears to be about Dan's age.

Eagle stares intensely at Dan. "On the football team, I played defensive back. I'd lock eyes on the opposing team's ball carrier and attack the ball carrier like an eagle dropping from the sky."

"Ugh, okay. Where do you play football?" says Dan.

"Kansas State, but I tore up my knee during my sophomore year and can't play any longer. Welcome to the Bell Crew." Eagle walks back into his room and closes the door.

The door to Room 2 is closed, but Lou stops briefly. "This room belongs to your brother Bill when he arrives next week."

Lou proceeds to the next door which is open. Standing in the doorway of Room 3 is a blonde-haired young man with blue eyes dressed in his bellman's uniform. His tan shirt is unbuttoned and his bolo tie has been loosened about eight inches. Lou nods toward this young man. "This is Cliffton Louis from Memphis, Tennessee, but we call him 'Chukker.' Chukker, this is Bill's younger brother, Dan."

Chukker steps forward with a big smile on his face. He takes Dan's extended hand and speaks in a Southern drawl. "Ya'll really Bill's little brother?" When Dan nods his head, Chukker pulls Dan close and embraces him in a big bear hug. "Well, I'll be G**D******. You are the little brother of that SonofaB**** Bill Johnson. Don't that beat all. Bill and I worked together on the Bells first at Canyon Village and then here for a year before Bill went into the Service. Welcome little brother to the Bell Crew."

Chukker squeezes him so hard that Dan is almost breathless. Chukker finally releases him and Dan says, "Nice to finally meet you Chukker. Bill has told me a lot about you, but I don't know how you got your nickname."

Chukker looks at Dan as if no one has ever asked him that question before. "Really? H***, I got that nickname a few years ago at a Pow Wow. The fire was burning low so someone asked me to put another log on the fire. H***, I had too much D*** beer but managed to find a log in the darkness. Because of my lack of sobriety, instead of walking over to the fire and carefully adding the log, I just chucked it into the fire from about thirty feet where I was standing. Somebody in an equal lack of sobriety yelled out: 'Chukker, nice toss.' Everyone heard it and the name kinda stuck."

Dan's arm is pulled from behind by Lou. "Dan, we have to keep going."

As they walk to the next door, Chukker calls out. "When will Bill arrive?"

"Next week," Dan yells back.

By now, Lou and Dan are standing in front of Room 4. Waiting in the doorway stands a casually dressed young man who has short traditional clipped brown hair and brown eyes.

"Dan, this is Theodore Nelson, III. We call him 'Ted,'" says Lou. "Ted, this is Dan Johnson."

Dan and Ted each take a step forward and shake hands.

"Dan, where are you from?" says Ted.

"Indiana, and you?"

"Alexandria, Virginia."

"Do you attend college?"

Ted nods his head. "Yeah. Harvard."

Dan doesn't expect this reply and decides it's best to switch the conversation. "How long have you worked in the Park?"

"This is my third year as a bellman at OFI."

"What does OFI mean?" Dan is uncertain with some words and acronyms expressed by Savages, but he's already learned that employees refer to themselves as "Savages" in Yellowstone.

Ted flashes Dan a 'how dumb are you' look, but catches himself and smiles at him. "OFI stands for Old Faithful Inn. Don't worry, Dan. You'll soon learn all the lingo. As with most places, Yellowstone has its own language. Welcome to OFI."

With that, Ted turns and resumes whatever he was doing before Dan arrived.

Lou and Dan walk a few feet and look through the open door into Room 5. The room is small but neat. There's a sink by a window that overlooks the boiler room of the Inn. The room contains a small chest with drawers for clothing on the right and a bunk bed on the left. The top bunk is neatly made up; the lower bunk contains only a mattress. Six hooks line the wall to the right with a single mirror over the sink.

"This is my room," says Lou. "As a new guy, they gave me this room but told me that I'll have to share this room with one of the other new guys. If you want, you can share the room with me. Your other choice is to share room 9 with several guys."

Dan takes a long look around the room and likes how neat everything appears even though it is obvious that the room will be cramped with two young men sharing it. Based on first impression, he also likes Lou.

Dan looks Lou in the eye. "I guess that you have a roommate. I assume that I'm taking the bottom bunk?"

Lou's face breaks into a big smile. He grabs Dan's hand and shakes it. "Great. I know that we're going to have a great summer together." Lou sets Dan's bag down on the floor. "C'mon, I'll show you the rest of Bats Alley."

The two walk out into the hallway and turn left to continue the tour of Bats Alley. Lou motions to his left. "The commode and shower are there. No sinks here since each room has its own sink."

Dan looks at the commode and shower which both seem a little grungy. "When does the maid service come?"

Lou starts laughing so hard that he begins to choke and has to bend over to catch his breath. While bent over, he looks up at Dan. "That's hilarious. The bellmen don't have any maid service. We have to clean our facilities ourselves. Don't worry. You can be sure you'll get your turn and often as one of the new guys. Mac posts a schedule every month on the inside of the bathroom door."

"Who is Mac?"

"Matthew McPherson is his given name, but everyone calls him Mac," says Lou. "Mac is the oldest bellman here and has been Bell Captain for several years. C'mon, let's go introduce you to Mac. He lives in Room 8."

Lou heads for Room 8 and points out the stairwell to their left. "That's the back staircase to Bats Alley. It goes down to the third floor of the Old House which is what we call the original part of the Inn. There are guest rooms below Bats Alley. I hear that the manager, Mr. Baxter, gets complaints from guests all the time about the guys making too much noise in Bats Alley. Mac continually tells all of us to keep the noise down. We aren't supposed to have girls in Bats Alley, but girls are here all the time. I have the impression that Bats Alley is party central around the Inn."

As he passes Rooms 6 and 7, Lou explains that guys who work in the bar occupy those rooms. Lou then knocks on the door to Room 8. The person who opens the door appears to be in his mid- to late-twenties. He has brown wavy hair with a bushy moustache and wears wire-rimmed glasses. His eyes seem to twinkle when he talks.

"Louis, who do we have here?" says Mac as he nods his head toward Dan.

"This is Dan, Bill's younger brother."

Mac gives Dan a long, appraising look and then extends his hand to shake hands with him.

"So, you are Bill's younger brother," says Mac. "You look a little small to be a bellman."

Dan is 5'7" tall and weighs less than 130 pounds with a slender frame. However, Dan's never felt small and believes he can carry his own load as well as any man.

Dan stares at Mac and pauses for a few seconds. "In Europe they used little dogs called dachshunds to go into badger holes and get the badgers out. People poked fun of these dogs and called them wiener dogs. But the truth is, they used them because they were smart and strong enough to hunt one of the fiercest animals known to mankind. I may look small, but I guarantee you that I'll carry my weight around here."

Mac returns his stare for a moment. "D***, I guess you are Bill's brother. Welcome to the Bell Crew, Daniel."

Mac looks at Lou. "Louis, Daniel will be on afternoon crew with you tomorrow. You can show him around and explain what we expect of our bellmen."

Mac nods at him. "Daniel, later this evening I'll bring you a uniform to wear. I'll also give you a master key for the Inn which all of the bellmen possess. It'll open all guest rooms and all of the linen closets located around the Inn. Only my master key will open the manager's suite which is located on the second floor of the Old House. Now if you will excuse me, I'm catching up on some paperwork."

Dan looks into Mac's room. He doesn't see any paperwork, but there is a Playboy magazine laying open on Mac's bed. Mac turns and shuts his door.

Lou tugs on Dan's arm. "Let's go to Room 9."

"Lou, can I ask you a question?"

Lou nods his head. "Why does Mac refer to us by our formal first names?"

Lou looks perplexed and ponders the question before answering. "I never realized it before, but as I think about it, I believe that Mac calls all the new guys by their formal first name. Not sure why though."

They are now standing in front of Room 9. The door's closed. Lou knocks on the door and turns the knob to open the door. He yells, "Anybody in here?" No response comes and Lou leads Dan into the room.

Dan looks around the room. It looks like a large attic with limited head-room. The roof slopes down steeply on each side. There are two sets on single beds on each side of the room. Two of the beds have bare mattresses. Two of the beds have sheets and blankets, but both are unmade. Clothes are strewn around the room. There is a partition wall located at the back of the room with a curtain covering an opening in the middle.

"The other two new bellmen, Larry Bowman and Steven James, live in this part of Room 9," says Lou. "Beyond that curtain, there's another part of the room with a double bed and a window which literally opens onto the roof of the West Wing. Carnival lives in that portion of the room."

Suddenly, the curtain is shoved to one side and there stands a young man with dark straight hair which appears rumpled. He's wearing boxers and a tee shirt. He has rose colored glasses and a thick braided gold chain around his neck. The young man takes off his glasses and rubs his eyes.

"What's happ'ning?"

"Carnival, I want you to meet the new bellman, Dan Johnson," says Lou. "Dan, this is Jerry Colson, but we call him Carnival around here."

Dan steps forward to shake Carnival's hand. "Why does everyone call you Carnival?"

Lou interrupts and says, "There's always a lot of action going on around Carnival."

Carnival smiles weakly. Dan has more questions, but decides it may be better to wait and ask them later.

"Where are Larry and Steve?" Lou asks Carnival.

Carnival shrugs his shoulders. "Working the Bells, I guess."

Lou turns to Dan. "I guess you'll meet them later. As for right now, I have to get dressed and down to work since the rush hour starts around here at 4:00 p.m. most days. Before I go, I'll take you down to the third-floor linen closet and get you some towels, sheets and blankets so you can make up your bed. When I take my dinner break, I'll come up and get you so I can show you the Staffateria where the staff eats."

Just then, they hear a booming voice out in the hallway. "Tour's in." Lou and Dan turn and walk into the hallway. Mac comes out of his room. He buttons the top button of his uniform shirt and cinches his bolo tie. He then shouts, "Okay guys. Let's get hustling. We OFI bellman have standards to maintain."

Like watching firemen answering an alarm, Dan sees Chukker, Eagle and Ted come running out of their rooms in uniform and follow Mac down the back staircase to meet the tour bus and the luggage that await them.

Lou turns around and shouts, "Carnival, are you working tour crew today?"

Carnival shouts back, "No, I'm working Fronts with you and the new guys. I'll see you downstairs in a little bit."

Lou turns back to face Dan. "Welcome to Bats Alley. Now, let's go and get that linen for you so I can get to work."

Later that night, Dan lays in his new bed and reflects on the day's events. Lou had invited Dan to join him and other individuals in some activity, but he indicated that he probably better get to bed early and would join them tomorrow night if anything was happening. As he reflects on the Inn and the individuals who he'd met that day, he thinks to himself that I'm really going to enjoy working in this magnificent place with these people.

Dan falls asleep a short time later with a smile on his face.

CHAPTER THREE

LEARNING THE BELLS

"Let's start talking about the Bells," says Lou.

Lou and Dan are finishing breakfast in the Staffateria. The sun rises early during late May in Yellowstone National Park. The night before, they had left the curtain which hangs over the only window in their room pushed to one side. That morning, the sun's early light had poured into their room and awakened first Dan and then Lou. Dan had gotten out of bed and stood up. Lou had slid down from his upper bunk and walked down the hall to use the facilities and shower. When he returned, Dan followed the same routine. They both finished cleaning up in their room. While getting ready, they worked out a general plan for the morning. Since they didn't have to report for work at the Bell Desk until 11:00 that morning, they decided to dress casually and then get an early breakfast. The Staffateria serves breakfast from 6:30 to 9:00 a.m. Once finished with their breakfast, their plan was for Lou to explain the nature of the work required for bellmen and show Dan more of the Inn.

Each takes a sip of the liquid in their respective cups. Lou's drinking black coffee. Dan's drinking watery hot chocolate which he got from a machine located next to the soda dispenser in the Staffateria.

"Tell me everything that you can about the work as a bellman," says Dan.

Lou takes a few moments to organize his thoughts. "The Bell Crew is divided into a morning crew, also known as the tour crew, and an evening crew. The morning crew normally handles luggage for tours groups that come to OFI by bus. Morning crew works a split shift. When tours arrive in the afternoon, usually between 4:00 and 7:00, they take the luggage from the bus to the Dudes' rooms."

Dan interrupts. "What are Dudes again?"

"Dudes are what we call tourists."

Lou continues with his description of the bellmen's duties. "In the morning, the Dudes leave their suitcases outside their rooms in the hallway. The morning crew collects the bags from the hallway and transport them outside where they line the bags up in rows of ten. They then count the bags to confirm that they have the same number of bags as they checked in. Someone will confirm the count with the tour escort. Once the count is confirmed, the morning crew loads the bags onto the waiting bus. If the crew has pulled luggage for more than one tour, the next bus is pulled forward and that tour's luggage is loaded onto their bus. Seems pretty straightforward, but sometimes there are four to five tours arriving or departing at the same time and it's a real zoo trying to keep the luggage from getting mixed up or delivered to the wrong room."

"The bellmen with the most experience only work the morning crew," says Lou. "These guys are Mac, Chukker, Ted and your brother Bill when he arrives. The rest of us are on afternoon crew, but every week one of the afternoon crew rotates onto the morning crew. Eagle has the rotation spot this week. Since I've only been here for a couple of weeks, I haven't worked on the morning crew yet and can't tell you a lot more about it. I'm sure you'll be on the rotation soon, but if you have more questions now, I suggest you ask Mac."

"No, that's okay," says Dan. "Tell me about the afternoon crew."

Lou takes a sip of his coffee. "The afternoon crew handles Fronts. We do other things as well like answering Dudes' questions at the Bell Desk (Lou lets out an audible groan), getting ice for guests, sometimes directing traffic outside, emptying the ashtrays in the lobby, sweeping the front and back porches, maintaining the fire in the fireplace, and basically doing whatever else we can to make our guests' stay as comfortable as possible."

Dan interrupts him. "What are Fronts again?"

"When a guest arrives, they check in at the Front Desk," says Lou. "They provide their name, address and the license number for their car if they drove one into the Park. They then pay for their lodging at which time the Front Desk clerk finds their assigned room number. Rooms are normally assigned at random the prior night by the night clerk. The Front Desk clerk then takes the key for the room, tears off a small slip of the intake sheet which contains only the guest's name and address and yells 'Front.' A bellman steps forward and takes the key and slip of paper from the Front Desk clerk."

"By the way, we keep a yellow tablet at the Bell Desk on which we write our name every time we return from a Front. This way we know whose turn is next. That bellman's name will be crossed off the list at the Bell Desk and the next bellman at the top of the list will step forward to await the next Front."

"I think I understand that," says Dan. "What happens once the bellman gets the Front?"

"Well, we ask the Dude if he or she needs help with their luggage. If they say 'no,' we provide directions to their room. If they say 'yes,' we follow them out the front door. If their vehicle is parked in front of the Inn, we help them unload their items and then carry their bags to their room. If their vehicle is parked in the front or back parking lots, we ask the Dude to drive their vehicle under the portico so we can help them unload their items. I've been here long enough to understand the saying 'time is money.' It takes too long to walk to the parking lot and back. More importantly, we work hard enough without having to carry bags twice as far."

"Once we get to their room, I unlock the door and let them enter if the room looks in order. Once they enter, I follow and put the luggage on any available luggage racks. I put hanging bags in the closet if the room has one, and if not, I hang the hanging bag on a wall hook. I look to make sure that housekeeping has cleaned the room adequately and that no towels, soaps or shampoos are missing. I always show guests where their thermostat is located and how to operate it since many nights are cold. You do know that Old Faithful Inn is situated at 7200 feet in elevation, don't you?"

Dan shrugs his shoulders. "Of course, I know that. When I started climbing all these stairs yesterday, breathing seemed difficult. I found that I was winded and had to stop several times to catch my breath. Fortunately, it seems much better today."

"In a few days, you'll be fully acclimated to the altitude and not notice it at all," says Lou. "Back to the Bells, you ask the guest if they have any questions or if they need anything else. You are still holding onto the room key. By then, they should be reaching for their wallet or into a pocket or purse to get some money for a gratuity. As you know, bellmen make most of their money on tips. The Company pays us minimum wage which is only $1.10 per hour.

Most people understand the concept of tipping and its importance to people like bellmen who get paid minimum wages. I've only been working the Bells for a couple of weeks, but I've already learned that there are people from certain regions like rural Midwestern states, or from certain areas overseas, where people must not be accustomed to the idea of tipping. However, it usually isn't a problem."

"Do not ever directly ask for a gratuity. If you do and the Dude complains to management, you can get fired. However, I've learned that if you hold the room key and delay leaving, the guest usually catches on and you get a tip."

Dan interrupts again. "How do you delay leaving?"

Lou shrugs his shoulders. "I don't know. Maybe you advise the Dude of the dining room and its hours for dinner and breakfast in the morning. H***, tell them the hours for lunch although 95% of the Dudes will be a hundred miles or more away from the Inn by lunch-time. Maybe you ask if they have seen Old Faithful Geyser erupt or give them the next estimated time. Maybe you suggest they visit the Visitor Center next door or take the boardwalk around the geyser basin. Maybe you indicate they can't leave the area without seeing Morning Glory Pool, Riverside Geyser or even Castle Geyser. Just be creative. Again, my experience is that the more you talk, the more likely they'll get the point!"

Lou stops to catch his breath and Dan says, "Maybe you can show me around a little more so I don't get lost."

They bus their trays in the Staffateria and walk toward the back entrance of the Inn. As they walk, Lou points to the left and says, "Those windows are the Bear Pit which is the Inn's lounge."

"What kind of lounge?" Dan asks naively.

Lou stops and turns to look at Dan. "A bar, you dummy."

Dan mutters, "Oh, that kind of lounge," and looks down at his feet.

"How old are you?" says Lou.

"Twenty, but my birthday is in July."

"Have you never been around alcohol?"

Dan looks up at Lou. "My church doesn't believe in consumption of alcohol. So, no, I haven't been around alcohol much."

Lou looks confused. "A life without alcohol? I've heard about people like that. I'm sorry that I asked the question."

"That's okay. Don't worry about it." Dan feels uncomfortable and puts his hands in the pockets of his trousers.

"Let's get back to your training," says Lou. "The Inn has about 325 rooms for guests. As you probably noticed when you arrived yesterday, the Inn faces north and overlooks the Geyser Basin. The rooms on the east side of the Old House and the east side of the East Wing overlook Old Faithful Geyser itself. It's pretty cool if Old Faithful erupts when checking a guest into one of these rooms. You can see the column of water and spray outside the window. If the window is open, you can hear the whoosh that Old Faithful makes when it erupts."

"Most of the rooms in the Old House don't have bathrooms in the room. There are sinks in the room, but no bathrooms. However, there are men and women's bathrooms in the hallways on every floor on each side of the lobby which are for the common use of the rooms without bathrooms. A few Old House rooms do have private bathrooms which must have been added long after the Inn opened. In the East Wing, most rooms have private baths, but a few don't. Again, there are common bathrooms on each floor for the common use segregated by sex. If you're checking Dudes into a room without a bath, be sure to point out to them where the bathrooms are located. Fortunately, all the rooms in the West Wing have private bathrooms. I guess by 1928, architects and builders had discovered the advantage of private bathrooms."

"The rooms in the Old House are very rustic. The walls, ceilings and floors of Old House rooms are made of wood planed right on the premises from local trees. Because the walls are thin, often you hear noises or voices from nearby rooms when checking Dudes into the Old House rooms. By contrast, the ceilings and walls of the East and West Wings are made from plaster or drywall. The rooms in both wings seem more modern, but they lack the character of the Old House."

By now, they have reached the back door to the Inn. Unlike the magnificent red double doors in front, the back door of the Inn looks rather unassuming. Dan starts to reach for the door knob when the door opens and two young women step out. He recognizes one of the two is Mary Ann, the young gal who he briefly met in the lobby yesterday.

Mary Ann's face lights up when she sees them. "Hi ya'll. Dan, isn't it?" Dan nods his head.

"Hi Sally, Mary Ann," says Lou and nods his head slightly toward both.

"Dan, have you met Sally?" says Mary Ann. "Sally works in the Indian Gift shop."

Dan and Sally exchange pleasantries. Dan turns toward Sally. "What's the Indian Gift Shop? Also, where is it located?"

Sally starts giggling. She puts her hand up to cover her mouth and then removes her hand.

"Honestly, I'd never heard of such a thing as an Indian Gift Shop until I arrived here and someone said 'you're going to work in the 'Indian Gift Shop,'" says Sally. "The Shop is located on your immediate right when you enter the Inn."

Dan vaguely remembers seeing the shop, but had no idea of what's sold in the shop.

"We sell all types of Indian things," says Sally.

"Do you mean things like tomahawks and feathered headdresses?"

Sally starts giggling again. "If you come in shopping for those items, we'll probably send you down to Lower Hams. We sell primarily Indian jewelry made with silver and turquoise and also a lot of woolen blankets made by Indians."

At this point, Mary Ann interrupts. "Ya'll are so cute together. Sally and I are headed to the girl's dormitory and have to get going. Bye guys. Hopefully, we'll see ya'll soon."

Mary Ann grabs Sally's arm and heads off in the direction from which the bellmen have just come.

Lou holds the door open to let Dan enter the building first. As they enter, Dan looks left and sees the lobby's enormous fireplace through the gnarled balusters of the main stairway that leads to the second-floor mezzanine. Dan looks right and sees an "L" shaped counter. The bottom of the counter is made of large coarse rhyolite rock similar to the stone in the lobby fireplace. The counter top is made of some type of Formica.

"This is what we call the Bell Desk," says Lou. "This is where the action happens."

Lou steps behind the counter and shows Dan the shelves underneath the counter. There is a double window at the back of the space which starts about two feet off the floor. Lou points to a wooden wall on the far side of the Bell Desk. "The Inn manager, Mr. Baxter, has his office on the other side of that wall."

Dan walks around the counter and notices a sign hanging above the doorway which says 'Manager.' He peeks in the manager's office. The office is small, but contains a large wooden roll-up desk, a wooden swivel chair pulled back from the desk, a side wooden chair and a couple of filing cabinets. No one's in the office.

Across from the Bell Desk, Dan sees the Front Desk counter which is also "L" shaped like the Bell Desk, but significantly larger than the Bell Desk. The Front Desk counter is made of the same coarse rhyolite rock and has a similar Formica top.

A young woman is leaning over the Front Desk facing them with her elbows on the countertop. Her arms are extended with her hands folded together as if praying. The expression on her face is one of boredom. It looks like the lobby is pretty empty and no one's near the Front Desk. The young woman lowers her head and lets out a long sigh.

Lou notices her and says, "Hi, Laura."

Lou walks toward Laura and Dan follows. "Laura, this is Dan Johnson-a new bellman."

Laura perks up and looks at them. "Hi, Dan. It's nice to meet you. Where are you from?"

"Muncie, Indiana. And you?"

"Madison, Wisconsin-you know, the dairy state," says Laura.

Lou interrupts. "Say, Laura, is Kitty here this morning? I want to introduce Dan to her."

"No, Kitty and Mr. B drove to West Yellowstone this morning to do some shopping. She told me they'd be back by 3:00 this afternoon so Kitty can help with the afternoon rush."

"Who are Kitty and Mr. B?" says Dan.

"Mr. B is Robert Baxter, the Inn's manager," says Lou. "Kitty is his wife. Kitty helps out at the Front Desk."

"Helps out?" snorts Laura. "She makes so many mistakes that we all have a lot more work."

Laura suddenly stops. "Did I really just say that out loud?" Laura puts the back of her left hand to her forehead and extends her right hand out and starts waiving it up and down. "Just ... just forget that I said that."

Lou gives Laura a big wink. "Don't worry, Laura," says Lou. "You're among friends. Our lips are sealed."

"Hello, is there anyone back there who can help me?" someone calls out.

"Sorry, but I gotta go," says Laura and she walks over to help a guest.

"Let's walk the Inn floor-by-floor so you can familiarize yourself with the rooms," says Lou.

The two proceed to walk the Inn floor-by-floor with Lou occasionally stopping to point something out to Dan or tell him something more about the Inn. The East Wing is connected to the Old House by a breezeway. The first floor of the breezeway is enclosed by glass with a door on the geyser side opening to the outside. The second floor of the breezeway is an open deck with railings on both sides. As they walk across this area, Lou glances at Old Faithful Geyser and stops.

"Why are we stopping?" says Dan.

Lou points to the geyser. "I think Old Faithful is about ready to erupt. Let's wait a few minutes and see if it does."

Dan turns to watch the geyser. "How do you know that Old Faithful is ready to erupt?"

"Old Faithful Geyser erupts like clockwork approximately every 30 to 90 minutes," says Lou. "The regularity of its eruptions is how the geyser got its name. After an eruption, someone at the Visitors Center computes the time for the next eruption and posts this information for the public. The estimated time is usually accurate within 10 to 15 minutes. You can often tell when the Geyser will erupt by looking at the numbers of people waiting along the boardwalk. If the boardwalk is fairly empty, it probably will be some time before the next eruption. If there are hundreds or thousands of people waiting, the Geyser probably will erupt soon."

"The funny thing is, you can look at the lobby in the Inn as another indicator. When the time approaches for Old Faithful Geyser to erupt, the lobby clears out and it looks deserted. Following an eruption, hundreds of people walk into the lobby to look around. I guess, in some ways, the people are like the ebb and flow of the tide in the ocean."

Lou pauses for a moment and then continues. "The other way to know that an eruption is coming is to look at Old Faithful Geyser itself. The Geyser has four or five small eruptions before the big event. I've heard some people refer to it as foreplay. I don't understand fully how geysers work, but it seems that these mini-eruptions are just the geyser releasing pressure before the big blowout."

The two wait and watch as the geyser starts making several small eruptions. Suddenly, a plume of water and steam bursts from the ground like a broken fire hydrant accompanied by the sound of a loud whoosh. Dan hears the crowd "ooh" and "awe" and then erupts like the geyser into a cheer of collective approval. Dan watches the spectacle in silent awe.

Lou doesn't take his eyes from this phenomenon. "The eruption of water reaches a height of 120 to 180 feet. The eruption lasts from 3 to 5 minutes typically."

The column of water and steam starts to gradually diminish and it becomes apparent to Dan that the eruption is over.

Lou turns to Dan. "Well, I guess you've now been officially welcomed to Old Faithful Inn by the Old Lady herself. Let's get going so we can finish walking the halls and get dressed for work."

Lou turns and starts walking. Dan starts to follow, but stops to take another look at the Old Lady before following Lou back into the bowels of Old Faithful Inn.

CHAPTER FOUR

ZIPPER CREEK FLOAT TRIP

"Hi, Dan. Come and join us."

Dan has only been a bellman at OFI for six days, but he's already learned that one of the bellmen's favorite hangouts is Hams-or more particularly, Lower Hams. Lower Hams is a log structure like Old Faithful Inn-only older. Henry Klamer built the building in 1897 to serve as the first store in the Old Faithful area. In 1915, Charles Hamilton purchased the Old Faithful Store. He founded Hamilton Stores and would operate a variety of concessions in Yellowstone National Park for the next 88 years. In the early 1970s, there are two Hamilton General Stores in the Old Faithful area: Upper Hams which is located adjacent to the Campers Cabins and Lower Hams which is located just west of Old Faithful Inn. When Savages in the Inn refer to "Hams", they mean the Lower Hams store.

In one end of Lower Hams, general merchandise is sold—all kinds of trinkets for tourists from shot glasses to cheap figurines and all types of clothing. Of course, almost everything has a Yellowstone Park themed logo or image like Old Faithful erupting, a solitary buffalo, a majestic bull elk, a silhouette of Old Faithful Inn or some crazy slogan. At the other end of Lower Hams, a small grocery caters to campers and tourists with essentials like milk, butter, bread, eggs, marshmallows, hot dogs, potato chips, candy, soda and beer.

In between the middle of the building, there is a grill where one can order breakfast in the morning and sandwiches, soups and the like after 11:00 a.m. This area looks like an old-fashioned soda shop. A long wooden bar with a Formica top runs the length of this area. Permanent metal swivel stools with red padded vinyl seats line the bar. Menus, salt and pepper shakers, mustard, ketchup and napkin dispensers are placed on the countertop about every four feet. Behind the counter, Hams employees dressed in white uniforms work the grill and deep fryers. They also serve the customers. On the customer side of the counter, there are about a dozen small tables with wooden chairs. This is the area in Hams where the Bell Crew likes to hang out when on break or not working.

Dan takes an unused chair from an adjoining table and joins Mac, Chukker, Ted and Eagle at their small table. Mac's drinking a cup of coffee. Chukker's slumped in his chair with his legs spread out in front of him. Although it is only 10:00 in the morning, Ted's slurping the last remaining portion of his milkshake through a straw. Eagle just sits in his chair apparently enjoying the comradery of his fellow bellmen.

Mac looks at Dan. "What time does your shift start today?"

"Noon. Have you guys finished pulling all the tours for the morning?" says Dan. He's learned that the bellmen use the term "pull" or "pulling" when referencing picking up the guests' luggage from the hallways, transporting the luggage to the bus and loading the luggage onto the bus when a tour group departs.

"Yeah, we had five tours leave this morning," says Ted.

"Did any of you see that crazy-a**** woman this morning who was carrying a bird cage with a chirpy little bird inside," says Chukker. Everyone shakes their heads and Chukker continues. "This lady comes up to me with her bird and asks if I can carry it to her car for her. I reply: 'Ma'am, we are precluded by National Park Service policy from touching any wildlife in the Park. That includes fowl. I'm truly sorry but I can't help you, Ma'am.'"

"Did you really say that?" says Ted.

Chukker snorts. "H*** yes, I said that. I ain't touching no dirty a**ed, f****** bird for anyone."

"Would the Park Service really stop you from carrying a bird cage for a guest?" asks Dan naively.

"H***, I don't know," says Chukker. "I doubt it, but there was no way in H*** I was going to carry that dumba** bird to that lady's car."

Everyone chuckles.

Two young gals are standing at the counter waiting to be served. Eagle leans back in his chair and says, "Are you new employees?"

The gals turn and look at the bellman. "Yes, we arrived two days ago," says one of the gals.

"Do you work at the Inn?" asks Eagle.

"We do," says the same gal.

"Where do ya'll work?" asks Chukker.

"We work in the dining room at the Inn," says the gal. "I'm a waitress and this is my younger sister Melody. Melody works as a bus person in the dining room. What do all of you do?"

"We're bellmen in the Inn," says Eagle.

"You're the ones who live in the place at the top of the Inn-Bats something or other- right," says the gal.

"Yeah, that's us alright," says Eagle. "Say, why don't you get your order and join us."

"That sounds great," says the gal.

Being the newest bellman, Dan gets up and takes two unoccupied chairs from another table. Everyone moves their chairs back to make room for the two gals. The gals get their sodas and join the guys at the table. The two gals sit down and the gal who's been doing the talking says, "By the way, I'm Penny Hobart. This is my younger sister Melody Hobart."

"I'm Andy Capehart," says Eagle. He then proceeds around the table and introduces each of the other bellman. After introductions are made, Dan tries to draw Melody into the conversation by asking her where the sisters are from.

"We were born in Canada," says Melody. "But we now live in Montana. How about you guys, where are all of you from?"

"A small town in Indiana," says Dan.

"Garden City, Kansas," says Eagle.

"Alexandria, Virginia," says Ted.

"Memphis, Tennessee," says Chukker.

"I guess I'm last. Lander, Wyoming," says Mac.

"Wow, everybody is from all over," says Penny.

There is a pause in the conversation. "Have either of you done anything fun since you arrived?" asks Eagle.

"Not really," says Penny. "We've been pretty busy getting settled and starting our new jobs."

"That's too bad," says Eagle. "There are so many things to do right here around the Inn."

"Oh," says Penny. "Like what kind of things?"

Eagle raises one eyebrow. "Like Zipper Creek float trips."

Penny looks perplexed. "Zipper Creek? I haven't heard of this creek. Does the Park Service really allow float trips on this Zipper Creek?"

"Oh, sure," says Eagle. "Normally only employees are allowed on the float trips. The Park Service is afraid that if word gets out there'll be too many tourists wanting to take these float trips."

Eagle leans back in his chair and winks behind the gals' backs at Dan.

"Say, what time do you have to report for work?" asks Eagle.

"We're working dinner today so we don't have to report until 3:00," says Penny.

"That's great. We could do a Zipper Creek float trip right now. Are you in?" says Eagle.

Penny and Melody look at one another and shrug their shoulders. "Sure, it sounds like fun," says Penny.

Penny, Melody, Eagle, Ted and Dan get to their feet and start to leave. Dan turns back and looks at Mac and Chukker.

"Do either of you want to join us on the float trip?" asks Dan.

Mac and Chukker look at each other and don't move from their chairs.

"I think Chukker and I will take a pass on this one," says Mac.

Dan turns and starts following the other four who are now walking through the east door of Hams. As he walks, Dan's brain starts churning because something seems amiss. Dan's been told that the tiny stream which runs between the Inn and Hams is called Zipper Creek. But Dan finds this strange because the so-called creek looks more like an irrigation ditch. It probably is two feet at its widest and not more than 18 to 24 inches deep. Tall green grass grows on each side of this creek. No one seems to know the source of this water, but it clearly drains into the Firehole River which flows through the Old Faithful Geyser Basin. Dan wonders where these float trips occur.

By the time Dan walks out of the east doorway of Hams, Penny, Melody, Eagle and Ted have crossed the small wooden bridge and are standing in the tall grass on the other side of Zipper Creek. Dan notices that Eagle and Ted have positioned themselves on either side of Melody. Dan stops and watches what happens next.

"When do we get to the raft?" asks Melody.

"We're there," says Eagle.

"I don't understand," says Melody.

As she says these words, Eagle firmly grips her left wrist and Ted firmly grips her right wrist. Melody screams as Penny starts running for the safety of the girl's dormitory which is located just up creek of Zipper Creek. Eagle and Ted reach down and grab Melody's ankles. They start to swing her back and forth.

Eagle starts counting. "One."

Dan doesn't believe it's possible, but Melody's screams get louder.

"Put me down. You can't do this!"

"Two," counts Eagle.

"Stop! Somebody help me, please!"

"Three," counts Eagle.

On the count of "three," Eagle and Ted release Melody at the top of her swing. Melody goes flying through the air and lands in the middle of Zipper Creek on her backside. Melody sits in Zipper Creek for a moment and then scrambles to climb out of the water. She stands up on the Hams side of Zipper Creek dripping wet with her hands balled into fists and sees Dan standing on the porch.

She points her finger at Dan and shouts. "You did this."

Shocked at the accusation, Dan sputters in disbelief. "Me? I ... I didn't know anything about Zipper Creek float trips. Honestly, I had no idea. I didn't know what was going to happen. I'm as surprised as you."

On the Inn side of Zipper Creek, Eagle and Ted are laughing. Eagle shouts, "Did you enjoy your Zipper Creek float trip?" With that, they turn and start walking back up the path to the Inn.

Melody watches them leave. She stomps her right foot. She takes one last glare at Dan and starts walking slowly toward the girl's dormitory. As Dan watches her leave, he thinks to himself that this is one float trip I hope not to take myself.

CHAPTER FIVE
THE GANG'S ALL HERE

"Front please."

Dan steps forward to the Front Desk and Laura hands him the room key along with a small slip of paper which contains the guest's name and address.

"Have a nice stay with us, Mr. Langford," Laura says to the guest. She then looks at Dan and gives him a quick wink. She raises her right hand over her head and says loudly, "Next guest please." A queue has formed in front of Laura and the next guest steps up after Dan motions his Dude to move a few feet away from the Front Desk.

Dan looks at the number on the room key and verifies that the guest is Donald Langford who lives in Evanston, Illinois. Inside, he does a little happy dance. He has now worked on the Bells for seven days and knows that Chicagoans are usually big tippers.

"Welcome to Old Faithful Inn, Mr. Langford," says Dan. "Do you have some luggage that I can help you with?"

Mr. Langford nods. "Yes, thank you."

"Is your car parked in front of the Inn?"

"Yes, right outside."

Mr. Langford heads for the front doors. The two of them walk outside to a Cadillac that is parked under the portico. Inside, Dan does another little happy dance because a Chicagoan driving a Cadillac is often an even bigger tipper.

Mr. Langford opens the trunk with his key as Mrs. Langford and their two young children get out of the automobile. Dan looks in the trunk and thinks to himself that this family isn't traveling light-that's a whole lot of luggage. Mr. Langford helps him take the luggage out of the trunk. Dan lines everything up on the concrete porch. There are four hard-cased Samsonite cases, two garment bags and a hatbox. Mr. Langford starts to reach for some pieces, but Dan says in a friendly way, "Please don't bother. I'll get everything."

Dan thinks to himself that this is his biggest challenge yet as a bellman. At the Inn, the Bell Crew have a few heavy wooden carts which are used exclusively by the morning crew for tours and two small metal carts. The morning crew has first priority of the metal carts, but they can be used by the afternoon crew if available. However, two thoughts occur to him. First, the Langfords are booked into Room 238 which is located on the third floor of the Old House. A cart wouldn't move the luggage very far before he would have to carry them up the stairs. Secondly, he remembers Lou's advice that the more bags you carry, the bigger the tip.

So, Dan positions the two large Samsonite bags with one on each side of his body. Fortunately, the other two Samsonite bags are slightly smaller. Dan puts one smaller Samsonite under each arm and rests them on the edges of the larger bags. Dan puts his right arm through the handle of the hat box. He then loops together the top of the clothes hangers which stick out the top of the two garment bags so that one garment bag is in front and the other behind his body. Dan picks up the handles of the two large Samsonite bags and starts walking into the Inn with the Langford family in tow.

As he walks through the lobby, Dan thinks to himself that Dudes must think that they are seeing an apparition-a pile of luggage with feet walking their way. Dan doesn't have to ask people to move unless their backs are turned to him. Instead, they move quickly to avoid being steamrolled by luggage. As he walks through the lobby, Dan smiles as he remembers carrying a similar load through the lobby a few days earlier and a tourist had asked him to stop so the Dude could snap a picture. He smiles as he remembers his reply—a curt "No!"

By now, Dan reaches the foot of the staircase located by the Bell Desk which leads upstairs to the second-floor mezzanine. He has noticed that when Lou carries similar loads, he's tall enough that he can just lift his arms a bit and walk up the stairs. Because Dan's shorter than Lou, he can't just lift his arms. Instead, he's learned that he has to drag the bags upstairs step-by-step. This results in a sound similar to someone driving a vehicle with a square tire-clunk, clunk, clunk all the way until Dan reaches the top of the stairs.

With great effort, Dan reaches the second-floor mezzanine. His arms burn from exhaustion and he's starting to sweat through his shirt. Dan stops for a minute and sets the larger Samsonite bags on the floor to rest his arms and catch his wind.

"Are you alright?" asks Mr. Langford.

"I'm fine, Sir. My palms are sweaty and I just need a moment to get a better grip on the handles of the bags."

Dan lets out a long breath and grabs the handles again. He repeats the agony again while clunk-clunking his way up the stairs to the third-floor mezzanine.

By the time Dan reaches the third floor, he realizes that he's audibly breathing heavily. His legs feel like spaghetti. He puts the large Samsonite bags down for a second time and tries to catch his breath.

"Not far from here," Dan says to assure the Langfords but, to be fair, more to assure himself.

From the top of the third-floor stairway to the Langford's room, Dan has to fight a mental game every step of the way to keep moving. Every muscle in his body cries 'stop,' but he fights back the pain and keeps shuffling his feet forward.

Finally, Dan reaches Room 238. Sweat is pouring down his face. His shirt is totally soaked. Dan reaches into his pocket for the key and opens the door to let the Langford family enter their room.

One of the children stops as he enters the room and stares at Dan. "Mommy, why is this man's face so red and why is he all wet?"

Embarrassed, Mrs. Langford rushes over and pulls her young son into the room. Without a word, Dan walks in and sets up the folded luggage rack. He puts one of the large suitcases on the rack.

"Mr. Langford, there is only one luggage rack in this room," says Dan.

"That's alright," says Mr. Langford. "Just put the bags in the room and we'll take care of it."

Dan puts the other bags in the room. He hangs the garment bags on wall hooks.

"Mr. Langford, is there anything else that I can do for you," says Dan.

"No, thank you." Mr. Langford then reaches into his back pocket, pulls out his wallet and hands a folded bill to him.

"Thank you, Mr. Langford. Enjoy your stay with us." Dan walks out of the room and closes the door on his way.

Alone in the hallway, Dan bends over and puts his hands on his knees to rest for a moment. A big smile breaks over his face as he looks at a $5 bill in his hand. This is the largest tip Dan has received so far. Normally, Dan would run at a slow gallop back to the Bell Desk to put his name on the sign-in list and then wait for his next Front. However, Dan notices the darkness of his sweat-soaked shirt. He decides it'd probably be better to stop by Bats Alley on his way back and put on a clean shirt. Dan stands upright and puts both hands on his back. He leans backward to stretch his back, then takes one final look at the door to Room 238 and starts slowly walking toward Bats Alley.

Dan's standing by himself at the Bell Desk waiting patiently for a Front. Mac walks up and stops in front of Dan.

"Say, Daniel, when is Bill supposed to arrive?"

"When we spoke last week on the telephone, Bill said he starts on the 8th. That would be tomorrow."

Mac strokes one end of his moustache and then the other end.

"Good," says Mac. "Bill will be the last bellman to arrive for the season. When he arrives, all the crew will finally be at the Inn."

Later that afternoon, business slows. Dan, Lou and Eagle are standing around the Bell Desk waiting for a Front. Eagle is next man up, but no guests are standing anywhere near the Front Desk.

"Do either of you have a date this evening?" asks Eagle.

Lou looks at Dan who shakes his head.

"I don't," says Lou. Although not necessary, Dan chimes in: "Me neither."

Eagle looks at them both and starts laughing.

"Why are you laughing?" asks Lou.

"I don't either," says Eagle. "Look at us-three bellmen at Old Faithful Inn. There are approximately 2,500 college kids working in the Park this summer. Old Faithful is the largest area in the Park in terms of numbers of employees. The ratio's about six gals for every guy. As bellmen, we're near the top of the money chain. And here we are-three bellmen and not one of us has a date for tonight. We're a pretty sorry trio."

Eagle pauses and then smiles. "You know what, I'm going to fix this."

Eagle turns and walks toward the Front Desk. Kitty Baxter, Laura and a young male clerk are standing idly behind the Front Desk chit-chatting with each other.

Eagle calls out, "Laura, can you help me?" He motions for her to come over to where he's standing.

Laura breaks away from the other two and walks to him. "Eagle, how can I help you?"

Eagle has a frown on his face. He lowers his head and whispers, "Laura, my two friends over there are newbies and a little shy. I thought that if you and a couple of your gal pals are free tonight, you could all come up to Bats Alley for a drink. It would help the new guys out."

"What are you offering," Laura whispers back.

"Oh, nothing fancy," says Eagle. "Maybe a few beers and some cheese and crackers?"

"What time?"

"Say 8:30?"

Laura stands up straight. "I'll see what I can do," she says loudly enough so everyone can hear her.

Eagle turns and walks back to Dan and Lou. A big smile breaks over his face.

"Boys, I think I've taken care of our predicament."

At approximately 8:30 that evening, Dan and Lou are sitting on the bed in Eagle's room talking with him.

"Do really think Laura will show and bring two girl friends?" Lou asks Eagle.

Eagle shrugs his shoulders. "Anyone want a beer?"

"I would love to have a brewski," says Lou.

Eagle walks over to his Styrofoam cooler and pops the lid off. The chest is filled with cans of Coors beer covered by ice. He reaches into the cooler and tosses a can to Lou. He then looks at Dan.

"How about you?"

"Thanks, but I brought a coke that I'm going to drink," says Dan.

Even though Dan will be 21 years old next month, a drop of alcohol has never passed his lips. The church that he grew up in had a long list of "Don'ts." Consumption of alcohol may not have been at the top of that list, but it certainly was pretty close. Dan's parents didn't drink alcohol. To his knowledge, none of his grandparents, aunts, uncles or cousins drank alcohol. None of his friends drank alcohol. In fact, before Dan's arrival in Yellowstone, he had never seen anyone consume alcohol. That changed quickly. Beer, and particularly Coors beer, seems to be the drink of choice among the Bell Crew. Dan doesn't feel comfortable drinking, but has been afraid to admit his abstention of alcohol to anyone at Old Faithful.

From the hallway, a female voice speaks. "Knock, knock."

"Come on in," says Eagle.

Laura walks through the door followed by two girl friends, Mary Ann and Sally. Dan looks at Lou who's watching the gals. Dan isn't certain, but believes that Lou's watching Mary Ann in particular.

"Glad you ladies could find your way to Bats Alley," says Eagle.

"Oh, I was talking with Chukker several nights ago and asked about this place called Bats Alley," says Mary Ann. "He was gracious enough to bring me up and show me around. Ya'll live in a very cool place."

Mary Ann flashes a big smile and winks at Lou. Lou's face begins to redden.

Mary Ann Betts practically oozes Southern charm. It's apparent that she takes great care with her makeup and clothes. She's dressed casually but smartly in the best sense.

"Eagle, I heard about your Zipper Creek float trips," says Laura. "Don't even try to fool me into a float trip." She flashes Eagle a big smile but no wink.

Laura Coats has previously told him that she lives in a sorority at her college and has worked one previous summer in the Park. Dan admires her self-assurance. She's clearly in charge of her life.

"What Zipper Creek float trips?" asks Sally.

Eagle jumps right in. "Do you have an interest in taking a Zipper Creek float trip?" He winks at Laura.

Before Sally can respond, Laura says, "Sally, don't fall for that baloney."

"Well then," says Eagle. "Would you gals like a drink?"

All of them nod their heads.

Eagle lifts the top of the cooler again and seems to studiously survey its contents. "It seems you have a choice. You can have Coors or, if you prefer, Coors."

The guys start chuckling at Eagle's humor. It must not have been as funny to the gals since none of them even smiles.

Eagle gives each gal a can of Coors. "Would anyone like some music?" Eagle has a record player sitting on his small dresser and a stack of vinyl records.

"That would be nice," says Sally. Eagle flips through his albums. He selects Abbey Road by the Beatles and starts playing it on the record player.

When the music starts, Laura says dryly, "Nice choice, Eagle."

For the next 45 minutes, the conversation becomes a get-acquainted session. By question and answer, each tells where they grew up, where they attend college, how they came to work at Old Faithful Inn and interesting experiences that have occurred since their arrival.

Suddenly, there's a loud bang at the door. From the other side of the door, a loud voice says, "Andrew, are you in there? Open the door!"

Eagle opens the door and Mac steps into the room. He doesn't look happy.

"D*** it, Andrew," says Mac. "You're playing your music so loud that I can hear it all the way down the hall in my room with the door closed. Turn it down!"

Eagle walks over to the record player to turn the volume down and Mac continues. "Mr. B called me into the office this morning again about a guest's complaint of loud noise coming from Bats Alley. He said that was the second complaint he'd received just this week. And one guest was so mad that he had to refund his money."

Mac pauses to catch his breath. "Mr. B threatened that if the bellmen can't stop partying so much, he's going to move us all into the boys' dormitory." Mac moved his index and middle fingers in synchronization up and down mimicking quotation marks around the words "boys' dormitory." "I'll be God D***** if some young bellmen are going to get us kicked out of Bats Alley! Have you got it?"

Eagle nods his head and looks at Mac. "Yeah, but I have one question?"

Mac glares at him. "What?"

"Do you want a beer?" Eagle smiles.

Mac pauses for a few seconds and looks around the room. He finally sighs. "Yeah, I'll have the regular."

Eagle returns to the cooler and gets a cold Coors for Mac. He tosses the can to him. Mac looks around and sits down on the bed between Laura and Mary Ann. He pops the tab on top of the can and leans his head back to take a long, slow swallow. No one says a word.

Suddenly, there is another knock at the door. Eagle opens it and Bill Johnson walks through the doorway. He spreads his arms wide and says, "I hear there's a party going on here."

Dan jumps up and runs across the room to embrace his brother.

Mac belches and his face then breaks into a big smile. "Well, I'd say the gang's all here now."

CHAPTER SIX
A NIGHT HIKE TO OBSERVATION POINT

The next morning, Dan awakens at 7:15 which is much later than usual, but Dan and Bill had stayed up until the wee hours catching up. Dan shared many of his experiences at the Inn and Bill wanted to learn about the new Savages-particularly the new female Savages.

Dan puts his bare feet on the ground and looks around for Lou, but then remembers that Lou has the split shift today. There's a knock at the door. Dan yells, "Come in" and Bill walks into the room.

"Do you want to have breakfast together?"

"I thought you'd be working this morning," says Dan.

"No. Today was my scheduled arrival date. Mac said to get settled this morning and just show up for work at 4:00 this afternoon."

"Great, just give me fifteen minutes and I'll be ready."

"No problem," says Bill. "I'll go on down to the Staffateria and get a cup of coffee. I'll see you in twenty."

When Dan walks into the Staffateria, he sees Bill sitting with two gals who Dan hasn't met yet. Dan gets his breakfast and walks over to Bill's table. "Do you mind if I join you?"

Bill looks up and motions for him to sit at an empty chair at their table. Dan sits down.

"This is my younger brother Dan," says Bill. "Dan, this is Debbie Wainwright and Betty Smith. Debbie works in the gift shop and Betty is a hostess in the dining room."

Before Dan can say anything, Debbie says in a Southern accent, "Why, Dan, I think you're even cuter than your brother." Debbie flashes a big smile and winks at Bill.

Dan looks at Betty. "Where are you from?"

Before Betty can respond, Debbie interrupts, "Why, Dan, did I embarrass you? Your cheeks look a little flushed." If Dan's cheeks weren't flushed before, they are now.

"No," Dan answers untruthfully.

"Dan, to answer your question, I'm from Boise, Idaho," says Betty.

"And Dan, where are you and Bill from?" Debbie asks.

"Oh, we're from a small town in Indiana."

Debbie claps her hands together. "How charming. A small town in Indiana. And to both be bellmen, too! Isn't the world a wonderful place."

Debbie's hazel eyes are twinkling. Dan's face turns a deeper shade of red. Bill just sits back and chuckles softly as the conversation unfolds, but finally jumps in to save his brother from further embarrassment.

"Dan, don't let your food get cold. Go ahead and eat."

Dan lowers his head and closes his eyes for a few seconds.

When Dan opens his eyes, he sees that Debbie's staring at him.

"Dan, are you not feeling well?"

Dan can feel his face flush. "No, I feel fine. Why do you ask?"

"You lowered your head and closed your eyes for a few moments. I thought that you're either not feeling well or hung over."

Bill starts laughing. "No, Dan and I come from a background where a prayer is said before every meal. We call it 'giving grace.'"

"Oh, I understand," says Debbie. "But I thought people folded their hands when they do a prayer."

Dan has a sudden flashback of going to lunch at a restaurant with his father and one of his father's longtime friends who took Bible courses in college taught by his father. The restaurant was popular and always crowded at lunchtime. When the food arrived, his father's friend suggested that his father say grace and then he got down on his knees beside his chair. To his astonishment, his father got down on his knees too and motioned for Dan to do the same. He didn't hear a word his father said as he prayed out loud. Instead, he kept his eyes open the entire time to see if anyone was watching them. Dan believes that he has never been more embarrassed in his entire life.

"No, many people say grace with their meal," says Bill. "But few fold their hands."

Bill changes the conversation. "Have you gals been to Observation Point yet?"

They both shake their heads.

Betty quickly jumps into the conversation. "Where is Observation Point located?"

"Observation Point's located on the mountainside behind Old Faithful Geyser," says Bill. "You walk outside the front of the Inn, turn right and follow the boardwalk around Old Faithful. You'll walk past Old Faithful Lodge and eventually come to a fork in the boardwalk. There's a sign at the fork to help visitors locate Observation Point. The path to the right leads to Observation Point which is 250 feet higher in elevation than Old Faithful Geyser. Observation Point overlooks the entire Old Faithful area and provides a majestic view of the Upper Geyser Basin."

"How far is the walk?" asks Debbie.

"Not too far. I would guess about a mile. Maybe a little more or less."

Betty chimes in. "It sounds like a place I need to visit."

Bill smiles. "You're in luck. A small group of us plan to hike up there tonight. Would you both like to join us?"

The two girls look at each other and Debbie answers for both. "Count us in. What time?"

"We are all meeting at 10:00 tonight by the Bellmen's Desk in the lobby," says Bill.

Bill gives them all the details and they get up to leave.

When the gals are out of earshot, Dan looks at Bill. "Is there really a small group of people going to Observation Point tonight?"

Bill grins. "There is now."

Dan leaves Bats Alley at approximately 10:50 a.m. dressed for work since he has the 11:00 to 8:00 shift today. As he approaches the Bell Desk, he sees that Mac is engaged in conversation with another guy who Dan guesses must be close in age to Mac. No one else is around. Mac sees Dan in his peripheral vision and motions for him to come over.

"Daniel, this is Scott Oakley, but everyone calls him 'Scotty.' I met Scotty a number of years ago when we were both newbie Savages. We played basketball on opposing teams and had to guard each other."

Scotty interrupts. "Mac, be sure to tell him who won the game that night."

"H***, don't interrupt me, Scotty."

Dan takes a step forward and shakes hands with him. Scotty is tall and clean shaven. His hands and face are deeply tanned. He's wearing jeans and a dirty baseball cap with the words "Ragin Cajun" embroidered across the front.

"Scotty's the manager of the Grant Village marina," says Mac. "Scotty and I are discussing a little business proposition."

Scotty interrupts Mac. "Yeah, I'm trying to build our guided fishing business at Grant Village. As you probably know, there are two marinas located on Yellowstone Lake-ours in Grant Village and the one at Bridge Bay. Bridge Bay gets far more business than my marina. Maybe it's because Bridge Bay's located near Lake Hotel and Lake Lodge. Anyway, I came over here to talk with Mac and see if you guys can help generate some new guided business for us."

Mac jumps back in. "So, Scotty and I've worked out a little business arrangement. Whenever someone makes an inquiry here about fishing, the bellmen will plug how successful tourists are using the Grant Village guides and direct them to Grant Village. If possible, we'll offer to call the marina and reserve a spot for the tourist."

Scotty nods. "In return, the OFI bellmen and their guests will have free use of our boats-not the cabin cruisers that our guides use, but good 16' long aluminum fishing boats with 20 hp Johnson motors. You don't even have to call beforehand to reserve one since we almost always have some available."

"Scotty, we still have one unfinished piece of business," says Mac. "If we're sending business your way, I believe that you should host the entire Bell Crew and their dates and take all of us on a YPCO Scenic Cruiser to a location on the Lake where we can have a Pow Wow."

Dan understands what Mac wants. The Yellowstone Park Company has several large boats which are used to take entire tours on scenic cruises around Lake Yellowstone. The boats probably hold up to 50 or 60 passengers. Without question, they're the largest boats on Yellowstone Lake. A Pow Wow is a Savage name for a party around a large campfire.

Scotty shakes his head slowly from side-to-side. "No, I can't do that, Mac. If I did and the Company found out, I'd probably get fired."

Mac pauses for a few seconds and methodically looks Scotty over from toes to head. Mac twists the corner of his moustache and finally says, "Scotty, I've got an idea. We agree on the free use of fishing boats, but not on the Scenic Cruiser and a Pow Wow. I know you think that you're a pretty good shooter in basketball. How about you and me have a little game of 'Horse.' If you win, no Scenic Cruiser. If I win, the Bell Crew gets the Scenic Cruiser and a Pow Wow on Lake Yellowstone. How about it, Scotty?"

Scotty considers the consequences and is obviously undecided.

"What's the problem, Scotty?" Mac asks. "Are you afraid I'm going to show your sorry a** up?" Mac laughs.

Scotty extends his hand which is accepted by Mac. The parties shake and say in unison, "Deal." They agree to meet the following week at the Old Faithful Lodge rec center and play their game of Horse.

Just then, Mr. Baxter walks out of his office and asks if Mac can see him. Mac walks into Mr. B's office and the door shuts.

Dan turns to Scotty. "I really enjoy fishing. Do you have any recommendations?"

"Fishing's always good around the West Thumb area. Have you ever been to the Southeast Arm of Yellowstone Lake?" Dan shakes his head and Scotty continues. "The Southeast Arm is closed to fishing until June 15th because the Cutthroat trout are spawning until then. If you can get to the Southeast Arm within a week or ten days of the 15th, the fishing's unbelievable."

Just then, Dan hears someone at the Front Desk yell, "Front."

"Scotty, it's been really nice to meet you, but I have to go. I hope to see you soon at the marina."

By 10:00 that evening, a small group of Savages has gathered by the Bell Desk. Bill had told Dan a few hours ago that several people were going to join the group, but Dan's surprised by how many people are actually gathered. The guys include Bill, Chukker, Eagle, Lou and a guy who works in the Bear Pit bar, Graham Callwood. The gals include Debbie, Betty, Mary Ann, Sally and a gal introduced as Mary Farmer. Sally tells Dan that Mary works with her in the Indian Gift shop.

"Is everyone here?" Bill asks. "Does anyone expect anyone else?" A murmur passes through the group, but no one says anything. "I guess we're all here. Onward and upward to Observation Point we shall go."

Bill turns and walks toward the Inn's front doors as the group follows him. As the group heads east on the boardwalk toward Old Faithful Geyser, Dan looks around and notices that the air has a definite chill. A light breeze blows from the west. The moon hasn't risen so the night is dark. Dan can see the small greyish white plume of steam rising from Old Faithful Geyser. When the steam hits the cold air, it dances back and forth like a ghostly Egyptian goddess as it trails into the night sky.

As they follow the boardwalk around Old Faithful Geyser, Dan walks with Lou, Mary Ann and Debbie toward the back of the group. Bill drops back to join them.

Mary Ann walks beside Debbie. "Like me, I notice that you have a Southern accent. Where ya'll from in the South?"

"I'm from Columbus, Georgia," says Debbie. "Where ya'll from?"

"Memphis, Tennessee."

Only about a third of the group has flashlights. Mary Ann stops. "Did ya'll hear that noise?" Dan can hear the anxiety in her voice.

"What?" says Bill. Mary Ann points in the direction of the nearest woods and Bill shines his flashlight in that direction. He plays the light back and forth. "I don't see anything."

"Are there bears in the Old Faithful area?" Debbie asks.

"Yes," says Bill. "But we don't see them too often in this area-not like the Lake or Canyon Village areas. But we do have them around at times. You have to be careful." Dan notices that Mary Ann steps closer to Lou and that Debbie also steps closer to himself.

Lou flashes his light on the sign indicating the turnoff to Observation Point. The sign points to the right. They step off the boardwalk onto a dirt path that disappears into the trees.

"I'm going to catch up with the rest of the group," says Bill and he disappears into the darkness.

They enter the woods which primarily consist of dense lodgepole pine trees. The dense trees blacken the night further. Lou and Dan use their flashlights to help Mary Ann and Debbie see the footpath. All four of them have their eyes trained on the ground to keep from stumbling as they hike uphill through the trees.

Suddenly, off to their right, a loud growl-Grrrrrrrrrrrrr-pierces the night silence. Something large and black bursts out of the darkness. Both girls start screaming hysterically. Mary Ann grips Lou's arm; Debbie grabs Dan's hand. Dan's frozen by fear. The hike to Observation Point has turned into their worst nightmare.

For a split second, Dan envisions the headline on the front page of tomorrow morning's Billings Gazette: FOUR YOUNG PARK EMPLOYEES MAULED AND KILLED BY BEAR IN YELLOWSTONE NATIONAL PARK. Dan can't perceive anything worse, but in another split second he envisions the headline on the front page of tomorrow morning's Billings Gazette saying: TWO YOUNG FEMALE PARK EMPLOYEES MAULED AND KILLED BY BEAR IN YELLOWSTONE NATIONAL PARK WHILE TWO OFI BELLMEN FLEE FOR THEIR LIVES. Dan thinks to himself that this headline would be definitely worse.

The growling stops as does the large black creature in the woods. Suddenly, all of them are blinded by a beam of light. A voice at the other end of the beam of light starts laughing loudly. Mary Ann shields her eyes from the light and bends slightly to see what, or perhaps more likely, who is at the other end of the light.

"Bill, is that you Bill?" Mary Ann asks weakly.

The light stops and Bill steps from the woods. He holds a flashlight in one hand and his jacket in his other hand. Bill has a big grin on his face. "Have you gals seen any bears tonight?"

Mary Ann puts a hand on her chest. "Bill, you almost scared me to death." She then starts laughing. Debbie stands with a disbelieving look on her face, but starts laughing with Mary Ann.

Tears of fear and joy stream down Debbie's face. "Bill, you scoundrel!" she says. "You scared me so much I peed my panties."

Now the guys are all laughing so hard that their eyes start tearing. Bill finally stands upright. "C'mon, let's catch up to the others.

The five of them don't catch the remainder of the group until they reach Observation Point. By the time they join the others, beers and a bottle of red wine are being shared by the hikers. Mary Ann reaches into her backpack and pulls out a box of Oreo cookies. Everyone shares the beverages and snacks and soon the conversation becomes more animated.

Dan's standing with his back leaning against the lodgepole pine railings that protect the public from venturing too close to the edge of the cliff. He's enjoying the camaraderie of the group, but turns around to survey the view from Observation Point. The Geyser Basin stretches from east to west with Old Faithful at its easternmost end. The steam from the geysers, fumaroles and hot springs drifts skyward like ghosts in the dark sky. The Inn stands tall like a fairyland castle with its lighted flags now flying intermittently as the wind blows and stops.

A shimmer of light from the East starts to slowly stream across the basin as a late moon begins to rise.

Suddenly, Old Faithful Geyser erupts into the night sky in all her glory.

Dan points and calls out, "Look everyone. Old Faithful's erupting."

The group finally decides it's time to return to the Inn. Once again, Lou, Dan, Mary Ann and Debbie find themselves trailing the group. As they're walking through the trees, they hear a deep growl from the woods to their right.

Mary Ann starts laughing. "Bill, you can't fool me twice."

Just then from up ahead, they all hear Bill yell, "Dan, where are you guys?"

"I think we better catch up to the group," says Dan.

His words disperse into empty air since Lou, Mary Ann and Debbie are already running down the path to catch the group. Dan turns and sees his friends disappearing into the darkness. Suddenly feeling very alone in the woods and frightened, he too starts running down the path into the dark.

CHAPTER SEVEN
BEST PICK UP METHOD EVER

The next morning, Bill, Dan and Chukker are sitting around a table at Hams. The morning crew has pulled all of the morning tours and are done working until the afternoon. Chukker loosens his bolo tie and the top button of his work shirt. He lies back in his chair with his legs stretched out as he sips soda from a paper cup. Bill finishes telling Chukker about the bear scare that he'd given the gals last night on the hike up to Observation Point. Dan thinks to himself that I'm glad he doesn't mention how scared Lou and I were too.

Chukker starts laughing so hard that he blows soda out his nostrils. Chukker wipes his nose with the back of his hand.

"Bill, that's one of the funniest stories that I've heard this summer. Did Debbie really say she peed her panties? That surprises me. She is one D*** fine Southern bred gal. I wouldn't have expected her to say something like that."

"It surprised all of us. Debbie has a lot of spunk."

Chukker finishes his drink and stands up. "Well, I'm going to head up to Bats Alley and then go over to the laundromat to wash clothes."

Bill raises an eyebrow. "Are you already doing laundry? Seems a little early in the season to be doing laundry."

"H***, I'm out of clean clothes." says Chukker. "If I don't do some laundry, I'll smell worse than a pig rolling in sh**. I'll see you brothers later today."

Chukker turns and starts walking toward the east door of Hams. When Chukker is out of ear shot, Dan looks at Bill.

"What was that all about-you know, being a little early in the season to be doing laundry?"

"Chukker is notorious for not doing laundry." says Bill. "He has more tee shirts, boxers, socks and other clothing than anyone I've ever known. He has three green canvas bags like military people use when they leave on deployment. He stuffs his dirty clothes into these bags until not one additional item of clothing can be added. He then takes the bags to the laundromat and will use every washing machine available. He lifts the lids of every washing machine and starts shaking clothes out of a bag. When I have watched, it reminds me a farmer walking along a feed trough continuously pouring feed out of a bag for the livestock. Chukker makes no effort to sort colors. Everything is washed together. When things come out of the dryer, his whites are normally pink. Weirdest way to do laundry that I've ever seen."

Bill pushes his chair back from the table and stands up. "I'm going to head back to Bats Alley and get cleaned up before lunch. I might take a short nap this afternoon before the tours start to arrive. It was a pretty late night. Do you want to come with me?"

Dan looks at Bill. "No, I'm going to stay and finish my coke."

Bill leaves and Dan starts thinking of his relationship with Bill and with their younger brother Dick. The three brothers have always been close. Bill is four and a half years older than Dan and six years older than Dick. Because of their age differences, Bill has always had a different set of friends from Dan and Dick. Bill has always been five years ahead of him in school. When he started high school, Dan quickly grew weary of being asked by teachers "Are you the younger brother of Bill Johnson?" Bill has always been a high achiever in everything he does whether scholastically, athletically or socially. Growing up, Dan had often felt the weight of having to meet the high standards that had already been established by Bill.

But, as Dan reflects, Bill himself has never put any pressure on him. He has always been positive about Dan's own successes and has continually encouraged Dan to try new experiences. He wouldn't be here in Yellowstone National Park at this moment but for Bill's encouragement and assistance.

From his perspective, Bill, as the oldest brother, has always viewed himself as the protector and nurturer not only for Dan, but also for their brother Dick. As with all siblings, the three have had differences at times over the years; but there has always been a strong bond between the three brothers based on love, mutual respect and acceptance.

Dan remembers an incident from their shared childhood that he believes typifies his thoughts. When he was 13 years old, he and Dick had a paper route delivering the local newspaper. Their route only had 67 customers, but it was located in a rural area. From start to finish, the route covered six miles. Normally they biked a mile to where their newspapers were dropped off and they then walked the route. Winters in central Indiana could be bitterly cold and snowy. Sometimes, if it was extremely cold or the snow on the ground was several feet deep, their mother, or their grandfather if visiting, would drive the route with them. Dan and Dick often made a competition of delivering their newspapers when aided by an automobile. They asked the driver to time the delivery from start to finish. Their best time had been 20 minutes.

That year, Bill started attending an out of state college and came home for the holidays. Dan and Dick had to deliver newspapers on Christmas morning-something neither of them particularly looked forward to doing. However, they learned that their newspapers would be dropped off at 12:30 a.m. Christmas morning if they wanted to deliver them early. When Bill heard this, he came to them and offered to help by driving them on their route on Christmas morning. Upon learning of Bill's assistance, they decided that it'd be best to stay up Christmas Eve, pick the newspapers up at 12:30 a.m. Christmas morning and deliver them at that time instead of waiting until 6:00 or 7:00 a.m. to start their delivery.

Now, years later, Dan can still visualize that night. He remembers sitting in the back seat of their mother's red Volkswagen bug at the local teen hangout in their small community. The time was 11:30 p.m. on Christmas Eve. Bill and Dick sat in the front seats. The temperature outside was below freezing. The windows were fogged. The small heater in the VW bug barely produced enough heat to warm the front passengers; any passenger in the back seat was simply out of luck. Christmas carols were playing on the radio. Dan vaguely recalls that the song being played was something about a Grandma being run over by a reindeer, but the sole speaker in the vehicle was not clear enough for him to be sure.

Bill cranked down his window to place an order. As he kept pushing the button on the squawk box, Dick said repeatedly: "Remember, Bill, I want a plain hamburger. Just a patty and the bun." For some reason, Dan guesses that his younger brother at that age must have equated Christmas Eve with a plain hamburger-just the patty and the bun.

Dan also remembers delivering the newspapers that night. There was a full moon and about two feet of snow on the ground. The snow had melted slightly during the day and had crusted over in the night's chill. Every step taken by Dan made a crunching noise. Many houses still had their outdoor Christmas lights on. The red, green, blue and white lights reflected off the snow like hundreds of sparkly prisms in the bright moonlight. As he ran from house to house putting newspapers between the glass storm door and the front door of each house, Dan could see through the windows of some homes that a few families were already awake and opening presents. These images are etched in his memory for eternity.

Dan thinks to himself that not many brothers returning home from college would stay up half the night to help his younger brothers deliver newspapers on a cold Christmas morning. Dan knows that he has a special older brother. And to think that I have the opportunity to work an entire summer with Bill in Yellowstone National Park!

As he pushes his chair back and returns to Bats Alley, Dan can't suppress the smile on his face.

Later that night, Dan has finished his shift and changed his clothes. He sits on his bed reading a novel. His door is open since Bats Alley seems unusually quiet. Bill, Mac, Chukker and Lou have driven into West Yellowstone for pizza and beers at the Gusher. Dan had turned down the offer to join them.

A knock on his door startles him. Dan looks up and sees Ted standing in the doorway.

"Are you doing anything tonight?"

"No. I'm just reading my book." Dan holds up his book in case Ted doesn't believe him.

"Since you aren't doing anything, why don't you join me and a couple of gals?"

Dan's curious. "Who are the gals?"

"That's not important. You'll just have to wait and see. I'm sure that you'll like them." Ted reaches his left hand backwards and pats the backpack on his back. "I have a bottle of wine, a box of Ritz crackers and a can of Cheese Whiz. That's all we need. Grab your coat and a flashlight and follow me."

Dan's still undecided, but figures he has nothing else to do. His book can wait. He stands up and grabs his jacket and flashlight. He then follows Ted down the hall.

When they exit the Inn through the front doors, Ted turns right and starts walking toward Old Faithful.

"Just curious, but where are we headed?" Dan asks Ted as they walk.

"To the girl's dormitory behind the Lodge."

"Are we meeting the girls there?"

Ted grins. "You'll just have to wait and see."

Dan wonders why Ted is being so mysterious, but continues to walk with him. They follow the boardwalk as it winds around Old Faithful Geyser. It is past 9:30 p.m. and only a few people are sitting on the boardwalk benches in the waning twilight. Up ahead, Dan sees Old Faithful Lodge.

Old Faithful Lodge is located opposite Old Faithful Inn. The Lodge is a wooden building dating to the mid-1920s which provides dining, social (recreation center), administrative and registration services. Guests stay in cabins located in back of the Lodge. The Firehole River flows past the back of the cabins and continues westward through the middle of the Upper Geyser Basin. Without question, the Lodge lacks the grandeur, charm or majesty of the Inn.

Ted leads them to the girl's dormitory which is located in back of the Lodge. When they arrive at the girl's dormitory, Dan sees that the dormitory is a two-story wooden structure with rows of windows spaced about ten feet apart on both floors. A wooden stairway leads up to a wooden porch with a single wooden door that apparently serves as the building's entrance. Dan starts to put his right foot on the bottom step, but Ted grabs the sleeve of his jacket and pulls him back.

"Not so fast."

Dan is perplexed. "What do you mean?" The thought occurs to Dan that this question is becoming more and more common as their short time together progresses.

Ted pulls Dan's jacket sleeve until they are standing 20 to 30 feet from the dormitory. Ted lets go of Dan's sleeve and bends over. He begins peering intently at the black volcanic gravel.

Dan's becoming impatient. "What are you doing?"

Rather than answering Dan's question, Ted looks up at him. "Help me find some small pebbles-big enough so they can be heard but small enough that they don't break glass."

"What in the world are you doing?"

Ted speaks brusquely. "Just do what I say."

Dan bends over and starts looking for the right sized small stones in the black gravel. It doesn't help that it's now dark outside. After several minutes of searching, he has a half dozen small stones and hands them to Ted. Dan still has no idea what Ted is doing, but keeps his mouth shut.

Ted begins pacing back and forth along the dormitory peering at the windows. Finally, Dan can no longer contain himself. "What are you looking for?"

"I'm looking for lighted rooms and any signs of activity."

Suddenly, a light bulb comes on-not in the building, but in Dan's head.

"We're not meeting dates here; you're looking for dates." Dan shakes his head in disbelief.

"Aren't you the bright one. You caught me."

As he says this, Ted tosses one of the small stones against one of the lighted windows on the second floor of the dormitory. Dan sees a silhouette of a gal appear and the window curtains are pulled back. The window is raised and the gal leans over to see what's going on outside. She then spots Ted and Dan standing under her window.

"What are you doing?" the gal asks.

"I'm Ted and this is my friend Dan. We work as bellmen at the Inn." Ted points at Dan. " Now, my friend Dan here has a problem tonight. Maybe you can help us out."

"What's the problem?"

"My friend is shy and would like female companionship tonight. Maybe you have a girl friend and we can all sit on the boardwalk and watch Old Faithful erupt."

"Get lost!" The gal slams her window shut.

Ted turns to Dan. "Well, that didn't go so well. Let's try another window."

Dan can't believe this is happening. He starts to tell Ted he's going back to the Inn, but Ted throws a small stone at another lighted window on the second story. Again, a silhouette of a gal appears before the window. The curtains are pulled back and the window opens so the female occupant can determine why a small stone has hit her window.

Ted repeats the same dialogue, but this time the gal doesn't say "Get Lost" or slam her window shut. Instead, she squints to see more clearly who's speaking and then holds her index finger in the air.

"Give me a minute."

The curtains are pulled shut again and the guys can hear the murmur of conversation occurring in the second story room. The curtains are pulled open and the gal pokes her head through the window. "Are we doing anything other than sitting on the boardwalk?"

Ted raises his right arm up with his fist balled except for the middle three fingers. "As a former boy scout, I'm obliged to tell only the truth. We aren't going anywhere else, I promise."

"Will there be any libations or food involved?"

"Only Old Faithful's finest. I have a bottle of wine, Ritz crackers and a can of Cheese Whiz."

"What kind of wine?"

"Red."

"Give me another minute." The curtains close again.

A few minutes pass and the curtains are again drawn back. "Give us ten minutes and we'll meet you outside on the front porch."

About ten minutes later, two gals walk through the front door of the girl's dormitory and introduce themselves to Dan and Ted. The gal who spoke with Ted through the window is Alice Pittman. The other is her roommate, Linda Larson.

Once introductions are made, the four walk to the boardwalk and take seats facing Old Faithful Geyser. Few people are around at this hour. Ted opens the wine bottle and offers both gals a plastic cup which they accept. Dan reaches into his jacket pocket and pulls out the Coke that he'd bought at the vending machine located in the West Wing of the Inn. Ted opens his box of Ritz crackers and takes the top off his can of Cheese Whiz.

For the next hour and a half, the four young people talk about their lives, how they happened to arrive in Yellowstone, their jobs (both gals work in housekeeping at the Lodge) and swap experiences since they arrived in the Park. They laugh frequently. Finally, after watching Old Faithful Geyser finish an eruption, Alice indicates that they need to get to bed. Ted offers to walk the girls back to their dorm.

Ted and Dan are walking back to the Inn.

"Thank you for this evening," says Dan. "At first, I thought you were nuts, but it really turned out to be a fun evening. What did you think of the gals?"

"Both were nice, but I really like the spirit and humor of Alice."

At the time, neither had any inkling that Ted and Alice would date each other for the duration of the summer.

Dan lies in his bed twenty minutes later. Lou was in his bed asleep by the time Ted and Dan had returned to Bats Alley. He hears Lou snore softly. Dan begins recalling the evening's events as he waits for sleep to come. He wonders who would've ever thought of finding a date by randomly throwing small stones at window panes in the girl's dormitory at the Lodge? It's nuts ... and to think, Ted is a Harvard guy. But as he thinks longer on the evening, Dan reaches a conclusion. Nuts? No, brilliant. This has to be the best pick up method ever.

And with that thought, sleep finally arrives.

CHAPTER EIGHT

SHOOT OUT AT OLD FAITHFUL LODGE REC CENTER

The big day has arrived. Tonight, Mac and Scotty will meet at the Old Faithful Lodge rec center to settle their bet by playing a game of "Horse." The bet doesn't involve any money, but that doesn't lessen the build up to the big game at all. Mac has downplayed the game with the Bell Crew, but every bellman knows that Mac has a lot of pride and doesn't like losing any game anywhere at any time. Besides, if Mac wins, the Bell Crew, and whoever their dates may happen to be, will win big. No one in the Old Faithful area has ever attended a Pow Wow on Yellowstone Lake and no one has ever, ever been chauffeured to a Pow Wow by Scenic Cruiser. Yep, there's no money on the line, but the stakes are enormous.

That morning, Dan's standing at the Bell Desk with Mac. Dan hears Kitty's voice.

"Mac. Oh, Mac, can you come over to the Front Desk please?"

Dan looks toward the Front Desk and sees that Kitty is motioning for Mac. Mac rolls his eyes and walks slowly toward the Front Desk.

"Yes, Kitty. Is there something I can do for you?"

Kitty leans over the countertop on her elbows and speaks in a low conspiratorial tone of voice. "What time do you and your friend start that Horsey game tonight?"

Mac removes his eyeglasses and starts wiping them with a corner of his shirttail. He emits a long sigh. "It's called a game of 'Horse.' We're supposed to start at 9:00 tonight. How'd you hear about it?"

"Well, everyone's talking about it. No one seems to know what the bet's about, but it seems pretty important. I know a lot of the employees plan to attend."

Mac gives another eye roll. "Great, as if I didn't feel enough pressure."

"I'm sure you're pretty good, especially if you made a big bet on the outcome. By the way, what's the wager?"

Mac smiles. "Kitty, the first rule for every bettor is that you don't show your cards."

Mac turns and returns to the Bell Desk. Mac looks at Dan. "Daniel, this is getting to be quite a kettle of fish."

After Mac leaves, Dan's standing by the Bell Desk when Graham Callwood walks by with a fly rod in one hand and a pair of waders folded over his other arm. Dan steps forward. "Graham, I didn't know that you're a fisherman."

Graham Callwood almost always has a smile on his face. He met Graham on his first Sunday at the Inn when he attended an interdenominational service that's held every Sunday morning. An organization called Ministries in the Parks supports young seminary or, in some cases, college students who conduct interdenominational services on Sundays throughout the National Park System. Graham happens to be assigned to the Old Faithful area. Dan recalls his initial conversation with Graham and his shock at the revelations resulting from it.

After the two had introduced themselves, Dan was curious about Graham's ministry in the Park.

"So, Graham, when do you have other services besides Sunday morning at the Inn?"

"After our Sunday morning service at the Inn, I walk to the Lodge and repeat the Sunday morning service there."

"Don't you have any other meetings during the week?"

"No. You seem surprised. Why?"

"Well, back home I attend a lot of church activities. I go to Sunday School before morning service. When I was in high school, I had Youth Group before Sunday evening service and of course we have a mid-week prayer service. Oh, and twice a year we have Spiritual Emphasis Week which people use to call revival. Do you have any prayer groups or Bible studies?"

"No, just the two Sunday morning services. I hope that you aren't disappointed."

Dan shook his head. "No, just a little different for me."

Dan thought it best to change the subject. "Do you work another job beside your pastoral duties on Sunday?'

Graham smiled. "Yes, my primary job is being a bartender in the Bear Pit."

Dan was perplexed. He had grown up hearing hundreds, if not thousands, of sermons preached from the pulpit on Sunday mornings, but never once had he met a minister or evangelist who left the pulpit to go tend Bar.

"How did you become a minister and a bartender?"

Graham laughed. "Where better to meet a sinner than in a bar?"

Dan left Graham that morning speechless. The idea of a minister also tending bar was almost incomprehensible to him. However, Graham did seem to be a really good guy.

"Yeah," says Graham in response to Dan's question. "I love fishing. I take off and go fishing every chance that I get."

"Do you only fly fish?" Dan asks.

"No. I have fished with bait and lures, but fly fishing is my favorite method of fishing."

"Say, do you know Scotty Oakley? He runs the Grant Village Marina."

"Yes, I have met him. Seems like a nice person."

"I agree," says Dan. "Listen, when I met Scotty last week, he explained that the Southeast Arm of Yellowstone Lake doesn't open to fishing until June 15th so the Cutthroat trout can finish spawning. He told me that if someone can get to the Southeast Arm within a week or 10 days of June 15th, the fishing's fabulous."

"I haven't been in the Southeast Arm myself, but I've also heard stories about it. It sounds really interesting."

Dan smiles since the hook is set. "Well, I talked with Eagle and Bill about taking a boat from Grant Village next week and going to the Southeast Arm after it opens to fishing. I then telephoned Scotty to see if it's possible to reach the Southeast Arm from Grant Village marina. Scotty indicates that not many people go to the Southeast Arm from Grant Village, but it can be done if we takes an extra tank of gasoline. Eagle, Bill and I are doing it next week. Would you like to join us?"

"Sounds like a great trip. What day next week?"

"Bill's going to clear it with Mac since there will be three of us bellmen taking off work the same day. We're looking at Wednesday subject to Mac's approval."

Graham nods his head. "If you get Mac's approval, I'm in. Sorry, Dan, but I have to run. I know a lot of trout are waiting for my flies." Graham leaves the Inn through the back door.

That evening, Dan's hanging around the Bell Desk when Mac walks down the steps at approximately 8:30. Mac's wearing sweat pants, a tee shirt, white socks and basketball high-top shoes. He has a sweatshirt draped over his shoulder.

"Are you headed over to the rec center?" asks Dan.

"Yeah, do you want to walk over with me?"

"Sure, I'd love to join you."

As they walk on the boardwalk toward the Lodge, Dan looks at Mac. "Are you nervous?"

"What do I have to be nervous about?"

When one approaches Old Faithful Lodge from the parking lot, there is a large separate building to the right. This is the rec center. Like the Lodge and Inn, this building is made of wood. There is a raised stage on one end of the building and a couple of small office like structures on the other end. The roof is held up by massive log posts and gables. The floor's made entirely of wood. A basketball court is outlined in paint on the floor between the stage and the small office area. The court is smaller than normal, but functional for multiple activities like basketball, volleyball, dances, pageants, and the like. There are basketball goals on either end of the court. Some benches, tables and chairs are situated on both sides of the court.

When they enter the rec center, Dan sees a crowd of 20 to 30 people waiting. He notices that all of the bellmen are present except for the two who are working the late shifts. Dan recognizes many of the other faces.

When Mac enters the rec center and the crowd sees him, a loud cheer goes up. Mac is being treated like a Roman hero returning home from a victorious conquest.

Mac speaks to Dan out of the side of his mouth. "Now I feel a little nervous."

Mac walks over to the rec manager, Rich Lang, and shakes hands with him. Rich originally started as a houseman cleaning cabins behind Old Faithful Lodge. When the real rec manager didn't show up in Gardiner for the start of his contract, someone at the Lodge appointed Rich to work part-time managing the rec center and part-time at his original housekeeping position. Mac had arranged with Rich to reserve the rec center for his little game of "Horse" with Scotty.

After shaking hands, Mac walks to the other side of the court and takes off his sweat shirt and pants. He's wearing gym trunks under his sweat pants. Mac picks up a basketball and starts warming up by shooting baskets.

A few minutes later, Scotty walks into the rec center with his entourage. Scotty brings with him 15 or 20 of his best friends or, perhaps to be more accurate, some of his co-workers and their friends. Scotty walks over and shakes Mac's hand. He then walks to the opposite side and takes off his sweats. He picks up another basketball and starts taking shots with Mac.

A little after 9:00, Rich walks to center court. He starts clapping his hands over his head and shouts. "Everyone, please. Quiet." He motions for Mac and Scotty to join him at center court. As the conversations stop and people quiet down, Rich sets the table for tonight's game.

"Ladies and gentlemen. Welcome to the Old Faithful Lodge rec center. Tonight, we've gathered to witness a friendly little game of "Horse" between Scott Oakley who hails from Grant Village (Rich raises his left arm toward Scotty and Scotty's followers cheer loudly) and Matthew McPherson who hails from Old Faithful Inn (Rich raises his right arm toward Mac and Mac's followers cheer even louder)."

Dan thinks to himself that Rich is being a little over-dramatic. After all, this isn't a prize fight.

Rich waits for the cheering to subside. "There can be different rules for the game of "Horse," but Scotty and Mac have agreed to the following rules for tonight's game. I'll flip a coin to determines who goes first. That person will call a shot and then attempt to execute the called shot. The other person will then attempt to execute the same shot. If one misses, the person who makes the shot gets a letter. If both make the shot or both miss the shot, then neither gets a letter. Then the person who lost the coin flip will call the second shot and we follow the same procedure. Mac and Scotty will alternate back and forth calling the shot. The first person to get h-o-r-s-e is the winner."

Rich looks at both players and asks if either has any questions. Both shake their heads. Rich takes a step back. "Scotty, do you want heads or tails?"

"Heads."

Rich reaches in his pocket and takes out a 50-cent piece. He flips the coin high in the air. The coin tumbles end-over-end and rolls when it hits the wooden floor before finally coming to a rest. Rich walks over and picks up the coin. "It's tails. Mac, you call the first shot. Let the game begin!"

Rich steps off the court. Mac walks about 10 feet to the right of the top of the circle. "Bank shot from this spot." Mac eyes the basket and bounces the ball three times. He then jumps up and releases the ball from his hands. The ball sails through the air, hits the backboard and bounces back through the net. As Mac's supporters clap and cheer, Mac raises his arms above his head in a "V" shape to signify "victory." Mac then turns toward Scotty. "Your turn. From this point." Mac puts his right toe on the exact spot on the floor where he had taken his shot.

Scotty steps forward to the spot marked by Mac's toe. He bounces the ball against the floor a couple of times and then jumps into the air. He releases his shot at the top of his jump. The basketball sails through the air and bounces against the backboard. The ball hits the rim and falls away. Scotty hangs his head. His followers let out a collective groan while Mac's followers stand and cheer.

Rich steps forward. "Mac has an 'h'. Your turn to call the shot, Scotty."

Scotty's standing on the right side of the circle where he had missed his shot. Scotty pauses. "Okay. Lay-up starting from the right side of the lane but you have to dribble under the basket and shoot the ball over your head with your right hand. Oh, and you have to spin the ball around your waist while in the air before releasing the ball."

Being from Indiana, Dan knows how difficult this shot will be. It requires skill to spin the ball around your waist before shooting, but shooting the ball over your head with your right hand requires an extremely high level of athleticism.

Scotty takes a couple of steps and starts dribbling toward the basket. He successfully makes the basket precisely as he'd called it. Scotty's supporters start cheering wildly.

Mac now tries the same maneuver. Mac dribbles down the right side of the lane and crosses under the basket. He jumps in the air, twirls the ball around his body and releases it over his head with his right hand. Perfect execution, result less perfect. Mac has misjudged the shot. The ball bounces against the bottom of the rim right back at him. Mac's supporters let out a collective groan while Scotty's supporters cheer and clap.

Rich steps forward. "Scotty gets an 'h'. The score is tied."

For the next twenty minutes the game proceeds with each call being crazier than the one before. Left-handed hook shot from 15 feet. Mid-court shot left-handed. Both Mac and Scotty are right-handed. Left-handed free throws and on and on. With each shot, the crowd cheers, groans, claps, laughs and/or boos depending on the result.

Both players play with heart and frankly, with the urging of their followers, both play above their abilities. The score see-saws back and forth. Scotty takes a one-letter lead (h-o-r vs. h-o) and then Mac leads by a letter (h-o-r-s vs. h-o-r). Scotty ties the score when he calls a "20 foot shot blindfolded". Both players are blindfolded and positioned facing the rim. Scotty's shot goes through the rim hitting nothing but net while Mac's shot falls short and never even touches the rim.

The score is now tied. The player who earns the next letter will win the game. Mac turns toward Rich and makes the "T" sign for time-out with his arms and hands. He walks over to the sideline. Dan's sitting next to where Mac left his sweat clothes. He picks up his sweatshirt and uses it to mop perspiration from his face. He then sits down next to Dan.

"Mac, you're doing great," says Dan. "Do you want some water?"

"Please." Mac takes the bottle offered by Dan and unscrews the top. He leans his head back and takes a long drink. Mac sits for a few moments saying nothing and then looks at Dan. "Daniel, you're from Indiana. Do you have any suggestions what to call next?"

"Mac, I really don't know what to tell you. I guess if I were playing the game, I would just keep it simple."

Mac considers Dan's words and mutters under his breath, "Just keep it simple. Yeah, just keep it simple."

Mac stands up and walks back onto the court. Rich steps forward and says loudly, "Okay, Mac. The game's on the line. Next letter wins. What kind of crazy call are you going to make?"

Mac calmly grips the ball with both hands. "Two handed, underhanded free throw."

Scotty is incredulous. "H***, Mac. No one has shot free throws that way since the '50s. Are you serious?"

Mac steps to the free throw line. "Watch me." He bounces the ball three times. He puts one hand on either side of the ball and pulls the ball back between his legs. He swings his arms forward and releases the ball at the top of the arc's swing. The ball hits the rim and rolls slowly around the rim. Like a roulette ball leaving the spinning wheel, the ball finally falls softly through the rim. Mac's arms fly upward in celebration. His followers are jumping up and down as they cheer.

Mac steps away from the free throw line. He bends over and with a sweep of his arm says to Scotty, "Thy free throw line awaits thee."

"Very funny wise guy." Scotty steps to the line.

Scotty looks at the backboard for a few seconds and then bounces the basketball twice. He grips the ball with a hand placed on each side. He shifts his legs to find the right pressure point and pulls the ball between his legs. He then swings his arms forward and releases the ball at the top of the arc's swing. Like Mac's shot, Scotty's ball hits the rim and rolls slowly around the rim. Unlike Mac's shot, Scotty's ball falls softly outside the rim.

Mac and his followers: Total elation. Scotty and his followers: Heartbreaking disappointment.

In the spirit of goodwill, Mac walks over to Scotty and extends a hand.

"Scotty, that was one H*** of a game. Too bad your last shot rimmed out, but look at the bright side. You and any friend you want, and of course your dates, are invited to join the Old Faithful Inn bellman and their dates on a long boat ride aboard a Yellowstone Park Company Scenic Cruiser for an evening Pow Wow on Yellowstone Lake."

Scotty shakes Mac's hand and both begin to laugh.

CHAPTER NINE

NEAR DISASTER ON YELLOWSTONE LAKE

The bow of the 16' aluminum boat glides effortlessly through the placid waters of Yellowstone Lake. Powered by a 20 horsepower Johnson outboard motor, the small craft moves at a slow, but steady pace. In the boat sit Dan, Bill, Eagle and Graham-each sitting alone on one of the four seats in the boat with Dan's hand on the tiller. The morning feels crisp, but the air is rapidly warming as the sun rises in the east. Dan suspects that layers will soon be shed.

The four young men are headed toward the Southeast Arm of Yellowstone Lake. At 7,732 feet above sea level, Yellowstone Lake is the largest freshwater lake over 7,000 feet in elevation on the North American continent. The Lake covers 136 square miles and has 110 miles of shoreline. Except for shallow waters covering hot springs, the Lake typically freezes over by early December. The ice can reach three feet in depth during winters and often doesn't totally melt until late May or early June.

Graham's facing Dan in the boat. "Did you know that the water's so cold that even in warm summer months, hypothermia can set in after 15 or 20 minutes if a person is in the water?"

Dan shivers at the thought of being in the cold water. "No, I didn't know."

The Southeast Arm of Yellowstone Lake can only be reached by boat or foot. That portion of Yellowstone National Park to the east and south of the Southeast Arm is considered to be the wildest, most remote and rugged area in the continental United States. This is the destination awaiting these four young men.

Dan surveys the distant mountains and the tree-lined shoreline. "Wow, this Lake is enormous."

"Hey, we're not even out of the Thumb," says Graham. "Wait until you see the main lake."

When Graham says the "Thumb," he is referring to a portion of Yellowstone Lake that resembles a human thumb on a hand. One of Yellowstone National Park's many thermal areas is located on the Lake and is called West Thumb. The Grant Village marina is located about two miles south of the West Thumb area.

"How long did Scotty say it would take us to reach the Southeast Arm?" asks Bill.

"He estimated over an hour and a half or maybe two hours," says Dan. "That's why he gave us an extra tank of gasoline and carefully showed me how to change tanks before we left the marina. If we don't change tanks before returning, Scotty said it might take a couple of days to row the boat back to the marina." Dan looks at the pair of wooden oars kept in the boat just in case the motor stops working.

"How did Scotty say we get to the Southeast Arm?" says Eagle.

"He said that once we leave the Thumb and reach the main Lake, we turn south and generally head southeast." Dan shades his eyes with one hand. "When the Lake appears to split, we veer left into the Southeast Arm and follow the Arm southward. There are no piers, picnic tables or other signs of human activity. There are several streams that feed into the Southeast Arm. This is where we should find Cutthroat trout spawning much like salmon do along the Pacific coast and in Alaska. Scotty says to find a stream and beach our boat. Scotty doesn't think that we'll see any people anywhere in the Arm because it's so remote and difficult to reach."

About 20 to 25 minutes after leaving the marina, the boat leaves the Thumb and enters the main part of the Lake.

"Wow, Graham," says Dan. "Now I understand your remark about waiting until we reach the main body of the Lake. This lake is really enormous!"

Dan slowly pushes the tiller to the left to make the boat turn right and sets his course southeast. As the boat slowly navigates the Lake, Bill raises his arm to the right and points.

"Look up there."

They all turn their heads and look up into the sky where Bill is pointing. A golden eagle is slowly circling. The great bird suddenly swoops down toward the water and grabs a Cutthroat trout that's swimming near the surface of the water in its claws. Burdened by the weight of the fish, the eagle flaps its wings harder and slowly gains altitude. As the four of them watch, the eagle flies to shore and eventually lands near the top of a huge pine tree.

"Wow," says Eagle. "I don't think I've ever seen anything like that."

The guys see a few boats on the Lake and assume that most of them are fishing. At one point, they pass an island and spot a female elk and her calf grazing on grass.

"I bet that the cow crossed to the island when the lake was iced over, had her calf and got stuck there when the ice melted," Graham says.

Bill looks at Graham. "Yeah, probably so, but elk can swim, you know."

"Sure, I know that. But that island is a long way from any shore. The cow can probably swim that far, but I'm not sure about her calf."

The boat finally reaches the entrance to the Southeast Arm and Dan guides the boat south.

"Start looking for streams feeding into the Arm," says Dan.

About 10 minutes later, Bill points toward the shoreline.

"It looks like there is a stream feeding into the Arm about 100 yards ahead."

Dan cuts the throttle to the motor and slowly passes the stream so that the four of them can take a good look. They pass the stream and Dan idles the motor.

"What does everyone think?"

"There's a fair amount of water flowing in the stream." says Graham. "Do you see that sandy beach on the north side?" Graham points to the sandy beach. "That would be a good place to beach the boat."

There being no objection to Graham's suggestion, Dan turns the boat around and cuts the motor when they are about 20 feet from shore to let the boat drift onto the sand. Dan remembers to lift the prop so it doesn't get damaged in the landing. As the boat's bottom hits the sand, Bill jumps out of the bow onto the sand with the rope for the anchor in his right hand. He has untied the anchor and now uses the rope to drag the boat farther onto the sand. Bill then ties the rope to a lodgepole pine tree located about 15 feet from the shore.

The remaining three guys stiffly climb over the seats and step onto the sandy beach. All four stretch their backs and disappear into the woods for a few minutes. Graham starts removing their gear from the boat and handing it to Bill on shore. Eagle and Dan help and they set the gear near a fallen tree log about 25 feet from shore. Several take drinks of water.

"I want to explore where this stream goes," says Dan. "Anybody care to join me?" Without waiting for an answer, Dan starts walking along the stream away from the Lake. The other three join him.

Dan loves nothing in life more than the sights and noises of a small stream. This stream is about 20 feet wide at its mouth, but quickly narrows to about 10 feet. Dan estimates that the stream is 12 to 20 inches deep. Dan can see that the stream bottom is a combination of rock and gravel. In the late morning light, Dan can see colors of gold, brown, orange, red, green and gray through the clear water. The stream gurgles and babbles as it flows over the brightly colored bottom.

Then, his heart starts to beat slightly faster. Dan can see dark flashes that dart up and down the stream. There are dozens of Cutthroat trout in this stream. Scotty was right-these Cutthroat trout are still spawning.

Dan points out the trout to the others, but they'd already seen the same thing. Everyone's excited. He looks ahead and sees a shaded area where the stream slows and tall grass grows along the bank. Dan's not exactly sure when or where or how he had acquired this knowledge, but he knows that trout like to rest in cool shady places during the midday heat.

Dan stops and takes off his long sleeve shirt. He hands it to Bill. He has a tee shirt on underneath. He then drops to his hands and knees and starts crawling forward. When he reaches the shady area, Dan slowly puts his right hand into the water. A trout brushes his hand and quickly swims away. Dan waits a couple of minutes and reaches further down toward the stream bottom. He crawls slowly forward and can tell there are a lot of fish resting in the shade. Suddenly, Dan makes a quick scooping movement with his hand. A Cutthroat trout comes flying out the water and starts flopping on the ground. He runs quickly and grabs the fish with both hands before it can flop back into the water.

Turning to the others with a 14-to-15 inch Cutthroat wiggling in his out-stretched hands, Dan grins and holds the fish up for everyone to see. "Think any of you can top this?"

Graham and Bill start applauding. Eagle's so excited that he's whooping and hollering and dancing from one foot to the other and back.

Eagle's eyes sparkle. "I want to do that."

Eagle gets down on his hands and knees and starts furiously splashing water out of the stream. Dan turns and releases the Cutthroat into the stream. He hears the splashing grow louder and sees Eagle on his hands and knees in the middle of the stream. Like a prospector looking for gold who's sure the Mother Lode is just beyond his nose, Eagle is moving upstream on his hands and knees frantically splashing with first his right hand and then his left hand.

"Hey, Eagle. I think the trout are on a lunch break," Dan finally calls out.

The group is eating lunch. Graham's sitting on a log and says, "After we finish, I would like to fish for a while."

Bill and Dan both like the idea, but Eagle isn't much of a fisherman. He didn't even bring a fishing pole. Dan's uncertain whether Eagle even owns a fishing pole.

"That's okay," says Eagle. "I'll either explore a little or read my book while the rest of you fish."

Graham is fly fishing while Bill and Dan are using spinners or, to be more precise, Jake's and Mepps spinners. When Graham's fly hits the water, the water roils with Cutthroat trout trying to grab his fly. Graham is virtually catching a fish on every cast. Bill and Dan are catching a fish about every third cast. After 60 minutes, they estimate that Graham has caught and released more than 40 fish and Bill and Dan more than 20 each. Absolutely incredible fishing!

Then they hear Eagle's voice. "Hey, have you guys looked at the sky lately? Looks like a storm may be moving in."

Dan, Graham and Bill have been so absorbed in their fishing that none of them has noticed that large, dark clouds have formed in the sky. All three look up into the sky. "We better get going," says Dan.

The four of them head immediately to the boat. The wind has picked up and the treetops are starting to sway back and forth. The temperature has dropped about 15 degrees.

"Dress warmly," says Graham. "It'll be chilly out on the Lake."

As they pack their gear back into the boat, Dan hurries and changes the gas tanks for the motor. Graham watches him do this. "Dan, do you want me to handle the boat on the way back?"

"Sure," says Dan.

Graham climbs into the boat first. He reaches under his seat and pulls out an old fireman's hat that he had brought along. When he had first seen this hat, Dan had asked Graham, "Why a fireman's hat?" Graham had explained. "A retired fireman back home gave me this hat and I brought it to Yellowstone as a gag. However, I've found that it can come in handy at times." Now, Graham puts the fireman's hat on his head.

Eagle climbs into the boat next and sits on the seat nearest Graham.

Bill yells toward Graham and Eagle, "Are you ready?"

When they nod their heads in agreement, Bill and Dan push the boat off the sand and jump into it as the boat starts to float in the water. Dan sits on the third seat located between Eagle and the bow seat. Bill sits at the bow seat.

Graham pulls the cord to start the motor. He brings the boat around and opens up the throttle heading north to exit the Southeast Arm. As they leave the sandy beach, Dan notices that the waves have picked up with the wind and there's probably a two-to-three foot chop.

By the time they exit the Southeast Arm and enter the main Lake, the sky has clouded over entirely. A piercingly cold wind blows from the northwest at a steady 15 to 25 mile per hour. The waves are now three-to-five feet tall. There are whitecaps everywhere on the Lake.

Graham sets course so that the boat is going perpendicular into the waves which is the only way to handle these waves. The ride quickly becomes the ultimate carnival attraction. As the bow of the boat crashes into the wave, the boat rides up and over the crest of wave and then smashes to the bottom of the trough. Each time, bone chilling spray soaks everyone in the boat and particularly the person riding in the bow seat. Within minutes of entering the main part of the Lake, all four guys are soaked to the bone and absorbing one chilling wave after another.

Graham lowers the visor on his fireman's helmet to protect his face from the wind and spray. He notices that the boat is taking on water. "Eagle, Dan, find something and start bailing!"

Eagle and Dan look around for something with which to bail water out of the boat. Dan spots what looks like a plastic bucket from the Inn at his feet and starts bailing water out of the boat furiously. He thinks to himself that this must not be the first time that somebody's had to bail water in this boat.

Eagle looks into his backpack and pulls out a thermos. He unscrews the cup and starts bailing water with the cup.

Dan looks at Eagle. "Really, a cup?"

Eagle returns Dan's stare. "You have a better idea?" Both get back to work bailing.

The motor continues pushing the boat against wave after chilling wave. After about 20 minutes, Dan takes a moment of rest from bailing and looks around. Graham sits like a frozen rock-albeit one wearing a fireman's hat-keeping the boat on course. Eagle and Dan are now taking turns bailing with the plastic bucket. Bill sits slumped over on the bow seat taking the brunt of every wave. Dan notices that the nearest shoreline is probably more than a mile away. Thinking of how fast hypothermia can start in Yellowstone Lake, Dan shudders at the thought of capsizing.

"Dan, I'm freezing cold. Can I sit on your seat with you?" Bill asks.

"No, it'll interfere with us bailing water." Dan continues bailing water out of the boat as fast as he can.

A few minutes pass. The wind seems to have gotten stronger.

"Dan, can I please sit with you?" Bill asks again. Dan is focused on his task of bailing and doesn't hear Bill.

Without another word to the others, Bill stands halfway up and moves to Dan's seat.

With the balance in the boat changed and the force of the waves, the boat abruptly turns 90 degrees and starts up the oncoming wave on its side instead of its bow heading directly into the wave.

The boat slowly, slowly climbs the oncoming wave and seems to linger just a split second at the top of the wave. If it falls back, the wave will probably swamp the boat and capsize it. If it falls forward over the wave, Graham may be able to correct the bow's direction and steer it into the next oncoming wave.

Dan watches as the boat slowly climbs the oncoming wave on its side. The moment seems frozen in time. He has a brief out-of-body moment where he feels as though he's watching a disaster unfold frame-by-frame. He's terrified of the boat capsizing, but the moment happens so quickly that he can't do anything but watch in horror.

Fortunately for the four young passengers, the boat just barely, and by barely it's probably by the width of a human hair, creeps over the crest of the wave and falls into the next trough where Graham's able to turn the boat 90 degrees to meet the next oncoming wave head on.

As the boat heads up the next wave, three voices in the boat yell in unison: "Bill, get back to your seat." It had taken several seconds for any of them find their voices.

Eagle is furious. "Bill, what the H*** were you thinking?"

Bill scampers to his seat on the bow with the speed of a cheetah and doesn't say another peep.

The boat continues powering through the waves toward the West Thumb entrance making slow time because of the power of the waves. As the boat nears the West Thumb, Dan sees a Park Service green cabin cruiser catching up to their boat. The Park Service boat is probably twice the size of their fishing boat and obviously has a motor with significantly more power. The Park Service boat pulls alongside them but about 100 feet away. The bellmen see someone dressed in a green uniform yelling, but they can't hear anything over the sound of the wind. The person starts to motion and they understand the gist of what's being communicated. The Park Service boat then pulls in front of them and starts breaking the waves for their fishing boat.

Although they have a sense of being saved, they're all miserable. They're soaking wet. The wind hasn't relented and adds to their misery. They're all shivering. Their teeth are chattering. Eagle and Dan continue bailing water while Bill sits huddled in the bow in a little ball.

When they finally approach the Grant Village marina, the Ranger in the Park Service boat gives them a wave and heads back out to the Lake. The four of them are so cold and miserable that they can barely return the wave.

The boat finally reaches the dock. Graham cuts the motor while Bill slowly climbs onto the pier and ties the bowline to the mooring. The rest of them start to slowly hand Bill the gear from the boat.

When they are all finally out of the boat and standing on the pier, Eagle looks out over the stormy Lake. "Today was quite an adventure. I don't know about the rest of you, but it may be some time before I get in a boat like this again."

Despite their misery, the others can't stop laughing.

That night Dan lies in his bed and replays the day's events in his mind. After a long busy day spent in the sun and wind, his body's weary, but his mind's still active. Dan recalls the beauty and the vastness of the Lake, the warmth of the morning sun, the slippery feel of a Cutthroat in his hands, and then the coldness of the spray and the boat just barely rolling over the wave. Whatever good images of the day he recalls, Dan's thoughts keep bringing him back to the near disaster this day on Yellowstone Lake. In his short life, this was without question the closest he has ever come to death.

As he continues to reflect on the day, Dan decides that Yellowstone National Park is like a wicked goddess: beautiful, enchanting, beguiling-but ever so dangerous. He thinks to himself, 'Danny boy, enjoy every day spent in this marvelous Park, but be very, very careful for danger lurks everywhere.'

Dan closes his eyes, but sleep this night is a long, long time coming.

CHAPTER TEN

HOTPOTTING AT NORRIS GEYSER BASIN

Several days after their adventure on Yellowstone Lake, Dan and Bill are sitting in Dan's room on his bed. Both have finished work for the day, but they're too tired to change out of their uniforms. Both are holding their bolo ties in their hands and have unbuttoned the top button of their uniform shirt. They're sharing their day's activities when Lou walks into the room.

"We have company," says Lou.

Laura, Mary Ann and Sally walk into the room.

"How are ya'll doing?" Mary Ann looks around the room. "The three of us were sitting in chairs on the second-floor mezzanine just chatting away when Lou walks by and stops to visit. Lou is such a nice bellman. He asked if we wanted to come up to Bats Alley for a visit. Ya'll bellmen are so gracious."

"Anyone want a drink?" Lou asks.

"I thought that you'd never ask," says Laura. "My throat is parched." She smiles at Lou. Mary Ann and Sally do not speak, but nod their heads in assent.

Lou goes to his Styrofoam cooler and lifts the lid. He takes out three cold cans of Coors and sets them on the floor next to the cooler. He turns to Bill. "Bill, do you want one too?"

"Sure," says Bill. Lou places two more cold cans of Coors on the floor-one for Bill and one for himself. Lou turns to Dan. "Dan, do you want a Coke?" By now, Lou knows that Dan doesn't drink alcohol.

"Please," Dan says. Lou reaches back into the cooler and finds a can of Coke. He sets it on the floor next to the cans of Coors.

Lou distributes the drinks to everyone. Dan watches silently as Lou hands Bill a can of beer. Dan is still getting use to seeing his brother drink alcohol.

Lou looks at Mary Ann. "So, Mary Ann. You said something about the Fabulous Five downstairs. What is the Fabulous Five? Is it some type of singing group?"

All three girls burst out laughing. Mary Ann regains her composure and grins. "No. I doubt that any of the Fabulous Five can carry a tune."

Laura starts to speak. "At Wurthering Heights..."

Dan interrupts Laura. "What is Wurthering Heights?"

"Wurthering Heights is the name of the girl's dormitory located in back of the Inn," says Laura.

"I didn't even know that the girl's dormitory has a name," Dan says. "When did the dorm get that name?"

"I don't know when or how the dorm acquired its name, but that's been the name I've heard used for the girl's dormitory since I arrived." Laura looks at Sally and Mary Ann. "Do either of you know?" Both gals shake their heads.

Laura looks at Dan. "Can I finish my answer now?" Dan nods his head.

"At Wurthering Heights, there are five of us girls who get together sometimes at night in one of the dorm rooms. We have a lot of fun together. One night, we decided we'd call ourselves the Fabulous Five."

"Who are the Fabulous Five again?" Lou asks.

"Well, there is myself, Mary Ann, Sally, Debbie Wainwright and Betty Smith. You all know Debbie who works in the gift shop and Betty who works in the dining room as a hostess, don't you?" The three guys all nod their heads.

"Wait a minute," says Bill. "Are you saying that the five of you have given yourselves a name-the Fabulous Five? Isn't that a bit presumptuous?"

Mary Ann batts her eyes at Bill. "Well, Bill, there are five of us and I know all ya' bellmen think we're fabulous, don't you?" Bill doesn't have a reply to this.

"What do the five of you do when you get together?" Dan asks.

"One thing we like to do is eat Oreo cookies," says Sally. "One of us will buy a box of Oreos at Hams and we eat cookies while we talk."

"What do you talk about?" says Lou.

"About you bellmen, of course," says Mary Ann. "Everyone loves the bellmen."

"Us?" Bill looks at Mary Ann. "What types of things do you discuss when talking about the bellmen?"

Mary Ann pauses for a moment. "Sally, tell them about your experience in Bats Alley a few nights ago."

Sally blushes slightly and hesitates to speak, but Laura urges her to talk. "Go on. Tell them, Sally. It's a funny story."

Sally shifts positions. "Well, one of the younger bellmen-I'm not going to say his name-asked me to come up to Bats Alley and watch the night stars with him last week. I say 'okay' and agree to meet him at 10:00 in the lobby. He takes me upstairs to Bats Alley. We go through Room 9 and onto the roof of the West Wing. There are a few mattresses lying around on the roof..."

Laura interrupts. "Those mattresses are disgusting."

Sally makes sure that Laura is finished speaking and continues, "This bellman offers me a glass of wine and we sit on a mattress while talking, sipping wine and watching the stars. Then he says, 'Sally, the stars look so much brighter when I look into your eyes' and he leans over to kiss me. I was surprised by his behavior and pulled away before he could kiss me. The next evening, the Fabulous Five had an Oreo party in Wurthering Heights. I shared this story with the other four and Betty says, 'I know who this bellman is because he used the same line on me.'"

Mary Ann jumps in. "And me too. I went up to the West Wing roof with this bellman to view stars and he said the same thing to me ...'The stars look so much brighter when I look into your eyes.' When he leaned in to kiss me, I told him that if he tried that again he'd be seeing stars alright—just not the ones in the sky."

All three of the gals start laughing. Pretty soon the three guys are laughing too.

Finally, Lou looks at Dan and Bill. "I bet I know who the bellman is."

Dan starts to open his mouth, but Mary Ann puts her hand out to stop him from speaking. "No, it's better to leave this person nameless. Otherwise, the stars may never seem as bright to any of us." All six break into laughter.

A short time later, Bill stands up. "I'm having a great time, but I need to change out of my uniform."

"I have to go, too," says Laura. She stands up and follows Bill out of the room.

Dan looks at the three remaining individuals in the room. "Have any of you ever gone hotpotting?"

"When I first arrived, a group of us went hotpotting late at night in a thermal pool called 'Bathtub,'" says Lou. "We didn't stay in the water long because the Rangers patrol the area frequently. If caught, it's a $75 fine."

"Excuse me," says Sally. "I don't want to sound dense, but what is hotpotting?"

Lou answers Sally's question. "There are geysers, fumaroles and hot springs all over Yellowstone National Park. Some of these contain boiling water. Some have very warm water, but it doesn't boil. For years, Savages have used some of these areas as hot tubs and soaked in them. It is called 'hotpotting.' Some areas-primarily rivers where hot water runs off a geyser or hot springs-are open to Savages. More popular areas, like Bathtub near here, are off limits by the Park Service. If you're caught by the Park Service hotpotting in a restricted area, you're arrested in the technical sense and pay a fine."

"Oh, like a traffic ticket," Sally says.

"Exactly."

Sally looks at Mary Ann. "It sounds like fun. I would like to try hotpotting."

Lou looks at Dan. "I've heard that there're some legal areas to hotpot around here. One's in the Firehole River where hot water runoff from Grand Prismatic flows into the Firehole. A couple of people have told me that the experience isn't great because you have to find the precise spot where to sit or else the water will be too hot or freezing cold. I've also heard that Savages in the Mammoth area hotpot in the Yellowstone River where hot water flows from the Mineral Pools into the river. However, Mammoth is too long of a drive from the Inn."

"Someone told me a few days ago that they hotpotted in a reservoir at Norris Geyser Basin." says Dan. "They said it was great, but a little tricky to get to the reservoir. I can check with them tomorrow to get better information."

Lou looks at the gals. "Would you two like to try this with us?"

Mary Ann winks at Sally. "What are ya'll doing tomorrow night?"

The next night, Dan, Lou, Mary Ann and Sally are riding in Bill's old four-door Plymouth sedan headed for Norris Geyser Basin. Bill agreed to let Dan borrow his car for this little adventure. Dan's behind the wheel. The car's headlights illuminate the road, but the darkness seems to swallow the light. Dan concentrates on his driving.

"How far is it from Old Faithful to Norris Geyser Basin?" Sally asks.

"About 30 miles," says Dan.

"What's at Norris Geyser Basin?" Mary Ann asks.

"I just read yesterday about thermal features in the Park," says Lou. "Yellowstone National Park contains at least 10,000 thermal features-geysers, fumaroles, hot springs and mudpots. Most of the more famous geysers are located in the Old Faithful area including Old Faithful, Castle, Lion, Beehive, Grand, Giant and Riverside Geyser. Norris Geyser Basin contains some more thermal features including Steamboat Geyser which is the tallest active geyser in the world[1]. There is also a warm reservoir located directly behind the caretaker's seasonal home. That's our destination tonight."

Dan sees a sign for the entrance to Norris Geyser Basin and turns left into a large parking area. He parks the car near the entrance of the parking lot.

"Hopefully, our car will be parked far enough away from the caretaker's seasonal home that the Ranger won't notice our car." Dan notices that there isn't another car in the parking lot and thinks to himself that this may not be his best plan.

Dan quickly turns off the engine and kills the headlights. The temperature has dropped precipitously since the sun set. A stiff wind from the northwest started blowing shortly before Dan and Lou picked up the gals at Wuthering Heights and has not abated since. The windows of the old Plymouth quickly fog over.

Dan rubs his hands together and blows his breath into them in an effort to warm them. "Let's go over the plans again."

From the passenger side, Sally groans but Dan continues anyway. "Now, the caretaker's cottage is around the bend in the parking lot to our left. I'm told that we literally have to walk over the front porch to get to the reservoir since the porch abuts a rocky outcropping which is too steep and dangerous to climb. So, we can't use our flashlights or talk at all. We have to find our way in the dark. Sally, I suggest that you hold onto my hand. Mary Ann, you hold onto Lou's hands. When we make it to the reservoir, we will take

---

1   Appendix 1.

off our clothes down to our bathing suits and slide into the water." Lou had instructed everyone to wear their bathing suits under their clothes. "Be sure to leave all of your clothes in a pile so you can find them when we get out of the water. No lights and no talking until we're back in the car. Anybody have any questions?"

"I have one," Mary Ann says. "Can we please get out of the car? It's freezing in here."

Dan opens his door and walks around the car to help Sally with her door. Sally doesn't wait for Dan and opens her door herself. She grabs Dan's extended hand and the two of them start walking slowly toward the caretaker's seasonal home. Dan can hear Lou and Mary Ann breathing behind them.

The parking lot turns slightly left. As they follow the turn, they see the caretaker' home. There's light coming through a couple of windows and a single low wattage bulb illuminating the front porch which is located on the left side of the house. The front porch looks like it's attached to a tall rock cliff, but there's actually a couple of feet separating the porch from the rock.

Dan and Sally slow their pace slightly as they approach the porch. Dan reaches the porch and goes first. He keeps ahold of Sally's hand, but watches the placement of his feet very carefully. They crouch over to avoid being seen from inside through the window in the door. When Dan and Sally reach the far side of the porch, Dan steps down onto the ground very cautiously. He waits for Sally to do the same and they proceed forward side-by-side.

As they leave the poorly illuminated porch, Dan peers into the darkness to find the reservoir. It takes a minute or two for his eyes to adjust to the darkness. He finally sees the outline of the reservoir. Careful not to stumble over something on the ground, Dan walks about 50 feet on the left side of the reservoir and stops. He whispers to Sally. "Let me test the water."

Dan lets go of Sally's hand and walks over to the water. He bends down and puts his hand in. The water feels wonderfully warm. Dan stands up and walks back to Sally. Mary Ann and Lou are now standing next to Sally. Dan whispers, "This is the place. Let's get our clothes off and into the water."

The air temperature seems to have dropped since they left the car. Dan doesn't need to issue this instruction twice. The gals separate a little from the guys and all four take off their clothes except for their swimming suits. They each put their clothes into small piles and walk to the water. Following Dan's cue, they sit on their butts and put their legs in the water. They slowly slide their bodies into the reservoir.

Ten minutes later, the four of them soak in the warm water in a row along the edge of the reservoir with their elbows resting on the ground. The reservoir's water has warmed both their bodies and their spirits.

Mary Ann whispers to the others, "I don't think life can be any more perfect than this."

Dan feels something cold and wet on his nose. He looks up and sees snowflakes drifting slowly downward from the dark sky. Dan motions for everyone to look up. As they look into the dark sky, the snowflakes become significantly larger. They multiply in number exponentially and seem to fall much more quickly.

As the four watch, Dan whispers to the others, "No, I believe that this is more perfect."

CHAPTER ELEVEN

HANGING WITH CARNIVAL

When Dan met Carnival, he couldn't imagine how two individuals in life could be more different.

Dan: a high achiever in almost all things he undertakes; Carnival: perhaps less achievement oriented.

Dan: serious minded; Carnival: carefree as a butterfly.

Dan: typically acts only after reasoned analysis; Carnival: mostly acts on impulse.

Dan: cares greatly what people think of him; Carnival: from outward appearances, could care less what others think of him.

Dan: abhors any form of smoking; Carnival: Lucky Strikes and rolled doobies are his preferred smoking material, but Dan suspects that Carnival on special occasions enjoys a fine cigar too.

Dan: doesn't swear at all. He took the commandment "Thou shalt not take the Lord's name in vain" seriously. He won't even say the words if quoting someone who's using profanity; Carnival: profanity is a mainstay in his vocabulary.

Dan: makes his bed and keeps his room immaculate; Carnival: never makes his bed and his room is a disaster unless his girlfriend straightens it up for him.

Dan: dresses neatly with shirt always tucked in except when wearing a tee shirt: Carnival: dresses less neatly and shirt normally untucked or partially tucked in his trousers.

Dan: wears no jewelry other than a watch sometimes. In fact, neither of Dan's parents wear their wedding rings for fear of disapproval from acquaintances at church or his father's college colleagues who consider a wedding ring as being worldly; Carnival: wears a fancy gold wristwatch, a thick gold chain around his neck and a jeweled gold ring on his right pinkie finger which he frequently twirls with his right thumb or the index finger and thumb of his left hand.

But, despite all their differences, Dan and Carnival have become good friends. Dan thinks it's because they see qualities in the other which they lack in their own lives and interact without any judgment. Whatever the reason, the fact is that they're good friends.

Dan and Carnival are standing at the Bell Desk one evening waiting for their shifts to end. The rush hours for Fronts have passed. Both have eaten dinner and now they just wait for something to do or the end of their shifts, whichever occurs first. They hear the back door to the Inn open and turn to see who enters. It's Mac and he doesn't have a smile on his face.

Mac walks up to Carnival. "Jerry, you and me need to have a little talk. Step outside to my office."

Mac motions toward the back door. He looks at Dan. "Daniel, you too. I may need a witness."

Mac turns and walks back outside. Dan looks at Carnival. "Do you know what this is about?"

Carnival merely shrugs his shoulders. "H***, I don't know." Carnival turns and walks outside followed by Dan.

When they get outside, Mac's waiting for them. He takes a step toward Carnival. "I've heard a rumor that you have a gal living with you in Bats Alley. Is that rumor correct?"

Carnival looks down at his feet. "Not really."

Mac twists one end of his moustache. "Let me ask you a few questions. Does a girl sleep with you in your bed every night?"

Dan thinks that something must be going on with Carnival's feet because he continues staring at them. Carnival looks up at Mac. "Yeah, I guess most nights."

"Does this same girl keep clothes in your room?"

Carnival looks down at his feet again. "A few."

"By a few, would that happen to mean all her clothes?"

Carnival is still looking at his feet. "Probably."

Mac practically shouts. "D***it, Carnival. A gal who sleeps in your bed with you every night and keeps all of her clothes in your room is living with you."

Carnival looks up again. "The poor girl has to have some place to live."

"Jerry," says Mac. "She has some place to live. It's called the girl's dormitory. I'll bet that she's even been assigned a room with a roommate."

Carnival shakes his head. "But she doesn't like her roommate."

Mac looks at Dan. "Daniel, are you hearing this? Can you believe this guy?"

Mac turns his attention back to Carnival. "Here's the bottom line. Gals aren't supposed to even be in Bats Alley, let alone live there. If Mr. B finds out that you have a girl living with you in Bats Alley, he'll fire your a** as well as the a** of the gal living with you and I won't be able to do a D*** thing to help either of you."

Carnival looks at Mac for a few moments. He finally reaches his right arm out and pats Mac on the back his shoulder. "Thanks for the little talk, Mac." Carnival turns and walks back into the Inn.

Mac shakes his head and looks at Dan. "Daniel, Carnival's going to get us all fired."

Dan grins. "If that happens, at least Carnival's girlfriend will probably still have a job. Carnival can move into her room at the girl's dormitory and become someone else's worry."

Mac laughs. "Thanks, Daniel. I needed that to make me laugh."

A few days later, Carnival and Dan are working the afternoon Fronts. As they stand around waiting for a Front, Carnival turns to him. "I see you're working the late shift tomorrow. I have to drive into West in the morning and pick up some things. I'm almost out of smokes. Do you want to ride along with me?"

Dan understands that Carnival is referring to West Yellowstone, Montana, a small, sprawling tourist town located just outside the West Entrance to the Park and only a 30-to-40 minute drive from Old Faithful. The town has dozens of motels, several small grocery stores, a bakery or two, many gift shops, a tee shirt shop, two sporting goods stores, a few restaurants and a Dairy Queen. Savages enjoy an occasional trip to West to shop and make frequent late-night excursions into West for pizza and beer at the Gusher.

"Yeah," says Dan. "That'd be great. What time?"

Carnival ponders the question. "Hmm. How about early although it's tough for me to get up too early. Say about 10:00?"

Dan wonders what this guy considers to be late. "Great."

The next morning, Carnival isn't as early as he suggested. Around 10:30, Carnival meets Dan at the Bell Desk. They walk down the steps to the parking lot in front of the Inn and to Carnival's car, a late model Pontiac GTO. It has the largest engine made for this model and is painted fire-engine red. There's a tachometer on the car's hood. Carnival has named his car the "Carnivalmobile".

Carnival unlocks the door and Dan sits down in the front passenger's seat. He immediately notices that there are about 15 to 20 empty beer cans littering the floor on the front passenger's side of the vehicle.

"Looks like you've been partying a lot lately," Dan says.

Carnival looks at the empty beer cans. "Oh, that. A few buddies and I got together last night and knocked down some brewskis. I haven't had time to clean them out yet."

"A few, you mean like four or five buddies?"

"No," says Carnival. "There were three of us."

Carnival turns the key in the ignition and the muscle car comes to life with a deep growl. He backs out of his parking spot. He then puts the car in gear and pops the clutch. The front of the car rears up slightly and the car jumps forward with its tires squealing.

"Easy there, Tiger," says Dan. "There are Dudes walking all over this parking lot."

Carnival smiles and lets up on the gas pedal. The car starts traveling toward West. They have driven less than two miles and are passing Biscuit Basin when Dan hears a siren. He turns his head and looks behind them. A forest green Park Ranger vehicle has its lights flashing and its siren screaming. Carnival looks in his rearview mirror and mutters. "Oh no, not again."

Carnival pulls the Carnivalmobile over to the side of the road and shuts off the engine. He rolls down his window. A Ranger gets out of his patrol vehicle and walks up to his window.

"Carnival, I haven't written a ticket for you since last week," says the Ranger. "This may be a record."

Dan notices that the Ranger is Rick Roberts. He's one of the younger Park Rangers in the Old Faithful area and very popular with the Savages. Most refer to him as "Ranger Rick." Ranger Rick works year-round in the Park as a law enforcement officer. He already has ten years of service. However, he's friendly, fair and relates well to the college kids who work in the Park.

"Okay, Carnival," says Ranger Rick. "You know the drill. I need your driver's license and registration."

"D***it, Rick. Do we have to do this again?"

Ranger Rick nods his head. "Carnival, have you been drinking?"

"Of course not."

Carnival then bends over to reach for his driver's license and vehicle registration which for some reason are lying on the front passenger floor. As he searches for the documents, Carnival starts pushing empty beer cans left and right to find the documents. The sound is akin to dropping a bag of empty cans into a large plastic trash container.

"Carnival, what are those empty cans on the floor?" Ranger Rick asks. "I thought you said you've not been drinking."

Dan holds his breath waiting for Carnival's response. Carnival picks up one of the empty cans and holds it up. "Oh, these cans? Anyone can see that they weren't drunk today. They're left over from the last Pow Wow that I attended a couple of weeks ago. I just haven't gotten around to cleaning them out of my car yet."

Clearly not convinced, Ranger Rick frowns and raises one eyebrow.

Carnival finds his driver's license and vehicle registration. He hands them to Ranger Rick who examines them.

"By the way," says Carnival, "what law do you think I've broken?"

Ranger Rick sighs. "There is a 25-mph speed limit through Biscuit Basin because tourists are always parking on the side of the road and walking across the highway. I clocked you going 60 mph."

"I didn't know that was the speed limit through here. Honestly. I thought I was going the speed limit." Dan knows that the maximum speed limit throughout the Park is only 45 mph.

Ranger Rick sighs again. "Okay, Carnival. I'm going to let you go this time with a warning. I know how many tickets you've received already. At some point the Park Service is going to revoke your right to drive in the Park. If I issue you another ticket now, I'm worried that it may trigger a revocation of your driving privileges in the Park. Just promise me one thing."

"What's that?"

"Please try to follow Park rules and regulations." He hands the driver's license and vehicle registration back to Carnival.

Carnival smiles. "Thank you, Rick. I really appreciate it."

Ranger Rick turns and walks back to his patrol vehicle. Carnival looks at Dan. "Whew. That was close."

Carnival starts the engine. He then revs the engine a couple of times and peels back onto the highway throwing loose gravel into the air.

They travel a few miles down the road in silence. Dan finally breaks the silence. "What was Ranger Rick talking about you having lots of tickets. How many have you received?"

"I dunno. A few, I guess."

Dan looks at him. "Carnival, how many?"

Carnival shrugs his shoulders. "I really don't know. You can check yourself. They're all in the glovebox." Carnival nods his head toward the glovebox located in front of Dan's seat.

Dan opens the glovebox and takes out a handful of pieces of paper that have all been wadded up into small balls. Dan slowly unfolds each piece of paper. As he does so, he carefully reads the content of each. "Wow. You have seven tickets here, Carnival. Two speeding tickets, one for running a stop sign and a ticket for illegal loitering."

Carnival interrupts him. "Oh, I remember that one. One night I went to West and had so much beer that I had to make an emergency pit stop on the way home. As luck would have it, a Ranger car passed just as I was zipping up my fly. That SonofaB**** actually turned around and gave me a ticket. All I was doing was watering the local fauna."

Dan looks at the next piece of paper. "Here's a ticket for driving without a license and also two fix-it tickets for your car."

Carnival smiles. "The Carnivalmobile is fairly new, but she's seen a little wear and tear."

"Have you taken care of any of these tickets?"

"No," Carnival says.

"Why not?"

Carnival smiles again. "Well, I thought they're maybe like green stamps. You collect enough tickets and you win a prize."

"Yeah. A prize," says Dan. "Like free room and board for six months in a jail cell."

With that, the two friends drive for a long time in silence.

One of Dan's favorite past-times that summer is walking the boardwalks around the Upper Geyser Basin and, in particular, the asphalt walkway that starts near Lower Hams and ends near Morning Glory Pool. The walk from the Inn to Morning Glory Pool and back is about two miles roundtrip. The walkway is closed to motorized traffic. Along this walkway, he admires several of the Park's best thermal features: Castle Geyser, Grotto Geyser, Riverside Geyser and Morning Glory Pool. Truly, each of these thermal features offers the very best of Yellowstone National Park.

A few days after his trip to West Yellowstone in the Carnivalmobile, Dan's sitting in his room reading a book. It has rained for about thirty minutes and the rain has just stopped. Carnival walks into Dan's room.

"Grab your jacket and come with me. I have something I want to show you."

"Is it still raining?" Dan asks.

"I don't think so, but bring your jacket anyway."

Dan is curious. "What do you want to show me?"

"Oh, c'mon. Trust me."

Dan grabs his jacket from a wall hook and follows Carnival.

Carnival and Dan stand outside the front of the Inn in the parking lot. A few drops of precipitation still fall from the sky, but it appears that the storm is passing. The pine trees glisten with rain droplets. The ground appears to be saturated with water. Puddles have formed in the parking lot during the rainstorm and the pavement is still wet.

Carnival walks over to a motorcycle parked in the lot.

"What do you think of her?"

Dan takes a long look at the motorcycle. It appears to be foreign built, but he doesn't recognize the manufacturer or model. Carnival is clearly excited. "This belongs to a buddy of mine who drove it from Idaho Falls. Isn't she beautiful?" Dan can tell that the motorcycle has exotic, clean lines. Carnival continues, "She was built in Italy. She has a 550-cc engine." Carnival acts as though he's describing a beautiful woman to Dan.

"My buddy gave me the key to her," he says. "Let's take a ride."

Dan hesitates. "Carnival, the road still looks pretty wet. It may not be safe."

Carnival lifts his right leg over the seat and straddles the motorcycle. He kicks back the kickstand. "Oh, nonsense. This bike is heavy enough that the rain won't slow her down at all."

Carnival pushes the start button. The motorcycle's engine comes to life and emits a low growl which grows louder and louder as Carnival races the engine with the hand throttle. Dan reluctantly climbs onto the seat behind Carnival.

"Where are the helmets?" Dan asks.

Carnival turns his head backwards and shouts over the noise of the revving engine. "You don't need one. Hold on tight to me."

With his left foot, Carnival puts the motorcycle in gear. With his right hand, he moves the throttle down. With his left hand, he pops the clutch and the motorcycle almost rears over backwards. Dan grabs Carnival around his waist and locks his hands together. The front wheel comes back down and grips the pavement. The motorcycle races out of the parking space.

"Carnival, I'm not sure this is a good idea."

No traffic appears to be in front of them so Carnival provides more throttle. As they shoot out of the parking lot, Carnival maneuvers the bike to the right onto the wet asphalt walkway to Morning Glory Pool.

Maybe 50 feet from the transition between the main road and the walkway, there is a sign which reads: "Closed to motorized traffic." By the time they reach this sign, Dan looks down at the speedometer and sees the needle hit 50 mph.

Dan yells against the wind. "Carnival, are we supposed to be on this walkway on a motorcycle?"

Dan feels a burst of speed as he watches Carnival's right hand work the throttle. Carnival yells so Dan can hear him. "Don't worry. No one'll be on the path because of the rain."

By now, they are passing Castle Geyser. Dan looks at the speedometer and the needle rests at 70 mph. Dan yells again. "Carnival, we are going too fast for this wet pavement!" Again, Dan feels a burst of speed as Carnival's right hand works the throttle.

Now, they are passing Grotto Geyser. Dan looks down at the speedometer and the needle is up to 80 mph. Dan doesn't know whether to continue hanging on tight or jump off the back of the speeding motorcycle.

Dan finally yells: "Slow down. I really want to live to see the dawn of another day."

Dan can feel the motorcycle slow and watches the needle on the speedometer drop to 50 mph. 50 mph still seems too fast for Dan's liking, but he keeps silent as Carnival slows the motorcycle at Morning Glory Pool and turns back toward the Inn.

Carnival returns the motorcycle to same parking space and kicks down the kickstand. Both hop off the motorcycle. Carnival has a big goofy grin on his face. "What do you think?"

Dan has less of a grin on his face and glumly looks at his friend. "Well, I suspect that I'll never take another motorcycle ride like this one in my entire life."

CHAPTER TWELVE

SOJOURN TO FLAT MOUNTAIN ARM

Mac stops Dan at the Bell Desk as he returns from lunch in the Staffateria.

"What's up, Mac?" Dan asks.

"I thought that you might not have heard the news."

"What news?"

"I received a call from Scotty this morning to settle up on our bet," says Mac. "He's arranging for us to have a Pow Wow next week at Flat Mountain Arm."

Dan starts to ask where Flat Mountain Arm is located, but Mac puts his hand up to signal "stop."

"I haven't been there, but Scotty says it's an area on the main Lake south of the West Thumb. He estimates it'll take 50 to 60 minutes on the Scenic Cruiser to get there from the marina. They have an area where the Grant Village Savages often go to have Pow Wows. The area has some picnic tables and a stream. Apparently, the area is only accessible by foot or boat. Scotty says he'll arrange for the permit with the Park Service and provide the transportation. The Bell Crew will provide everything else."

Mac pauses for a moment. "All of the bellmen can participate. I've arranged with Mr. B for a couple of housemen to cover the Bells. We'll leave the Inn next Wednesday evening at 7:00 sharp and everyone will car pool to Grant Village marina. If we're aboard the Scenic Cruiser by 8:15, Scotty believes we'll reach Flat Mountain Arm well before dark. In the morning, we have to back to the Inn by 7:00 so morning crew can pull a tour and afternoon crew can relieve the housemen who'll cover for us."

"Is it easy to get the housemen to cover?" Dan asks.

Mac looks at Dan as though he's lost his mind. "H***, Dan. They're housemen. They would like nothing more than to be bellmen next year. This might be their big break. Besides, I'm going to pay them well and I assume they'll receive some tips while working the Bells. D***, as I think about it, these housemen will probably earn more working the Bells for a few hours than they normally make in 2 or 3 days working as housemen."

Dan starts to leave but Mac catches his arm. "Oh Dan, one more thing. You'll need a date for the Pow Wow."

Dan walks up the stairs to Bats Alley. When he enters his room, he finds Lou bending over Dan's lower bunk looking at a map that's spread across his bed.

"What are you doing?" asks Dan.

Lou looks up at Dan. "I heard about this place called Hayden Valley. Do you know about it?"

Dan shakes his head.

"Hayden Valley is located between the Lake and Canyon Village areas," says Lou. "It supposedly has the largest concentration of grizzly bears in the continental United States." Lou doesn't have to ask Dan if he's heard of grizzly bears. "I was talking with a Savage a few days ago who claims he hiked through Hayden Valley. Apparently, this person started from a turnout that's located between Lake and Canyon. Hayden Valley is a barren plain with a tiny stream running west to east through the valley. He estimates that the valley is several miles wide in places and 10 to 12 miles long. Lodgepole pine trees line the north and south ridges on either side, but there are few trees in the valley itself-just sagebrush and grasses." Lou shows him the location of Hayden Valley on the map.

"If I'm reading the map correctly, you enter the forest and follow the trail to Lake Mary." Lou traces the trail on the map with his index finger. "We'd walk around the lake and continue hiking west on the other side of the lake. The trail reaches Nez Pierce Creek and we would follow the creek to the highway that goes from Old Faithful to Madison Junction." Dan's already familiar with this road since it's the one which Savages take when driving to West Yellowstone.

"I notice that you're using the word 'we,'" says Dan. "Do you intend for you and me to take this hike together?"

"Right. I need a partner in crime. What do you think?"

Dan puts up his right hand to signal "stop." "Before I answer that question, how far is the hike?"

Lou shrugs his shoulders. "Not sure, but I'd guess 22 to 26 miles."

"Whew. That's a long hike." Dan smiles. "I'm probably nuts to say this, but count me in."

Before Lou can respond, Dan says, "Wait a minute. Didn't you just say that Hayden Valley supposedly has the greatest concentration of grizzly bears in the continental United States?"

"Yes, I did say that," Lou says. "However, this person says that although he saw bear scat everywhere, he didn't even catch a glimpse of a bear all day."

"Yeah, I'm definitely interested, but let me think about it. Say, Lou. Not to change the subject, but have you heard about the Pow Wow next week on Flat Mountain Arm?"

"Yeah, Mac told me about it an hour ago."

"Do you have a date for the Pow Wow yet? Mac said I should have a date."

"Not yet, but I have an idea who I may ask."

"Who?"

"Possibly Mary Ann. Who are you taking?"

Dan shakes his head. "Not sure. Do you know if anyone has a date yet?"

Lou nods his head. "Mac told me he's taking Carol from housekeeping. I suspect Ted will take Alice since they've been seeing each other a lot. Oh, and I'm sure Carnival will take his girlfriend. Things might get a little frosty in Room 9 if Carnival were to take someone else. Other than that, I don't really know."

Dan thinks about who he should invite to join him on the Pow Wow. He's already learned that a few bellmen have steady girlfriends, but most guys date more casually—meaning they may date one gal from time-to-time, but go out with other gals in the meantime. Dan has noticed that it's common to see the same gal with different bellmen at different functions. No one seems upset by this. As a result, males and females mix well and become good friends. Good lovers? Dan has no idea, but he seriously doubts it.

"Do you think Mac would mind if I ask Gloria to go to the Pow Wow with me," says Dan. Gloria White works as a waitress in the Dining Room. She's cute and fun to be around. Best of all, she grew up in Southern Indiana and attends Indiana University. However, he also knows that Mac and Gloria have been together at a number of functions. Even if he can find the courage to ask her, Dan wonders whether Gloria will agree to be his date for the evening.

Lou has a quizzical look on his face. "Probably not, but I would sure as H*** ask Mac before asking Gloria."

Later that afternoon, Dan stops Mac. "I hear that you've invited Carol from housekeeping to accompany you as your date next week for the Pow Wow at Flat Mountain Arm."

Not sure where this conversation is headed, Mac says guardedly, "Yes, that's correct."

"Can I ask you a question?"

Mac nods his head.

Dan looks down at his feet. He then squares his posture and looks Mac in the eye. "Mac, would you have any objection if I ask Gloria to be my date at the Pow Wow?"

Mac apparently hasn't anticipated this question. He starts twisting the end of his moustache while thinking. "Daniel, do you plan to be the perfect gentleman that I know you are?" Mac's eyes seem to twinkle.

"Yes," says Dan weakly.

Mac's face breaks into a smile. "Then I see no reason why you shouldn't. Gloria would enjoy the Pow Wow."

Dan and Gloria are talking.

"Do you miss home?"

"I've been having so much fun here that I haven't even thought about home," says Gloria.

Dan is trying to work up his nerve to ask Gloria to the Pow Wow. "Have you attended any Pow Wows?"

"Oh yes, Mac took me to one at Goose Lake. It was so much fun."

Dan feels like a deflated balloon upon hearing that Mac had already taken Gloria to a Pow Wow.

"Front" someone calls from the Front Desk. This brings Dan back to reality.

"Listen, Gloria. I need to ask you something," says Dan. He fidgets with the change in his pants' pocket.

"What do you want to ask me?" Gloria watches Dan intently.

"Well, the bellmen are having a Pow Wow at Flat Mountain Arm in a couple of days. We're going to the Pow Wow on a Scenic Cruiser. And, I wondered if you would like to go with me?" Dan hopes that he wasn't stuttering when he asked his question.

"I would love to go to the Pow Wow with you," says Gloria to Dan's great relief.

"Front," someone at the Front Desk yells a little louder.

"Look, I have to take this Front. I'll give you the details later." Dan doesn't wait for a reply, but runs to help the Dude who's checking in.

For the next week, the Bell Crew and their dates (as they are asked) become increasingly excited with anticipation as the big day draws closer. Plans are made for the Pow Wow and then executed. On the morning of the event, Chukker and Larry drive into West Yellowstone to buy supplies and pick up a keg of beer. Firewood is taken from the Inn's enormous firebox so a bonfire can be built at Flat Mountain Arm.

That afternoon, Dan passes Chukker's room while walking down the hallway of Bats Alley and sees that three bellmen are inside. Dan stops. "What's everyone doing?"

"We're making Yucca Flats for the Pow Wow," says Eagle. "H***, we have a keg and I don't believe it's necessary to make Yucca Flats, but Chukker here insists it just isn't a bellmen's Pow Wow without Yucca Flats. C'mon in and join us."

Dan steps inside the room and watches the activity of those present. "Pardon my ignorance, but what are Yucca Flats?"

Ted corrects Dan. "The verb should be 'is,' not 'are.' Yucca Flats is a drink traditionally made by bellmen for Pow Wows. The drink consists of orange and lime juices, maraschino cherries, sugar, a little vodka and lots of ice. The formula is a bellman secret that's been handed down from generations of bellmen at the Inn."

"Not a little vodka—a lot of vodka," Eagle snorts. "That's why the bell-man sometimes call the drink 'Virgin's Doom.'" Eagle laughs mischievously and rubs his hands together vigorously.

Chukker has a large plastic pail on the floor. Eagle and Ted are cutting limes and oranges on two small cutting boards. Once the citrus is cut into eight or ten slices, they squeeze the juice into the plastic pail and then throw the rinds in as well. While they're doing this, Chukker's adding other ingredients into the mix—two small bottles of maraschino cherries and a five-pound bag of white granulated sugar.

"Should we make a separate Mormon Yucca Flats?" Chukker asks.

"How's that different from regular Yucca Flats," says Dan.

Chukker looks at Dan. "No vodka in Mormon Yucca Flats."

Eagle responds to Chukker's original question. "No. I don't want to cut up any more citrus. If any Mormons get thirsty, they'll just have to drink Yucca Flats tonight."

Chukker pours the entire contents of a large bottle of vodka into the pail and starts mixing the brew with a wooden paddle. He offers Eagle a spoonful of the brew and asks how it tastes. Eagle puts the spoon in his mouth and takes it out. He smacks his lips and looks at Chukker. "No, more vodka."

Chukker picks up another unopened bottle of vodka. He unscrews the cap and adds about half of the bottle to the pail.

Eagle isn't satisfied. "Chukker, add the rest of the bottle."

Chukker shakes his head from side-to-side. "People are going to get so F***** up that no one will be able to climb back on that D*** Scenic Boat in the morning."

Chukker and Ted then lift the plastic pail and pour its contents into what looks to Dan like a five-gallon plastic jar that probably once contained mayonnaise. Chukker then fills the jar to the top with ice from his Styrofoam cooler and screws the top onto the jar. Chukker lifts the jar with both hands above his head and his face breaks into a big grin. "Ya'll, I do believe we're ready to Pow Wow."

And thus is Dan's introduction to Yucca Flats.

Gloria and Dan stand leaning over the railing with their elbows resting on the highly polished wood. The Scenic Cruiser's big twin diesel motors power the huge boat slowly through the calm waters of Yellowstone Lake. The evening is warm although some have put on sweatshirts over their tee shirts as the air cools. Gloria has a plastic glass half-filled with Yucca Flats. Dan points toward an osprey in the sky that is winging its way home with a fish clutched in its claws to feed hungry mouths in its nest.

As the Scenic Cruiser sails toward Flat Mountain Arm, there's an air of anticipation and excitement aboard the boat. There also is a lot of noise. Dan marvels at just how much noise 12 young men and 12 young women can make on a boat. Of course, most of the individuals aboard, including the boat's captain (Scotty), are holding onto a plastic glass which has been drained and filled several times. By the time the Scenic Cruiser reaches Flat Mountain Arm and Scotty navigates the boat's bottom onto a sandy beach, this group is primed and ready for a really big Pow Wow at Flat Mountain Arm.

Darkness has enveloped Flat Mountain Arm. The smoke from the blazing fire drifts silently into the night air. By now, the party is in full swing.

Mary Ann calls out across the crackling spits of fire. "Larry, the trout is delicious."

Larry had been fishing yesterday with his co-bellman, Steve James, at Riddle Lake and caught dinner. They put the fish on a stringer and into the lake to keep chilled with the intent of bringing them to the Pow Wow. After the fire was built, Larry filled the body cavities of the fish with onions and tomatoes. He smeared butter on the skins and carefully wrapped the fish in tin foil. He used a stick to dig a small hole in the burning coals and put the fish directly into the coals for thirty minutes. And then, voila, some of the best tasting trout one'll ever experience.

Larry sits on a log on the other side of the fire and acknowledges Mary Ann's compliment with a tip of his cowboy hat.

Sitting on another log close to the fire, Dan and Gloria are holding wire coat hangers over the fire with a hot dog at the end of each hanger. Dan's dog looks fairly charred; Gloria's dog looks uncooked. Dan looks at the two hot dogs. "Here, Gloria. Mine's ready to eat. Please take mine and go get a bun. Put whatever you like on your hot dog and eat while it's hot. Hand me yours and I'll finish cooking it."

"Thanks," says Gloria as she hands her hot dog stick to him. She takes Dan's cooked hot dog and stands up to walk over to the picnic table to get a bun. Dan watches her as she walks to the table and notices her steal a glance at Mac and Carol who are standing near the fire talking. Each holds a plastic glass. This isn't the first time he's caught Gloria glancing at Mac. Dan knows that this Pow Wow is just getting started and he can tell he's with a gal who would prefer the company of another bellman.

Laura walks by and then sits beside him. "Wow," she says. "That's not Pow Wow—-just Wow. Sorry, that was a feeble attempt at a joke. This is quite a shindig in an amazing setting. We don't do anything like this back home."

Laura has a plastic glass. "What are you drinking?" asks Dan.

Laura holds the glass out and peers into the bottom as though she has no idea what the glass contains. Finally, Laura looks at him. "I'm not sure-some kind of punch. It's really sweet."

"It's called Yucca Flats. Be careful with the punch. I watched the guys make it."

"Why be careful?" Laura asks. "Is there something wrong with the punch?"

"No, nothing wrong with the punch, but there's a lot of alcohol in the punch."

Laura shrugs. "Humph. It sure tastes good. I better go fill my glass."

Laura has a little difficulty rising from the log and Dan helps her to her feet. She stands up and looks around as if she's not sure what she's doing. She finally walks slowly toward the picnic table where the Yucca Flats container sits.

Dan remembers Eagle's alternative name for Yucca Flats-Virgin's Doom-and thinks to himself that Laura better be very careful with that punch.

Dan looks up to find Gloria and spots her talking with Mac and Carol. Dan wonders whether he should go over and talk with Carol, but decides this isn't such a good idea.

Dan sees Bill off to his right talking with Penny and goes over to join them. As he approaches, Bill and Penny are laughing. "What is so funny?" Dan asks.

"I was just telling Bill about something that happened in the kitchen this week," says Penny.

"What was it?"

Penny looks at Bill who nods his head as if giving his assent.

"Well, a waiter was serving a Dude's family," says Penny. "It was during the busiest time of the evening. The dining room was packed. Anyway, this waiter whose name I shall not repeat comes back to the kitchen with a steak and hands the plate to the chef. The chef asks 'What's the problem?' The waiter answers that the meat is undercooked according to the Dude. The chef was furious, but he took the steak and put it back on the grill for another five minutes."

Penny pauses to take another sip from her plastic glass. "After five minutes, the chef replates the steak and sends the waiter back to serve the meal to the guest. A few minutes later, the waiter returns and says that the guest complained that the steak was still undercooked and demanded that it be returned to the kitchen. The chef was furious. As the waiter handed the plate to him, the chef accidentally upset the plate and the steak fell to the floor."

"What happened next?" Dan asks.

Penny continues with her story. "The chef told the waiter to return to the guest and tell him that the chef would be delighted to cook the meat more. When the waiter turned to go back to the dining room, the chef took a clean plate, picked up the steak and set the plate on the counter. The waiter returns and the chef tells him that the steak is ready to go. The waiter picks up the plate and takes it back out to the guest."

Dan stares at Penny in disbelief. "What did the guest do?"

Penny and Bill start laughing. "The waiter returned in about five minutes and told the chef that the Dude had eaten the entire steak," says Penny. "The Dude specifically asked him to tell the chef that it was the best steak he had ever eaten."

Penny, Bill and now Dan start laughing again. Silly Dudes!

The three hear two loud voices. They turn and see Eagle and Scotty's friend Kipper standing about three feet apart from one another. They're arguing.

"Your guy cheated," says Kipper.

Eagle is clearly indignant. Dan can see from where he's standing that the veins on Eagle's neck are pulsing. Eagle speaks forcefully. "Mac doesn't cheat! How do you think he cheated?"

"By calling a two-handed, underhand free throw."

Eagle inches closer to Kipper. "I don't know where you grew up, but back home that would be an entirely appropriate call."

Kipper steps toward Eagle. "Don't worry about where I grew up. No one shoots a ball underhanded—at least not for 25 years."

"You're just angry because Mac was savvier than your guy," Eagle says.

By this time, Mac and Scotty are hurrying over to break up this little dust-up.

Mac and Scotty manage to get their bodies between Kipper and Eagle.

"Whoa, boys," says Mac. "You both have probably had a little too much to drink. We're all friends here."

Mac puts his hands on Eagle's shoulders and starts to gently push him back.

Scotty also puts his hands on Kipper's shoulder and tries to gently push Kipper back, but Kipper pushes his hands away. Scotty looks his friend in the face and speaks softly. "Kipper, it was only a game of 'horse' and I lost fair and square."

Kipper looks over Scotty's shoulder at Eagle and then turns his back to Eagle. He bends down and pulls down his jeans, and his underpants too, to moon Eagle.

The gals gasp; the guys stare in disbelief.

As for Eagle, he calmly watches and says, "I was right. Kipper isn't from the same town as me."

By 3:00 in the morning, the fire burns low. A few people sit idly by the fire trying to capture any warmth remaining in the spent logs. Most people have fallen asleep.

Dan has brought his cotton sleeping bag that he had purchased in Eagle's Sports store in West Yellowstone. He likes the sleeping bag because it's old fashioned and big-not like a backpacker's lightweight, coffin shaped bag. Dan had crawled into his sleeping bag around 12:30 and was awakened sometime after 1:00 by Gloria when she crawled into the sleeping bag with him. She awakened him as she struggled to get into his sleeping bag. Dan suspected that Gloria must have been cold. He smelled her perfume, but she curled into a fetal position with her back to him and fell asleep. Dan soon fell back asleep himself.

Scotty's voice booms. "Okay, campers. It's time to head for home!"

People wake up and start gathering their things. Everyone seems to move so slowly that Dan feels as though they're all playing a part in a Zombie movie. The bellmen douse the fire and sweep the area to ensure that all trash and debris have been removed. While the bellmen are busy cleaning the site, Scotty and Kipper are busy readying the boat for the return trip.

Once everybody is aboard, Scotty starts the motors and allows them time to warm. Finally, Scotty slips the gear into reverse. Kipper and a couple of bellmen help push the bow of the boat off the sandy beach and hop aboard. The boat slowly moves backward. When the boat reaches deeper water, Scotty puts the gear in the forward position and slowly eases the throttle forward.

All 24 people onboard are sleep deprived, but what a great Pow Wow at Flat Mountain Arm. Despite bringing the wrong gal, Dan realizes that he and everyone else had a fabulous time. The ride aboard the Scenic Cruiser on the Lake was magnificent as the colors and shadows of the lake and shoreline changed from evening to dawn. The bonfire at the Pow Wow was spectacular against a star strewn dark night sky. The fresh trout and other goodies that people shared were delicious. Except for Kipper and Eagle's little dust up, people mixed well and collectively enjoyed each other's company. As he reflects on the Pow Wow, Dan refuses to allow his poor choice of dates to detract from the specialness of this experience.

As the Scenic Cruiser approaches the entry to the West Thumb, it passes a forest green Park Service cruiser going in the opposite direction. Daylight has arrived. The Park Service craft is about 600 yards off their starboard side as the boats pass. Scotty waives at the Park Service Ranger piloting the other boat. Mac's standing beside Scotty. Scotty looks at Mac. "I hope this doesn't mean trouble."

Two days later, a couple of bellmen including Dan are standing around the Bell Desk talking. Mac walks down the stairs and over to the bellmen.

"I had a call from Scotty about an hour ago," says Mac.

"Any problems?" Lou asks.

"Scotty says he got a call from someone at YPCO headquarters yesterday," says Mac. "That person indicated that he had received a call from the

Park Service wondering why the Scenic Cruiser was on the Lake at 6:00 a.m. Thursday morning. Apparently, headquarters was also curious."

"Are we in trouble?" Dan asks. "Is Scotty in trouble?"

Mac twists one end of his moustache. "Naw. Scotty told them that he and Kipper had been up all night fixing a mechanical problem on the motor and had taken the boat for an early morning test drive to make sure everything was working. I guess there was some truth somewhere in that answer."

Mac smiles and everyone begins laughing.

CHAPTER THIRTEEN

THANK TAUCK FOR THE BEER

In the early 1970s, one of the most upscale tours staying at Old Faithful Inn is Tauck Tours. Tauck runs two tours per week through Yellowstone National Park. Each tour spends one night at Old Faithful Inn. The OFI bellman have become well acquainted with the tour escorts and bus drivers. Their favorite Tauck escort and bus driver are Benny Stout and Jimmy Greaves. Benny and Jimmy have worked together as a team for Tauck close to ten years.

Jimmy has an incredible knack for handling his bus and became legendary with the Inn bellmen after he and Benny had been invited the previous summer to a Pow Wow at Goose Lake. According to the older guys, Jimmy drove them to the Pow Wow in the Tauck bus which, by the way, can hold 46 passengers. Jimmy used one hand on the steering wheel and somehow managed to back the bus up to park between two lodgepole pine trees. The older guys swear that Jimmy had no more than six inches of clearance on either side. But the best part of the story is that Jimmy consumed six or eight beers before leaving the Pow Wow. Jimmy got in the bus and somehow managed to drive the bus out of an incredibly tight spot. He had to put the gears in reverse and back up repeatedly. The older guys still marvel that he didn't get a single scratch on the bus.

The bellmen like Benny because he always tips them well since he knows that his tour always receives service before any other tours at the Inn. To show his appreciation, and perhaps to ensure that his tours continue to receive the OFI bellmen's best service, Benny has started a custom of bringing the OFI bellmen a case of Coors beer every week. He purchases the beer during his stop before Old Faithful. He ices the beer cans in a Styrofoam cooler filled with ice and leaves this for the bellmen in one of the luggage bays underneath the bus. Jimmy parks the bus in the parking lot behind the Inn after it's unloaded. He leaves the bay unlocked so the bellmen can access the beer, but he locks the bay later in the evening.

The bellmen aren't the only Savages who like Benny. He enjoys flirting with the young female staff at Old Faithful Inn. This year, Benny seems to really like Mary Ann. Some of the Bell Crew have seen Mary Ann dining with Benny in the Inn dining room and think that Mary Ann might enjoy Benny's company as well.

Chukker, Bill, Ted, Eagle, Lou and Dan are sitting in a luggage bay of the Tauck bus. They're all drinking chilled Coors from a can except for Dan who's drinking his usual Coke. The bay is tall enough that they can sit up with their legs crossed or stretched out in front of themselves or, if they prefer, sit on the edge of the bay's floor with their legs hanging down to the pavement. They're all still dressed in their uniforms. All have finished their work for the day. Since it's early July, the evening stays light for another hour. This night is warm, but the clouds to the west are starting to build.

Eagle takes a drink from his can and sighs. "This is the life. Tell me again what the poor people are doing?" Eagle laughs at his joke. Perhaps the others don't believe the joke is so funny because none laugh. A faint smile on Chukker's face is the best Eagle gets.

Eagle is undeterred. "Ted, tell me again about soap and geysers."

"I read recently that decades ago people would put soap down thermal features to trigger a reaction," says Ted

"What kind of reaction?" Bill asks.

"I'm not sure," says Ted. "But I assume it must trigger a small eruption."

Eagle shakes his head. "Naw. I don't believe that."

"H***, why don't we try it someday," Chukker says.

Lou joins the conversation. "I don't know. You probably won't find a Park rule or regulation that explicitly says you can't pour soap into a thermal feature, but I'm pretty sure the Park Service would give an emphatic 'no' if you asked for permission."

Eagle looks around the group. "What if we could find a thermal feature that's dormant?"

The guys hear a familiar female voice. "Hi, ya'll. What's this about a dormant thermal feature?"

The guys look up and it's Mary Ann and Penny. Penny's still wearing her waitress uniform, but Mary Ann is all dolled up and wearing a skirt and high heels.

"What are you two doing?" Bill asks.

"Business was really slow this evening and they let me leave early," says Penny. "I ran into Mary Ann who needed something from Upper Hams and was heading that way. So, I decided to walk to Upper Hams with her."

Bill looks at Mary Ann. "Mary Ann, you look dressed up tonight. Any special occasion?"

Mary Ann looks down at her skirt and pretends to brush a piece of lint off. "Oh, no. Just getting together with some friends."

"Some friends?" says Bill. "Anybody we know, oh, you know, like a certain handsome male tour escort?"

Mary Ann blushes. Bill notices that Lou blushes a little too. Mary Ann looks at Bill. "Bill Johnson, ya'll are so funny. No, nothing special, but I'm having dinner."

Eagle interrupts. "You girls want to join us for a beer?"

"Sure," says Penny. "A cold beer sounds great right now."

Eagle reaches in the cooler and hands Penny a Coors. He looks at Mary Ann. "How about you, Mary Ann."

"Eagle, you are so gracious. I would love to stay and have a Coors with ya'll, but I have to meet someone in twenty minutes. Bye ya'll."

As Mary Ann turns and starts to walk away, Bill calls out, "Say hello to Benny from all of us. Tell him we're enjoying the Coors." Dan thinks that Mary Ann must have a problem with her hearing this evening because she just keeps walking.

Dan looks at Penny. "Penny, do you have any funny stories to share from the dining room?"

Penny looks perplexed. "Funny stories?"

"Yeah, you know, like the one you told at the Pow Wow about the guest sending his steak back because it was undercooked?"

"What was that story?" Chukker asks.

"Oh, it was nothing."

"No, it was funny," says Bill. "Share it with the rest of us."

Reluctantly, Penny tells the story again. Everyone laughs when she finishes.

"I think I need another brewski," says Eagle. "Anyone else?"

As Eagle reaches into the cooler and starts to pass cans to those who want another Coors, Bill sees Debbie and Betty walking around the Bear Pit and heading toward the back door of the Inn. Bill calls out to them.

"Debbie, Betty. Over here." He motions for both gals to come to the bus. Debbie and Betty stop and speak with each other for a moment. They then turn and walk to the bus.

When they reach the bus, Debbie takes a moment to survey what's happening. "Well, well. What mischief are ya'll up to?"

"Would a southern lady drink a Coors?" Bill asks.

Debbie winks at Dan and then looks at Bill. "As part of our southern upbringing, a can of Coors is an absolute requirement as long as there's one for the southern lady's friend as well."

Everyone laughs and Eagle gets two more cans of Coors out of the cooler.

Debbie pops the tab off her can. "Are ya'll having a little party under this bus?"

Bill nods his head. "Something like that. When we unloaded this bus today, we noticed that there was a Styrofoam cooler filled with iced beer. Since it's so nice this evening, we thought the owner wouldn't mind if we helped ourselves to a cool one."

Debbie gasps. "No, ya'll don't have permission to take these beers?"

Bill shakes his head with a frown on his face. For a moment, Dan thinks Debbie is going to spit her beer out of her mouth. But Debbie suddenly realizes that Bill is kidding and plays along.

Debbie uses her best exaggerated Southern accent—as if she needs to exaggerate her normal accent.

"Why, Bill. Are you really going to involve a poor, naïve Southern belle in your dastardly scheme to steal these beers from this outstanding Tauck company?" Debbie glances at the name on the side of the bus to finish her sentence. "How could you entice me into a life of crime? All this time, I thought ya'll bellmen were virtuous, upstanding young men of character. But the illusion has been shattered. I shall never ever view ya'll the same. Oh, the shame of it all." Debbie puts her right hand to her forehead and thrusts her left arm backward to visibly illustrate her shame. Everyone breaks into laughter.

For the next hour, the group swap stories and banter back and forth. There's a lot of laughter. The sun has set and the wind has begun to blow steadily.

"This has been so much fun," says Debbie. "I love ya'll so much, but tomorrow morning is an early one for me and I have to go back to Wuthering Heights."

Debbie stands to leave. Betty and Penny take Debbie's cue and stand as well. All three gals thank the bellman and start walking toward the girl's dorm.

Chukker stands. "Well, I have to get going too." Eagle, Ted and Bill stand as well.

Bill turns to Dan before leaving. "We have an early pull in the morning. I'm not going to bed very late, but if you get back soon, c'mon down to my room."

"I have to run over to Upper Hams before they close," says Lou. "Dan, do you want to walk over with me."

"Sure," says Dan. "Bill, if I don't see you in a little while, I'll talk with you in the morning."

Lou shuts the door for the luggage bay of the bus with a big bang. Chukker, Bill, Ted and Eagle head for the Inn. Dan and Lou head in the opposite direction for Upper Hams.

Dan notices that the wind has picked up even more. The tops of the pine trees are swaying back and forth in the wind. About halfway to Upper Hams, Dan feels cold.

"Shoot, I left my jacket in the bus bay," says Dan.

"Do you want me to walk back with you to get it?" Lou asks.

"No. I'll go back to the bus while you go to Upper Hams. I think that I'll just walk back to the Inn and see if Bill's still up. Don't worry if I'm not in the room when you return. I'll be in Bill's room talking."

Lou continues toward Upper Hams and Dan returns to the Tauck bus. He feels raindrops start to fall. The temperature has dropped several degrees in a matter of minutes. The bus is parked in the back of the parking lot. The lighting is so poor that it takes a minute for him to find the handle for the bay's door. Dan finally manages to slide the door upward on its two hinges.

The rain starts to fall harder. Dan climbs into the bay but has to wait for his eyes to adjust to the darkness. He can't see anything. He starts crawling on his hands and knees searching in the dark for his jacket. He feels the Styrofoam ice chest and some cans next to it. Finally, he touches what he assumes is his jacket on the opposite side of the bay. He puts the jacket on and is pretty sure that this jacket belongs to him since it fits.

Suddenly, Dan hears a voice over the rain falling on the metal of the bus and the howl of the wind. "It's raining like H***. It's so dark I can't see a D*** thing."

The door to the bay slams shut. Dan is so surprised that he's speechless. Then he hears a noise that's barely audible through the steel bay door and the wind. Suddenly, he realizes what the sound is—it's the metallic click of a lock engaging.

Dan starts yelling at the top of his lungs. "Wait. I'm in here. Stop. Open the door."

He crawls quickly in the pitch blackness to the other side of the bay and bangs on the metal door with both of his bare fists.

Dan uses his hands to search all over the bay door for an inside handle. His search is futile.

After twenty minutes of yelling, pounding and searching, Dan realizes that he's trapped in the bay of the Tauck tour bus. In silent resignation, he leans his back against the side of the bay door and waits for any sounds other than the storm that's raging outside.

Dan sits in the pitch blackness with his eyes wide open. He puts his left wrist within inches of his face and sees from the luminated hands of his wristwatch that it's almost midnight. He hopes that someone will notice that he's missing and come to rescue him. But, with each passing minute, Dan slowly accepts the obvious conclusion that he's going to spend the night in the luggage bay of the Tauck bus.

Dan finally curls into a fetal position on the cold metal floor of the bay and uses his arm as a pillow. He puts his jacket over himself like a blanket, but he's cold and uncomfortable. Although tired, sleep comes slowly. Eventually, his eyes close and his breathing slows as he finally falls asleep.

Dan awakens with a start. He's disoriented for a moment, but then remembers his predicament. The bay of the bus is still black, but he notices a few small beams of light coming from the cracks where the bay doors don't align precisely with the sides of the bus.

Dan looks at his wristwatch. It says 6:30. He believes that it must be morning.

A few minutes later, Dan hears the muffled sound of someone whistling. He bangs on the bay door with both fists and yells, "Let me out of here."

He hears the click of the lock mechanism as it disengages. The door suddenly opens and morning light streams into the bay.

"What the H*** are you doing in here?" Jimmy has a look of incredulity on his face.

Too embarrassed to confess that he got trapped in the bay of the bus, somehow Dan manages to put a smile on his face.

Dan steps out of the bay of the bus and yawns. Nonchalantly, he stifles his yawn with his hand and says, "The bellmen wanted to make sure that we get your tour pulled on time." Jimmy's mouth flies open as he watches Dan slowly walk toward the Inn.

As he walks away, Dan wonders if he'll become legendary with the OFI bellmen like Jimmy.

Dan walks into the Staffateria and spots Bill and Lou eating breakfast. He walks over to their table.

They stop eating and look intently at him. "What happened to you?" Bill finally asks.

"I got locked in the bay of the Tauck bus last night. Why didn't either of you come and get me?"

Dan recognizes the look of incredulity on Lou's face. "Wait, did you really spend the night in the bay of the Tauck bus?"

Dan briefly explains what happened and again asks, "Why didn't you come and get me?"

"I didn't even know that you never made it back to Bats Alley," says Bill.

"When I left," says Lou, "you indicated that you were going to get your jacket and then might visit Bill in his room. I just assumed that you were with Bill."

"Hey, you're not mad at either of us are you?" Bill asks.

Dan sighs. "No, I have no reason to be mad at anyone. It was just one of those things that happen in life."

Bill smiles.

"Why are you smiling," asks Dan.

"Oh, I was just thinking. If Benny hadn't brought the beer, you wouldn't have ever spent the night in the luggage bay of the bus. I guess you should thank Tauck for the beer."

Bill and Lou laugh. After a moment, Dan somewhat reluctantly begins laughing with them.

CHAPTER FOURTEEN

RAID ON BATS ALLEY

All of the Bell Crew except Mac and Steve are in Mac's room awaiting his arrival. Earlier this morning, Mac called an emergency meeting of the Bell Crew for 10:00 in his room. The morning crew has finished pulling all tours. Steve's working the split shift for the afternoon crew and only he is excused from this meeting so someone can handle the Bell Desk. Dan's surprised that Carnival is present since he doesn't work until noon.

Dan whispers to Lou. "How did Mac get Carnival out of bed so early?"

Lou whispers back. "I heard Mac went into Room 9 and literally rolled Carnival out of bed onto the floor by picking up one side of the bed. Do you know why we're all here?"

Dan whispers. "Not a clue."

Mac strides into the room and slams the door shut. If there was any doubt whether he would have everyone's attention this morning, Mac shuts the door with enough force to capture everyone's intense attention.

Mac takes off his eyeglasses and rubs his eyes. "Gentlemen, we have a crisis in Bats Alley. Mr. B called me into his office this morning and read me the riot act. Apparently, he was upset about refunding two guests their money this morning because the loud noise from Bat Alley kept them up most of the night. What the H*** is going on up here?"

Mac puts his eyeglasses on and looks around the room. Larry starts to say something, but Mac puts up his arm to signal "stop." Apparently, he isn't finished.

"I don't get paid enough to be a babysitter. If someone gets fired for playing music too loud, partying, having girlfriends live with them or whatever screw up happens simply because that person isn't being an adult, I'm not going to bail you out. You're all put on warning as of right now. Stop whatever you're doing that might result in me getting called into Mr. B's office!"

A long silence ensues while Mac looks around the room at each bellman. Most are looking at their feet. Mac finally breaks the silence. "Any questions?"

A murmur passes through the room. Mac closes the meeting. "Get back to whatever you were doing. No more F***ups."

Mac opens his door and the bellmen silently file out of his room one-by-one. Most head into their rooms, but Bill walks into Lou and Dan's room.

"Wow," says Bill. "I'm not sure that I've ever seen Mac that angry."

"I understand why Mac and Mr. B are angry," Lou says. "Some nights I can hardly fall asleep because of the noise in Bats Alley-especially from Room 9." Lou pauses for a moment. "Hey, guys. I have a few things to do before my shift starts. I'll see you later." Lou leaves the room.

Bill looks at his watch. "It's 10:20. Aren't you working the late shift today?"

"That's right. What do you have in mind?"

"If we hurry, we might be able to fish for a couple of hours at Sandpoint before our afternoon shifts start."

"Let's do it," says Dan. He's already reaching for his fishing gear, his hat and a sweatshirt.

Dan loves fishing with Bill. As children, their family visited their grandparents' farm in Wyoming every summer. Because both of their parents had summers off from their teaching jobs, they usually drove from central Indiana to Wyoming, but on a few occasions took the train instead. Bill, Dan and their younger brother Dick literally grew up fishing for trout with hook and worms.

In Yellowstone National Park, Bill and Dan fish with spinners or lures, but their interest in fishing is just as keen as when they were children. Sometimes they drive to the Grant Village marina and use one of Scotty's boats to troll for Cutthroat trout on Lake Yellowstone. Sandpoint is a gravel sandbar along Lake Yellowstone located a few miles south of the Lake area. Sandpoint's popular with tourists since they can stand and cast lures or spinners into the Lake and reel their line in slowly. Amazingly, Bill and Dan have caught a lot of trout at Sandpoint.

Although they're avid fishermen, neither particularly likes the taste of trout. However, they discovered that Mr. and Mrs. Baxter love fresh trout for dinner. The Baxters have a standing table reserved in the Inn dining room every night at 8:00. Bill and Dan have developed the habit of cleaning their fish at the Lake and bringing them back to the Inn so they can be put in the kitchen's refrigerators and cooked for the Baxters that evening or the following evening. The Baxters are very appreciative and consider Bill and Dan to be the foremost fishermen in all of Yellowstone National Park.

Bill and Dan have fished for 90 minutes with only moderate success. They only have two keepers. Fishing's never very good in the middle of the day.

Dan looks at his watch. "Bill, it's already 1:30. If we don't get started back to the Inn soon, we may get caught in a traffic jam and I'll be late for my shift."

The speed limit in Yellowstone is generally 45 mph. Unless a Ranger vehicle is in sight, most Savages ignore the speed limit. However, there are two potential problems which can significantly delay travel around the Park during the daytime. First problem: too many Dudes on the road who drive slowly to take in all of Yellowstone's wonders or, worse yet, who stop mindlessly and uncaringly in the middle of the road to get just the right picture without any regard to the traffic that backs up behind them. Second problem: black bears working the tourists like carnival hawkers for marshmallows, crackers, bread or whatever morsel a Dude tosses from their vehicle. The Savages call these bear jams.

It is 2:00 and traffic's at a standstill. Bill and Dan are stuck in traffic about three miles north of the West Thumb area. Neither can see what's causing the traffic jam, but both are pretty certain it's a black bear sow maybe with cubs. People are pulling their vehicles to the side of the road; others are just abandoning their vehicles in the middle of the road and getting out with cameras in hand or hanging from their necks.

"Bill, we have to get moving," says Dan. "I'm going to be late for work."

Bill edges his vehicle slowly forward. If an inch of space opens, he steers his car into it as long as they are moving forward. After 20 minutes, the jam clears enough so they can finally see the cause of the delay. A brown sow sits on her rump by the side of the road with her shoulders, head and paws up in the air. She's fielding marshmallows with her mouth like Mickey Mantle playing baseball in center field. Tourists stand in the road snapping pictures like photographers surrounding the red carpet at the Academy Awards.

One last vehicle sits in the middle of the road while the driver snaps one photo after another. Bill finally loses patience and intends to tap his horn to get the Dude moving. Instead, he accidently hits his horn too hard. The loud nose startles the bear. She quickly gets all four paws on the ground and vamooses into the trees.

Bill drives his vehicle slowly since people are still on the road. People turn and glare at Bill for ruining their fun. Finally, Bill has clear road ahead and quickly accelerates.

Dan turns to Bill. "Well, that's what I call bearly getting through."

Bill never turns his head, but mutters, "Not even close to being funny."

Dan's late for work that afternoon because of the bear jam. Dan has eaten dinner and has just completed a Front. The time is approximately 7:45 in the evening. He's walking back to the Bell Desk along the east side of the second-floor mezzanine and happens to see Mr. Baxter slowly climbing the stairs to Bats Alley step-by-laborious step. Dan's heart almost stops.

Robert Baxter is a large man. When Mr. Baxter walks, he walks slowly like his knees are tied together with his shin bones bowed outward. No one knows his age, but if asked to guess, Dan would guess about early to mid-sixties. Mr. Baxter seldom smiles or laughs, but when he does on rare occasion, Mr. Baxter can actually deliver a funny quip. Now, however, as Dan watches in horror, Mr. Baxter is near the top of the staircase to Bats Alley. A movie scene flashes across Dan's mind of Godzilla standing twenty feet tall as he's about to wreak death and destruction on an unsuspecting village.

Dan alters course and runs around the second-floor mezzanine and up the back steps to Bats Alley to warn everyone. Too late. As Dan reaches the top of the back staircase, he hears Mr. Baxter's booming voice somewhere down the hallway. "What's going on in here?"

Dan slowly peeks around the corner and doesn't see Mr. Baxter in the hallway, but hears animated voices coming out of someone's room. He quickly turns left and runs into Room 9 fearing that Carnival's girlfriend may be in the room. To his relief, the room is empty. He decides that there's nothing else he can do in Bats Alley and runs down the steps and back to the lobby.

Dan finds Carnival standing with his back leaning against the Bell Desk. He runs over to him and explains what just happened in Bats Alley. Dan and Carnival move into the lobby so they can watch the stairway from the third-floor mezzanine to Bats Alley.

About 10 minutes later, the door to Bats Alley opens and people start slowly walking down the stairs to the third-floor mezzanine. Laura leads the way, followed by Sally, Mary Ann, Bill, Eagle and Chukker. Mr. Baxter follows in the rear. The whole scene reminds Dan of a sheriff in the wild, wild West bringing the bad guys into town to lock them up in jail.

Even from a distance, Dan can tell that Mary Ann and Sally are crying softly. A streak of Mary Ann's mascara is running down one of her cheeks. Everybody has a somber look on their faces.

The group reaches the Bell Desk. "Where's Mac?" Mr. Baxter asks.

"I don't know, Mr. Baxter," says Dan. "I haven't seen Mac since eating my dinner in the Staffateria."

Carnival isn't sure what he should do and merely says, "Me neither."

Mr. Baxter points to the group he found in Bats Alley. "You all stay here." He goes into his office and closes the door.

To lighten the mood, Eagle looks around and smiles. "Anybody up for a drink in Bats Alley?"

"Not now, Eagle," says Chukker. "Now isn't the time for your G**d***** twisted sense of humor."

Mary Ann and Sally have stopped crying, but Sally is sniffling her nose. Dan reaches into the back pocket of his trousers and pulls out his handkerchief. He hands it to Sally. "Here, Sally. This may help."

Sally dabs the corners of her eyes with the handkerchief and then blows her nose into it. "Thanks, Dan." She extends her arm toward Dan to return his handkerchief.

Dan looks down at the handkerchief and shakes his head. "No, Sally, keep it. You may need it again."

"How much trouble are we in?" Mary Ann asks. "Do ya'll think any of us may be fired for this?"

Dan doesn't believe the mood can become any gloomier, but suddenly it does.

"It's possible, but I doubt it," says Bill. "We're all good employees. The Company has enough problems with staffing to fire all of us."

The back door of the Inn opens and Mac walks through the door. Everyone turns.

"Mac! Thank goodness you're here," says Mary Ann.

Mac steps forward and looks around the assembled group. "You all look terrible. Did someone die?"

"No one died, but Mr. Baxter made an unannounced raid on Bats Alley this evening," says Bill.

"What happened?" Mac asks.

The six unlucky Savages who were caught in the raid proceed to tell Mac the story quickly-or, for the sake of correctness, as quickly as six people can tell one story.

"So, let me make sure that I have the story correct," says Mac. "Mr. B catches three bellmen with three female employees in Bats Alley all drinking alcohol. Of course, women and alcohol aren't permitted in Bats Alley or any other male housing. Have I missed anything?"

The six Savages all look pretty glum. Bill nods his head. "That's the essence of it."

Mac takes off his glasses and wipes them with a corner of his shirt. "So, Mr. B asked for me?"

"That's right," says Mary Ann. "Oh, Mac, is there anything you can do to help us? I don't want to be fired."

Mac looks at Chukker, Bill and then Eagle. "Based on my little chat with the Bell Crew this morning, I shouldn't do a D*** thing." Mac sighs loudly. "Let me go talk with Mr. Baxter."

Mac walks over to the door to Mr. Baxter's office and knocks lightly. The door opens and he disappears into Mr. Baxter's office. Everyone hears the door shut.

Twenty minutes pass and Mr. Baxter's door hasn't opened. Finally, they all hear the sound of the iron latch on the door and the hinges creak as the door to Mr. Baxter's office opens. Mr. Baxter walks out of his office followed by Mac.

No one standing at the Bell Desk can tell what happened behind his closed door since Mr. Baxter and Mac both have poker faces.

Mr. Baxter walks over to the Front Desk. Kitty's still behind the counter supposedly working, but she's been listening intently to try and figure out what's happening.

"Kitty, get your things together and let's go have dinner," says Mr. Baxter. "We're already an hour and a half late and I'm hungry."

Mr. Baxter then walks over to the group gathered by the Bell Desk. "I'll deal with all of you in the morning. Right now, I'm tired, hungry and have a migraine starting. For now, you can all leave."

No one moves except for Kitty. Kitty joins her husband and the two of them walk slowly toward the dining room. When they've disappeared around the lobby fireplace, Mary Ann breaks the silence. "Mac, I'm dying to know what happened. Are we going to be fired?"

"I don't know," says Mac. "Mr. B talked of termination as a possibility, but I did my best to talk him out of it. Sorry, but I'm tired and going to my room in Bats Alley. We'll all find out tomorrow."

Mac turns and walks up the staircase to the first-floor mezzanine as he heads toward Bats Alley.

When Dan's shift ends at 11:00 that night, he immediately returns to Bats Alley and finds the door to Mac's room open. Chukker and Bill are sitting on the side of his bed. Mac sits in a chair with his feet propped up on a low table. All three have a can of Coors in their hand. When he sees Dan, Mac motions for him to come into the room and join them.

"Did the meeting with Mr. Baxter go okay?" Dan asks tentatively.

Mac smiles. "Daniel, I've told this story three times now and I'm not going to repeat it again. You know what happened."

"What did you say to Mr. Baxter in his office," says Dan.

"Well, I had to do some fast thinking. Mr. B asked me what I thought he should do. I told him that if I were him, I'd be very cautious before terminating anyone. I reminded him of the 'S*** rolls downhill principle.'"

Dan's puzzled. "What's that?"

"Funny thing, Mr. B asked me the same thing. I reminded him that Chukker, Bill and Eagle are three of our most experienced and hardest-working

bellmen. If Mr. B fires them, it'll be difficult to find replacements mid-sum-
mer. It would definitely impact the quality of service that the bellmen provide
to tours and guests. Our service would be slower and there'd be a greater
chance of mistakes like misplaced bags. An escort could complain to his home
office. That person could contact someone at corporate in Gardiner who would
undoubtedly contact Mr. B and ask what kind of operation is he running at
the Inn. I told Mr. B that once the S*** starts flowing, it probably will flow
back to his doorstep."

Dan's impressed. "That's brilliant, Mac."

Mac holds up his hand to stop Dan. "I then reminded Mr. B that the
three gals are young women. If he terminates them, they'll have to go home
and confess why they were terminated. Undoubtably, some parent is going
to be very upset that their young adult child has been unfairly terminated
or concerned that their child's honor has been impugned. That angry parent
telephones someone at corporate who in turn calls Mr. B. Again, I reminded
him that the S*** would end up on his doorstep."

"Mac, how did you think of this?" Dan asks.

"Oh, I almost forgot. I then reminded Mr. B that your brother is a veteran who starts law school in the fall. If some Veteran's Rights Group learns
of Bill's termination for drinking alcohol with young women, they probably
wouldn't view the infraction as constituting sufficient cause for the punish-
ment since drinking alcohol with young women seems to be a military tradition. I started to remind him of the S*** rolls downhill principle again, but
he told me to stop. He was rubbing the temples of his head and indicated that
he had a migraine headache. He said he needed to eat and we walked back to
the Bell Desk."

"Mac, do you think anything will happen in the morning?"

Mac looks at Dan. "Daniel, go to bed. What will happen tomorrow will
happen. Now, I'm going to bed. Everyone out of my room."

Mac ushers everyone outside his room and closes his door.

The next morning around 10:00, a group has gathered around the Bell
Desk. Mr. Baxter had arrived at 9:00 as usual. He walked into his office and
shut the door—not usual. Mac and the morning crew finished pulling all the
tours by 9:30. Mr. Baxter called Mac into his office about 9:50 and shut his

door. The group around the Bell Desk started to form shortly afterward. As though anticipating a puff of smoke from the Sistine Chapel when the Vatican is electing a new pope, the group gathered around the Bell Desk to await news of what, if any, action will be taken as a result of last night's raid on Bats Alley.

A short time later, Mac walks out of Mr. Baxter's office and says, "Let's take a little walk outside."

The group follows Mac through the red double front doors. Mac heads toward Hams and stops at the entrance of the West Wing. The group closes rank around him.

Mac's face breaks into a smile. "No one gets terminated." The group doesn't cheer, but there's a collective sigh of relief. Mac continues. "Mr. B said that he thought long and hard about everything during the night and concluded that it isn't in anyone's best interests, including his own, to terminate anyone. In fact, Mr. B told me that he never wants to set foot in Bats Alley again."

"So, Mr. Baxter's attitude is one of 'what happens in Bats Alley stays in Bats Alley?'" Dan asks.

"Not exactly what he said, but that's the essence of what he meant," says Mac. "I promised to continue working with the bellmen on keeping the noise down at night and Mr. B will stay out of Bats Alley unless a complaint reaches Gardiner."

Now a collective cheer erupts from the group.

The bellmen didn't know at the time, but, true to his word, Mr. Baxter never stepped a foot in Bats Alley ever again.

CHAPTER FIFTEEN
GRIZZLY ENCOUNTER IN HAYDEN VALLEY

Dan and Lou have a topographical map of Yellowstone National Park spread out on the lower bunk of their room when Larry walks through the door.

"What are you looking at?"

They look up and acknowledge Larry with nods of their heads.

"Dan and I are going to take our day off next week and hike Hayden Valley," says Lou. "I was just showing Dan on the map what I expect our route will be."

"Do you mind if I look too?"

"Sure." Lou bends over the map again. He uses his right index finger to point things out on the map and show them the proposed route.

"So, Dan," says Lou. "You indicate that Bill will let us use his car and Chukker's said we can use his car as well. I suggest that on the day before our trip, we take both cars and park one at the turnout closest to Nez Perce Creek so it'll be waiting when we finish our hike."

Lou points to the Nez Pearce Creek area on the map[2] and continues, "We'll drive the other car back to the Inn. I suggest that we get up early on the day of our hike and have a quick breakfast before leaving the Inn. We'll drive to the turnout for Alum Creek." Lou points to Alum Creek on the map. "The trail for Hayden Valley starts along Alum Creek. With any luck, we'll be on the trail by 9:00 in the morning."

Dan interrupts Lou. "What do we do with the second car that we leave at Alum Creek?"

---

2   Appendix 2.

Lou nods his head. "Good question. On the morning after the hike, you have the 12-8 shift and I have the 3-11 shift. We'll have to drive the car which we pick up at the Nez Perce Creek turnoff and return early the next morning to pick up the car left at the Alum Creek turnoff. We'll each drive a car back to the Inn. I know it's a lot of driving, but I can't figure any other way to do it."

Dan's nods his head.

Lou puts his finger back on the map. "At Alum Creek, there's a game trail that runs west along the north side of the creek. Hayden Valley is several miles wide with hills on the north and south sides that have lodgepole pine forests starting near the ridge line. The valley consists mostly of grasses and sagebrush. We'll be walking for five or six miles in the open through grizzly country."

Lou's description is generally correct, but none of these three bellmen have ever hiked in Hayden Valley. To be more accurate, Hayden Valley is a high-altitude plateau approximately seven miles in length and seven miles wide. The valley contains abundant grasses and chapparal, but trees are sparse in the valley and instead grow starting near the ridge lines of the hills on both the north and south sides of the valley[3].

The most famous inhabitant of Hayden Valley is the grizzly bear. In the early 1970s, black bears are more commonly viewed by tourists, but grizzly bears are more elusive and widely feared by people. A grizzly bear has a large muscle mass on its shoulders and a concave face. A male grizzly can weigh as much as 700 pounds and can run up to 35 mph. Most people believe grizzlies can't climb trees, but this is a myth. Although some grizzles can climb trees, most don't because the claws on their massive paws are curved and can be over 5.5 inches long. Grizzlies are unpredictable and can be extremely aggressive. Without question, grizzlies are at the very top of the food chain in Yellowstone National Park. All three bellman understand the dangers presented by hiking through Hayden Valley.

Lou still has his finger on the map. "We'll run into the Mary Mountain trail and continue heading west along the forested northern fringe of Hayden Valley. We'll ultimately reach the top of Mary Mountain and then enter a corridor of lodgepole pine forest through the Central Plateau which leads to Mary

---

3   Appendix 3.

Lake. Our path will descend from Mary Lake and eventually we'll break into open meadowland where we'll find Nez Perce Creek. We then follow the path along the creek until we reach the highway that runs between Old Faithful and Madison Junction."

"That sounds like a really long hike," says Dan. "How long will the hike be?"

Lou shrugs his shoulders. "I'm not sure, but I guess it'll be 21 to 25 miles."

Dan whistles softly.

"Wow, this sounds like a great adventure," says Larry. "Can I join you next week?"

Dan looks at Lou. Lou thinks for a minute and turns to Larry. "I don't have any objection and assume Dan doesn't either. If we were to encounter a bear in Hayden Valley, there may be safety in numbers. Dan, do you object to Larry joining us?"

"No, but Mac may object. He didn't like three bellmen being off at the same time when we went into the Southeast Arm. He finally approved it because some of us were morning crew and some were afternoon crew. This would involve all afternoon crew. But, if Mac approves it, you're more than welcome to join us."

"Thanks, guys. I'm going to find Mac and ask him if it'll be okay."

"Rather than asking Mac yourself, I think it's better if we all approach Mac together," Lou says.

"Good idea, Lou," says Larry.

"What? All three of you want the same day off?"

Larry, Lou and Dan are pitching the idea for a threesome in Hayden Valley and Mac doesn't seem particularly receptive to the idea.

Larry pleads his case. "Mac, I missed out on the Southeast Arm adventure and I don't want to miss out on this trip. You gave three bellmen the same day off so they could go to the Southeast Arm together."

"Big difference," says Mac. "They weren't all on morning crew or all on afternoon crew. You three guys are all on afternoon crew. I'm concerned that we'll not have sufficient crew to provide the same quality of service that we always provide to the Dudes."

Larry sees that he's losing the battle. "What if one of the morning crew guys is willing to cover for me? Could I do it then?"

Mac twists the corner of his moustache. "H***, I doubt any of the morning crew guys will be willing to do that. But, if you get one morning crew guy to go along, okay, then you can do it."

When Mac leaves, Larry immediately turns to Dan. "Since Bill is your brother, can you ask him for me?"

Dan starts laughing. "Really? That's a pretty big ask from my brother. Bill already agreed to let me borrow his car so Lou and I can do the trip. If you want to go, you'll need to ask him yourself." Frankly, he doesn't want to put his brother on the spot by asking on Larry's behalf.

About thirty minutes later, Larry walks into Room 5 with a big grin on his face. He didn't need to say anything-both Lou and Dan know that Bill has agreed to cover for Larry and he'd be going to Hayden Valley with them.

On the evening before the big hike, Dan drives Bill's car to the turnout closest to Nez Perce Creek and Lou follows in Chukker's car. He parks Bill's car in the turnout and locks the doors. He climbs into the passenger seat of Chukker's car for the return ride. When they reach the Inn, Dan and Lou walk straight to their room in Bats Alley and methodically lay out their gear for the following day on the lower bunk bed. Lou lays the items on the bed while Dan carefully checks the items off the joint list which they'd prepared several days earlier. Lou's day pack-check. Lou's topographical map neatly folded into a 6" by 6" square-check. Lou's 35mm camera-check. Lou's binoculars-check. Dan feels guilty that Lou's getting all the checks. Dan's old metal canteen with brightly colored wool sides and shoulder strap-check. Dan thinks that it's not much of a contribution, but it's something. Provisions for lunch and snacks-check. Four chocolate candy bars-check. And so the process continues.

When all items on the joint list have been checked, Lou carefully packs the items into his day pack. Since Dan doesn't own a day pack, Lou graciously agrees to carry the day pack and he will carry the canteen of water. Each then lays out their clothes for the next day. Being mid-July, the forecast is for highs in the mid-to high 80s with clear skies. It'll be cool when they start the hike, but the day will warm quickly. Thus, both plan to dress in layers which can be removed as the day heats up.

The next morning, both arise around 5:45 and get ready for the day. They're waiting outside the Staffateria when it opens at 6:30. Larry joins them five minutes later. The three eat quickly and agree to meet at the Bell Desk in twenty minutes. Dan and Lou are waiting for Larry when he comes down the staircase located next to the Bell Desk. Larry's wearing shorts, a tee shirt, a sweatshirt wrapped around his waist, knee length socks, hiking boots and a big cowboy hat on his head. He's carrying a rather large day pack in his right hand.

Lou takes a look at Larry. "Are you dressed for a hike or a rodeo?"

Larry grins good-naturedly.

Dan notices that Larry's day pack has a big bulge. "Say, Larry, what do you have in your day pack?"

"Just the usual things for a long hike."

Dan's question prompts Lou to look at Larry's day pack. "Larry, Dan's right. Your day pack has a big bulge in it."

Larry looks at Lou and smiles. "It's a surprise for the hike."

Dan and Lou look at each other.

"I'm not sure that I like surprises," says Dan. "Especially in the middle of grizzly country."

"Really, don't worry about it," says Larry. "I know you'll like it."

Lou looks at Dan and shrugs his shoulders. "Gentleman, we have a long, long day ahead," Lou says. "Let's get going."

It is about 10:30 and the temperature must already be in the mid-80s. The three bellmen have walked a couple of miles in treeless terrain. They're all now wearing sweat-stained tee shirts.

Lou's leading the group and stops to take a drink of water. The others follow suit. All three feel the same sense of foreboding-they're in the middle of grizzly country and the nearest tree is probably a half mile away.

Lou scans the valley and points to something on the south side of Alum Creek.

"What do you see, Lou?" Dan asks.

"It's difficult to see with a naked eye, but I think I see a bear about a mile away walking up the south slope of the valley."

As Dan and Larry strain to see what he's describing, Lou takes off his day pack. He pulls out his binoculars and trains them on the area he's spotted.

"Yep," says Lou. "It's a sow grizzly with a cub following her. I can see the hump on her back."

Lou hands the binoculars to Dan and then to Larry so they can both view the mother and cub grizzly bears.

Although the bears are walking away from them and are over a mile away, Lou returns his binoculars to his day pack and hoists the pack onto his back. "I think we better get moving. I suggest we hike another hour or two and then stop for lunch."

There being no dissenting opinion, Lou leads the other two westward through Hayden Valley.

About two hours later, the group still hasn't left the treeless portion of Hayden Valley. They come upon a large knoll which has a dozen or so pine trees clustered at the top of the knoll. Most of the trees are lodgepole pines, but there are a couple of Western Douglas fir. The group decides to stop here in the meager shade of the trees and eat lunch.

After taking off their day packs and, in Dan's case, his canteen, Lou looks around the area. "Before we do anything, lets each pick out a tree in case a bear wanders by and decides to take a peek at us."

Larry starts laughing, but Lou holds his hand up. "Stop laughing. We're still in the middle of grizzly country and I want to be prepared just in case."

Each selects a tree. Lou and Dan go first and choose the two Western Douglas firs because the branches are lower. Larry selects a lodgepole pine which has a sturdy looking trunk, but the first branch is about ten feet high.

Dan and Lou are busy looking at the map which Lou has unfolded when they suddenly smell smoke. Both look up and see that Larry has gathered some dead tree branches and built a small fire which is just catching hold.

Lou is incredulous. "Larry, what the H*** are you doing?"

A big grin breaks across Larry's face. "Surprise!" He pulls a cast iron skillet out of his day pack and plops it on a larger branch over the fire. He then reaches back into his day pack and pulls out a rather large packet wrapped in butcher's paper.

"What's in your hands?" Dan practically screams the words at Larry.

Larry grins again and holds the package up. "Two pounds of West Yellowstone's finest bacon." Larry quickly unwraps the bacon and throws it into the skillet which is now quite hot. The bacon immediately begins to sizzle and pop.

Dan and Lou absolutely lose their cool. Lou shouts at Larry. "Larry, you fool. Are you trying to get us killed?"

"Hey, guys," says Larry. "Don't get mad at me. I talked with someone who hiked Hayden Valley and he never saw a bear. Why come to Hayden Valley if you don't want to see a grizzly. I just didn't want us to make this big hike and leave empty handed."

Lou's posture suddenly freezes. Lou lowers his voice and speaks quietly. "Guys, don't make any sudden moves. We've got company."

Dan and Larry follow Lou's stare and understand why his posture has frozen.

A rather large grizzly bear stands about 300 yards away. Dan knows it's a grizzly by the large-no, humongous, hump on its back. This monster of a grizzly is standing still with its huge nose pointed in the air. The beast slowly swings its massive head back and forth trying to pinpoint the source of the scent it smells.

Grizzly bears have notoriously bad eyesight, but Mother nature compensated by giving them an extremely keen sense of smell. When they would later reflect back on this moment, the three bellmen were never sure whether it was the scent of bacon frying over an open fire or the scent of fresh red meat, but the grizzly pinpoints the direction of the source of the scent and starts walking slowly toward them.

"Start slowly walking backward toward your tree," says Lou. He has the presence of mind to pick up his day pack with one hand while backing up very slowly. Dan and Larry join him in a slow backward walk.

The grizzly suddenly starts running. Dan yells. "Run!" No further instructions are necessary.

All three bellman turn and each runs to his predesignated tree. They frantically start scrambling up their respective tree as quickly as humanly possible.

The grizzly runs past the bacon frying in the cast iron skillet and heads directly for the lodgepole pine tree where Larry's now perched near its top with his arms tightly wrapped around the trunk. The bear emits a screeching sound somewhat between a growl and a howl. The bear stands on its rear paws and tries to reach Larry with its forepaws. When it can't touch Larry, the bear leans back and crashes forward against the tree trunk in an attempt to dislodge Larry from the top of the tree. The bear continues trying to dislodge Larry by repeatedly leaning back and crashing forward against the tree trunk.

"Larry, hold on tight," Dan yells, probably needlessly. The bear quickly whirls around and looks up into the Western Douglas fir tree where Dan sits perched near its top on a branch big enough to support his weight. The grizzly races over to his tree and again stands on its rear paws to reach him. Dan wonders if he's going to survive to tell this story to others, but then thinks that nobody will ever believe him if he does survive.

When unsuccessful in reaching him, the bear returns to a position of having all four of its paws on the ground. At that moment, a gust of wind blows Larry's cowboy hat off his head. The hat falls out of the tree and lands about twenty feet from the bear. Apparently frightened by the sudden appearance of the hat, the grizzly emits a loud roar and charges toward the hat. The bear grabs the hat in its teeth and shakes it violently. The grizzly seemingly realizes that the hat isn't either a threat or food and lets the felt hat fall from its mouth to the ground.

Larry looks at the others and just shakes his head.

The bear slowly looks around and then saunters to where the bacon's still frying in the iron skillet. The bear sniffs carefully into the smoke. It doesn't step into the coals, but instead knocks the iron skillet from its place in the fire with one swipe of its massive paw. The bacon flies out of the skillet and rolls on the ground before coming to a halt. The bear walks over to the bacon and waits patiently for the hot grease to cool before devouring two pounds of West Yellowstone's finest bacon.

Satisfied with this meal in its tummy, the bear walks over to the lodgepole pine tree where Larry's still perched near the top. The bear sniffs around for a few minutes. It then circles the tree several times and finally curls up into a ball with its back against the tree's trunk. The bear becomes very still. Dan didn't know that bears snore, but this bear is snoring loudly five minutes into its slumber.

Forty minutes pass and the bear continues to sleep like a baby-actually, like a snoring baby. The three bellmen grow impatient sitting in the tops of their respective trees. At first, the three are hesitant to speak verbally and only communicate with gestures and by mouthing words. However, as the bear keeps sleeping at the bottom of Larry's tree, they become bolder and start whispering.

Lou whispers. "How long is this D*** bear going to sleep?"

Larry whispers. "Can either of you smell the stench of this flea-bitten monster? When it let out that thunderous noise below me, I thought for a moment that the stench alone would knock me out of this D*** tree."

Dan whispers. "I'm glad that the gals at the Inn can't see us now. Three bellmen sitting at the tops of three trees while a grizzly snoozes below us."

Larry whispers. "At least the grizzly's snoozing. I prefer that to the bear trying to shake me out this D*** tree."

Dan whispers. "I have an idea how we might get rid of the monster. Lou, can you reach those candy bars in your day pack?"

Lou takes his day pack off while holding onto the tree with his left hand and manages to open the top flap with his right hand. Lou sticks his right hand into his day pack and after a moment nods his head. "I found them."

Dan whispers. "Good. Now take the four candy bars and throw them as far as you can in the direction from where the bear appeared. Maybe two pounds of West Yellowstone's finest didn't fill the big guy up."

Lou whispers back. "Good idea. I'll try it."

Lou grabs the four candy bars with his right hand while tightly clutching a stout tree branch with his left hand. With his right arm, he throws all four chocolate bars as far as he can in the direction where the bear had originally appeared.

For a few minutes, the bear doesn't move, but keeps snoring loudly. Then, they notice that the bear's nose starts to twitch. The grizzly opens its tiny eyes. It lifts its massive head and starts smelling the air with its twitching nose. Finally, the bear stands on its paws and slowly lumbers over to the four chocolate candy bars. The bellmen watch in fascination as the bear slowly works the chocolate free from the candy wrappers with his tongue and forepaws and swallows each bar in one big bite. Its appetite apparently not satisfied, the grizzly walks slowly back to where it had first appeared and disappears over the knoll.

Forty-five minutes later, Lou grows impatient waiting at the top of his tree. "How long do you think we have to wait before it's safe to climb out of these trees?"

"I don't know," says Larry. "But I need to relieve myself."

"What if that grizzly's waiting for us to climb down and then ambush us?" Dan asks.

"I can't answer that question," says Larry. "But I do have to answer the call of nature." He starts climbing down out of his tree. After Larry's feet hit the ground and he's taken care of his business, Lou looks at Dan. "Well, maybe we should climb down too." Both of them start climbing down from their respective trees.

The fire has died. Larry kicks the ashes just in case the fire isn't totally out. Larry then goes over to retrieve his cast iron skillet. Dan watches him and says, "Larry, I guess you'll not be bringing home the bacon tonight." No one laughs.

Larry then retrieves his battered cowboy hat. He brushes the dust off and puts it on his head.

With one last look around, Lou starts hiking westward. Dan and Larry silently fall in line behind him. All three bellmen from Old Faithful Inn know they have a lot of ground to cover before this day will end.

Late that evening, three weary bellmen sit in Room 5 of Bats Alley. Lou and Larry are sipping their cans of Coors beer. Dan has his usual Coke. They're reminiscing about their day.

"Wow," says Dan. "That grizzly encounter was unbelievable."

Larry smiles and picks up his hat. "I'm the only one who has a souvenir to prove it." Larry sticks his finger through a hole near the crown of the hat and starts wiggling it.

Lou looks at Larry. "You're just lucky that you weren't wearing that D*** hat when that monster made the hole."

"Hey, I've been thinking about our grizzly encounter and two things seem interesting," says Dan.

"What's that?" Larry asks.

"First, do you remember that the bear ran past the bacon frying in the pan to try and attack us," says Dan.

"Yeah," says Lou. "I hadn't realized that until now. What's the significance?"

Dan pauses. "Probably we were much larger and the bear charged the biggest threat first. But, maybe the bear passed the bacon because it thought we were a bigger meal."

"Kind of a grim thought," says Lou.

The silence in the room becomes palpable.

"What's your second thought?" Larry asks.

"Do you remember that the bear didn't burn itself by reaching in the pan to get the bacon," says Dan. "It swatted the pan from the fire and then waited for the bacon to cool before eating it."

"So, what's the significance of that?" says Larry.

"The significance is that this probably wasn't the grizzly's first encounter of this type," Dan says. "It means that the grizzly probably has interacted with people before and is pretty savvy."

Lou looks at Larry. "I think that Dan's telling us that we got lucky today with this grizzly."

Dan nods his head. "Yeah, it was a great adventure. But it's one I don't have to repeat."

As the group breaks up for the night, Dan thinks to himself that today's adventure gave a whole new meaning to the term 'a grizzly encounter.'

CHAPTER SIXTEEN

RESPECTING OTHERS' CULTURE AND CUSTOMS

"Front please."

It's approximately 4:15 in the afternoon. Dan's next up on the bellmen's list and walks to the Front Desk to assist the guest. Laura hands him the room key and the slip of paper with the guest's name and address. Dan looks at the slip of paper which reads "Samuel Jones", but the address portion is blank. The room key reads "208" which is located on the third floor of the main house of the Inn.

Dan looks at the guest. "Mr. Jones?"

Mr. Jones is a heavier older man. He wears a flamboyant yellow tie with a bright blue peacock embroidered on the front and sandals on his bare feet.

Mr. Jones is looking at the lobby. Dan isn't sure that the guest heard him. "Mr. Jones, do you have any luggage that I can help you with?"

Mr. Jones realizes that he's speaking to him and turns to address Dan. "Yes. You can call me 'Sir.'"

Dan is slightly taken aback. "Where is your luggage located, Sir?"

Mr. Jones points toward the front doors. "Follow me, Boy." Dan cringes at being called 'Boy.'

Mr. Jones turns and starts shuffling toward the front doors of the Inn with Dan in tow. He notices that this individual has a foreign accent, but he can't place the origin of the accent.

"Sir, I notice that you provided no address. Where are you from?"

Mr. Jones looks puzzled by the question. Dan rephrases it believing that this might help him understand. "Where is your home?"

"Oh, I have traveled from a long, long distance."

Dan's still curious. He isn't sure that the man's name is really Jones, but decides it may be best to let it go.

When they step out onto the front porch, Mr. Jones points directly ahead to a Yellowstone Park Company bus that's parked in front of the portico.

At Old Faithful Inn in the early 1970s, the bellmen deal with two types of tours. Most tours ride in their company owned bus or a bus leased by the tour company. These are group tours which usually have 20 to 45 tourists. The morning crew handles the luggage for these tours. The other type of tours are individual tourists who book their tours through the Yellowstone Park Company and tour Yellowstone National Park aboard a Company owned bus. The bus driver has a microphone and provides commentary as the Company bus travels around the Park. The afternoon crew handles the luggage for these individuals as normal Fronts. The afternoon crew doesn't particularly like handling these individual tourists since they generally are small tippers. But it's part of the job if you want to be a bellman at Old Faithful Inn.

Mr. Jones walks over to the back of the bus and points to a dilapidated old carpet bag which still sits in the back of the Company bus. Dan looks at the bag which is literally made out of old floral-patterned carpet. It's the largest bag that he's ever seen in his entire life. The bus driver comes over to him and says, "I think that you're going to need my help lifting that bag out of the bus."

Dan looks more closely at the bag. The sides of this enormous bag seem to bulge out. The bag has a single leather handle which is frayed and looks as if it may break apart if used. Masking tape has been wrapped around portions of the handle.

Dan grips the handle with his right hand and starts to lift the bag out of the bus, but it doesn't budge. The bus driver leans over and together they lift the bag out of the bus and carry it to the porch of the Inn. Mr. Jones follows them to the porch.

Dan thanks the bus driver for his help and turns to Mr. Jones. "Sir, the bag seems really heavy. Are you a geologist collecting rocks?" Dan is attempting to put a smile on Mr. Jones' face. The plan fails miserably.

Mr. Jones stares at Dan. "Boy, why do you ask me a question like that?"

"Sorry, Sir," says Dan. "I was just trying to make a joke."

"Not funny," Mr. Jones says and turns his back on him.

Bystanders start to ooh and aah. Old Faithful Geyser is erupting. Mr. Jones opens an old weathered leather bag that he's carrying on his shoulder and pulls out an old 35mm camera.

"Stay here with the bag, Boy." He then walks in the direction of Old Faithful Geyser holding his camera in his hand. Dan soon loses sight of Mr. Jones as he pushes his way through the crowd which is watching the eruption. In the interim, Dan decides to return to the Bell Desk and get a metal cart so he can wheel the bag to the stairway.

Mr. Jones returns fifteen minutes later. "Now, Boy, you can take me to my room."

By now, crowds of tourists are thronging into the lobby of the Inn as usual following an eruption. Dan tries to wheel his cart through the crowd, but gets jostled by tourists eager to see what the big wooden building looks like inside. Dan manages to reach the Bell Desk, but turns around and discovers that Mr. Jones isn't there. Dan leaves the bag-after all, no one's going to steal an old dilapidated bag like this and especially one that weighs as much as this one does-and retraces his steps to find Mr. Jones. He finds him across the lobby leaning backward to take a picture of the Inn's fireplace.

"Sir, I seem to have lost you," says Dan. "Please follow me so I can take you to your room."

"Boy, do not bother me until I take my photo."

"Sir, we bellmen are very busy," says Dan as patiently as he can. "Please, I need to show you to your room so I can get back and help other guests."

Mr. Jones finishes taking his photo and slowly puts his camera back in the leather shoulder bag. He says nothing, but nods his head. Dan starts walking toward the staircase by the Bell Desk and this time Mr. Jones silently follows behind.

When they reach Mr. Jones' bag, Dan notices that Carnival is standing by the Bell Desk. Dan calls to him. "Carnival, this bag is incredibly heavy. Can you help me get it to the third floor?"

Carnival laughs. "Did someone forget their spinach today?" Dan understands the reference is to the cartoon character Popeye, but at the moment Dan doesn't have much humor in him.

Carnival comes over and Dan instructs him to lift one end of the bag while he lifts the other end. Carnival lifts his end and grunts. ""J****, you weren't kidding."

The two bellmen strain as they carry the bag to the third-floor mezzanine. Carnival sets down his end on the floor of the third-floor mezzanine and pulls a handkerchief from his back trouser pocket. He mops sweat from his forehead. "Do you want me to help you get it to the room?"

"No, I'll take it from here," says Dan. "Thanks for your help, Carnival. I don't believe that I could 've carried this up the steps by myself."

Carnival returns to the Bell Desk and Dan grabs the handle of the bag with both hands. He starts shuffling toward Room 208. Dan has almost reached the room when the leather handle breaks and the bag drops to the floor. Dan looks up at Mr. Jones. "Sir, it looks like your handle finally broke."

Mr. Jones frowns. "Boy, you broke the handle of my bag."

By now, Dan's patience is pretty thin. "Sir, the leather on your handle was badly frayed before I even touched the bag. It looks like it has broken before and someone taped it together. With the weight you have in your bag, I suspect it has broken numerous times before."

Mr. Jones glares at him. "Boy, you break the handle, you fix the handle."

Dan is furious. Mr. Jones has already taken 45 minutes of his time during the busiest time of the day. However, Dan knows the guest is always right.

"Sir, let's get you and your bag into your room and I'll see what I can do to help you fix your bag."

Dan grabs one end of the bag and starts dragging it across the floor. Mr. Jones makes no effort to help. He finally reaches Room 208 and opens the door for Mr. Jones to enter. Mr. Jones walks around the small room inspecting everything as though he's the housekeeping supervisor. Dan drags the bag into the room using both hands.

"Boy, I don't like this room. I want another one."

In fact, the Inn is normally 100% booked most nights during the summer. It is further fact that by now Dan could care less what Mr. Jones thinks. Besides, even if there were another room available, Dan isn't going to carry, push or pull that old carpet bag another inch.

Dan speaks evenly. "Sorry, Sir, but I know the rooms are all taken. If you prefer to have your money back and leave, I'm sure the Front Desk will refund the money you paid for the room."

Mr. Jones is not too keen on the "Boy's" reply, but decides it's best not to press the issue unless he's willing to sleep in the woods with the animals that evening.

"Boy, are you going to fix the handle that you broke?"

Dan can hardly contain his anger, but again manages to speak evenly. "Let me work on that."

Dan walks out of the room and returns to the Bell Desk. Lou's standing by the Bell Desk and sees Dan walking toward him. "Where have you been? We've been really busy."

"I've been helping the Dude from Hell," says Dan. "The guy's impossible and claims I broke the handle on his old dilapidated carpet bag. He now expects me to fix it. Do you know where I can find some duct tape?"

"Check with the Inn's electrician. He works in a space out back near the laundry."

Dan walks out the back door and spends the next thirty minutes trying to locate the Inn electrician. After finally finding him and explaining why he needs duct tape, Dan returns to Room 208 with a roll of duct tape in his hand. He knocks at the door and Mr. Jones opens the door to let him enter. Dan spends the next ten minutes wrapping layers of duct tape around the handle. When he's finished, Mr. Jones bends over to examine the newly duct taped handle of his carpet bag.

"Boy, this is no good."

Dan can't believe what he's hearing. "What do you mean this is no good?"

"This is no good because the tape will not hold the handle together for very long."

Dan is incredulous. "Sir, the handle was taped with masking tape when I first saw it. Duct tape is much stronger than the masking tape that you had on the handle."

Mr. Jones shakes his head from side-to-side. "I need the handle to last until I return home. I have a long, long trip ahead of me. Boy, you need to make this right."

Dan's becoming too weary to argue with this person. "Let me see what I can figure out." He walks out the door for the second time.

When Dan reaches the Bell Desk, Lou is there again waiting for another Front.

"Lou, do know where I can find some rope?"

Lou scratches his head. "How about the Inn's carpenter?"

Dan sighs. "Where can I find the carpenter?"

"I'm not sure, but I think that he has his shop somewhere out back near the boiler."

Dan walks out the back door of the Inn again and spends the next thirty minutes trying to track down the Inn carpenter. He finally finds the carpenter and explains why he needs a piece of rope.

"I don't have any rope, but I have some twine that might work." He finds a spool of twine and cuts off a large piece for Dan. He hands Dan the twine. "I hope that this works."

Dan thanks him for his help and walks back to Room 208. He knocks on the door and Mr. Jones again lets him into the room. Dan spends the next twenty minutes looping the twine back and forth between the handle brackets and then taping the twine with duct tape. Dan picks up the bag by its new improved handle and shows Mr. Jones its strength. "Sir, I believe that this will get you back home."

When he sets the bag back on the floor, Mr. Jones comes over to the bag and gives the handle a couple of hard pulls. Dan notices that he doesn't lift the bag off the floor.

"This should do," says Mr. Jones.

Dan turns and starts to walk back out of the room.

"Boy, stop," Mr. Jones says.

Dan stops and faces Mr. Jones who reaches into his front trouser pocket and pulls out a small coin purse. He slowly unzips the top of the coin purse and finally removes something with his right index finger and thumb. Mr. Jones reaches his right hand toward Dan.

"This is for you, Boy."

Dan puts his right hand out palm facing upward and Mr. Jones drops something into the palm of his hand. He raises his hand closer to his face and sees a tarnished dime resting in the middle of his palm.

Dan's face flushes. For a second, he considers flipping the dime back to Mr. Jones. Instead, he closes his hand slowly around the coin and says, "Thank you, Sir,"

Dan walks out of the room and shuts the door to Room 208 behind him.

Later that evening, Dan, Bill and Lou are sitting together in Bill's room. Dan has just finished his tale of the foreign guest. Both are laughing at Dan's misfortune.

"This Dude took over two hours of my time during the busiest time of day," says Dan. "Normally, I would make $15 to $20 during those two hours. What did I receive? A lousy dime."

Bill kids Dan. "A whole dime? The Dude thought you were overpaid."

Bill and Lou laugh; Dan does not.

"Did you ever find out why the Dude's bag was so heavy?" asks Lou.

"I did. You're not going to believe this." Dan pauses and smiles.

"What?" says Bill. "Don't keep us in suspense."

"Well, when I went back to the room the third time, the Dude asked me for directions to the restroom. After he walked out of the room, I peeked inside his bag. There were normal things like clothes, jackets and shoes. But there also was a set of old encyclopedias."

"No way," says Lou. "Are you sure?"

"Yeah, I'm absolutely sure. I counted the volumes. There were eighteen volumes. Maybe it wasn't a full set, but it must have been pretty close."

"Why do you think he was carrying all those encyclopedias in his bag?" Bill asks. "Do you think that he was an encyclopedia salesman?"

"No, he definitely didn't have a salesman's personality."

"Do you have any ideas?" Lou asks.

"Yeah, I think that I may. The Dude said he was a long, long way from home. Based on his dime tip, I'm guessing that he had an old set of encyclopedias and took them on his trip rather than spending money to buy a guidebook like most tourists."

All of them begin laughing so hard that their eyes tear.

When the laughter stops, Dan looks at Bill and Lou. "You know what bothered me more than the dime? The Dude treated me like the hired help by always calling me 'Boy.'"

"Dan, remember that you don't know where this person lives or the culture and customs of his home," says Bill. "This person may live in a society that has some type of class system."

Dan shakes his head. "Yeah, but don't you think someone from overseas traveling in this country would take the time to learn a little bit about our culture and customs? Just show a little respect for our culture and our customs?"

"You know, we can learn from others who set a good example for us," says Bill. "We also can learn from others who set a bad example for us. Maybe you might want to take the high road and learn something positive from this experience that you can use in the future."

Dan pauses for a moment to process what Bill just said and then says, "Now I understand why you're my big brother." They all laugh.

"I am going to take the high road," says Dan. "I'll probably never miss the few dollars that I lost this afternoon. But I've learned a couple of valuable lessons. I'm going to try to never treat anyone as the hired help and, if and when I'm able to travel in the future, I'm going to try to learn about the culture and customs of the places I visit so I'm never the dreadful foreign guest."

"Oh, and one more thing. I promise to never, ever give anyone a dime tip for service."

All of them start laughing so hard that tears begin rolling down their cheeks.

CHAPTER SEVENTEEN
DANCING IN YELLOWSTONE

"Dan, are you going to the dance with me tomorrow night?"

Dan knows exactly what Lou's talking about, but plays dumb. "Tell me about the dance again."

Lou seems exasperated. "As I've told you repeatedly, there's a dance tomorrow evening at the Lodge rec center. Everyone's going to be there. I want you to join all of us. You'll have a great time."

"What's the name of the band again?" Dan senses that he may be overplaying his role.

"They're called the Singing Squirrels," says Lou. "They've played all over the Park and will be here tomorrow night."

Dan knows that the Yellowstone Park Company has rec centers at Mammoth Hot Springs, Canyon Village, Lake Lodge and Old Faithful Lodge. He also knows that YPCO pays bands to play at each rec center three or four times during the summer. Some bands are just traveling through the Park and are hired by circumstance. Sometimes, the band members have jobs with YPCO in the Park and play at night.

"I'm not much of a dancer," Dan reminds Lou.

"Yeah, you've told me that before. If you don't want to dance, just come and enjoy the music and the conversation."

Bill walks into their room. "What are you guys talking about?"

Lou points at Dan. "I was just talking to your brother about going to the dance tomorrow night with us."

Bill knows why Dan's reluctant to attend the dance, but says nothing.

"Bill, are you going to the dance?" Lou asks.

"Yeah, I'm looking forward to it. I hear that the band's pretty good."

"That's what I was just telling him." Lou looks at Dan. "Okay, it's settled. You're coming with us to the dance."

"But, Lou, I didn't agree to go," says Dan.

"Nope, you're going with us. Right, Bill?"

Bill looks at his brother. "Dan, I guess you're coming with us."

The next evening, Dan, Bill and Lou walk together to the Lodge rec center. They can hear the band playing well before their arrival.

"I don't know how good they are," says Bill. "But they certainly play loudly enough."

A large number of employees are attending the dance. Most are inside the rec hall, but many are standing around outside.

"I see a lot of familiar faces, but I don't recognize a lot of these people," says Dan.

"A lot of employees come from different locations in the Park," Bill says.

"Why are so many people standing outside?" Dan asks.

"Some people find it hard to hear inside over the music," says Lou. "Some go outside for a smoke. Also, it can get really warm inside. Some go outside to cool off."

They step inside. Dan's surprised by how many employees are there. He's also surprised by how loud the music is playing.

Lou shouts to be heard. "I see Mary Ann over there. I'm going to see if she wants to dance."

Dan watches Lou stroll over to Mary Ann and in a few minutes, they're dancing together on the dance floor.

Dan looks at the band. Suddenly, he realizes that he knows one of the guys playing a guitar.

The band leader speaks into the microphone. "You all are a great crowd this evening. The band's going to take a short break. We'll be back soon."

People start applauding as the band members put down their instruments and walk down from the stage.

Dan stares at the band members and then looks at Bill. "I think that I know one of the band members. I'm going to go over and talk with him. Do you want to come with me?"

"No thanks. I see Penny and Debbie and I'm going to talk with them."
Bill heads across the floor toward the gals and Dan walks over to the band
member who he's spotted. This individual's walking toward the exit. Dan cuts
him off.

"Hi, do you remember me?"

The band member has long hair and wears a tee shirt and black leather
jacket. He looks him in the face. Dan can tell that he's struggling to remember who he is or where he met him.

"Kyle. That's your name, right?"

"Yeah, how do you know that?"

Dan smiles. "I met you in Gardiner when your parents dropped you off
to work in the Park."

"Yeah, I remember you now. My parents got a room for both of us."

"That's right. I didn't realize then that you play in a band. I thought that
you were working in the Park this summer."

"Yeah, that was the original plan. I missed the bus that morning and
showed up late at Canyon Village. They put me to work as a dishwasher. The
job was horrible. After a couple of days, I planned to quit but they fired me
before I could quit."

Dan's curiosity is peaked. "Why did they fire you?"

"Someone caught me smoking a joint. Apparently, that's not allowed in
the Park."

"Sorry to hear that." Actually, Dan isn't surprised at all. "How did you
end up with the band?"

"While waiting for a ride home, I met someone who was traveling through
the Park with a band. I told this dude that I used to play guitar in a band
back home and asked if they needed a musician. It turned out that their lead
guitarist had to return home for an emergency and they gave me an audition.
I've been playing with the band all summer."

"Hey, man, nice seeing you again," says Kyle. "If you don't mind, our
break's going to be over soon and I need to go outside and have a smoke." Dan
wonders whether it's a cigarette or a joint.

The band starts playing again. Dan's standing by himself watching everyone on the dance floor when Laura walks up.

"Hi, Dan. You look lonesome over here." Laura smiles at him.

"Hi, Laura. I'm not lonesome—just enjoying the music."

"Do you like the band?"

"Yeah, they're pretty good."

"Why don't you come and dance with me?" Before he can respond, Laura grabs his hand and starts leading him toward the dance floor.

Dan pulls his hand away and turns back.

Laura grabs Dan arm and pulls it hard so he's facing her.

"Why'd you do that?" asks Laura.

"I'm not much of a dancer," says Dan as he looks at his feet.

Laura gently pushes his chin up with one hand until their eyes meet. "Now, tell me what this is really about."

Dan hesitates. "I, I don't know how to dance."

Laura seems to pause for a moment to digest this information. "Didn't your high school have dances after football and basketball games?"

"Yeah, I went to the games but not to the dances."

Laura is dogged. "Did you go to your prom in high school?"

Dan's feeling very uncomfortable. "No, but I went to a substitute prom."

Laura's face is one of puzzlement. "What's a substitute prom?"

"Some parents at my church organized an event where the guys rented tuxes and the gals bought dresses. We attended a banquet and afterward they showed a Christian film."

"So your church doesn't approve of dancing?" Dan at that moment knows how a fish must feel when it's gutted.

"Yeah, that's right."

"How do you personally feel about dancing? Do you believe there's anything wrong with it?"

"Since I've never danced, I'm not sure how to answer that question. My church has a lot of what I call 'don't rules.' I'm not sure I personally agree with a lot of them. To a Christian, the Bible is supposed to be our guide but it doesn't address a lot of these 'don't rules.' Dancing is one of those 'don't rules,' but I have never read anything in the Bible that condemns dancing. In fact, it kinda looks like fun."

Laura's eyes don't blink as she stares at him. She finally sighs and says, "You poor dear. We're going to fix this right now."

Laura grabs his hand and holds it tightly so that he can't pull away again. She leads him to the edge of the dance floor. She stands facing him. "If I let go of your hand, do you promise not to run?"

Dan grins. "I promise not to run."

The band is playing a loud rock and roll song. Laura stands beside Dan. "Now do what I do."

She bends her knees and balls her hands into loose fists. She then puts one foot forward and starts swiveling her hips.

"Move your feet back and forth like you're putting out a burning cigarette butt."

Dan mimics her movements.

"Now, do it in rhythm to the music. That's it. You're a natural."

Dan can't believe that he's actually dancing. His posture loosens and he can feel his body gyrate to the rhythm of the music.

The song ends and the band begins to play a slow piece of music. The lights in the rec center dim. Dan watches as other couples start to slow dance and he begins to walk away. Laura grabs his arm.

"Wait a minute, buster. We're not done with your lesson yet."

Laura faces Dan again. She takes his right hand and places it on her left hip. She then takes his left hand and places it on her right hip. She puts her elbows on Dan's shoulders and begins to slowly sway her hips right and left.

Laura looks in his eyes. "Do what I do. Can you feel the music?"

Dan nods his head.

"Now take a small step forward with you left foot. Good. Now take a small step sideways with your right foot."

Dan looks down at his feet and she says, "No. Look me in the eyes. Don't look at your feet."

When she has eye contact with him, Laura speaks again. "Now, take a small step backward with your right foot. Good. Now take a small step sideways with your left foot. Good. Now, let's repeat it."

Dan's concentrating on her instructions, but he feels like he's dancing with a goddess.

Laura presses her body against Dan's and wraps her arms around his neck.

"Look in my eyes. Feel the music."

They slowly sway and dance around the floor.

"Do you like dancing?"

Dan grins. "Very much."

Laura rests her head on his shoulder. He can hear the lyrics of the slow melodic song being sung by the band. He can smell her hair and the faint scent of the perfume she's wearing. He can feel her body pressed against his as the two slowly move around the dance floor. Dan breathes deeply and savors all of the new and wonderful sensations of dancing for the first time in his life.

As they dance together in the dim light of the rec center, he can't help but wonder why anyone would ever disapprove of dancing.

CHAPTER EIGHTEEN

FISHY BUSINESS WITH ONE OF AMERICA'S FOREMOST TRIAL ATTORNEYS

Dan's in his room when Bill walks through the doorway. "Guess who's staying in the Inn?"

"I have no idea."

Bill is excited. "Clive Carter."

"Who's Clive Carter?"

Bill looks puzzled by the question. "Clive Carter. You know, probably America's most famous trial lawyer."

"Is he that lawyer who I sometimes see on network news—the one who always says 'You'll get a better barter with Carter?'"

"Yeah, that's who I'm talking about."

"Well, I always thought that line 'You'll get a better barter with Carter' is pretty cheesy."

Bill nods his head. "Yeah, but that cheesy tagline was Clive's entre to the big time."

"What do mean?"

"About 30 years ago, Clive was a young attorney who came up with his catch phrase for advertising in his local media," says Bill. "Someone in the area was seriously injured in an auto accident and heard the catch phrase on local radio. That person hired Clive to represent him and the negligent driver's insurance company refused to settle. He had to try the case in court. The jury came back with a $5,000,000 verdict and Clive suddenly had more business than he could handle."

"Where is Clive from?"

"Clive grew up in the South and attended Vanderbilt Law School. After he hit the $5,000,000 verdict, he was able to set up shop anywhere he wanted. He chose Charleston, South Carolina because he loved the charm of the city. He has a large law firm in Charleston and takes cases all over the country. In the legal community, he's considered one of the top trial lawyers in the entire country, but he still uses that silly catch-phrase any time he gets in front of a camera."

"How did you find out that Clive's staying in the Inn?"

"Kitty Baxter called me over to the Bell Desk and could barely contain her excitement over Clive staying in the Inn. She told me that she and Mr. B are dining with Clive and his ten-year-old son in the dining room tonight."

Late that evening, Bill and Dan walk into the Inn at around 11:00. They're returning from West Yellowstone where they'd joined some other Savages from the Old Faithful area for pizza at the Gusher. As they walk by the Front Desk on their way up to Bats Alley, they hear a familiar voice calling to them.

"Oh, Bill and Dan." They look to their left and see Kitty Baxter behind the Front Desk motioning them to come toward her.

They walk to the Front Desk and Bill says, "Kitty, isn't it a little late for you to be working?'

"Oh no," says Kitty. "Bobby and I just finished having dinner with Clive Carter and his adorable son Auggie. And guess what?"

Dan notices that Kitty's slurring her words a bit which isn't an uncommon practice.

Dan plays along. "What?"

Kitty leans her elbows on the countertop of the Front Desk and speaks in a conspiratorial voice. "During dinner, Clive said he's going to be in Yellowstone two more days and he wants to take Auggie fishing one of those days."

Kitty's eyes practically twinkle with excitement. "So, I told Clive that two of the best fishermen in Yellowstone work right here in the Inn." She extends an arm and points at them without taking her elbow off the countertop. "And, I told him that those two fishermen are you! What do you think about that?"

"That's great Kitty," says Bill. "But do you think you were perhaps over-selling our abilities a little bit?"

Kitty shakes her head. "Oh no! You two bring Bobby and me fish all the time. And guess what else?"

Dan plays along again. "What?"

"He wants to meet both of you tomorrow and set up a time for Auggie and him to go fishing with you."

Bill winks at Dan. "Kitty, we'd be more than happy to accommodate Clive and Auggie."

The next morning, Dan and Bill are standing at the Bell Desk talking with several other bellmen. The morning crew has just finished pulling all tours and are done for the morning. Bill's dressed in his uniform; Dan's dressed in shorts and a tee shirt. Kitty and an older man approach the group.

"Bill and Dan, can we talk with you?" Kitty asks.

Bill and Dan step away from the group and Kitty says, "Clive, I want to meet Bill and Dan Johnson. These are the two fishermen that Bobby and I were talking about at dinner."

Clive Carter steps forward and warmly shakes hands with both bellmen.

Clive Carter is an older man with a pure white mane of hair that's immaculately trimmed and piercing blue eyes. He's wearing dress slacks and a polo shirt with a sweater tied around his neck. When they shake hands, Dan notices that his fingernails are well manicured.

"It's nice to meet you gentlemen," says Clive. "I hear that you're quite the fishermen."

"We enjoy fishing a lot and spend a fair amount of time on the water," Bill says.

Clive seems interested. "Where do you normally fish?"

"Different places," says Dan. "But we primarily fish on Yellowstone Lake with spinners."

"Would the two of you consider taking Auggie and me fishing with you tomorrow morning?" asks Clive. "We're staying in the Inn tonight and tomorrow night we'll be staying at Jackson Lake Lodge. It would work out perfectly for us if you could take us fishing tomorrow morning."

"Mr. Carter, we'd be happy to take you, but we don't provide guided fishing experiences," says Bill. "Grant Village marina has guided fishing available with professional fishermen and much nicer equipment. Dan and I use a 16' aluminum boat with a 20 hp motor."

Clive smiles his best television smile. "First, call me Clive. Secondly, I prefer an authentic fishing experience for Auggie. The boy's pampered too much already. What time does the marina open?"

"Why don't we meet you and Auggie here at 8:30 and you can follow us in your car to the Grant Village marina," Bill says. "That way you can drive onto Jackson Lake Lodge when we finish fishing."

Clive shakes hands with the two bellmen and says: "It's a deal."

The next morning, Bill and Dan are up early to prepare for their fishing trip with Clive Carter and his son Auggie. They plan to eat breakfast early in the Staffateria and are walking by the Bell Desk when Dick Larson calls to them. They turn and see Dick who motions for them to come to the Front Desk. No one else is around the area.

Dick's the night clerk. He starts work at 11:00 at night and is normally relieved by a morning clerk at 7:00. As night clerk, Dick handles really late check-ins, fields late night calls and other duties performed by a desk clerk, but his main responsibility is to post the rooms for the guests arriving the next day. This may sound like a mindless task, but it's actually quite difficult. The night clerk has to see which guests will be checking out and how to assign rooms for the next night and even multiple nights. The night clerk must also coordinate the rooms for tour groups which all want the members of their particular tour to be lodged close to one another. Dan has watched Dick work late at night and it reminds him of a general sitting in front of a war map moving all his pieces around to formulate a winning battle plan.

Dick is from Laguna Beach, California. He's tall and handsome with blonde hair and blue eyes. Dan knows that Dick and another Front Desk clerk from Pasadena, Monica Stephenson, are an item this summer. Monica's also tall and has a shapely figure. Dick will be a senior at UCLA for the fall term; Monica will be a senior at USC this fall. Dan has heard a rumor that the two met at a USC sorority party and decided to spend their last college summer working together in Yellowstone National Park.

When Bill and Dan reach the Front Desk, Dick leans over the countertop and looks to his right and then to his left. When he's certain that no one else is around, he looks at them. "Have you guys seen this Clive Carter character in the Inn?"

"Yes, we've met him," says Bill. "Why do you ask?"

"I've heard that he's been flirting with Monica and he invited her to dinner last night."

Both bellmen separately saw Clive talking with Monica at the Front Desk yesterday. Both reached the same conclusion that Clive was flirting with Monica but she wasn't interested.

"How do you know that he asked Monica to dinner last night?" Dan asks.

Dick reaches into the back pocket of his pants and pulls out an envelope that's been folded several times.

"Mr. Carter came to the Front Desk about 11:15 two nights ago and asked if I knew Monica," says Dick. "When I indicated that I did, he handed me this envelope and asked if I'd give it to her. I assured him that the matter would be handled alright."

Dick unfolds the envelope and pulls out a piece of paper. He then unfolds the paper and hands it to Bill. "Read this."

Bill holds the piece of paper so he can read it while Dan looks over his shoulder. A handwritten note in blue ink is penned on a piece of Yellowstone Park Company stationary found in every guest room. The note reads:

"My dearest Monica,
It has been such a delight to meet you. You are a
lovely person. I would be honored if you would join
me tonight for dinner at 8:30 p.m. in the Inn dining
room.

>Yours truly,
>Clive"

"Did Monica have dinner with Clive?" Bill asks.

Dick looks embarrassed. "No, Monica never received the envelope. I'd appreciate it if neither of you ever say a word about this to anyone and especially not to Monica." Bill and Dan both nod their heads.

They say goodbye to Dick and walk out the back door of the Inn headed toward the Staffateria.

"What do you make of all that?" says Dan when they are alone outside.

Bill smiles. "I think our boy Clive Carter is a player. I also think our friend Dick is as smart as a fox and as dangerous as a wild stallion protecting his mare."

Both brothers start laughing.

At the agreed time, Dan and Bill are waiting at the Bell Desk when Clive and his son Auggie arrive.

"Good morning, Bill and Dan," says Clive. "I want you to meet my son, Clive Augustus Carter. We call him Auggie."

Auggie sticks out his right hand and politely shakes hands with his new friends.

"Where's your car parked?" Bill asks.

"In the lower parking lot in front of the Inn."

"Great," says Bill. "Our car is parked in the same lot. It's a green four-door Plymouth sedan. I'll wait for you at the end of the parking lot and you can follow us over to Grant Village marina in your car."

They all walk out of the Inn together. Bill and Dan walk directly to Bill's car. They had loaded all the fishing gear beforehand. Bill starts his car and backs out of his parking space. He drives to the end of parking lot where he pulls over and waits for Clive.

Dan's looking over his shoulder and whistles. "You won't believe this, but Clive's driving a burgundy Rolls Royce with a South Carolina license plate that reads 'Clive.'" Bill quickly looks in his rearview mirror and sees a Rolls Royce pull behind his car.

"First time I've ever seen a Rolls Royce in Yellowstone National Park," says Bill. "Not sure the Park has seen many of them."

On arrival at Grant Village marina, Bill goes into the marina office to check out a 16' aluminum fishing boat with a 20 hp Johnson outboard motor. Bill later tells Dan that he paid the normal rental rate in case Scotty and the boys see the Rolls Royce sitting in the parking lot and wonder why its owner got in a boat with two OFI bellmen rather than in a YPCO guide boat. While

Bill's checking out the boat, Clive heads toward the restrooms and Auggie helps Dan carry the fishing gear from the car to the boat. As they walk toward the docks, Auggie's curious as to which boat they'll be using.

Auggie points to the Scenic Cruiser which is by far the biggest boat in the marina. "Is that the boat we are taking?"

"No."

Auggie points to the next largest boat in the marina, which is an extremely large cabin cruiser that some wealthy individual has moored in the marina for the summer. "Is that our boat?"

"No."

Auggie then proceeds to point to the next largest boat (in descending size) in the marina and asks the same question. "Is that our boat?"

Dan keeps giving Auggie the same reply. "No."

After about ten questions and answers, Auggie seems stumped. "Well, which boat are we using?"

Dan points to the row of 16' fishing boats. "One of those."

Auggie's mouth flies open. All he can say is "Oh." Dan suspects that Auggie's accustomed to a somewhat larger boat.

The day is sunny, warm and beautiful on Lake Yellowstone. While driving over to Grant Village marina, Bill and Dan had decided that they'd not fish but just assist Clive and Auggie. Bill sits on the aft bench seat and handles the motor; Dan sits on the bench seat behind the bow seat and handles the fishing gear. Clive sits on the bench seat between Bill and Dan; Auggie sits on the bow bench seat.

When they are about 100 yards offshore of the West Thumb Geyser area, Bill cuts the speed of the motor to a slow trolling speed and heads the boat westerly parallel to the shore. Dan puts a Mepps lure on the swivel at the end of the fishing line on one pole and casts to the starboard side of the boat. He lets the line play out. When enough line has played out, he sets the bail on the reel and hands the pole to Clive. They had instructed Clive and Auggie on how to use the equipment before they left the docks.

Dan picks up the second pole and attaches a Jake's lure to the swivel at the end of the fishing line. He starts to cast to the port side of the boat when Clive yells. "I think I've got one."

Dan looks at the tip of Clive's fishing pole which is bending downward and springing back as the fish tries to fight free of the three-pronged, barbed hook at the bottom of the lure. Bill has cut the power to the motor and lets the boat drift. Dan gives Clive instructions. "Set the hook and then start to reel the fish slowly toward the boat."

Clive follows the instructions and soon Dan sees the Cutthroat trout alongside the boat. Dan takes the fishing net and dips it into the water behind the fish. He scoops the fish into the boat with one smooth motion. The fish flops around the bottom of the boat. Clive has a big smile on his face. Auggie is clapping his hands in delight. Dan bends over and picks up the fish. He then takes the hook out of its mouth.

Dan holds the fish up. "Auggie, what do think? Is this a keeper?"

Auggie squeals in delight. "Wow. The fish is beautiful. I want to keep it."

In the early 1970s, anyone could fish for free in Yellowstone National Park, but a person still had to obtain a license. A license could be obtained at any of the Visitor Centers located throughout the Park or at most Hamilton General Stores. The license was good for the entire season.

Later, Dan and Bill are sure that they were given a pamphlet which contained the fishing rules and regulations when they obtained their fishing licenses, but both are also pretty sure that neither of them bothered to read the pamphlet. Dan does later recall that when he first fished with Bill on Yellowstone Lake, Bill's memory from prior years was that Cutthroat on the Lake could be kept if 12 inches or longer and that each person could keep three fish per day.

Although they don't have a tape measurer, Bill and Dan are certain that Clive's first fish is a keeper. So, Dan pulls out a metal stringer and opens one loop. He runs the loop through a gill to keep the fish from swimming away and puts the stringer with the fish into the water. He ties the other end of the stringer to the oar lock of the boat.

Dan casts the line of the second pole to the port side of the boat and lets the line run out. He sets the bail and hands the pole to Auggie who has returned to his bow seat bench. Dan then casts the line of the first pole to the starboard side of the boat and lets the line run out. He sets the bail and hands the pole to Clive.

During the next two hours, Clive and Auggie fish while Bill handles the motor and Dan handles the fishing gear. As they fish, Clive and the two bellmen talk about a variety of subjects. Clive wants to know more about Bill and Dan—things like where they grew up, what kind of family, their education (Clive's particularly interested when Bill explains he's just finished his military service and is starting law school in the upcoming fall term), what types of recreational things they do in Yellowstone and so on. As time passes, Clive seems less guarded about himself and shares more about his life. Clive's just been the featured speaker for a conference for the United States Eighth Circuit judges. He decided to drive rather than fly so he and Auggie could have some bonding time. He particularly wanted to visit Yellowstone and Teton National Parks. However, Clive shares that he won a big case against the National Park Service some years before and has ever since had the perception that the Park Service has a continuing grudge against him because of his success on that case.

The group finally decides that the day's been a great success and they should return to the marina. Clive and Auggie have caught many fish that day, but more are released back into the water than kept. They keep ten fish which Dan will clean on their return to the marina. Clive will take these fish to Jackson Lake Lodge and have them for dinner that evening. One of the ten trout is only about 10 inches long, but Auggie caught the fish and wanted to keep it. Bill and Dan finally agree with Auggie because the hook had badly torn the trout's mouth and it probably wouldn't survive if released.

As the boat returns to the marina, Bill and Dan notice a Park Ranger in uniform standing near the cleaning station. This doesn't seem normal. When they reach the dock, Dan jumps on the dock and ties the rope in the bow to a tiedown on the dock. He helps Clive and Auggie out of the boat and then Bill hands him the fishing gear and the stringer of fish. Clive and Auggie head to the restrooms and Bill heads to the marina office to check out the boat. Dan picks up the stringer with ten trout and walks over to the cleaning station.

Dan takes the fish off the stringer and starts gutting the trout one-by-one. He runs his knife up the belly of each fish and then holds the fish in his left hand and uses his right hand to remove the gills and guts of each fish. He then runs his right thumb up and down the spine under running water from a faucet to clean the fish. He then lays the fish in a row after they're cleaned.

When Dan's almost finished, the Park Ranger comes over and looks carefully at the fish. The Ranger then picks each fish up and holds it against a red line painted on the cleaning table.

Dan's starting to feel a queasy sensation in his stomach. Bill and Dan have often noticed a similar red line painted on the boats near the aft bench seat. Neither knew why this red line was painted on the boats.

By the time Dan finishes cleaning all of the fish, Clive and Bill have joined him at the cleaning station.

The Ranger lifts his head as they approach. "Gentlemen, it appears you have seven fish under the limit of 14 inches. You'll all have to follow me over to the station."

As Bill and Dan follow the Ranger to the station, Dan looks at his brother. "Did you know that the regulation on Yellowstone Lake this year is that all fish being kept have to be 14 inches or longer? Apparently, if the fish is less than 14 inches, you have to release it back into the water."

"No," says Bill. "It used to be 12 inches or longer."

"Did you know that the red lines painted on the fishing boats are 14 inches long?"

"No. Neither of us understood why those lines were painted on the boats."

At this moment, there are two Old Faithful Inn bellmen who are feeling pretty stupid.

When they arrive at the Ranger station, Clive's Rolls Royce pulls up beside them. Everybody gets out of their vehicles. The Ranger goes into the station. Clive tells Auggie to play while his Dad attends to some business inside.

As they make their way into the station, Clive talks with the two bellmen. "You two keep quiet unless asked a direct question. I'll handle this."

Dan thinks to himself that I'm definitely going to let Clive handle this. Afterall, he's the guy who always claims that you get a better barter with Carter.

When inside the station, the three are escorted into the only office in the tiny building. The three are asked to take a seat. The Ranger from the marina takes the seat behind a desk and another Ranger enters holding a chair in one hand. The second Ranger puts the chair down beside the first Ranger and sits down.

The first Ranger introduces himself. "I'm Officer Hanson and this is Officer Brown."

"Can I see fishing licenses for all of you?" Officer Hanson asks. Fortunately, Bill and Dan had insisted that Clive get a fishing license while in the Old Faithful area. All three produce their fishing licenses.

"Now, may I see driver's licenses for all of you," says Officer Hanson.

Clive starts talking. "Officers, are we being charged with anything?"

"It's my understanding that the three of you had seven fish which were undersized, meaning they were not 14 inches long," says Officer Brown.

"To answer your question, we're merely investigating this incident at the moment," says Officer Hanson.

Dan thinks to himself, 'Incident? When did seven undersized fish become an incident?'

"Where are those fish now?" Clive says.

"They're in the other room," says Officer Hanson.

Clive stares at Officer Hanson. "Are they being properly refrigerated?"

Officer Hanson seems unsure where this conversation's headed. "No. Why does it matter?"

Clive explodes. "Why does it matter? For every minute of delay, each fish shrinks a little bit more. For God's sake, man. You're not preserving the evidence appropriately. I demand that you immediately refrigerate all of the fish. I want each one tagged and photographed before you bungle this further."

Officer Brown excuses himself, stands up and leaves the room. Dan's pretty sure seven fish are being put in the office's small refrigeration unit alongside the Officers' lunches for today.

"I'll ask the question again," says Clive. "Are any of us being charged with something?'

Dan notices that a small bead of sweat starts to drip down Officer Hanson's forehead.

"Mr. Carter, as I said, we're merely investigating a possible violation of Park rules at this moment," says Officer Hanson.

Clive's not deterred. "If any of the three of us were charged with a misdemeanor, when would the arraignment date occur?"

"A traveling federal magistrate handles misdemeanors twice a month in Gardiner," says Officer Hanson. "The next arraignment date will be in twelve days."

Clive snorts. "Twelve days? I have an oral argument before the Supreme Court in Washington D.C. in twelve days. By the way, who's the traveling federal magistrate?"

"I believe it's Judge Franklin," says Officer Hanson.

"Is that Richard Franklin? I just had a long talk with Judge Franklin a few days ago at the Judicial Conference for the Eighth Circuit judiciary where I was the featured guest speaker. Get Judge Franklin on the telephone for me and we can resolve this matter in a few minutes."

The drop of sweat on Officer Hanson's very red face now drips into one eye. Officer Hanson pulls a handkerchief out of his rear pants pocket and starts wiping his eye. Officer Hanson excuses himself and exits the office. He closes the door as he leaves. The three individuals still in the office can hear muted conversation through the closed door, but can't understand any words.

In a couple of minutes, Officer Hanson returns to the office. "I think this will do it for now. We may have a few more questions so I'll need to know where to contact you later today."

Bill indicates that he and Dan stay in Bats Alley at Old Faithful Inn. Clive says he'll be at Jackson Lake Lodge in the Tetons for the next two nights.

Office Hanson thanks them for their cooperation and shows them to the front door of the station. When outside, Clive pulls his wallet from his back trousers' pocket and takes out a business card.

Clive looks at them. "Thank you for a great day of fishing. Auggie and I really had fun. I doubt that you'll hear anything more about undersized fish, but if you do, I want you to call me immediately."

Clive hands Bill his business cards. "All of my contact information's on the card."

"Dan and I should have known the new regulation this year," says Bill. "It's all our fault. We feel really sorry to have gotten you into this situation."

Clive waves his right hand in a dismissive motion. "Nonsense. I told you that I've felt that the Park Service has been holding a grudge against me since I won that big case against them. I beat the Park Service once and I can do it again. I'm serious. If the Park Service pulls a stunt and tries to charge either of you with anything, I have 25 attorneys in my firm in Charleston and I'll fly every one of them to Wyoming if necessary to defend you."

Clive sticks out his right hand. "Thank you both."

They shake his hand and Clive turns to find Auggie again.

As Clive walks away, Dan calls out. "Wait. You forgot the three remaining trout."

Clive doesn't miss a step, but raises his right arm above his head and waves it again in a dismissive manner. Clive yells so they can hear him. "I've lost my appetite for trout this evening."

That afternoon, Dan and Bill are sitting on the bed in Bill's room when Carnival appears at the door. "These two guys want to talk with you."

Carnival steps aside and Officers Hanson and Brown walk into the room.

"We just want to follow up on our meeting in the station this morning," says Officer Hanson. "Tell me again what happened?"

"We were introduced to Mr. Carter two days ago here at the Inn," says Bill. "The subject of fishing came up while talking and Mr. Carter expressed an interest in joining us for an outing on Lake Yellowstone."

"Who caught the fish?" Officer Hanson asks.

Bill sighs. "Mr. Carter and his ten-year-old son Auggie."

"Did you two catch any of the fish?" says Officer Hanson.

"No, Officer," says Dan.

"Can Officer Brown and I have a moment alone?"

Bill and Dan leave Bill's room, but they leave the door open. Down the hall, they hear the two men laughing. When they're called back into the room, Officer Hanson thanks them both for their cooperation and the two Park Rangers leave.

As they hear the sound of the Park Rangers' footsteps going down the stairway from Bats Alley, Dan looks at Bill. "Do think we're going to get into any trouble?"

Bill grins. "Little brother, relax. We aren't going to get into any trouble and neither is Clive. These Rangers are just small minnows nibbling on a Big Fish trapped in a small pond."

Neither can contain their laughter any longer.

CHAPTER NINETEEN

FIRE AT OLD FAITHFUL INN

When one lives in a log structure, nothing strikes fear in that person's heart quicker than the thought of the wooden structure catching on fire. Well, there may be one thought which induces greater fear—living in a seven-story wooden structure that catches on fire. Yikes! That's a lot of combustible fuel for a fire. Such were Dan's thoughts throughout the summer while living at the top of Old Faithful Inn.

Dan and Lou are visiting with Bill in his room one day when the fire alarm sounds. The building engineer is conducting his monthly test of the alarm system. The fire alarm is a steam whistle which blows continuously until turned off. The sound is similar to a factory or mine whistle that signals a change of shifts or an alarm. The Inn's alarm is located near the boiler room right behind Bats Alley. To merely call the Inn's fire alarm loud is akin to calling the Civil War a little difference of opinion.

When the fire alarm starts shrieking, Dan almost levitates off the bed. He isn't watching Bill or Lou, but suspects they have the same initial reaction.

Dan covers his ears with his hands and shouts above the noise. "How much longer will this last?"

Lou and Bill also have their ears covered with their hands and can't hear Dan, but shake their heads anyway. Dan isn't sure whether they're shaking their heads to indicate they don't know how long the alarm will continue or to indicate that they can't hear what he said. At any rate, the alarm suddenly stops.

Bill takes his hands off his ears and sighs. "I hope that I never hear that in the middle of the night. That would give me a headache."

"If the Inn has a fire," says Lou, "a headache would be the least of your problems."

Dan shivers as though he's cold. "Sometimes I almost start shaking when I think of a serious fire burning in the Inn. There are seven stories of kindling in the Inn—kindling that's dried out for 70 years."

"Yeah, it's a grim image," says Lou. "At least we have the Grinnell system that hopefully would save the Inn."

In the early 1970s, the Inn has metal pipes located near the ceiling that run throughout the Inn. The pipes are a sprinkler system that carries water to suppress any fire outbreak. In every room and most nooks and crannies throughout the Inn, there are small extensions to the metal pipes. Each extension has a capsule on top which melts under heat to open the sprinkler head so the water in the pipe is released. Savages refer to this fire suppression system as the 'Grinnell system.' To Dan's knowledge, no one knows how the system got its name or when the system was installed.

Dan recalls a conversation with Lou on his first day about this fire system.

Dan had pointed to a metal pipe that ran up the steeply pitched ceiling of the lobby.

"What's the metal pipe for?" Dan said.

"It's a fire suppression system. The metal pipe carries water. The pipes run all over the Inn. If a fire breaks out, sprinklers start spraying water and hopefully put out the fire."

Dan had looked around the lobby and noticed metal pipes in multiple locations. "That's interesting."

"Yeah," Lou had said. "The bellmen are considered to be part of the front line of defense in the case of a fire."

"Why the bellmen?"

Lou had shrugged his shoulders. "I'm not sure I know the answer, but guess it's because the bellmen know every nook and cranny in this building. We're constantly walking around the Inn and into the guest rooms. You'll soon understand."

"Do the bellmen receive any training on what to do if a fire occurs?"

"Not that I'm aware of," Lou had said.

As he now reflects on this conversation weeks later, Dan knows that Lou's statements had been pretty accurate. The fire chief for the Old Faithful area tests the alarm system regularly, but there hasn't been a single drill or any other type of instruction provided to the bellmen. Dan just hopes that a fire doesn't start while he's a bellman at the Inn.

"The Grinnell system? Are we even sure that it works? Let's hope we never have to test the system," says Bill. Dan believes that he's been reading his mind.

Every summer, the "Green Wave" hits Old Faithful Inn. What is the "Green Wave?" It is hundreds, if not thousands, of Boy Scouts ages 10 to 12 wearing their green uniforms who travel by the busloads to their annual Jamboree Camp. Many of these buses stop in the Old Faithful area to view the sights including Old Faithful Geyser and, of course, Old Faithful Inn. Some of these Boy Scouts actually stay in the Inn as guests. Dan's sure that these are all good kids, but quickly concludes that their frazzled adult leaders are happy to get a break from their charges and let the little green monsters run unimpeded throughout the Inn.

For afternoon bellmen on duty, the Green Wave can be challenging.

Dan and Larry stand by the Bell Desk waiting for a Front. A cute little kid dressed in his Boy Scout uniform comes up to the Bell Desk.

"Where do I get ice?"

Dan looks at the kid. "The bellmen get the ice for guests. There isn't an ice machine where guests can help themselves."

The kid pauses for a moment. "Are you a bellman?"

"I am," says Dan.

"Can you get me some ice?"

"What room are you staying in?" Dan wants to make sure this kid's a guest in the Inn.

The kid digs in his pockets and pulls out a room key. He shows the key tag with its room number to him. Dan looks at Larry and sighs. "Okay, I'll go get you some ice."

Dan walks across the lobby and down the stairs to get a small bucket of ice. He returns and hands the ice bucket to the kid.

"Do you want a tip?" asks the kid.

Dan smiles. "That's the polite thing to do."

"Here's my tip," says the kid. "Get another line of work."

The kid-not so cute now-laughs loudly and runs up the staircase toward the second-floor mezzanine spilling ice out of the bucket as he goes.

Dan turns to Larry and expects him to be laughing at the prank, but Larry's face looks grim.

"I've had it with these little green monsters," says Larry. "I'll show them."

Larry goes behind the Bell Desk. He finds two pieces of cardboard and a black felt pen in one of the drawers. Larry works for a couple of minutes and grabs one small and one large plastic ice bucket. The bellmen have two different sizes depending on how prosperous the Dude requesting ice looks. Larry places both buckets on the countertop of the Bell Desk and sticks one of the cardboard pieces in front of each bucket. The sign in front of the small bucket reads "50 cents" and the one in front of the large bucket reads "$1.00."

In a few minutes, another cute kid dressed in his Boy Scout uniform comes up to the Bell Desk and asks Dan for some ice.

Larry steps in front of Dan. "Do you want the 50-cent size or the $1.00 size?" Larry points to the buckets to reinforce the cost of the ice.

"Gee, the guys didn't tell me I'd have to pay for the ice," says the kid. "Uh, I guess I'll take the 50 cent bucket."

Larry walks across the lobby and returns with a small bucket of ice. He holds the bucket of ice behind his back with one hand and extends his other arm out with his palm up. The kid fishes in his pocket and finds two quarters. He puts them in Larry's palm.

Larry gives him the bucket of ice and grins. "Thank you."

When the kid leaves, Dan looks at Larry. "Genius."

Funny thing is, the demand for ice runs from Boy Scouts quickly stops.

About thirty minutes later, Larry returns to the Bell Desk. His face is flushed. "You'll never believe what I just found."

"What," says Dan.

"I took a Front up to Room 212. On the way back, I saw a bunch of the green monsters on their knees in a circle on the south side of the second-floor mezzanine. There was something in the circle but I couldn't tell what it was. I thought that I better walk that way and check out what these kids are doing. When I got closer, I saw some sticks and twigs piled in the middle of the circle. One kid was just starting to light a match, but I shouted at them and they all ran away."

Dan flinches. "I can't believe those kids would do something that stupid."
"Believe it. One never knows what the Green Monster is capable of doing."

It is 2:00 in the morning when the fire alarm starts blaring. Dan and Lou are both sleeping soundly when the alarm begins. Dan sits up in bed and is disoriented for a few seconds, but the shrieking of the fire alarm and the scent of smoke quickly focus his orientation. Dan jumps out of bed and slips on his shoes. Dan's wearing his summer pajamas-short sleeves and boxer type bottom, but he could care less about his appearance. Lou also jumps out of bed wearing only the long bottom portion of his pajamas. Lou doesn't take time to put on shoes. He runs out of their room followed closely by Dan. Lou flies down the back stairways three steps at a time and races toward the lobby.

When they reach the lobby, they stop but can't detect any signs of smoke.

Lou turns to Dan and yells. "Check with the Front Desk to see if anyone knows the location of the fire. I'm going to check the kitchen."

Dan runs to the Front Desk and sees Dick Larson behind the counter. "Dick, where's the fire?"

Dick shakes his head. "I'm not sure, but I think in the kitchen."

Dan runs through the dining room and into the kitchen. Lou and a couple of other people are looking up at the Grinnell system which is spraying copious amounts of water from the ceiling throughout the kitchen.

Lou notices Dan. "There was a fire in the kitchen, but the Grinnell system worked and extinguished the fire. Now we have to figure out how to shut the sprinkler off."

Lou looks at the sprinkler for another moment. "I have an idea."

Lou runs out the door of the kitchen toward the dining room and returns in about sixty seconds. Lou's holding a small triangular piece of wood in his right hand.

"I remembered seeing this being used as a doorstop to keep the door open in the dining room."

One of the building maintenance engineers has arrived with a six-foot step-ladder. Lou asks to use the step-ladder and positions it under the sprinkler. The sprinkler continues to emit copious amounts of water. The kitchen now has about an inch of water flooding the floor. Lou climbs the ladder and jams the narrow end of the wooden block into the space where the material had melted to trigger the sprinkler. Lou uses the butt of his right hand like a hammer and hits the thicker end of the wooden block several times. Once the piece of wood is firmly jammed into the space, the water which was gushing from the sprinkler stops.

While still standing on the ladder, Lou looks around and makes an announcement to the small crowd that's gathered.

"The show's over. The fire's out. The wooden block will work until maintenance can repair the sprinkler in the morning."

Somebody in the crowd yells, "Hey, buddy. This is the morning."

More as a collective release of tension than a response to the attempt at humor, the crowd starts laughing and then clapping.

Lou climbs down the ladder. He's soaking wet from the top of his head to the bottom of his feet. Mr. Baxter has arrived attired in his finest robe and slippers. His pajama bottoms extend below the bottom of his robe.

Mr. Baxter walks over to Lou and shakes his hand.

"Good job, Lou," says Mr. Baxter. He begins to walk away, but turns and faces Lou again. "By the way, I like your pajama bottoms."

Mr. Baxter turns to the crowd and speaks loudly. "Okay, thank you all for coming. The problem's solved. Let's all get back to bed."

Dan suddenly realizes that the fire alarm has stopped. He walks over to Lou. "Hey, Hero. Can I get you a towel?"

Lou just grins as he shakes his body like a wet dog.

As they walk out of the dining room, Dan sees a woman with two small children standing at the Front Desk. The woman has curlers in her hair and is dressed in pajamas covered by her bathrobe. She has fuzzy slippers on her feet. The two small children are dressed in similar fashion. Both are yawning and rubbing their eyes. Dan then notices the suitcase sitting on the floor beside the woman. The bag was apparently packed so quickly that pieces of clothing were hanging outside of the suitcase when it was shut.

Dick's helping the woman. Out of curiosity, Dan walks toward the Front Desk and listens to their conversation.

"It was just a minor fire in the kitchen that was quickly extinguished," says Dick. "There's nothing to worry about. We're very sorry that you and your family were awakened in the middle of the night."

The woman seems rather testy. "I don't care. I want my money back. My family and I won't spend another hour in this death trap."

Dan decides that he's heard enough and better get to bed.

By the time Dan reaches his room, Lou has dried himself with a towel and is back in bed. Dan relates what happened at the Front Desk.

Lou remains silent for a few moments before speaking. "I hope Dick gave the poor woman her money back. You know, she's right. This place could be a death trap."

On that happy note, Dan turns off the light.

CHAPTER TWENTY

TWENTY-FIRST BIRTHDAY SURPRISE

Dan and Bill are having breakfast in the Staffateria when Mary Ann walks
over to their table with her breakfast tray.

"Ya'll mind if I join you?"

"Please, sit down and join us," says Dan

Mary Ann puts her tray on the table. She pulls out a chair across from
them and sits down.

"You both look chipper today."

"This is a big day for celebrating," Bill says.

Dan gives Bill that younger brother look—the one where 'older brother is
about to embarrass younger brother' look.

Mary Ann raises one eyebrow. "What are ya'll celebrating?"

Bill grins. "Oh, I'm not celebrating. It's Dan who's celebrating today."

Mary Ann looks at Dan as his face reddens. "Dan, what're you celebrating
today?"

Dan looks at Mary Ann and pauses. "It's no big deal, really."

Mary Ann gives him her best Perry Mason look. "Dan, what's no big
deal?"

Dan looks like a cornered animal. "Today's my birthday," he says
softly.

Perry Mason, rather Mary Ann, pursues her line of questioning. "Dan,
which birthday is it today?"

Dan pauses again and then speaks even more softly. "My twenty-first
birthday."

Mary Ann clasps her hands together. "Dan, this is just so precious."

Then to Dan's eternal chagrin, Mary Ann stands up and raises her arms over her head. She starts clapping her hands loudly above her head—very, very loudly. Everyone stops eating and looks at her. Mary Ann yells. "Ya'll, today is Dan Johnson's twenty-first birthday."

A few people clap, but Mary Ann isn't finished. "This is a big day for Dan. We should all clap."

Everyone in the room starts clapping.

Debbie Wainwright is sitting at a nearby table and stands up.

"A twenty-first birthday is special," says Debbie. "I think we should all stand and sing Happy Birthday to Dan. Everybody up on your feet." Vickie makes a big sweeping motion with her arms urging people to stand and participate.

Dan's sitting quietly, but his face now shows colors of scarlet.

Mary Ann yells so everyone can hear. "On the count of three, we'll start." Mary Ann starts flapping her arms back and forth like an orchestra conductor. When she counts "one," her arms drop below her waist. On the count of "two," her arms ascend high over her head. On the count of "three," Mary Ann dramatically drops her arms and thrusts them forward.

Surprisingly, every person is on their feet singing "Happy Birthday" to Dan. Perhaps a few are offkey—well, maybe most are offkey since Mary Ann began the first note offkey. But people sing with vigor to wish Dan well on his twenty-first birthday.

When the last "to you" is sung, everyone in the room starts clapping. Debbie cups her hands to her mouth and shouts, "Speech, speech."

Dan is uncomfortable being the center of attention. The others in the room sense this and it only fuels the energy of the crowd when Mary Ann yells above the clapping, "Dan. Dan. Dan."

Soon the sound of the chant "Dan. Dan. Dan" starts reverberating off the walls and seems even louder.

A bemused Bill looks at Dan and shouts over the din, "You better stand up and give'em what they want."

Dan breathes deeply and slowly rises to his feet. The chanting stops.

"Thank you all for such a rousing verse of Happy Birthday," he says. "I didn't expect this and will truly remember this day forever."

Before Dan sits down, Bill leans over to Mary Ann and whispers, "Dan hasn't seen anything yet."

When Dan sits down, people resume eating their breakfasts. Mary Ann smiles at Dan. "Are you doing anything special for your birthday?"

"Bill's taking Lou and me into West tonight for pizza at the Gusher."

"Bill, what time are ya'll leaving the Inn?"

"About 8:30," Bill says.

Mary Ann laughs. "This may sound a little presumptuous, but would you mind if I joined ya'll? I might even be able to arrange for a friend or two to join us."

Bill shrugs his shoulders. "Mary Ann, it's alright with me if it's alright with Dan and, of course, only if you arrange to bring a couple of friends along."

Mary Ann winks at Dan. "Would it be okay with you?"

"Sure, it sounds like a good time," says Dan. "One condition though."

"What's that?"

Dan grins. "You don't get the crowd at the Gusher to sing another round of Happy Birthday to me!"

Everyone at the table laughs.

Dan and Bill walk up to the Bell Desk later that evening. Lou's waiting patiently at the Bell Desk, but neither Mary Ann nor her two friends are there.

Bill looks at Lou. "Have you seen Mary Ann or whoever she's bringing with her?"

Lou shakes his head. "Not yet."

Bill turns to Dan. "I have to walk over to the Staffateria. I believe that I left my jacket there after dinner. Do you want to come along?"

"No, I think I'll wait here with Lou."

"Dan, why don't you walk over with Bill," says Lou. "I forgot my wallet and have to run back up to Bats Alley to get it. You two can get Bill's jacket and we'll probably all arrive back here about the same time. Hopefully, Mary Ann and two gals will be here when we all return."

Dan nods his head in agreement and follows Bill out the back door of the Inn as Lou heads up the stairs toward Bats Alley. When they reach the bottom of the stairs to the Staffateria, Bill motions for Dan to lead the way. As they climb the stairs, Dan notices that there are no lights on inside but it doesn't strike him as anything unusual. Dan pauses at the top of the stairs.

"Open the door," Bill says. Dan turns the door knob and pushes the door. "Surprise!"

Dan's disoriented for a moment. When the lights are suddenly switched on, Dan sees 35 to 50 Savages crammed into the Staffateria. Dan recognizes most of the people. All of the Bell Crew are here except for Larry who's working the late shift. Dan notices Mary Ann, Debbie, Betty, Sally, Laura, Penny, Melody, Graham, Dick, Monica and other employees from virtually every department in the Inn. Dan suspects that the party started awhile ago since people definitely seem to be in a party mood. Most have a beverage in one of their hands. Dan spots a plastic bucket sitting on a table which appears to contain an enormous quantity of Yucca Flats and plastic glasses stacked alongside the bucket. Dan sees a number of coolers sitting against several of the walls of the Staffateria.

Bill steps to the center of the room and motions for Dan to come toward him. Bill claps his hands to get everyone's attention.

"For any of you who may not know Dan, this is tonight's birthday boy." People whoop and holler.

Bill turns to his brother. "Dan, I promise that we won't sing another verse of Happy Birthday to you." Now people really whoop and holler.

Bill holds up his hands to quiet the crowd. "

"To get the party started, we're going to divide into four groups and have a 21st Birthday Scavenger Hunt."

This group is really happy tonight— they whoop and holler some more. Bill waves his hands to quiet everyone again.

"I'm going to go around the room and assign each of you a number at random- one, two, three or four. You need to remember your number."

Bill looks at Carnival. "Carnival, do you have a pen and paper to write down your number so you don't forget?" Carnival's face breaks into a big goofy grin.

"Once I'm done assigning each of you a number, I want you to find the other people with the same number and form yourselves into a group."

Bill proceeds to give everyone a number. When he finishes, he yells so everyone can hear. "Find everyone with the same number and form into your group."

Absolute bedlam ensues as everyone starts talking or shouting their number in an effort to identify their fellow group members. About ten minutes later, the four groups are loosely formed.

Bill begins to clap his hands over his head to get everyone's attention.

"Here are the lists for the scavenger hunt. There are twelve items on each list. Each list is the same. You have one hour from when I say 'go' to find as many items on your list as you can. Since everyone has the same list, you may want to be careful who you share any ideas with. We'll all meet back here in one hour and see which group wins the scavenger hunt."

Someone yells. "What do we get if we win the scavenger hunt?"

Bill waits for the chatter to stop. "Good question. You'll earn Dan's undying respect (Bill pauses until the laughter finishes) and dinner for two of the group with Mr. and Mrs. Robert Baxter in the dining room."

People clap and cheer. Someone yells, "How do we determine who the two from the group will be?"

Bill pauses again. "The names of all members of the winning group will be put in a hat and two names will be drawn out of the hat by none other than Kitty Baxter." More whooping and hollering follow.

Bill passes out three copies of the scavenger list to each group. Each group breaks up into smaller clusters as everyone attempts to review the items on the list. The items are: 1) a cloth baby diaper, 2) a button from a Park Ranger uniform, 3) an Oklahoma license plate, 4) a receipt from Hams that's at least 24 hours old, 5) a cocktail napkin from the Old Faithful Lodge Bar, 6) one of Kitty Baxter's bras, 7) a $2 bill, 8) a copy of one of Carnival's speeding tickets, 9) a basketball autographed by Rich Lang, 10) a buffalo chip, 11) a buffalo head nickel and 12) a Lady Liberty dime. As people examine the list, Dan hears much laughter and a few sighs.

Bill raises his hands over his head and claps them. "Remember, you have to be back in one hour. Each group has a lot of work to do in the next sixty minutes. On your mark. Get set. GO!"

There's a traffic jam at the door to the Staffateria as everyone tries to leave through the only exit at the same time.

Almost everyone reassembles in the Staffateria in sixty minutes. All groups discover that locating the items on Bill's list presents a tougher task than they first imagined.

Bill shouts so everyone can hear. "Okay, quiet please. Everyone, please reassemble with your group."

Bill then starts working through the list item-by-item. No group has all the items. Probably the biggest laughter comes when Bill calls, "Who was able to obtain one of Kitty Baxter's bras?"

Two people hold up what appear to be two rather large bras.

The holder of the first bra waives it back and forth over his head like a flag. "I knocked on Kitty's door and said I was from the laundry and needed any dirty bras to add to the load we were doing in the laundry," he says. "Kitty looked quizzically at me, but said 'Sure, I have one' and goes and gets a dirty bra for me."

When the laughter dies down, the holder of the second bra steps forward and holds a bra over his head. "I too knocked on Kitty's door and said I was collecting used clothing for the less fortunate in West," says the second guy. "I told Kitty that we especially needed undergarments like bras. Kitty looked at me and says, 'That's funny. Someone from the laundry just came and got my dirty bra. What is it with bras tonight?' Then she took a long swig of her vodka martini and walked away. She came back to the door in a couple of minutes and hands me one of her bras."

People are laughing so hard that Dan worries that some are going to drop to the floor in a convulsion of laughter and roll around the linoleum.

As to a copy of one of Carnival's speeding tickets, the only group that could produce anything is the group of which Carnival's a member. Actually, Carnival doesn't have a copy. Instead, he holds up two original speeding tickets and asks Bill, "Will these do?" Dan will later recall that the entire assembly laughed pretty hard at that item too.

As Bill's finishing his list of items, Eagle bursts into the room and flops down on a chair. His face is red. He has sweat running down his forehead and he seems out of breath. Bill and Dan walk over to Eagle.

"What happened to you?" Dan says.

Eagle takes a gulp of air. "I got an Oklahoma license plate." He holds it up as proof of his assertion.

Dan looks apprehensive. "Where did you get that?"

Eagle looks at Dan. "I know this is your birthday party, so I won't say anything unkind. But one obviously finds an Oklahoma license plate on a vehicle from Oklahoma."

Dan looks aghast. "Well, you're going to put it back on the vehicle, aren't you?"

"Sure. But, the more important thing is that I started thinking about where could I find a cloth baby diaper," says Eagle. "The thought occurred to me that most baby diapers become soiled and need cleaning, so I thought that maybe I could find one in the laundry. I found a window that was open in the laundry and let myself in. The lights suddenly go on and the laundry manager's standing in front of me accusing me of unlawfully breaking and entering. I explained that I was only looking for a baby diaper because it's on the scavenger list. The manager said he was going to call the Park Rangers and have me arrested. When I started to leave, he reached in his back pocket and pulled out a pistol. He pointed it at me and threatened to shoot me if I tried to leave."

Bill has a look of disbelief. "What'd you do, Eagle?"

"I started bawling—no, no, not out of fear but play acting. This guy puts his gun down to his side and I ran like H*** to get out of the laundry."

"You need to report this," says Bill. "No one should be permitted to point a gun at a fellow employee."

Eagle nods his head. "I met Mac leaving the party when I was coming up the stairs and I've already reported it."

The guests to Dan's surprise twenty-first birthday party continue the merriment well into the night. Sometime past midnight, Dan's sitting alone on a chair watching the revelry. Chukker walks by and notices Dan sitting by himself.

"Great G**D***** party, Dan. Did you get any of the Yucca Flats? It's about gone."

Dan shakes his head. Chukker pulls up a chair and sits next to Dan. He puts his arm around Dan's shoulder.

"You know, Dan, I understand your background and how people from your home are opposed to alcohol. Did you know that when I first started working in Yellowstone, I didn't drink alcohol?"

"Why not?"

Chukker chuckles. "My Daddy and Momma are good Southern Baptists. Neither of them consume any type of alcohol. The Church frowns on consumption of alcohol, although I'm not sure that was the Church's position during bootlegging days. Anyway, I arrive in Yellowstone and didn't drink any alcohol, no sir'ee."

"One night I'm at a Pow Wow and this Savage offered me a beer. When I refused to accept the beer, he looked at me and said, 'Do you know what Jesus' first miracle was?' Do you know Dan?"

"Sure, it was when Jesus turned the water into wine."

Chukker starts laughing. "G**d***, you know your Bible, Brother. So, I start really thinking about what the fellow told me. If Jesus is God's Son and Jesus' first miracle is to turn water into wine, how could God make consumption of alcohol a sin. As I thought about it more, I became convinced that God couldn't possibly consider drinking alcohol a sin. Rather, I came to believe that it was people—not God—who decided to make it a sin."

"What do you mean 'people made it a sin?'"

"Well, I don't know how to answer that," says Chukker. "Maybe there were people who had a relative who was an alcoholic or maybe there were people who liked spirits a little too much. But to say that God believes it's a sin to consume alcohol, it just seems disingenuous to me. That's why I started drinking alcohol and I've liked it ever since."

Chukker pauses a moment. "Listen, Brother. I'm not trying to preach to you. I just want you to consider what my friend asked me some years ago."

Chukker squeezes Dan's shoulder with his hand and stands up. As Chukker walks away, Dan calls to him. "Chukker?"

Chukker turns back to face him. "What?"

"Thank you."

"You're welcome." Chukker turns to walk away.

"Chukker?"

Chukker turns again to face him. "What is it, Brother?"

Dan grins at Chukker. "Do you know where I can find a glass? I need to find out for myself what this Yucca Flats tastes like."

The next morning, a lot of employees arrive late to work. Two additional things happen that morning.

First, the manager of the laundry is summarily fired and instructed to leave the Park. It turns out that pointing a pistol at a fellow employee isn't only against Company policy, it's against Park regulations for anybody to have possession of a weapon of any sort in Yellowstone National Park.

Oh, the other thing? There's one angry Dude from Oklahoma who discovers that he's missing one Oklahoma license plate.

CHAPTER TWENTY-ONE
LESS THAN RESPECTFUL ACTIVITIES?

When Dan later reflects back on that summer in Yellowstone National Park, he recalls a few occasions on which Savages, including himself as one of those Savages, engaged in activities which some might deem disrespectful of Yellowstone's marvelous natural wonders.

Dan, Lou and Steve stand by the Bell Desk waiting for a Front. Lou's next up on the list. The lobby's empty of people. All three assume that Old Faithful Geyser must be ready to erupt soon.

At nineteen years of age, Steven James is the youngest member of the Bell Crew. He prefers to be called "Steve." He'll be a sophomore this coming fall at New Mexico State University.

The three bellmen chat as they wait for something to do.

"Have either of you heard of the IPIOF Club?" says Dan.

Steve shakes his head. "Yeah, I've heard of it," Lou says.

Dan scratches his bare arm. "I keep hearing people talk about the IPIOF Club, but I don't have any idea what it is or what IPIOF means."

Lou turns to Dan. "Stop and think for a minute. The letters are "I-P-I-O-F".

Dan thinks for minute. "Beats me. I have no clue. What do the letters stand for?"

"The letters stand for: 'I peed in Old Faithful.'"

"Do they mean Old Faithful Geyser?" Steve asks.

Lou looks at Steve and sighs. "I doubt they would form a club for people who pee in restrooms while visiting the Old Faithful area."

Dan is incredulous. "You mean to tell me that Savages walk right up to the lip of Old Faithful, unzip their pants and then pee into the geyser?"

Lou nods his head. "That's exactly what some Savages do."

"Are there female members of the Club?" asks Steve.

Lou looks up in the air. "I don't think you receive an actual award when you join the Club, but sure, I've heard several gals indicate that they're members."

Dan now scratches his head. "How can that even happen? I can see guys taking a whiz into the geyser, but a gal would have to hold her butt over the geyser opening and hope she doesn't lose her balance and fall backwards."

All three young bellmen wince at the thought of a gal falling into Old Faithful Geyser while attempting the initiation rite.

Steve pounds his fist on the Bell Desk. "I want to become a member of the Club. How about you guys? Do you want to join me? We can all become members at the same time."

Dan and Lou aren't much older than Steve, but enough older to proceed cautiously with the way this conversation's headed.

"I don't know," says Dan. "It sounds dangerous. I'm not sure that the Park Service would approve."

Lou looks at Steve. "I'm with Dan. I'd have to think about it."

Steve's undeterred by their reluctance. "We're all done working by 9:00 tonight. Why don't we walk out to Old Faithful Geyser together about 11:00 and wait for an eruption. It'll be late enough that there should be nobody around that late. We know that we'll have at least 35 to 40 minutes before Old Faithful Geyser erupts again. That'll give us time to check it out. If you guys chicken out at the last minute, that'll be okay with me because I want to become a member of the Club."

Dan and Lou look at one another. "Okay, I'll come with you," says Dan. "But no promises on becoming a member."

Lou nods his head. "Ditto for me."

Around 11:00 that night, three bellmen walk out the front doors of the Inn and head toward Old Faithful Geyser. The night's very dark since the moon hasn't risen yet. They follow the boardwalk until they find the last bench on the boardwalk. That bench is located near Old Faithful Lodge. The bellmen sit in a row on the bench and await the Old Lady's next eruption.

The next eruption occurs shortly before midnight. Ten minutes later, they can't see any people in sight. They all stand and walk further along the boardwalk until Old Faithful Geyser stands between them and the lights of the Inn.

Steve pulls a flashlight from his jacket pocket and turns it on. Dan notices that he's wrapped a handkerchief around the light end and secured it with a rubber band in order to prevent the light from beaming more than five feet.

"Steve, it was a good idea to restrict the light by using a handkerchief," says Dan.

"Thanks."

Lou turns toward Steve's silhouette. "Since this is your party, you lead the way. Dan and I will follow."

Steve steps off the boardwalk followed by Dan and Lou. A thin vapor column drifts upward from Old Faithful Geyser and can be seen against the darkness of the night. The three walk very cautiously since they know that areas around thermal features in the Park can be very thin and fragile. When they're about fifteen feet from the geyser's opening, Steve stops as do the other two.

Old Faithful Geyser is the most famous geyser in all the world. If one were to play a word association game with someone who's never visited the Park, there's a 50% probability that if one said "Yellowstone National Park," the person who'd never visited the Park would say "Old Faithful"—meaning the geyser. Yet, as Dan stands here looking at this world-famous attraction, what strikes him is that up close there's nothing striking at all about Old Faithful Geyser. There's simply an opening in the ground surrounded by a thin bleached white chemical deposit created by the silica in the water that's sprayed regularly by Old Faithful Geyser.

"Are you guys going to join me?" Dan notices that Steve's voice cracks and assumes that he's nervous.

"No, I'm not cut out for membership in the Club," says Dan.

Steve looks at Lou's silhouette. "How about you, Lou?"

Lou doesn't hesitate. "I'm still with Dan on this. I'm going to sit this one out. You're on your own."

"Okay," says Steve. "I guess that I'll just have to show both of you the kind of balls it takes to become a member of the IPIOF Club."

Steve hands Dan the flashlight and walks another ten feet toward the geyser. When Steve is about five feet from the geyser opening, he unzips his pants and starts to prepare for his initiation rite into the IPIOF Club. At that moment, Old Faithful Geyser belches a small column of water about four or five feet high out of her opening.

Dan's seen these small mini-eruptions from Old Faithful Geyser repeatedly during the summer. Dan and others refer to these mini-releases of boiling water as "foreplay." Perhaps he hasn't spent as much time watching Old Faithful Geyser as him, because Steve totally freaks out. He turns and runs past Dan and Lou until he's standing back on the boardwalk.

Dan and Lou turn and walk back to join Steve on the boardwalk.

Something sparkles for just a split second from Steve's pants. Dan's eyes follow the trajectory of the light. He looks at the Inn and realizes that the sparkle was caused by the lights of the Inn reflecting off Steve's zipper. He concludes that Steve was so frightened by the mini-eruption that he forgot to zip his pants up.

Dan turns toward Steve. "You better pull your zipper up so you can keep those big balls in your pants." Dan can't see his face due to the darkness, but can see Steve's silhouette zipping his pants up.

When he later reflects on that evening, to Dan's knowledge, none of the three bellmen who were together on the boardwalk that night ever became members of the IPIOF Club.

"Do you guys remember when we started talking about soaping a geyser a while back?" Ted asks.

Ted, Bill, Chukker, Eagle and Dan are sitting in the baggage bay of a Tauck tour bus. Four of them are casually sipping beer from a can of cold Coors.

No one responds to his question. Ted arches his back to stretch it and says, "Remember, I had read a historical piece on Yellowstone National Park. The article indicated that decades ago the Park Service would 'soap geysers' to produce an eruption for tourists. We got interrupted when some gals showed up."

"I know that they use to do some crazya** things like feeding grizzly bears in Hayden Valley while tourists watched from wooden bleachers," says Chukker.

Bill seems perplexed. "So, soap can really create a chemical reaction that results in an eruption?"

"Apparently so," Ted says.

Eagle's eyes sparkle. "Why don't we try it?"

Chukker frowns. "One reason not to attempt it would be that we'd all be thrown out of the Park if the D*** Park Service learned of it."

"Why not attempt it," says Ted. "Perhaps we can find a geyser that's been inactive for awhile and soap it to see if it produces a reaction."

"Hey, Ted," Bill says. "Since this is your idea, why don't you find the inactive geyser for us to soap."

Ted nods his head and accepts the challenge. "Okay. Let me see what I can come up with."

A couple of evenings later, Dan and Bill are talking with Chukker in his room. Ted and Eagle walk into Chukker's room.

"Guess what?" Ted says. No one answers his question, so Ted continues, "Remember talking about soaping a geyser?" Heads nod in agreement.

"Well, I dropped by the Visitor Center and talked with a naturalist about dormant geysers. This naturalist pulls down a three-ring binder from a bookshelf and opens it up. Apparently, the naturalists in the Old Faithful area keep records on every geyser in the area as they receive information from tourists and other sources. He identified a small geyser located in Fountain Flats which has supposedly been dormant for more than two decades. He showed me where to locate it. I'm calling it No Name Geyser. Who wants to join me in a little expedition to No Name Geyser?"

Four arms shoot into the air in unison.

Several days later in the early evening, the five bellmen (Ted, Bill, Chukker, Eagle and Dan) gather and carpool to Fountain Flats in Bill's and Chukker's cars. The cars are parked in a pullout. The bellmen climb out of their cars with $20 of laundry detergent that they purchased in West Yellowstone. In the early 1970s, $20 buys a lot of detergent. They also have several dozen bars of soap obtained from the Inn's stock for guest rooms.

Ted looks at the map in his hands. "This is the trail. Follow me."

Ted leads off followed in single file order by the other bellmen. After a brisk twenty minute walk, Ted stops and starts turning in a circle looking for No Name Geyser. The other four start looking as well.

"I think that I see No Name Geyser," Eagle yells. He points to the northwest and the others see a small cone of silica about two to three feet high with a circumference of approximately ten feet.

The group walks carefully over to the cone and start tapping against the silica with their toes to test the strength of the crust of No Name Geyser. When they're sure that the crust will support their weight, they gingerly walk onto the cone. The opening of the geyser is approximately two feet in diameter and contains a pool of very hot water starting about a foot below the rim of the opening. Tiny wisps of steam rise from the opening in the cone.

Bill breaks the silence. "Well, let's try this."

He steps to the center of the cone and pours all of the laundry detergent that he's carrying into the water located in the center of the cone. One-by-one, the other bellmen follow Bill and pour all of their laundry detergent into the center of the cone. They pull the bars of soap from their pockets and toss these into the water as well.

The five bellmen take a step back and watch No Name Geyser, but nothing happens.

Five minutes pass. Eagle grows impatient. "How long are we going to stand around here waiting for something to happen?"

As if on cue, the level of the water in the cone suddenly drops about two feet as though a toilet has been flushed. Simultaneously, the ground under their feet starts shaking violently. Without a word, all of the frightened bellmen scramble off the cone of the geyser and step back another 50 or 60 feet from the edge of the cone. Their eyes don't leave the center of the cone of No Name Geyser.

Suddenly, boiling steam and water erupt out of the cone of No Name Geyser in a column about 40 to 50 feet high. The water pulsates into the air sending columns of steam billowing into the blue sky.

The bellmen stare at the eruption with their mouths wide open.

Chukker finally manages to speak first. "I'll be G**D*****—that soap made the SonofaB**** dormant geyser erupt!"

Bill speaks in a hushed tone. "Chukker, I couldn't have expressed it better myself."

Dan shakes his head in disbelief. "I never would have believed this could have happened if I wasn't here in person."

The eruption of boiling water and steam lasts about five minutes. Then, just as quickly as the eruption began, No Name Geyser goes back to sleep for a long, long rest.

On the hike back to the cars, the bellmen walk in silence. Bill finally stops and the others also stop. Bill turns to the others. "I've been thinking. This is probably something that we should keep to ourselves. If we tell others about what just happened, word will spread rapidly and the Park Service may want to speak with us."

"H***, the G**d***** Rangers may want to put our a**es in jail," says Chukker.

"Everyone agree to keep silent about this?" Bill asks. The others nod their heads in agreement.

At the time, Dan wonders whether five people can ever all keep a secret. But somehow, they manage to keep the story secret out of fear of what would happen if word leaked out of their success soaping a dormant geyser. However, the mere mention of soaping a geyser will always make them smile.

CHAPTER TWENTY-TWO
FLIRTING WITH A DON'T RULE

From Dan's perspective, some rules on the Don't List seem pretty black and white; others perhaps a little murkier. For example, the Don't rules of "Thou shall not kill" and "Thou shall not steal" seem straightforward, particularly since they are two of the Ten Commandments enumerated in the Old Testament. On the other hand, the "Don't have premarital sex" rule seems less clear to Dan.

His parents certainly believe in the "Don't have premarital sex" rule as do his grandparents, his aunts and uncles and most of his cousins. Over the years, Dan has heard countless pastors and evangelists rail from the pulpit that "Thou shall not have premarital sex." He's read in the Bible that "Thou shall not commit adultery." In fact, that's another of the Ten Commandments. But he can't recall ever reading any passage from the Bible that explicitly says, "Thou shall not have premarital sex."

Dan's parents never had the "birds and bees discussion" with him. He recalls that the subject of an unwed young woman becoming pregnant came up during family discussions on more than one occasion. To his recollection, his mother couldn't bring herself to use the word "pregnant." Rather, she would lower her eyes and say softly, "Isn't it sad that so and so is 'PG.'" Dan for a long time wondered what "PG" even meant.

Dan also recalls that his only sex education in public schools occurred during his high school freshman biology class. The teacher was so clinical and detailed in discussing how the male's sperm fertilizes the female's egg that he left class wondering how it actually happens. As his classmates were gathering their books and papers at the end of the class, confirmation of his confusion came when Dan overheard one female classmate say to another female classmate, "I don't know how the sperm gets to the woman's egg" and the other classmate said, "Me neither."

Like most teenagers-male and female, Dan has hormones and is attracted to certain members of the opposite sex. Perhaps because of the lack of discussion of sex in his personal circle, or more likely, the absence of any meaningful dialogue of sex whatsoever, Dan's somewhat shy and feels awkward with the opposite sex when romantic feelings surface. In high school, he started dating a little during his senior year but on a very superficial level. In college, he began dating more gals with some dates ending in what some refer to as "a good old make out session." Suffice it to say, by the time he arrived in Yellowstone National Park, Dan hadn't come even close to breaking the Don't rule of "Thou shall not have premarital sex." Dan's summer at Old Faithful Inn will change his perspective forever on this Don't rule.

Her name is Kathleen O'Connor. Dan met Kathleen one night at a Pow Wow at Deer Tracks. Dan recalls their chance meeting.

One morning Lou and Dan were having breakfast together in the Staffateria.

"Do you have any plans for this evening?" Lou asked.

"None tonight."

"Do you know Brenda Hightower? She works as a maid in the Inn."

Dan shook his head. "No, I don't think that I know her. Why?"

"Apparently, all of the housekeeping departments in the area are having a joint Pow Wow tonight at Deer Tracks. This includes the Inn, Lodge and Campers Cabins staff. Brenda invited me to join her this evening."

Dan interrupted. "Is she expecting you to be her date or is this just a friendly invitation?"

"That's the problem. I don't know which she intends. That's why I thought you might want to go with me. If she intends it to be a date, then you can meet some new people. If two of us show up and she doesn't intend it to be a date, I won't look like a total idiot."

Dan started chuckling. "Yeah, you would look like a total idiot if you showed up solo and Brenda has no romantic notions."

"So, will you go with me?"

"Where is Deer Tracks located?" Dan asked.

"Deer Tracks is located behind Old Faithful Lodge on the Firehole River. We'll walk behind the Lodge and head down the hill toward the Firehole. When we reach the Firehole, we turn right and follow the river to the Pow Wow. I'm pretty sure that we'll see lights or hear noise before we find the Pow Wow."

Dan sighed. "Against my better judgment, I'll go with you and be your wingman."

Later that evening, Dan and Lou found the Pow Wow by following the noise. When they arrived, they saw that Savages were standing around a bonfire. They looked for anyone they knew. Brenda spotted Lou and walked over to them.

"Hi, Lou," said Brenda. "Who's your friend?"

"Hi, Brenda." Lou turned to Dan. "This is my roommate, Dan."

Brenda looked at Dan. "Are you also a bellman at the Inn?"

Dan smiled. "Someone has to keep an eye on Lou."

Everyone snickered.

Brenda looked at Dan again. "Can I borrow Lou for a little bit? I want to introduce a few of my friends to him."

Without waiting for a reply, Brenda grabbed Lou's arm and led him to the other side of the fire. They joined several gals who were holding their hands toward the fire to warm them. Dan remembers thinking to himself that Brenda apparently believed this was a date.

Dan stood alone for a few minutes and finally stuck his hands in his front jeans pockets. A few minutes later he moved to an empty log near the fire and sat down.

A voice behind Dan spoke. "You look pretty lonely sitting on that log by yourself. Is there room on that log for two people?"

Dan looked over his shoulder and saw an attractive young gal standing behind him. The light was dim since the fire had been allowed to burn low, but it provided enough illumination for him to get a good look at her. She was shorter than himself and had a slim figure. She was wearing woolen mittens and a knit stocking hat on her head. Locks of curly red hair hung down from her hat and her face was covered with freckles. Dan could tell from her reddened face that she spent plenty of time outdoors.

Dan moved over to make room on the log. The gal came around the log and sat next to him.

She offered her right hand and smiled. "Hi. I'm Kathleen O'Connor."

He shook her hand. "I'm Dan Johnson. Do you work in the area?"

Kathleen nodded her head. "It's a little complicated, but I currently work in housekeeping at Camper Cabins. My contract was to work in housekeeping at the Inn which I did for two days. I moved into Wurthering Heights and was assigned a roommate. But after two days, they desperately needed help at Campers Cabins. When I showed up for work on my third day, my supervisor told me to walk over to Campers Cabins where I've been ever since."

"Were you reassigned to a cabin at Campers Cabins?" Dan had heard that Savages who worked at Campers Cabins were housed in a few of the cabins.

Kathleen shook her head. "No, they told me to just stay at Wurthering Heights. I room there, but I eat most meals with the other Savages at Campers Cabins. Even I get confused sometimes. What do you do?"

"I'm a bellman at the Inn."

"Do you live in that place at the top of the Inn?"

"Yep. Bats Alley." Dan looked at the fire since someone had thrown another log on top and the bark of the log flamed as it caught fire. "Kathleen, where are you from?"

"Kalamazoo, Michigan, but I go to school at Michigan State in Lansing."

Dan grinned. "No way. I'm from central Indiana and attend a small college there."

Kathleen looked at Dan. "Well, I guess we have something in common."

Turned out that Dan and Kathleen had a lot in common. Both were from the Midwest. Kathleen was born and raised in Kalamazoo. She would be a sophomore at Michigan State and was only a year younger than him. Her parents were staunch members of a conservative Presbyterian church in Kalamazoo which had a definite evangelical bent. Like him, Kathleen had grown up with a lot of Don't rules—both written and unspoken. The only difference from Dan was that her Don't rules were significantly fewer than his. But the more they talked, the more each realized how many similarities each had to the other.

They talked while sitting on the log for over two hours until Lou came over and told Dan that he was walking back to the Inn.

Dan turned to Kathleen. "Would you like to walk back to the Inn with us? I'll make sure that you get safely back to Wurthering Heights."

"I'd like that," said Kathleen. Dan noticed that her eyes practically seemed to sparkle in the light of the fire.

Dan walked her to the porch of the girl's dormitory.

Before leaving, Dan paused for a moment. "Kathleen, would you like to get together again?"

"Is it safe to date a bellman?" said Kathleen teasingly.

Dan grinned. "I'm not sure about all the bellmen, but I think you're pretty safe dating this one."

Kathleen chuckled. "Then I'd love to get together again."

Kathleen stepped forward and kissed Dan on his cheek.

Dan and Kathleen begin spending considerable time together. During the day while not on duty, he often finds the need to walk to Upper Hams and frequently locates her working out amongst the cabins. Whenever he arrives, Kathleen always takes ten or fifteen minutes to stop working and chat with him. Since meeting at the Pow Wow, they've had five "official" dates and also spent a day off together in the Tetons. They've grown comfortable with each other and have discussed a wide range of topics. And, it should be mentioned that Dan thinks Kathleen is a terrific kisser and is pretty sure that she, if asked, would say the same about him.

Dan finds Kathleen working among the cabins and stops to personally invite her to Bats Alley that night. Lou has the day off and is backpacking overnight somewhere in the Beartooth Mountains with two individuals. Dan locates Kathleen in one of the cabins.

"Knock, knock. Caught you working again."

Kathleen's on her hands and knees. She looks up and smiles brightly when she sees him.

"Someone has to work in this Park. We all know it's not going to be the bellmen."

Dan chuckles. "Say, Lou's backpacking overnight with a couple of friends. Would you like to come up to Bats Alley this evening? I can make popcorn and I'm sure that Lou wouldn't mind if you drink a couple of beers from his cooler."

Kathleen pretends to look at an imaginary watch on her wrist. "What time?"

"Why don't I meet you at Wurthering Heights about 8:00. By the way, I like your fake Timex."

Kathleen sticks her tongue out. "I'll have you know that my wristwatch is an expensive Rolex. I'll be ready at 8:00."

Punctuality is one of the things that Dan likes about Kathleen. He arrives at Wurthering Heights at 8:00 and is surprised that Kathleen isn't waiting for him on the porch. About 8:15, Mary Ann walks out the front door of Wuthering Heights. He notices that she's all dolled up. He then remembers that Tauck Tours and Benny Stout are staying at the Inn that evening. Dan and Mary Ann say hello to each other. He's ready to ask Mary Ann if she would let Kathleen know that he's waiting when the door opens and Kathleen walks out of the dormitory. Mary Ann walks down the steps and heads for the Inn.

Dan greets Kathleen with a hug. "You look nice this evening, as always."

"You don't look so bad yourself."

Dan then remembers Mary Ann. He turns and calls to her, "Mary Ann, enjoy your dinner in the dining room. Be sure to say hello to Benny from me."

Mary Ann turns back toward Dan and starts to open her mouth, but decides not to say anything and resumes walking toward the Inn.

Dan looks at Kathleen again.

"Sorry that I'm late, but I'm ready for some popcorn," she says. Kathleen slips her arm into the crook of Dan's right arm and the two of them walk down the stairs of Wuthering Heights together.

The aroma of fresh popped popcorn fills his room. Dan has the door closed to keep the smell from wafting through Bats Alley. Kathleen has a can of cold Coors in one hand. He's wondered whether her church doesn't have a

'Don't Rule" prohibiting consumption of alcohol or whether she just ignores the rule. Kathleen uses her other hand to select just the right kernels of popcorn from the plastic bowl. They're both sitting on Dan's lower bunk bed.

The conversation starts innocently enough.

"How's the popcorn tonight," says Dan.

Kathleen pops another kernel into her mouth and says, "Delicious." She then leans over and kisses him.

Dan grins at her. "By the way, I didn't ask you before. What made you late this evening? You're always so punctual."

"I was helping my roommate find her medicine."

"Her medicine? Is your roommate alright?"

Kathleen nods her head. "She's fine."

Now, Dan will learn later in life that it's probably better not to ask too many questions when discussing certain topics. Dan hasn't yet learned this valuable life lesson. "What kind of medicine?"

Kathleen blushes. "It isn't actually medicine for a health issue."

Dan's still a little slow understanding. "What is it then?"

Kathleen hesitates for a second. "It's her birth control pills."

"Oh." Now Dan blushes.

"They're my roommate's birth control pills—not mine."

Dan hesitates for a second. "Have you ever taken birth control pills?"

Kathleen blushes again. "Well, I've never had any reason to take birth control pills."

"Oh, you've never had sexual relations with anyone." Dan isn't sure whether it's a statement or a question.

Kathleen shakes her head. "No. How about you?"

Dan grins. "Well, let's just say that we're both virgins."

Kathleen giggles. "Have you ever wanted to try it?"

"By 'it,' I assume that you mean sex?" Kathleen nods her head and Dan continues, "Sure, I've had thoughts about it."

Kathleen pauses. "Are you curious about sex?"

Dan grins again. "Sure, what 21-year-old guy hasn't had thoughts about sex? How about you?"

"Of course. Gals are no different from guys when it comes to curiosity about sex."

A minute passes in silence as if neither knows where the discussion should go from here.

Then Kathleen's face lights up. She looks at Dan and says, "Let's do it!"

Dan looks back at Kathleen. "Do what?"

"You're silly. I mean have sex together," says Kathleen. "Let's lose our virginity together. Right now."

Dan hesitates. "Umm, Kathleen, are you sure that this is a good idea?"

Kathleen smiles at Dan. "I like you a lot and I assume that you feel the same way about me, right?"

Dan nods his head. "I do like you a lot."

"We both are curious about sex. We both have sexual desires. We're both virgins. Why not lose our virginity with someone we really care about who happens to be a virgin as well?"

In a convoluted way, Kathleen's logic makes some sense to Dan. "I don't have any protection."

"Don't worry. I 've been taking some of my roommate's birth control pills for six weeks now." Kathleen smiles a wicked little grin.

"Kathleen, I'm surprised that a sweet gal like you brought up in a conservative church would do such a thing."

"Look, we both grew up in strict religious environments. Maybe that's the reason why we should do this together right now." Dan nods his head. He clearly hears and understands this comment from Kathleen.

Dan looks at Kathleen. "Okay, you're right."

They sit in silence for a minute. Then, Kathleen stands up and Dan does as well. She unbuttons the top two buttons of her blouse. She takes Dan's hand and places it on the third button of her blouse. Kathleen looks toward the front of her blouse and nods her head. Dan reaches out and slowly unbuttons the remaining buttons. He holds the blouse as Kathleen slips out of it. Kathleen turns her back to him and says softly, "Will you please unhook my bra." Dan fusses with the fasteners, but she becomes anxious over his delay and reaches back and undoes her bra herself. She pulls her bra off and then turns to face him bare breasted.

Dan can't recall having ever seen a bare breasted woman in person before this moment. He looks at Kathleen's breasts and feels a tingle of excitement. He just stares until she takes his right hand and places it on one of her breasts.

She then pulls his tee-shirt up over his head and places both of her palms on Dan's skinny chest.

Kathleen unbuttons the button of his jeans and unzips his zipper. She pulls the jeans down to his ankles and he steps out of them. Dan reciprocates and does the same with her jeans. Both then remove their own undergarments and lay down on the lower bunk of the bed.

Dan has never lain with a naked woman before and suspects that Kathleen has likewise never lain with a naked man before. Both are somewhat tentative as to what they should do next so they start kissing passionately. Then, Kathleen places her hand on his inner thigh and rubs it slowly up and down his thigh. Dan can feel his body tingling and knows he's getting aroused. Dan places his hand on her inner thigh and starts stoking it slowly just as she had done. He can feel Kathleen's excitement and anticipation. By now, both are laboring with their breathing.

Kathleen rolls onto her back and spreads her legs apart. Dan gets on his hands and knees to position himself over her. She reaches up and gives him a long, slow kiss.

Kathleen drops onto her back and whispers, "Now, Dan."

Dan looks into her eyes and slowly shuts his. Suddenly, he pushes himself up and rolls over onto his back so that he's lying alongside her on the mattress.

Dan looks at her and whispers, "I'm sorry, Kathleen. I really like you, but I'm just not ready to do this yet."

Kathleen looks into his eye, but says nothing. He can tell that she's disappointed. After a few moments, she turns her head toward the bottom of the upper bunk and just stares at the mattress. Dan also turns his head toward the bottom of the upper bunk and stares at the mattress too.

Ten minutes pass and neither says a word. Their breathing returns to normal. They just lie side-by-side next to each other with their bodies touching.

Dan thinks to himself that he has never felt so naked in his whole life—not a physical nakedness, but rather a feeling of being totally drained emotionally.

Kathleen finally breaks the silence. "Dan, I have to go home."

Dan nods his head. "I'll walk you back to the dorm."

They dress slowly in silence. After they're both dressed, Dan opens the door for Kathleen and follows her out of his room. They walk side-by-side back to the bottom of the stairway to the porch of Wurthering Heights, but not a single word is said by either of them.

When she turns to face him, Dan isn't sure what Kathleen will say.

"Thank you, Dan," she says quietly.

Dan's perplexed. "Thanks for what?"

"Thank you for stopping me from making the biggest mistake of my young life."

Kathleen takes ahold of Dan's hand and squeezes it tightly. She then stands on her tiptoes and kisses him on his cheek. Kathleen turns, walks up the stairs and disappears into Wurthering Heights.

Twenty minutes later, Dan's lying in his bed in his room. The room is dark, but his eyes are wide open as he replays the evening's events over and over in his mind. After about 15 minutes, he exhales a long, audible sigh. He thinks to himself that if I'm with the right gal at the right time someday, it wouldn't be the most terrible thing in the world if I broke the "Don't have premarital sex rule."

And with this thought, Dan's eyelids finally shut.

CHAPTER TWENTY-THREE
THE SHRANER CART

Dan loves working on the morning crew. When Lou had first showed him around the Inn and taught him about working the Bells, he'd explained that Mac, Chukker, Bill and Ted work only the morning crew because of seniority, but Mac rotates the afternoon guys into the morning crew one at a time. This week is his second rotation onto the morning crew. Dan likes the split schedule. He likes the heavy work taking luggage to guest rooms in the afternoons and pulling the luggage in mornings. He likes that morning crew seldom handles Fronts and that he avoids the hundreds of mindless questions asked by Dudes every day. He likes the money that he makes on morning crew which is considerably better than what he earns on afternoon crew. But most of all, he likes morning crew because there's a lot of down time waiting for tour buses which allows him a lot of time to flirt with the gals. Dan doesn't know that this aspect of morning crew may create a problem for him one day.

Morning crew does one primary thing: move luggage from tour buses to guests' rooms in the afternoon and from guests' rooms back to tour buses in the morning. Since an average tour typically has 30 to 60 bags, the bellmen use carts to carry the baggage from the buses to the general area where the rooms are located. In the early 1970s, there are no elevators in the Inn. If rooms aren't located on the main floor, bags must be hand carried up or down stairs depending on the location of the guest rooms.

To assist in transporting large quantities of luggage from the buses to the general area where guests are staying, there're three wooden carts for the bellmen to utilize for this purpose. The bellmen don't know the origin of these carts, but all appear to have been built by craftsmen on the premises. Two larger carts have two small wheels on the front end and handles on the rear end. The bellmen have to pick up the rear handles and shift the weight to the front wheels much like a two-handed wheelbarrow. The third wooden cart is smaller and has four wheels with small wheels in the front and larger wheels in the rear. The two larger carts can carry more bags per load—approximately 28 to 32 bags depending on the size of the bags. The smaller cart can carry fewer bags per load—approximately 22 to 26 depending on size. However, the smaller cart is prone to tipping over if top-loaded, i.e., unless the heavy bags are loaded toward the rear of the cart.

The smaller cart has its own name—the Shraner cart. Apparently, the cart was named after Howard Shraner, who worked as a bellman at the Inn years before Dan arrived. Some of the older bellmen had worked with Howard, but no one could ever provide Dan with a satisfactory explanation as to why this particular cart was named after the former bellman.

Dan will later recall two additional things of note. First, although the Front Desk staff who work with Kitty Baxter aren't too sure of her competence, Kitty, as the manager's wife, has taken the prime responsibility of greeting tour groups after they disembark from their bus and then leading them to their assigned rooms. She always has a copy of the same guest list that's provided to the Bell staff and a plastic ice bucket which contains the individual room keys for all the guests in a particular tour. After Kitty greets the tour group, she leads them to the area of their assigned rooms and personally hands out the keys as she calls names from her list.

The second thing that Dan will later recall is that the OFI Bell Crew has an esprit de corps mentality. Every single one of the OFI bellmen believes that they're the hardest working, most efficient bell crew west of the Mississippi. This perception is especially evident with the morning crew. After all, what other bell crew west of the Mississippi works in a huge multi-storied building without any elevators? The goal for the morning crew on afternoons is to always have the luggage waiting in the room when the guest opens the door. Does this always happen? If the truth be told, it doesn't because there are circumstances beyond even the control of an OFI bellman—such as multiple tours arriving at the Inn in close proximity. But, more often than not, a tour guest staying at Old Faithful Inn in the early 1970s opens the door to their room and discovers their luggage resting on luggage racks just waiting to be opened.

"Whew, that was a G**D***** lot of bags that we loaded onto buses this morning," says Chukker.

Chukker's body is stretched out across a chair in the dining area of Lower Hams with his legs stretched out away from the small table. Mac, Bill, Dan and Eagle are sitting on chairs around the table. Ted has the day off and is hiking in the Park. Mac asked Eagle to cover for Ted since Dan's working the morning crew rotation this week. Dan's sipping his butterscotch malt through a straw. This has become his morning treat since he gets plenty of physical exercise in Yellowstone and really never puts any weight on his 130-pound frame. Mac and Bill are sipping their coffees. Eagle and Chukker are simply enjoying the morning comradery of their fellow bellmen.

"Pulling six tours in one morning involves a lot of physical work," says Bill. "Thankfully, our first tour this afternoon isn't supposed to arrive until 4:30 so I can take a little nap after lunch."

Mac looks at the sheet with the estimated arrival time of this afternoon's tours and the number of guests for each tour. He then looks at Bill. "You may need more than a little nap. We have seven tours arriving this afternoon. Four of them have an ETA of 5:30. Some are large tours. It's going to be a zoo for us the get everybody's bags to the right room without some mix-up."

Dan takes a big slurp on his straw to drain the rest of his butterscotch malt from the bottom of his glass. Dan looks at Mac. "Mac, what were you saying about increasing the rates for tour groups?"

Before Mac can reply, Chukker interrupts. "Dan, we're getting ripped off by these tour escorts. Currently, we receive 25 cents per bag in and out— meaning we receive 50 cents total per bag. We know that most large hotels have started charging 35 cents per bag. H***, Benny pays us 35 cents per bag without us even having to request an increase."

Mac jumps into the conversation. "That's correct, Daniel. Benny pays more than what I've told him that he owes. Benny says, 'Mac, your Bell Crew provides the best service that I receive anywhere. Everyone else is charging 35 cents per bag in and out. Tauck gives me 35 cents per bag in and out. Why would I short-change your Bell Crew when you guys provide the best service?' I thanked Benny and told him that we'll continue to give his tours our very best service. If Benny's tour arrives close in time to any other tour, the Bell Crew's going to handle Benny's tour first."

"Wait a minute, Mac," says Bill. "Are you saying escorts are getting 35 cents per bag, but the escorts are paying us only 25 cent per bag and padding the difference?"

Mac nods his head. "Sadly, I think that's been happening all summer."

Dan's incredulous about what he's just heard. "Isn't that dishonest for the tour escorts to do that?"

"Probably, but the escorts' bosses never know that their escorts are pocketing the money," says Mac. "The bosses just assume that their escorts pay the bell staff the monies which they're given for that purpose."

"Why don't we charge 35 cent per bag in and out?" Dan asks.

Mac takes off his glasses and wipes them with a corner of his uniform shirt. Mac looks at him. "That's a good question, Daniel. The Company's policy is that we can't charge escorts. Occasionally, an escort will totally stiff us and pocket the money. Nothing we can do about it. The Company won't help us. In fact, the Company occasionally will receive a complaint about us squeezing an escort too hard. Those complaints probably come from escorts who stiff us and don't like being called out on it."

"H***, some of our former colleagues took care of people who stiffed them," says Chukker and smiles. "Do you remember Buster Jackson. He got so angry after getting stiffed that he took one of the Dude's bags and put it on a bus headed to Alaska. I'm not sure the Company ever figured that one out."

"Look, maybe I'm getting old, but we're not going to do things like that as long as I run this show," says Mac. "Don't worry, I promise to use every trick of the trade so that we don't get stiffed. But I'm not going to get fired for pulling a stunt like that."

"Yeah, but what about starting to charge 35 cents per bag in and out?" Bill asks.

Mac looks sternly at Bill. "When the time seems right, I promise that I'll start charging 35 cents per bag in and out."

Mac has the final say on the subject.

That afternoon the first tour arrives right on time at 4:30. The morning crew unloads the luggage and has the bags waiting for the guests when they enter their rooms. But then things really get busy. Between 5:00 and 6:00, four buses with large tour groups arrive within 20 minutes of each other. The buses have to wait their turn to pull into the bus loading zone which can only accommodate two buses at once. The morning crew works hard and has the luggage from all four tours in the guests' rooms by 6:30. By the time they return to the front of the Inn, another tour bus has arrived and is waiting to pull into the loading zone. When this bus finally parks in the loading zone, the morning crew quickly unloads the bags and marks the room numbers on each luggage tag. They then begin loading the luggage onto a couple of wooden carts.

As the crew starts loading the carts, Laura appears on the concrete apron where the bellmen are working. She leans against one of the Inn's wooden posts and initially watches the bellmen work, but then just stares vacantly at the ground. She looks very weary. Dan sees her and walks toward her.

"Are you okay, Laura?"

Laura's eyes are still staring at the ground. She looks up and smiles when she sees him. "Hi Dan. Everything's fine. I just needed a little break from Kitty."

"What's the problem?"

"Oh, you know Kitty," says Laura. "I know she means well, but she always creates additional work for the rest of us behind the Front Desk. This afternoon, she managed to book three different guests into the same room. We had three unhappy Dudes at the Front Desk at the same time. It took me an hour to straighten everything out."

Laura gets on a roll. "Do you know what else Kitty did this afternoon?"

Dan shakes his head. "No, what else did she do?"

"Apparently, she was supposed to have lunch with Mr. B in the dining room at 1:00. Mr. B was called away from his office to deal with a problem and left Kitty waiting behind the Front Desk. About ten minutes later, Kitty becomes impatient and grabs the microphone for the lobby's public address system. She speaks into the mic and says: 'Mr. Robert Baxter. Mr. Robert Baxter. Please report to the Front Desk.'"

"Did Mr. Baxter come running to the Front Desk?" They both giggle.

"No. He doesn't appear," says Laura. "Kitty waits another ten minutes and picks up the mic again. This time she announces, 'Mr. Baxter. Mr. Robert Baxter. Please return immediately to the Front Desk. There's an emergency.'"

Laura pauses and Dan asks, "What happens next?"

"Kitty waits another ten minutes and now she's really steamed. She grabs the mic and announces, 'Bobby, please return to the Front Desk. I'm really hungry.'"

Dan can't believe this. "No, you're kidding me."

Laura shakes her head. "No, I wish I were. It was really embarrassing. But, on the bright side, the lobby was pretty empty since everyone was outside watching Old Faithful erupt."

Dan scratches his arm. "Wow, I wonder what made her do that?"

Laura shrugs her shoulders. "I don't know for sure, but I suspect Kitty may've had a couple of vodka martinis for breakfast."

While Dan's having this conversation with Laura, the morning crew loads one of the large carts with about 30 bags. They're starting to load the Shraner cart when Eagle looks over at Dan and Laura who are laughing. Eagle nods his head toward them and says, "Looks like Dan's doing a little flirting on Company time. Let's teach him a lesson. Let me load the Shraner cart."

Mac, Chukker and Bill laugh and step back so Eagle can load the Shraner cart.

"Chukker, hold the back handles of the Shraner cart while I load it," says Eagle.

Chukker holds the back handles to keep all four wheels on the ground while Eagle carefully loads the cart. Of course, Eagle carefully selects the heaviest bags to load high above the cart on the cart's front end.

When the Shraner cart is loaded to his satisfaction, Eagle walks to the rear of the cart and carefully takes the cart handles from Chukker. Eagle looks at the others and says, "Are you ready to push the carts to the West Wing?" He gives the other three a wink.

Eagle starts wheeling the Shraner cart toward the West Wing. He motions to Dan. "Can you give me a hand here?"

Dan quickly tells Laura good-bye and runs over to help. Eagle looks at him. "Dan, why don't you take the Shraner cart?"

Eagle steps aside but keeps one arm pressing down on one of the cart handles so the Shraner cart doesn't tip on the spot. Dan takes both handles of the Shraner cart and begins pushing the cart toward the West Wing. Chukker picks up the back of the larger cart which is also piled high with bags. He falls in behind Dan and the Shraner cart. Mac, Bill and Eagle walk on either side of the Shraner cart warning people to stand clear of the oncoming carts.

Now, the patio area on the eastern front of the Old House looks like the concrete was poured at the same time as the concrete porch under the portico of the Old House. Where the portico ends on the other side of the porch, there's a steep concrete ramp which drops about five feet in elevation over twenty or thirty feet of ground. A short stretch of concrete walkway continues with a small inclined ramp ending at the double doored entry to the West Wing.

As he's pushing the Shraner cart toward the steep ramp, Dan notices that the Shraner cart seems a little top heavy, but he doesn't suspect that anything's amiss.

When the front wheels of the Shraner cart hit the downward slope of the ramp, Dan suddenly realizes that the Shraner cart is top heavy. Dan puts every ounce of his 130 pounds into keeping the rear wheels on the concrete. What's that expression about trying to stop a speeding locomotive? Dan tries to remember it, but has more pressing issues at hand.

About halfway down the ramp, Dan can't keep the back wheels on the concrete any longer. The Shraner cart tips over and catapults him through the air like a clown shot from a cannon at the circus. The bags which Eagle so carefully loaded onto the Shraner cart scatter in every direction. Dan flies through the air maybe 15 or 20 feet and lands on top of a mixture of large Samsonite bags and smaller canvas bags.

Whenever he recalls this event later, he's never sure whether he momentarily lost consciousness or not. However, he does recall seeing black splotches when he finally opened his eyes. He also recalls that his bare arms had multiple bruises and abrasions and that his entire body hurt like crazy. He also recalls that he was lying on top of bags of various sizes and shapes. But, what he recalls most vividly are the other four bellmen laughing so hard at him that tears were streaming down their faces.

As If his embarrassment couldn't be worse, Dan's mishap occurs just as Kitty's leading the tour group to the West Wing. Not only does Kitty watch this disaster unfold, so do approximately 40 tour guests—most of whom are white haired and widowed. As he regains his senses, Dan hears an older woman scream, "My Gawd, my bag, my bag!" While still lying on his back, two of these white-haired older women are literally using both hands with their feet braced against the ground trying to pull their precious bags out from under him. Dan thinks to himself that there's not much sympathy from this crowd.

Dan finally recovers his composure enough to slowly roll off the bags onto the concrete. He remains on all fours for a few moments while his head clears and then slowly gets on his feet. He notices that his uniform's filthy dirty. Blood from an abrasion is running down one arm. His eyeglasses seem bent.

The other bellmen finally quit laughing and begin clearing a path through the scattered luggage so the guests can reach their rooms. The tour group passes Dan in single file. Some look sympathetically at him as they pass; others glare at him in disgust. Two white-haired older women pass holding onto the handles of their large bags with both hands.

After the tour group disappears into the West Wing, Eagle comes over and looks at Dan.

"So, how do you like the Shraner cart?"

Four bellmen laugh loudly.

CHAPTER TWENTY-FOUR

MS. YELLOWSTONE IS A SLEEPER

Dan and Lou are standing by the Bell Desk waiting for a Front. Bill walks up with news.

"Guess who's entering the Miss Yellowstone pageant?"

In the early 1970s, the Yellowstone Park Company sponsors an annual Miss Yellowstone pageant for its employees. Gals around the Park are selected to represent their area at the final competition which is being held this year at the Old Faithful Lodge rec center. Dan doesn't know how representatives are selected in each area, but he certainly has heard of the Miss Yellowstone pageant.

"Who?" Dan asks.

"Debbie Wainwright."

"I wouldn't think that a beauty pageant would be something that'd interest Debbie," says Dan.

"I wonder what she'll do for the talent portion of the pageant?" Lou asks.

Just as luck would have it, Debbie and Sally walk through the back door of the Inn.

"Hey, Debbie," says Bill. "Is it true that you're entering the Miss Yellowstone pageant?"

Debbie and Sally stop. Debbie winks at Dan and then looks at Bill.

"Why, Bill, you seem surprised that I would enter the Miss Yellowstone contest. Are you?"

Bill grins sheepishly. "Yeah, just a little."

Debbie puts her hand on her chest and feigns disappointment. "Why, Bill Johnson. You have so little faith in one of your co-workers?" Debbie grins and winks again at Dan.

Bill's eyes twinkle mischievously. "How were you selected to represent the Old Faithful area? Did anyone else apply?"

"Bill, you are just so cute," says Debbie. "I guess it had something to do with my good looks, my good figure and especially my talent."

Lou interrupts. "Say, Debbie. What are you going to do for the talent portion of the pageant?"

Debbie smiles at Lou. "Oh, I have many talents, but it'll be a surprise. Ya'll just have to wait and see."

Dan thinks to himself that he's had enough surprises this summer, but he merely smiles.

"When is the pageant?" Lou asks.

"A week from Wednesday. Be sure to put the date on your calendar so you can come and support me."

Lou pauses for a moment. "D***, that's my day off and I have plans to be in the Tetons that night. Good luck though. I'm sure that you'll be terrific."

"Ya'll will have to excuse us," says Debbie. "Sally and I need to get to work."

As the two gals walk across the lobby, Dan looks at Bill. "Do you think Debbie can win the Miss Yellowstone pageant?"

Bill shakes his head. "Not a chance."

On the night of the pageant, Dan and Bill walk together from the Inn to the rec center and find seats near the front of the stage. Folding chairs are neatly arranged in rows on the hardwood floor where Mac had won his game of "Horse" with Scotty. As show time approaches, Dan glances around the rec center and is surprised that the center's nearly filled with people. The lights dim and Rich Lang walks to the front center of the stage where a microphone stand is located. When he grabs the microphone stand with both hands, a spotlight from the other end of the building illuminates him on the stage. Rich looks at the audience and talks into the mic.

"Ladies and Gentlemen, welcome to this year's Miss Yellowstone pageant. I'm Rich Lang. I'm the rec center manager and tonight I'll be your host. This year, we have representatives from locations all over the Park. Our young women will compete in swimsuit, talent and evening gown. The final three contestants will answer questions from our panel of judges. Our panel of judges tonight are ...."

The spotlight flashes on the front row of the audience. A table has been set up in the center of the seats and three people sit behind the table with pens and paper in front of each.

"Robert Baxter, who's the manager of Old Faithful Inn." Mr. Baxter stands up while the audience politely applauds. He waves to the crowd.

"Samuel Smith, who's the manager of Lake Hotel." Samuel stands and waves to polite applause.

"And William Buckley, who is a senior vice-president of the Yellowstone Park Company located in Gardiner, Montana." William also stands and waves to the politely clapping audience.

Rich steps back from the microphone and clears his throat.

"Now as to the introduction of our contestants, each young woman will come on stage so you can meet them."

Rich calls each contestant by name and their title. The contestants include Miss Mammoth Hot Springs, Miss Lake Area, Miss Fishing Bridge, Miss Canyon Village, Miss Grant Village, and Miss Old Faithful Area. Dan still wonders how Debbie became Miss Old Faithful Area. At any rate, the gals walk onto the stage as their names and titles are called and form a line in the middle of the stage facing the audience.

The crowd politely applauds each contestant. Each contestant seems to have brought a cheering section with them who are definitely not impartial. When their friend's name is called, they stand and cheer loudly. Dan can quickly tell where the various cheering groups are located in the rec center.

The contest begins with the swimsuit competition. Dan isn't overly impressed by any of the young women. Debbie wears a conservative one-piece outfit which he believes is probably the appropriate selection by her.

The talent competition comes next. The first contestant, Ms. Mammoth Hot Springs, plays a classical piece on a flute. She is followed by a gymnast who does a tumbling routine, a soloist who sings-slightly offkey- America the Beautiful, a baton act performed by a gal dressed in a sparkly sequined outfit (Dan suspects she was a baton twirler for her high school band), a soloist who plays another classical piece on a cello and a gal dressed like a clown who does a magic act. The audience applauds each gal politely, but none of the contestants has thoroughly engaged the crowd.

The next individual up will be Debbie. Dan feels anxious while waiting for Debbie to appear.

Rich Lang walks onto the stage and grabs the microphone stand. He pulls the mic toward his mouth.

"Now, Ladies and Gentlemen, we have our last contestant of the evening for the talent competition. Here is Miss Old Faithful Area, Debbie Wainwright!" The volume of Rich's voice rises as he introduces Debbie and he makes a big sweep of his arm and hand to bring her onstage.

The crowd claps politely. A few people in the audience-definitely from the Debbie camp- yell, "Go Debbie."

Several people help set up a few props on stage. From the audience's view, four large suitcases are lined up on the right side of the stage with a couple of hat boxes and a garment bag placed on top of them. One of the bellmen's metal carts is rolled on stage and placed at the back center of the stage standing up. On the left side of the stage, a large piece of cardboard is propped up facing the audience. A hole is cut in the center of the cardboard. Someone has used a black felt tipped pen and written above the hole in large block letters "Bank Teller".

Debbie walks to the front center of the stage and stands facing the audience. She's dressed in one of the uniforms which the bellmen wear at Old Faithful Inn. She grabs the microphone stand with both hands and flashes a huge smile at the audience.

"How are ya'll doing tonight? Are you enjoying the show?"

The audience is coming to life. They clap and a few people whistle.

Debbie pauses to let the noise stop.

"For my talent, I'm going to sing a little song that I wrote called 'Ode To The Old Faithful Inn Bellmen.' I'll sing this song a cappella to the tune of a children's song, 'The Wheels On The Bus Go Round And Round.' I dedicate this song to all of the fine young men who are bellmen at Old Faithful Inn."

Dan isn't sure how many bellmen are in the audience, but those who are all stand to their feet and start cheering.

Debbie walks to the right side of the stage and begins singing in a clear voice.

"The bellmen pull the bags from the bus, yessiree, yessiree.

The bellmen pull the bags from the bus, all through the Inn."

As she sings, Debbie picks up each piece of baggage stacked on stage and turns to stack the bags behind her in the precise order in which they'd been set on the stage. The audience doesn't know that the bags are all empty. She does a great job of acting as though she's straining really hard to lift the bigger items.

Debbie walks over to the cart and pushes it toward the stack of luggage. She continues singing.

"The bellmen put the bags on the cart, bags on the cart, bags on the cart.

The bellmen put the bags on the cart, all through the Inn." As she sings, Debbie loads all of the items onto the cart.

The audience is loving Debbie's performance and claps after each verse.

Debbie rolls the cart to front center stage and sings the next verse.

"The bellmen take the bags off the cart, bags off the cart, bags off the cart.

The bellmen take the bags off the cart, all through the Inn."

Debbie sets the cart down and unloads the bags again acting as though she can barely lift the larger pieces. Debbie then starts arranging the luggage as the bellmen do at the Inn. She places the two largest pieces on either side of her. While facing the audience, she hangs the wire loop of the garment bag to the back of her shirt collar. She sticks each arm through one of the looped handles of the two hat boxes and tucks the two slightly smaller suitcases under her armpits. She then picks up the larger suitcases by their handles. She acts as though she's straining to pick up all items. Dan thinks the acting is terrific, but wonders if possibly it's not all acting.

Debbie then starts lifting one knee high and then the other as though marching in place. She sings the next verse.

"The bellmen slowly climb up the steps, up the steps, up the steps.

The bellmen slowly climb up the steps, all through the Inn"

The audience is going wild and cheering enthusiastically.

Debbie goes back to the right side of the stage and lets the bags drop to the floor in a jumble. She then extends her right arm out with the palm of her hand facing up. She looks up at an imaginary guest and begins the next verse.

"The bellmen want a big, big tip, a big, big tip, a big, big tip.

The bellmen want a big, big tip, all through the Inn."

Debbie looks out at the audience and scowls. She turns her head back toward the imaginary guest and wags her right index finger and her head back and forth as if admonishing this imaginary guest. She then leans over and pushes her butt back. She extends her right arm again with her palm facing upward and sings the next verse.

"The bellmen won't leave without a tip, a big, big tip, a big, big tip.

The bellmen won't leave without a tip, all through the Inn."

Debbie's face lights up and she pretends to accept a big tip from the reluctant guest. She stuffs the money into the pocket of her shirt. Debbie then walks to the left side of the stage and stands in front of the cardboard teller's window. Debbie begins her next verse.

"The bellmen take their money to the bank, money to the bank, money to the bank.

The bellmen take their money to the bank, all through the Inn."

The audience laughs, claps and roars its approval.

Debbie takes a bow and walks to the microphone. When the audience quiets, Debbie speaks into the microphone. "To the Old Faithful bellmen, I love ya'll."

The audience claps and whistles again as Debbie blows kisses to the crowd and walks offstage.

Bill turns toward Dan. "Wow, I didn't see that coming. Can you believe that was our Debbie who just wowed the crowd?"

Dan is fighting back tears and is so emotionally overwhelmed by Debbie's performance that he can't speak. Instead, he just nods his head in agreement.

Rich announces each contestant's name and title for the evening wear competition and each gal struts across the stage in high heels. Almost all of the gals are wearing the same outfits that they wore during their introduction. None of the gals wears an actual evening gown. Dan suspects that none of them anticipated any occasion in Yellowstone National Park where they would need formal evening attire.

The judges then confer among themselves. One of the judges writes three names on a piece of paper and puts it in an envelope. He motions for Rich to come and get the envelope. Rich walks off the stage and takes the envelope. He returns to the stage and opens the envelop while standing in front of the microphone. Rich looks at the names written on the sheet of paper and speaks into the mic.

"Our three finalists are ....." Rich pauses to build drama with the audience.

"Miss Mammoth Hot Springs." The audience applauds and she comes back on stage to stand beside Rich.

"Miss Lake Area." The audience applauds and she joins Rich and Ms. Mammoth Hot Springs on stage.

"Our last finalist is Miss Old Faithful Area." The audience claps much louder and a few people whistle. Debbie joins Rich and the other two finalists on stage.

"Now, for the final part of our contest," says Rich. "Our judges have pre-selected three questions which I hold in my hand. I will read each contestant one question in the order that they appear on the piece of paper in my hand. Contestants, are you all ready?" All three nod their heads.

Rich motions for Miss Mammoth to stand beside him. She steps out of line and stands by Rich facing the audience.

"Miss Mammoth Hot Springs. What's been your favorite thing about working in Yellowstone National Park this summer?"

Miss Mammoth Hot Springs ponders the question for a moment.

"It would have to be the beauty of Yellowstone and all of the magnificent animals in the Park."

"Thank you, Miss Mammoth Hot Springs," says Rich. He motions for Miss Lake Area to stand beside him for her question.

"Miss Lake Area, what one experience will you take home at the end of the summer and share with your classmates in college?"

Miss Lake Area thinks for a moment before beginning her answer.

"I've met some delightful tourists and made many friends this summer. I plan to share with my classmates what a wonderful country we live in."

Rich thanks Miss Lake Area and asks Miss Old Faithful Area to join him.

"What's been your most exciting moment in Yellowstone National Park this summer?"

As Debbie considers the question, Dan thinks to himself that she could tell them about the hike to Observation Point and that she was so scared by the bear that she peed in her panties or that she got busted in Bats Alley by Mr. B. Dan decides those responses probably wouldn't be proper.

Debbie steps forward and speaks into the microphone.

"My most exciting moments have been shared with the friends who I've make this summer-especially the bellmen at Old Faithful Inn. I've done things and seen things this summer that I never could have imagined-hiking at night to Observation Point, meeting bison or elk unexpectedly on a hike, fishing in Lake Yellowstone and rafting on the Snake River in the Tetons. But, none of these exciting moments would have happened without the friends I've made this summer."

Debbie flashes a big smile at the audience and the crowd loudly applauds.

The judges confer a few minutes and seem to reach a consensus choice. They write the winner's name on a piece of paper and put it in an envelope which one of them seals. Rich watches the judges and walks down to get the sealed envelope. Rich returns to the stage. As he unseals the envelope and reads the name of the winner while Miss Mammoth Hot Springs and Miss Lake Area hold hands onstage.

Rich looks at the audience and speaks into the microphone.

"And the winner is….Debbie Wainwright, Miss Old Faithful Area. Congratulations!"

Debbie walks over to the microphone and Rich steps aside to let her say a few words. Debbie grabs the microphone stand with both hands and looks at the audience.

"I just want to thank ya'll for this honor." She looks directly at Bill in the audience and continues. "I know some of you had doubts about my ability to compete in this pageant, but I hope that those doubts have been answered tonight. Thank ya'll."

Debbie raises both of her hands high above her head and claps for the audience as the spotlight is turned off.

Dan and Bill walk home in the darkness.

"Wow, can you believe that Debbie was that good this evening?" Dan asks.

"No, I'm sorry that I ever doubted her even if I was only kidding," says Bill. "Debbie was a real sleeper of a contestant."

Sometime after midnight, Dan is awakened by a loud knock on the door of his room. He gets out of bed and opens the door. Debbie and Betty burst through the doorway and push him onto the mattress of his bed. Both are kissing Dan on his arms, his neck and his face. Still half asleep, he finally manages to speak after his initial shock dissipates.

"Whoa, what's going on here?"

Debbie grins a mischievous smile. "We're celebrating." She pushes him back onto his mattress and both gals start kissing him again. Dan notices that Debbie's hair is still pinned on top of her head just as she had worn it for the pageant. He also notices the smell of alcohol on the breath of both gals. He doesn't understand why their celebration has ended up in his room during the middle of the night, but what the heck—one can party at any time.

The noise being made in Dan's room awakens Bill. He gets up and walks into Dan's room.

"What's going on here?" Bill asks.

Bill gets the same answer as Dan. "We're celebrating."

When Dan recalls this moment later, he vaguely remembers that Betty started kissing Bill and then left. He also recalls that he and Debbie ended up making out for awhile before Debbie fell asleep on his bed. Dan also vaguely remembers that he was uncertain what he should do as Debbie snored loudly and then he too fell asleep at some point.

Dan's awakened early by the morning light pouring into his room. He rolls over and sees Debbie sleeping next to him. He notices that both of them are fully clothed although he's only wearing the pajamas that he wore to bed last night. He then remembers the craziness of late last night.

Dan touches Debbie's shoulder and shakes her lightly.

"Debbie, it's morning. You need to wake up. I want you to get back to Wurthering Heights before anybody finds you here."

Debbie opens her eyes and is disoriented for a few moments. She looks around and suddenly realizes that she's in Bats Alley. Debbie looks at Dan in terror and quickly sits up.

"What will people think?"

"Relax," says Dan. "We didn't do anything for which we should feel ashamed. You fell asleep and then I feel asleep. Com'n, I'll walk you back to the dorm."

Dan pulls on a pair of jeans and a sweatshirt over his pajamas. He gives Debbie a jacket to wear in the cool morning air. On the way to Wurthering Heights, he tells Debbie what a great job she did in winning the Miss Yellowstone pageant and how much pride he feels for her. When they reach the dorm, Debbie returns his jacket and starts to rush up the stairs of the porch, but stops and runs back down the steps to him.

"Thank you, Dan, for everything."

She hugs Dan and then quickly kisses him. She then runs back up the steps and vanishes into Wurthering Heights before anyone sees her.

Later that morning, Bill comes into his room.

"Dan, what was that all about last night?"

"I have no idea. All I know is that I was awakened sometime after midnight. I opened the door and was attacked by Debbie and Betty. I'm pretty sure that they both had done a little too much celebrating before they arrived at my door. Then you arrived and left with Betty. What happened with you and Betty?"

"Oh, we went back to my room and talked for awhile. Then I walked her back to the dorm. What happened with you and Debbie?"

Dan shrugs. "Oh, nothing really. We made out for awhile and then Debbie fell asleep. I eventually did too. When we woke up early this morning, I walked her back to the dorm."

Bill grins at him. "So, you slept with Miss Yellowstone."

Dan throws his hands up in protest. "No, it was nothing like that at all. Honestly, we didn't do anything but make out a little."

Dan looks at Bill and realizes that he's only teasing him.

Dan thinks to himself that nothing happened at all, but, in a technical sense, I really did sleep with Miss Yellowstone last night. Dan will later recall that the mere thought put a smile on his face for the rest of the morning.

CHAPTER TWENTY-FIVE

BUFFALOED ON THE WAY TO FAIRY FALLS

Dan and Bill are finishing breakfast in the Staffateria when sisters Penny and Melody Hobart walk through the door. Bill spots the pair and motions for them to come over to their table. Melody gets in line for breakfast and Penny walks toward Dan and Bill.

"When you get your food, come over and join us," Bill says.

"Sure," says Penny. She gets back in line behind Melody. The sisters get their food and join Dan and Bill at their table.

"I haven't seen the two of you for awhile," says Bill.

"Oh, you know how it goes," says Penny. "We've just been busy."

Bill takes a sip of his coffee and looks at the sisters. "Dan and I were just talking about organizing a hike to Fairy Falls. Have you hiked to Ferry Falls?"

"I haven't even heard of Fairy Falls," says Melody. "This isn't another Zipper Creek float scam, is it?"

Bill has heard the Zipper Creek story and grins. "No, Fairy Falls is 200 feet tall and one of Yellowstone National Park's most spectacular waterfalls."

"Where is Fairy Falls located?" Penny asks.

Bill takes another sip of his coffee. "Well, you reach Fairy Falls by one of two ways. You can drive to the Fairy Falls parking lot which is located about one mile south of Midway Geyser Basin or drive to the end of Fountain Flats Road near Goose Lake. The hike to Fairy Falls is about the same length from either spot. But, I think it'd be fun to park at a pullout just past the Fountain Paint Pots and actually walk across Fountain Flats. On the map, there appears to be a trail to Fairy Falls."

"Are you planning to hike to Fairy Falls?" Melody asks.

"We were just talking about it," says Dan.

Penny seems interested. "The hike sounds like fun. How long is the hike?"

"Honestly, I'm not sure but I'd guess we're looking at 5 to 6 miles," says Bill.

Melody seems interested too. "When do you plan to do this?"

"Bill and I were just trying to figure out when to do the hike," says Dan. "I'm working the 3 to 11 shift this Friday. Bill says the last tour bus that morning leaves the Inn around 10:00. We thought we could leave around 10:00 and have enough time to be back at the Inn before 3:00. However, we'll have to keep an eye on the time. If it starts getting too late, we can just hike back to the pullout so we can all get to work on time."

"Melody and I are working the dinner shift Friday," says Penny. "I think the timing would work."

"Great. It's a date," says Bill. "No, I didn't mean it that way." The sisters giggle and Bill continues. "Let's do it. You can invite anyone who wants to join us and we'll do the same thing."

"Agreed," says Penny. "Shall we meet by the Front Desk around 10:15 on Friday? If other people join us, I assume some will have cars and we can all carpool to the pullout."

Bill looks at his watch. "I'm sorry, but I have to get back to work. Dan, are you going to join me?"

Dan nods his head and both stand up to bus their trays.

"We'll see you Friday morning," says Dan.

Later that day, Graham Callwood walks by the Bell Desk while Dan's waiting for a Front.

Dan calls to Graham. "Hey, Graham, did you do something to your knee?"

Graham's wearing a tee shirt and shorts, but has a black brace on his left knee. Graham stops in front of Dan.

"I was fishing on the Firehole River last week and stepped in a pothole. I twisted my knee and went to the Hospital in the Lake area."

Dan knows there's a small medical center located in the Lake area which is staffed by a doctor and a nurse. Many Savages refer to this medical center as the "Hospital," but the use of the term "Hospital" is somewhat of a stretch.

Graham rubs the leg with the brace. "The doctor x-rayed my knee. Fortunately, there aren't any breaks of any bones and no torn muscles. The doctor believes that I just strained the ligaments in the knee. However, the doctor suggested that I use this brace for a week to ease the strain on my knee."

"Did the doctor place any restrictions on your activities?" Dan's thinking about Friday's hike to Fairy Falls.

Graham shakes his head. "No. In fact, he suggested that moderate activities like walking would help the healing."

"Is hiking okay?"

Graham pauses. "Probably, but I'm not sure. Why do you ask?'

"A group of us are planning to hike to Fairy Falls on Friday by walking across Fountain Flats. If you're interested, we plan to meet near the Front Desk around 10:15 in the morning and car pool to a turnout on the highway. We plan to be back at the Inn in time to report for work at 3:00."

Graham seems interested. "Hmm. Friday?"

Dan nods his head and Graham says, "I have to check the schedule again, but I believe I work the 3 to 11 shift in the Bear Pit on Friday. If I do, I'll definitely join the group."

Dan hears someone at the Front Desk yell "Front."

"Sorry, but that's me," says Dan. "I have to take this Front. I hope to see you Friday morning."

Dan walks to the Front Desk as Graham continues on his way.

It's around 10:15 on Friday morning when Dan walks down the stairs from the second-floor mezzanine and sees a rather large group of Savages gathered near the Front Desk. The group includes Bill, Chukker, Eagle who's working the split shift on the afternoon crew today, Penny, Melody, Sally, Graham who's still wearing the brace on his left knee, and two other girls from the dining room staff who Dan recognizes by sight only. It's now mid-August. Dan has learned to appreciate his older brother's ability to come up with an idea for a group activity and then be able to sell the idea so it does in reality become a group activity.

Bill sees Dan and turns to the group. "Here's Dan. I think we have everyone."

No one speaks up to object.

"I'm driving," says Bill. "I believe Chukker and Graham also have cars. Why don't we all carpool in those three cars. I'll lead and park in a turnout located in Fountain Flats. Chukker and Graham, please follow and park your cars in the same turnout."

Bill leads the group outside and walks down the steps to the parking lot where all three drivers have their automobiles parked. The group automatically splits into three groups and get into their respective cars to start their adventure to Fairy Falls.

Everyone's standing in the turnout that Bill selects and is ready to begin the hike to Fairy Falls. The temperature is predicted for mid-to high 80s so everyone's dressed in tee shirts and shorts. Some individuals wear long sleeved shirts to protect their arms from the sun. Almost all are wearing hiking boots which Dan believes are a necessity for a Savage to truly enjoy the wonders of Yellowstone National Park. Some individuals carry day packs. Most have applied white sun screen to their faces, necks, arms and legs. Almost all have some form of hat on their heads.

The "trail" that Bill has selected seems to be an animal trail. It's a narrow, dusty path. Apparently, the animals who made and use the trail proceed primarily single file. Dan suspects that the trail was probably made by buffaloes.

In the early 1970s, bison, more commonly referred to as buffaloes, roam throughout the prairie regions of Yellowstone National Park. Bison are the largest land-dwelling mammals in North America. A mature bull (male) weighs up to 2,000 pounds; a mature cow (female) can weigh up to 1,000 pounds. Both sexes are generally dark chocolate-brown in color, have long hair on their forelegs, head and shoulders but short, dense hair on their flanks and hindquarters. All bison have a protruding shoulder hump and horns on their large heads. Breeding season (known as the rut) occurs in July and August. During the rut, bulls show their dominance by bellowing, wallowing and engaging in fights with other bulls. Following the rut, mature males typically separate from the herd and spend the rest of the year alone or in small groups.

Despite their enormous size, bison are agile and can run up to 35 miles per hour. One additional thing should be noted about bison. They may look docile, but they can be very aggressive.

The group sets off on the hike with Bill leading along the buffalo path. Rain hasn't fallen for several weeks. The trail has dried to the extent that the group's footsteps kick up a lot of dust. Some in the group have kerchiefs tied around their necks which they take off and tie around their mouths.

The group has walked about a quarter of a mile when they see a lone buffalo about a quarter of a mile ahead of them. The buffalo apparently is headed in the direction of Fairy Falls too. As the group watches, the buffalo plods slowly along the trail kicking up small dust clouds every time its hooves strike the dirt.

The group continues walking behind the buffalo, but Dan realizes that the group's walking faster than it and catching up to the enormous creature. The buffalo finally catches the scent of humans and stops. It slowly turns its massive head around and assesses the threat level of the group's presence. After a minute or two, the buffalo turns its head and continues plodding along the trail.

When the buffalo stops, the group stops. When the buffalo starts walking, the group starts walking. Although being very cautious with this enormous animal, the group gradually closes the gap between themselves and the buffalo.

By the third time that the buffalo stops, the group is now only 200 yards from the buffalo. This time the buffalo turns its entire body around so the group of young Savages are directly looking at the buffalo's massive head. Everyone stands very still. The buffalo paws the ground with its right front hoof and then its left front hoof. This sends dirt and dust flying into the air behind the buffalo. The buffalo lifts it nose in the air and bellows.

By now, many in the group are frightened.

Dan senses that Penny is nervous.

"What should we do if the buffalo charges?" Penny asks.

"I just read about this in a book," says Graham. "The author suggests that we form a single line across the trail. We should make ourselves as big as possible by standing on our tiptoes and waiving our arms above our heads while screaming as loudly as possible."

Most in the group collectively shake their heads. Some say in unison, "I'm not going to do that."

Eagle looks at the brace on Graham's left knee. "The way I see it, I have to beat only one person if we all run. My legs aren't in the best of shape after my football injuries, but I believe I can beat one person." Eagle points at Graham. "And that person is you, Graham."

Everyone laughs except Graham.

"Why don't we just wait and see what the buffalo does," says Bill.

As they wait, the group talks quietly among themselves. After a few minutes, the buffalo turns around and starts plodding along the dirt trail heading in the direction of Fairy Falls. The group waits for a few minutes and then resumes hiking behind the buffalo.

Again, the group gradually closes the distance between the buffalo and themselves. The buffalo again stops and turns around on the trail so the buffalo's again facing the group. The buffalo again paws the ground with first its right hoof and then its left hoof. A cloud of dust and dirt flies into the air behind the buffalo. The buffalo again raises its nose into the air and bellows. The group watches in apprehensive silence.

Suddenly, the buffalo starts charging toward the group. Dan wonders at that moment whether anyone ever mentioned to any of this group of young Savages that a buffalo is agile, can run up to 35 miles per hour and can at times be aggressive? Two tons of chocolate-brown mass are charging at full speed toward ten extremely frightened young Savages. Despite the heat, the hiking boots of the ten Savages are seemingly frozen to the ground since none of them move their feet. Several of the gals manage to scream. Several of the guys have the presence of mind to raise their arms high over their heads and wave them back and forth as they yell at the buffalo.

The buffalo quickly closes to within fifty yards of the group and abruptly stops. The buffalo's now close enough that Dan can see its nostrils flaring. He notices that the sides of the buffalo expand and contract as it sucks oxygen into its lungs and then exhales.

The mid-day sun beats down on the ten Savages and one massive buffalo. Neither the buffalo nor any of the young Savages flinch while waiting for the other to make the first move. Finally, Dan thinks that the buffalo must have decided that it's too hot for a battle because it turns around and resumes plodding slowly along the trail in the direction of Fairy Falls.

"Wow," says Bill. "I think that we just witnessed what's called a 'false charge.'" I think that our buffalo friend is just trying to intimidate us. What does everyone want to do? We can probably walk around the buffalo and still get to Fairy Falls, but the delay has seriously affected our timing."

"I don't have to look at my watch," says Penny. "If that buffalo was trying to intimidate me, it worked really, really well. I just want to go back to the Inn. Fairy Falls will have to wait for another day."

The gals in the group agree unanimously with Penny. The guys in the group? What are guys always going to do when the gals are united? The group turns around and returns to the Inn with visions of charging bison flashing through their minds.

That evening, Bill and Dan are in Dan's room relating the events of their Fairy Falls adventure to Lou.

Lou ponders the story for a minute before saying anything.

"Too bad that you didn't make it to Fairy Falls," says Lou. "The Falls are definitely worth the hike. I guess one could say that you were all buffaloed by a buffalo on the way to Fairy Falls."

All three bellmen have a good laugh.

CHAPTER TWENTY-SIX
THE BELLMEN'S BANQUET

The Bellman's Banquet is another tradition that's been handed down from generation-to-generation of bellmen at Old Faithful Inn. In the early 1970s, none of the current OFI bellmen knows when the tradition started or how it started. Nonetheless, the bellmen hold an annual banquet at the end of every summer. Each bellman invites a guest or date to attend the event. This is the one night of the summer when all of the bellmen will wear coats and ties and the gals will dress up in their finest outfits—excluding Mary Ann, of course, who has dressed up a number of times during the summer to dine with Benny. This year, the bellmen have also invited Robert and Kitty Baxter to attend.

This year's Bellmen's Banquet will be held at the Crazy 8 Dude Ranch located in Jackson Hole. The bellmen have reserved the Dude Ranch's dining room from 8:00 in the evening to 1:00 in the morning. With Mr. Baxter's approval, the bellmen are again paying three housemen to handle the Bells during the absence of the entire Bell Crew. There'll be a cocktail hour followed by a late dinner. The bellmen have reserved a number of guest rooms at the Crazy 8 Dude ranch so no one has to drive home late or while they may be too impaired to drive. The bellmen and their dates will drive back to the Inn early the next morning so everyone can be at work by 8:00. To everyone's surprise, Mr. and Mrs. Baxter accept the bellmen's invitation, but they plan to drive back to the Inn late that night rather than spending an overnight.

As the date of the Bellmen's Banquet draws near, there's a great deal of excitement among the bellmen and their friends—particularly their gal friends. About two weeks before the event, Dan comes up with an idea to build excitement for the event. His idea seems brilliant at the time.

He searches around the Inn and finds three different colors of felt-tipped pens—black, green and orange. He also locates an easel and a large piece of white cardboard about 2 feet by 3 feet in size.

Dan writes in big black, block letters at the center top of the cardboard: "Countdown to Bellmen's Banquet." Under this caption, he draws on the far-right side in bright green and orange ink an image of a rocket ship blasting off from earth. To the far left, he writes "Bellmen" in bold black letters and underneath this caption writes the names of all ten bellmen in a straight line going down the cardboard. To the right of the caption "Bellmen," he writes another caption: "Guest." He draws ten lines underneath this caption with one line to the right of the name of each bellman. Dan positions the easel next to the Bell Desk and puts the large cardboard poster on it. As each bellman selects his date for the banquet, her name will be added to the poster.

Unfortunately, no one can walk out the back door of the Inn or pass the Bell Desk without seeing this poster.

When he recalls this in later years, Dan always feels considerable regret for making this poster. With the passage of time and the benefit of maturity, he came to realize that this poster was arrogant, obnoxious and insensitive. He could probably add a few more adjectives, but he eventually realized that this was an immature and possibly hurtful idea—particularly to anyone not invited to the Bellmen's Banquet that year.

However, at the time, the bellmen had some fun with this poster. For example, Dan and Bill knew that Lou intended to invite Mary Ann as his guest, but he kept procrastinating in making the invitation. About 80 percent of the guests' names had been added on the poster, but the line next to Lou's name remained blank.

One afternoon, Dan, Lou and Larry are standing by the Bell Desk while waiting for Fronts. Bill walks up and checks the poster to see if any new names have been added. Bill looks at Lou.

"Lou, are you ever going to ask Mary Ann to the Bellmen's Banquet?"

Lou nods his head. "Yeah, I intend to do it."

"When are you going to do it?"

Lou looks down at his feet. "Soon."

Someone from the Front Desk yells "Front" and Lou walks away to take the Front.

When Lou leaves, Bill looks at Dan and Larry. "Lou may need a little nudge to ask Mary Ann to the Bellmen's Banquet. Why don't we help Lou a little?"

Dan wonders how Bill's going to help.

Bill walks behind the Bell Desk and finds a black felt-tipped pen. He walks to the poster and writes "Mary Ann" next to Lou's name.

Bill turns and grins mischievously at Dan and Larry.

A short time later, Lou returns to the Bell Desk from his Front. The other three are still there. Lou starts talking about his Front when Bill grows impatient and casually says, "Lou, have you looked at the poster lately?"

Lou turns and looks at the poster for a moment before realizing that someone has added Mary Ann's name on the line next to his name. Lou's face drains of color and then turns scarlet.

Lou looks at Bill. "J****, Bill, did you do this?"

At that exact moment, the bellmen hear a familiar voice.

"Well, hello ya'll. How's everyone doing this afternoon?"

Dan's surprised that Lou's face seems to turn a darker shade of scarlet.

Lou quickly jumps in front of the poster so that Mary Ann can't see it.

"Say, Mary Ann, there's something I've been meaning to discuss with you," says Lou.

Lou places his hands on Mary Ann's shoulders and turns her back in the direction from which she'd just come. He leads her well away from the Bell Desk so they can talk in private.

As the other three bellmen watch, Mary Ann's face breaks into a big smile and they overhear her saying to Lou, "Of course I'll go with you to the Bellmen's Banquet."

Bill grins at Dan and Larry. "Mission accomplished."

The Bellmen's Banquet starts with a cocktail hour. Including Mr. and Mrs. Baxter, there are eleven gentlemen wearing coats and ties and eleven ladies wearing dresses and heels in attendance. To be precise, Mac wears a bolo tie and Larry wears a bowtie, but Dan believes that these are within the parameters of the evening's dress code. Everyone has a drink in their hand. Everyone's in a festive mood and mixing well.

Dan's conversing with Laura and Sally when Kitty laughs loudly across the room. Laura rolls her eyes. "I'm not keeping track of how much Kitty's drinking, but I've seen her at the bar three times ordering another vodka martini. Hopefully, a couple of those were for Mr. B."

Laura looks at the drink in his hand and asks, "What are you drinking, Dan?"

Dan holds his glass up and looks at it. "Rum and coke." He smiles at Laura.

Laura winks at Dan. "My, my, how things have changed this summer."

Dan decides to change the conversation and looks around the room. "What do you think of our Bellmen's Banquet?

"So far, it's been really, really fun," gushes Sally.

"By the way," says Laura. "If I forget to thank Larry myself, be sure to let him know how much the rest of the Fab Five appreciated him inviting Betty so all of us could attend the Bellmen's Banquet."

Dan nods his head. "I'll try to remember to mention it to him. Larry does some crazy things at times, but he's really a good guy."

Mary Ann walks up holding a package of Oreo cookies in one hand and a drink in the other. She extends the arm holding the cookies and shakes the package like a rattle. "Do any of ya'll want an Oreo cookie?"

"An Oreo cookie at cocktail hour?" Dan asks. "What's with the Oreo cookies?"

Mary Ann bats her eyes at him. "When the Fabulous Five get together in Wurthering Heights, we almost always eat Oreo cookies. Oreos have become the Fabulous Five's symbol."

Mary Ann pauses. "Oreos are a symbol of a good time. I just knew that ya'll bellmen were going to have a good time at your banquet and thought I'd just add to the fun by bringing Oreos."

Dan looks at Laura who shrugs her shoulders.

Someone claps their hands and yells, "Dinner's ready."

"It looks like we should maybe put the Oreos on hold until later," says Dan. "What do you think?"

The four of them join the others in the Crazy 8's dining room.

Chukker walks to the front of the room and grabs ahold of the microphone stand with both hands. Dan isn't sure whether he's just being theatrical or needs both hands on the microphone stand to keep from swaying. Chukker taps the face of the mic to determine if it's live. No sound comes from the speakers which are mounted on both sides of the wall behind Chukker. He looks all over the microphone and the stand, but can't locate an on/off switch anywhere.

"D***. I can't figure out how to turn on this G**D***** microphone," Chukker finally says. "Can anyone help me?"

Larry gets out of his seat and walks to the front of the room to help him turn on the microphone.

As Larry returns to his seat, Chukker again grabs the microphone stand with both hands and looks at his audience.

"How ya'll doin' tonight?"

Chukker has a big grin on his face. There's some chatter from the audience, but apparently not enough crowd response for Chukker. He shouts into the microphone.

"I asked, how ya'll doin' tonight?"

This time the audience catcalls and claps.

Chukker takes one hand off the microphone stand.

"How about the food tonight? Did ya'll enjoy your meal?"

The audience claps in approval.

Everyone had three courses to their meal. Each started with a garden salad with their choice of dressing. For the main course, you could have prime rib or almond trout sauteed in butter. Dan thought his prime rib was a little tough and the trout looked a little oily. The dessert was a strawberry cheesecake something or other. Frankly, a food critic probably wouldn't have given the dinner a very high rating-if one at all. But after a summer's fare of Staffateria food, everyone seemed to eat their meals with gusto as if the food had been prepared by a top French chef.

"How did ya'll enjoy the open bar?"

Now the audience really claps and shouts its approval. Dan looks around and thinks to himself that Chukker probably didn't need to ask that question since everyone seems to have consumed a lot of alcohol.

"The bar's still open. If any of ya'll need to refresh your drink, just help yourself."

Chukker starts to sway backward and again puts both hands around the microphone stand to steady himself.

"Ladies and Gentlemen, welcome to this year's Bellmen's Banquet. I especially want to thank our guests, Mr. and Mrs. Baxter, for attending this year."

Chukker points at the Baxters who stand up and wave to the audience.

"Now it's a tradition at the Bellmen's Banquet to announce the winners of the Belly Awards. This year we have five categories: the Buster Award, the Fooled 'Em Award, the 'Gee, I Peed My Pants' Award, the Most Exciting Moment Award and the Best Feel Good Award. The honorees are nominated by the Bell Crew and voted on by all of the bellmen. The votes are tabulated and the results are placed in sealed envelopes which I hold here in my hand."

Chukker holds five plain white envelopes in his right hand. He raises his right arm above his head and waives it back and forth.

"If your name's announced, please come forward to accept your Belly."

On a small table to his right sit the five Belly statues. Each one is a plastic buffalo mounted on a small wooden base. In reality, Chucker found them in a tourist shop in West Yellowstone and purchased all five for $5 plus tax.

Chukker clears his throat. "Now, our first award is The Buster Award. Our presenter is our own Mac McPherson. Please give Mac a warm welcome."

The audience starts clapping and cheering as Mac gets out of his seat and saunters to the microphone. Chukker hands him an envelope and a "Belly statue." He then backs away to let Mac make the presentation.

Mac tucks the Belly statue under his arm while he opens the envelope. He reads the enclosure and looks at the audience.

"The Buster Award this year goes to Robert Baxter. Come and get your Belly Mr. B."

To loud applause and catcalls, Mr. B climbs out of his chair and walks slowly toward him. Mac reads the enclosure with Mr. B standing by his side.

"The Buster Award goes this year to Robert Baxter. Thank you, Mr. B, for raiding Bats Alley and for not firing any of us. Signed ... The Fabulous Five."

The audience bursts into uproarish laughter. People start clapping. Some start stomping their feet on the floor. But the most animated individual of all is Kitty Baxter. She stands up, throws her arms in the air and shouts, "Yeah, that's my Bobby!"

When the noise from the audience dies, Mac hands Mr. B his Belly and asks if he has anything to say to the audience. Mr. B turns to face the audience.

"I think I made a big mistake. I should've fired all of you." And then, something extremely rare happens. Bobby Baxter's face breaks into a big smile.

The audience erupts again. This time, Kitty Baxter stands up and with tears streaming down her cheeks, she shouts, "Bobby, I love you."

When the noise abates, Chukker steps forward and takes the microphone from Mr. B. As Mr. B and Mac make their way back to their seats, Chukker speaks into the mic.

"Mr. and Mrs. Baxter, if you need to excuse yourselves and leave, we'll all understand." He reaches into his pocket and holds up his room key. "If you need to borrow this, I'll understand."

The audience catches the meaning and roars again.

He waits until the noise subsides. "Our next Belly is the "Fooled 'Em" Award. To present this award, please welcome Bill Johnson. C'mon up, Bill."

Bill stands up from his chair and walks to the microphone. He takes the envelope and the Belly statue from Chukker and addresses the audience.

"This year we had several nominees for this category. Carnival was nominated after a bellman thought he caught Carnival reading a book, but it turned out to be only a Playboy magazine."

Laughter ripples through the audience. Bill opens the envelope and pulls out the enclosure. He slowly reads it and then looks at the audience.

"This year's "Fooled 'Em" Award goes to Debbie Wainwright. C'mon up Debbie."

Debbie stands up and walks toward him. Bill hands her the Belly Statue and then reads the card to the audience.

"Debbie: We didn't think you had a chance, but you sure fooled the bellmen by winning the Miss Yellowstone contest. Apparently, your charm, wit and beauty fooled the judges as well. Congrats. Signed ... All the Bellmen."

The audience starts clapping and cheering.

When Bill asks her if she'd like to say a few words, Debbie seizes the microphone from his hand and turns to face everyone.

"Ya'll bellmen are just so cute. How clever of you to honor me with this award. I'm thrilled to the bottom on my heart that ya'll bellmen are kind enough to award me this expensive tiny little buffalo statue." Debbie holds her arm out and stares at the tiny statue as though it were a Faberge egg. "I can assure you that it'll grace the mantel of my fireplace forever, unless this little creature has an unfortune accident and burns in the fireplace instead. Thank ya'll so much."

To whistles, claps and cheers, Debbie puts her free hand to her cheek, bends slightly over and does a perfect Marilyn Monroe pose. Flashbulbs from the audience start popping. Debbie stands up and swishes her skirt to the accompanying applause of the audience.

As Bill and Debbie walk back to their seats, Chukker returns to the microphone.

"Now, for the "Gee, I Peed My Pants" Award. The presenter's Dan Johnson. Come on up Dan."

Dan walks up to the microphone and Chukker gives him an envelope and a Belly statue. Dan opens the envelope and reads the name of the winner.

"I'm very excited. The honor goes to my brother, Bill Johnson. Com'n up and accept your award, Bill."

When Bill reaches him, Dan hands him the Belly statue and then reads the enclosure card to everyone.

"Bill: You turned a memorable trip to the Southeast Arm into an unforgettable one. By the way, Eagle, Graham and your brother Dan want to be reimbursed for the cost of laundering the underwear that they were wearing that day. Signed... Your loving bother Dan, Eagle and Graham."

By now, everyone in the audience has heard the story of the adventure to the Southeast Arm in June. The audience erupts in laughter and clapping. The faces of both Bill and Dan redden slightly.

Dan looks meekly at Bill. "Honest, I didn't know who would win this award or what the card said before opening the envelope."

Bill starts laughing. Dan sees this and starts laughing too. The audience laughs even harder.

Dan hands the microphone to Bill.

"I'm only happy that I created an unforgettable moment for my brother and for Eagle and Graham too. I graciously accept this award on behalf of all the people who have accidentally peed in their pants this summer in Yellowstone National Park." Bill looks directly at Debbie as he says the last part of his acceptance speech.

The audience howls in laughter as Bill bows to the audience.

As the brothers walk back to their seats, Chukker speaks into the microphone.

"Our next category is the "Most Exciting Moment" Award. The presenter of this award is our own Louis Chamborg. Lou, c'mon up and present this award."

Lou walks to the microphone and takes the envelope and a Belly statue from Chukker. Lou opens the envelope and reads the winner's name.

"The winner of the Most Exciting Moment Award is Larry Bowman. Larry, c'mon up and accept your award."

Larry's already out of his chair and halfway to Lou by the time he finishes his announcement. When Larry reaches the microphone, Lou hands a Belly statue to Larry and then reads the enclosure card to the audience.

"Larry: What an exciting two hours we spent with you at the top of three pines trees while that grizzly bear took a siesta. It was one of the most exciting two hours of our lives. Thank you for bringing the bacon. Signed: Lou and Dan."

The audience is whistling, laughing and clapping. Lou raises his arms with palms downward to quiet the crowd. The noise finally stops.

Lou turns toward the award recipient. "Larry, since I have a little personal knowledge of how you earned this honor, I just want to add that if you ever again bring bacon on a hike with me in Yellowstone National Park, you won't live to see the end of that hike."

The crowd howls in glee.

Larry grabs the microphone from him and looks at Lou.

"Lou, the next time the two of us hike together in Yellowstone National Park, I promise not to bring bacon—-I'll bring ham instead."

The audience starts laughing again. Larry and Lou look at one another and both join the audience in laughing.

As they return to their seats, Chukker steps up to the mic again.

"For ya'll afternoon crew bellman, the owner of this place just advised me that there's a Front waiting at the Front Desk, just in case you might need a few extra bucks."

Some people start laughing, but none of the afternoon crew guys laugh. Then Chukker adds, "The owner said something about this Dude being from Podunk City, Iowa."

The afternoon crew begin to boo and hiss. Chukker shrugs his shoulders. "Okay, I'm not Dean Martin. Give me a break."

"Now, our final category is the "Best Feel Good" Belly. Our presenter of this award is Carnival. C'mon up, Carnival."

Everyone turns and looks at Carnival. Dan thinks to himself that Carnival seems to be daydreaming again.

Chukker says again, "C'mon up, Carnival."

Carnival finally realizes that it's his turn. He puts his hands on the table and pushes himself up from his chair. He slowly walks toward the microphone. Chukker hands him the last envelope and the last Belly statue. Carnival slowly rips the envelope open and reads the name of the winner.

"The winner of this award …." Carnival looks at Chukker. "What's this award called again?"

The crowd laughs and Chukker whispers loudly, "The 'Best Feel Good' Award."

Carnival shrugs, "Oh, that's right. The winner is Mac McPherson." Carnival peers into the crowd. "Mac, are you here tonight?"

By now, the audience is laughing so hard that some are finding it difficult to remain seated in their chairs. Mac stands up and walks forward to receive his award. Carnival hands Mac the last Belly statue.

Chukker leans forward and whispers so loudly that the microphone catches his voice. "Carnival, read the enclosure card that's in the envelope."

Carnival nods his head. "Oh, right." He digs around his pockets to find the envelope—-which is in his right hand all the time.

The audience is almost having convulsions, they're laughing so hard.

Carnival holds the enclosure card up. He takes his eyeglasses off and squints his eyes to read the card.

"Mac: Your two-handed, underhand free throw was a brilliant idea. We all loved the moment, but loved the Pow Wow at Flat Mountain Arm even more. Thank you. Signed: Your Appreciative Bell Crew."

As the audience applauds, Carnival stuffs his hands back into the front pockets of his pants. Mac reaches over and grabs the microphone stand. He pulls it towards himself and looks at the audience.

"Thank you, Jerry, for the smooth delivery. And thank you Bell Crew. I'm only happy that I was able to provide the summer's best feel good moment for all of you."

Mac pauses. He reaches into the inside pocket of his sports coat and pulls out a roll of paper. The paper is actually an adding machine roll of paper. Mac holds the end of the roll in his hand and acts as though he's starting a lengthy acceptance speech.

"First, I want to thank both of my parents for giving birth to me so one day I could become a bellman at Old Faithful Inn…" Mac holds the end of the adding machine tape and lets the rest unravel. When it hits the floor, it just keeps rolling and unraveling.

The audience now realizes it's all a big gag and everyone starts laughing, clapping or whistling.

Mac picks up the paper on the floor and then grabs Carnival by the elbow. They walk slowly back to their seats.

Chukker returns to the microphone.

"And that's it, folks. Those are your Bellys for this year. The bar's still open. Drink up."

About thirty minutes later, Dan's talking with Sally when May Ann comes over and tells him that he's needed for the group bellmen photo. Dan excuses himself and follows Mary Ann to the other side of the room where the bellmen are all standing in a line with their arms wrapped around the waist of the young men next to them. Dan sees Bill and Lou in the center of the line and squeezes between them. They wrap their arms around his waist as he wraps his arms around their waists. He sticks his head out and looks up and down the line at each and every one of the OFI bellman. Dan thinks to himself that he's spent the summer with some of the best friends he'll ever have and that they're all his brothers.

Just then, Dan hears Mary Ann's voice. "Say Oreo cookie." And the flashbulbs start popping.

CHAPTER TWENTY-SEVEN
FAREWELL TO OLD FAITHFUL INN

It's late August and Dan's contract terminates in ten days. He's sitting alone in his room when there's a knock at the door. He opens the door and there stands Mac.

"Hi, Daniel. Do you have a few minutes?"

"Sure." He steps aside to let Mac enter the room. Mac sits down on his lower bunk and motions for Dan to join him.

"Daniel, do you plan to return to the Inn next year?"

"I haven't given it a lot of thought, but I've had the best summer of my life the past three months. I probably will return next summer," says Dan. "I've been thinking about attending law school after I finish college and could possibly work here summers during law school."

"So, you're going to follow Bill by going to law school?"

"That decision is at least a year away. Who knows? How about you? Do you anticipate returning next summer?"

Mac shakes his head. "Probably not. I'm old enough that I need to find a permanent year-round job and settle down. But, that brings me to the point of this discussion. I anticipate that there may be some turnover on the Bell Crew next year. I want to make sure that I thoroughly train a few of you younger guys on the ins and outs of morning crew so any transition next year will be as seamless as possible. That's why I rotate an afternoon guy onto the morning crew every week. As you probably know, Ted leaves this Friday so morning crew will be short a person next week. Lou's already scheduled for the rotation spot on morning crew. I want you to fill in for Ted next week since it'll be your last week of the summer."

Dan smiles. "Sure. That'd be great. What about afternoon crew? Will three guys be able to handle the Fronts?"

"Don't worry about it. That's my problem. That's why they pay me the big bucks." Dan knows that Mac doesn't receive a single cent for the additional responsibility and work that comes with the title of 'Bell Captain.' Mac continues. "You and Lou may have to help take Fronts at times if it's really busy. However, I know that we'll get the job done. Afterall, we're Old Faithful Inn bellmen."

Mac and Dan both start laughing.

The following week, Dan's working on a morning pull. Several tours are leaving at the same time and the morning crew's working hard so the tour buses can all leave the Inn on time. One tour consists of foreign tourists who seemingly don't speak English.

Mac walks up to him.

"Daniel, it's time for you to learn how to collect our money from the tour escort. I want you to meet with the escort and collect our money for handling the baggage."

Mac looks at the three tour buses waiting in front of the Inn and says, "That foreign tour group's fairly small. Why don't you take that tour escort?"

Dan nods his head. "What am I supposed to do?"

"Locate the tour escort and then introduce yourself to him. I normally ask if the Bell service has been satisfactory. Most escorts at that time are reaching for their money bag. If not, I make small conversation until they do reach for their money bag. Always count the money in front of them to make sure that the amount's correct. Then I usually ask if there's anything else the Bell Crew can do for them and wish them a safe journey."

"Sounds pretty simple," says Dan. "I think I can handle this."

"Daniel, if you have any problems, just come and get me."

"Thanks, Mac. I'm sure there won't be any problems."

When the bus with the foreign tourists is loaded, Dan tries to find the tour escort. The first four people don't speak any English and just smile at him when he asks for the tour escort. He sees the bus driver who is Caucasian and decides that he may be his best resource to locate the escort. Dan approaches the bus driver.

"Do you know where I can find the tour escort?"

The bus driver points to a middle-aged man wearing wire-rimmed spectacles and holding a leather briefcase. "That's David Lee, the tour escort." Mr. Lee looks like he may be foreign, but Dan isn't sure.

Dan thanks the bus driver and walks over to Mr. Lee.

"Are you Mr. Lee, the escort for this tour?" Dan asks.

Mr. Lee responds in good English. "Yes, I'm David Lee. I'm the tour escort for this tour."

"I'm Dan Johnson." He shakes hands with Mr. Lee and continues speaking. "I work on the Bell Crew. Was the luggage service to your satisfaction?"

Mr. Lee is quite gracious and nods his head. "Oh, yes. The service was quite satisfactory."

Dan stands waiting for Mr. Lee to open his briefcase to remove his money pouch, but Mr. Lee instead turns and starts to leave.

"Mr. Lee ..." Dan remembers his instructions to keep the escort engaged.

Mr. Lee turns around to face Dan.

"Mr. Lee, is there anything else that the Bell Crew can do for you today?"

"No, but thank you." Mr. Lee again turns and starts to leave.

Dan's desperately trying to think of something to say in order to get Mr. Lee to reach for his money pouch. "Mr. Lee ..."

Mr. Lee turns around again to face him, but Dan can tell that this escort is becoming annoyed.

"We loaded 40 bags onto your bus," says Dan. "I want to verify that 40 bags is the correct count."

Mr. Lee nods his head. "Yes, thank you." Dan wonders whether the 'thank you' is really sincere. Mr. Lee continues, "Now, if you'll excuse me, I really must attend to my tour guests."

Mr. Lee turns and walks away from Dan. Dan feels like a total failure—his first time to collect from a tour escort and he gets da nada.

Dan runs and finds Mac. He quickly explains what happened.

"Daniel, follow me and do as I say," says Mac.

He walks back to the tour bus with Dan in tow. By the time they reach the bus, all of the tourists have boarded including the tour escort. Mac steps up into the bus and waits for Dan to join him. He whispers to him, "Stay here."

Mac faces the back of the bus and then begins to walk slowly—very slowly—up the aisle of the bus. As he walks, he looks left and right into every occupied seat. By the time he reaches the back of the bus, every pair of eyes on the bus is trained on Mac except for the tour escort who has his back turned to the aisle. Mr. Lee's engaged in conversation with an older lady on the tour.

Mac turns to face the front of the bus and practically yells in a booming voice, "Daniel, where's the tour escort who didn't pay us for our services? Please point the escort out to me."

Dan walks up the aisle and stands next to the escort. He extends his right arm and index finger toward Mr. Lee. "This is him."

Mac starts walking toward Dan. The escort now turns and realizes that he's the object of discussion between these two bellmen. The escort looks around and sees that all eyes on the bus are staring at him. The escort's face reddens and he seems to shrink down into his seat.

"Mr. Lee, this young man and three other bellmen carried 40 bags up to the rooms of your tour guests yesterday and carried all of them back this morning and loaded them onto this bus," says Mac. "Do you think that this young man and the other three bellmen should work for free?"

What's Mr. Lee going to say in front of his tour group—who, incidentally, are probably expected to give him a gratuity at the end of their tour? Mr. Lee shakes his head. "Of course not."

Mac isn't finished. "Mr. Lee, do you know that Daniel is in college?"

This seems to come as a revelation to Mr. Lee. "No, I didn't know that."

"Do you know that most of the other bellmen who helped young Daniel here carry 40 bags belonging to you and your tour guests up to your rooms yesterday and back this morning also attend college?"

Mr. Lee's humiliation is reaching new limits. "No, I didn't know that either."

"Mr. Lee, do you know that if these young bellmen don't make enough money this summer, they may have to drop out of college?"

Mr. Lee flinches at the very thought. "No, I didn't."

"Mr. Lee, you don't want any of these fine young men to drop out of college, do you?"

Mr. Lee shakes his head again. "No, of course not."

Mac isn't finished. "Mr. Lee, don't you think that it's only fair that these young men should be compensated for their labor?"

Dan can see that Mr. Lee realizes Mac has trapped him. "Why don't we step off the bus and take care of this little matter," says Mr. Lee.

Mac gestures for Mr. Lee to walk toward the front exit of the bus. They follow him off the bus and step outside. Mr. Lee walks to the rear of the bus so that they're out of sight of his tour group. He opens his briefcase and takes out a money pouch. He counts out $20 in fives and ones and offers it to Mac.

Mac shakes his head and says, "Give the money to Daniel."

Dan accepts the money. Mac looks at him. "Daniel, please count it."

Dan counts the money and looks at him. "20 dollars, Mac."

Mac twists one end of his moustache. "Daniel, I'm not really good with math. How much is that per bag in and out?"

"25 cents per bag in and out."

Mac turns to Mr. Lee. "Do you know how many stairs Daniel and the three other bellmen climbed in order to handle your tour group's luggage?"

Mr. Lee shakes his head.

Mac looks at him and smiles. "I don't know either, but I do know that it required a lot of hard physical work. I also know that every other bell crew who handles your luggage has elevators in their hotels and that they will all charge 35 cents per bag in and out."

Mr. Lee shows no emotion.

Mac looks at him again. "Daniel, how much more does Mr. Lee need to pay you so that we receive 35 cents per bag in and out?"

Dan quickly does the math in his head. "Eight additional dollars."

Mac looks at Mr. Lee. Mr. Lee then reaches into his money pouch and finds an additional eight dollars. He hands the money to Daniel without any further prompting by Mac.

Mac looks Mr. Lee in the eye and grabs his hand to shake it. "Mr. Lee, have a great day."

Mr. Lee turns with a scowl on his face and rejoins his tour group on the bus. Mac and Dan turn and walk together back toward the front doors of the Inn.

"Mac, I thought that you weren't ready to charge 35 cents per bag in and out," says Dan when they finally reach the front doors.

Mac grins at him. "Well, Daniel, things sometimes change in life. This just seemed like the right time."

Bill and Dan are reminiscing about the summer while Dan carefully packs his suitcase for the return trip home.

"Before you arrived at the Inn," says Bill, "did you ever imagine any of the experiences that you've encountered this summer?"

Dan shakes his head. "Not in my wildest imagination."

"Who could have imagined that we'd almost capsize in a small fishing boat in the middle of Yellowstone Lake?"

Dan stops packing long enough to look at his brother. "I believe that you mean we almost died in Yellowstone Lake. Thank you, brother."

Bill shrugs his shoulder. "Or what about the Scenic Boat adventure to Flat Mountain Arm?"

Dan smiles. "Yeah, that was really cool. You weren't there, but sitting at the top of a pine tree in Hayden Valley for a couple of hours while a grizzly bear slept off its bacon hangover is an experience that I'll never forget."

Bill hands him a small pile of tee shirts. "What about soaping No Name Geyser in Fountain Flats? That was an amazing experience, too."

Dan takes the tee shirts and wedges them into his suitcase. "It's probably better that we keep quiet about that little adventure. Oh, what about our little fishing trip with Clive Carter and being detained by the Rangers?"

Bill shakes his head as in disbelief. "I'll never understand why the Rangers ignored us. We were the employees who should have known the rules—not Clive."

"No, like you said, they were just having fun with a well-known national name. They couldn't have cared less about two unknown bellmen from Old Faithful Inn."

Bill stands up and looks out the window. "How about Mr. Baxter's surprise raid on Bats Alley. I didn't believe that any of us would be fired, but it certainly created a lot of anxiety at the time."

Dan stands up and stretches his back. "Again, like our fishing mishap, the focus should've been on us—you know, the bellmen—and not on the gals."

"Dan, they call that crime by association."

Dan picks up some socks and searches for a place to cram them in his suitcase. "I'll never forget my 21ˢᵗ surprise birthday party. By the way, thank you again for throwing the party for me. Who would've ever suspected that the laundry manager would pull a gun on Eagle?"

Bill looks serious for a moment. "The Company did the right thing by firing the laundry manager the next morning. I wonder if that poor Dude from Oklahoma has ever discovered that he's missing a license plate?"

"I'm sure that he has," says Dan. "Maybe Eagle will track him down and return the plate." Both laugh at the thought.

Dan closes the top of his suitcase to see if it can be zipped. "One night that I'll never forget is the night of the Miss Yellowstone pageant. I'm still amazed whenever I think of that night how poised and creative Debbie was that evening. She deserved to win the title without question."

"Have you forgotten about what happened after the pageant?" Bill asks teasingly.

Dan looks at him. "Of course not, but that's something neither of us should ever discuss with anyone else."

Dan walks over and picks up his electric popcorn popper. "Bill, I can't take this on the airplane with me. Can you use this at law school this year?"

Bill looks at the popper for a moment. "Since I'm driving to school, I'll have room for it. Why not? Maybe I'll need to find a kernel of truth occasionally in my studies."

Dan smiles. "Ha, ha."

"What about the Bellmen's Banquet at the Crazy 8 Dude Ranch?" Bill asks. "I thought that the Belly Awards were hilarious this summer."

Bill then becomes serious. "What do you think is the most important thing that happened to you this summer?"

Dan ponders the question for a moment. "It's difficult to answer that question. I can't in my mind prioritize or even separate everything that's happened to me. I love the people who work with us. The Savages come from all over the United States from so many different backgrounds and have so many unique personalities. I love the Inn with its grandeur and history. I love our work as bellmen and the traditions that have been passed down from generation-to-generation of bellmen. I love all of the beauty of Yellowstone National Park and all of its diversity—wildlife, lakes, rivers, waterfalls, canyons and, of course, all of the thermal features. Being able to live and work for three months in Yellowstone National Park has been such a unique, thrilling experience."

Bill looks at his brother. Dan notices that his eyes seem misty.

"What?" Dan says.

Bill glances down for a moment and then looks at him. "Dan, I'm proud of you."

"Why?"

"Look at yourself," says Bill. "You're a different person from the brother who greeted me when I arrived early in the summer."

Dan shakes his head. "No, I don't think so."

Bill shakes his head. "No, you are, Dan. Think about it. You have experienced so many new things this summer and met so many people. That includes the Savages we work with and the Dudes who pass through the Inn. You have learned to deal with difficult people like the Dude with the carpet bag who gave you a dime tip or the tour escort this morning who tried to stiff the Bell Crew."

Dan walks to the sink and washes his hands as Bill continues, "And then there are all the religious issues from our past that have challenged you."

Dan starts to speak, but Bill holds up a hand to stop him and says, "Think about it. We were raised in a loving family deeply rooted in a conservative evangelical church. Our father teaches Bible to ministerial students at one of our church's colleges. Our church and college communities were synonymous. We attended public schools and participated in scholastic and athletic activities there, but our social activities always centered around the church."

Dan nods his head in agreement as Bill continues. "Our parents didn't enforce church practices strictly, but we grew up with all of the 'Don't Rules' as you like to call them. No one in our church community danced. No one consumed alcohol. No one used profanity. We couldn't go to movies like other kids. Our parents didn't even wear wedding rings only because they feared disapproval from their church friends and college colleagues. Conversely, no one from our school community attended as many weekly religious activities as we did. Growing up, we had some type of church event four to five times a week."

Bill pauses for moment and a crease appears across his forehead as he thinks. "Our parents loved us and provided a wonderful home for us. But many people would consider our upbringing as being abnormal and too restrictive."

"Yeah, I know," says Dan.

"Dan, this is the first time in your life that you've really been able to get away from the religious environment that permeated every aspect of our lives growing up. I know that this summer hasn't always been easy for you, but you've been challenged to examine many of the customs and practices of our childhood. You've had the opportunity to be around other individuals our age and observe them. Some dance. Some consume alcohol. Some smoke. Some use profanity. Some are sexually active. But, as I think you now realize, they're still good, decent people."

Dan nods his head. "You're right. The people I've met in Yellowstone do have different practices and customs than what I've always been taught, but they're all really good individuals."

Bill smiles at him. "I'm proud of you, Dan, because you've been challenged this summer to look at life differently and decide for yourself what's really important. I'm proud that you've had the courage to try new things."

Dan sits down on his bed. Bill sits next to him. They sit together in silence for a few minutes.

Bill finally looks at him and grins. "If I had to sum up your summer, I'd say that you came of age in Yellowstone National Park during your twenty-first summer."

Both laugh at Bill's sage observation.

That night, Dan lies in bed thinking about Bill's statement that he came of age in Yellowstone National Park during his twenty-first summer. He knows that the phrase 'coming of age' can for some mean attaining one's twenty-first birthday, but he understands that the phrase can encompass so much more than simply reaching a certain age. Although he's only spent three months working in the Park, Dan knows that the things that he's learned and experienced this summer have truly changed his life. He feels that his world has greatly expanded. He no longer accepts many of the customs, practices and beliefs which were so important to him when he arrived in Yellowstone National Park. He knows that when he leaves Yellowstone in the morning, he will return home as a different person. Home will not have changed, but he definitely has. Dan feels a wave of anxiety course through his body because he doesn't know if, or how, he'll fit into his old life.

Sleep comes slowly on his last night in Yellowstone National Park.

Dan stands under the portico at the front of Old Faithful Inn waiting to board the Yellowstone Park Company bus to return home. He's chatting with Bill and Lou when they hear a familiar voice.

"Dan, wait for us to say good-bye."

They turn and see Mary Ann and Debbie walking out of the red double front doors of Old Faithful Inn. Mary Ann's carrying something that's covered in wrapping paper and tied with a ribbon. Debbie comes over and gives Dan a big embrace.

"Dan, we're all going to miss you so much," says Debbie. He feels Debbie squeeze him more tightly and then she releases her embrace and steps back.

Mary Ann walks over and hugs Dan with her free arm. She steps back and gives him the package that's she's holding in her hand.

"This is a little present from the Fabulous Five for your trip home."

"Go ahead and open it," says Debbie.

Dan tears off the paper and discovers a bag of Oreo cookies.

Dan smiles. "I can't think of a better parting gift. Thank you both and thanks to all of the Fabulous Five. You'll always be fabulous in my mind."

Dan hears the bus driver yell, "Last call. This bus will depart in two minutes."

Dan quickly hugs all of them. Tears are rolling down Mary Ann's and Debbie's cheeks. He turns so they can't see the tears that have formed in his own eyes. He walks toward the door of the Yellowstone Park Company bus. Dan pauses at the foot of the steps to take one last look at Old Faithful Inn before boarding the bus.

Dan then steps up into the bus to start his return home. He walks up the aisle of the bus and takes a seat with a window facing the Inn. As the bus pulls away from the portico of Old Faithful Inn, Bill, Lou, Mary Ann and Debbie all wave good-bye to him. Dan watches as Old Faithful Inn disappears from sight and thinks to himself that Bill was right—I truly came of age this summer in Yellowstone National Park in every sense of that phrase.

Dan leaves Yellowstone National Park with a big smile on his face.

EPILOGUE

Dan sits alone on a bench located on the portico porch of Old Faithful Inn facing Old Faithful Geyser. As always happens when in Yellowstone National Park, all of his senses seem alive and sparking on all cylinders. Dan sees the tiny wisp of hot steam drift slowly from the mouth of Old Faithful Geyser into the ever-lightening sky. He feels the crispness of the early morning chill on his unprotected neck. He hears the caw-cawing and flapping of wings as a raven flies close to the Inn in search of breakfast. He smells the scent of pine from the lodgepole pine trees that surround Old Faithful Inn. He tastes the bitterness of the black coffee that kitchen staff leave outside the dining room's door for early risers.

More than five decades have passed since Dan Johnson first arrived at the doorstep of Old Faithful Inn and stepped from the yellow Yellowstone Park Company bus to view the grandeur of the Inn. As with all people, much has happened in the intervening time. Dan completed college and then obtained his law degree. He practiced law for 40 years before retiring. He was happily married for over 25 years before his wife died suddenly. Dan remarried and is now as happily married as he was in his first marriage. He and his first wife raised two children who are now well into adulthood and have families of their own. He has permanently said good-bye to countless relatives and friends and has welcomed countless new relatives and friends into this world. As one might say, Dan has experienced many, many transitions over the past five decades.

However, he reflects that there have been two of constants in his life: his Yellowstone family and his love of Yellowstone National Park itself. After his initial summer at Old Faithful Inn, Dan returned for three more summers to work on the OFI Bell Crew. In those four summers, he and other Savages forged friendships that have lasted a lifetime. About 15 years after his first summer in the Park, a group of former Savages from Old Faithful Inn decided to hold a reunion at the Inn. The reunion was so successful that the group determined to meet at the Inn tri-annually. As the group aged and some members passed, the group decided they should meet bi-annually. Dan and his family have been attending these Yellowstone reunions for over 35 years. He likes to joke that his children believe that the Yellowstone reunions are a birthright. Now his grandchildren attend with their parents. As with bellmen traditions passed down from generation-to-generation, so are the reunion traditions being passed from generation-to-generation. Dan and his family are visiting Old Faithful Inn yet again in connection with such a reunion.

As he sits alone in the early morning stillness, Dan suddenly senses another presence. He looks to his right and sees his five year-old granddaughter Allison standing patiently next to him.

"Oh, good morning, Allison. Does your mother know that you're here?"

Allison nods her head. "Yes, Grandpa. Mommy thought that you'd be here. When she found you, she told me to join you. She went back to our room to finish getting ready."

Dan smiles and pats the bench next to him. Allison accepts the invitation and sits down on the bench very close to her Grandpa. The two sit in silence watching Old Faithful Geyser until Allison looks up at him.

"Grandpa, did you really work here once?"

Dan nods his head. "Yes, sweetie, I worked here a long, long time ago."

Allison is swinging her legs since her feet don't reach the ground. "Did you like working here?"

Dan pauses for a moment and looks down at Allison. "Yes, I loved working here. Old Faithful Inn, Yellowstone National Park and the people who worked with me changed my life forever. Perhaps someday you'll work here too and let Yellowstone National Park work its wonders on you."

Allison slips her small hand into his hand. Dan squeezes her hand softly.

At that moment, both hear the whoosh of boiling water and steam as Old Faithful erupts yet one more time.

Grandfather and granddaughter sit side-by-side holding hands as they silently watch the Grand Old Lady provide another dazzling show. As he watches the show, Dan thinks to himself that I came of age that first summer in Yellowstone National Park, but the magic of Yellowstone National Park has never stopped for me and never will.

Connection—an essential of life. Such is Old Faithful Inn and Yellowstone National Park for Dan Johnson. A connection that will remain for the rest of his happy life.

APPENDIX

1. Much of Yellowstone was formed as a result of volcanic activity over the last two million years. The Yellowstone Caldera is the largest volcanic system in North America. The magna chamber that lies under Yellowstone was created by a cataclysmic eruption which occurred 640,000 years ago. It is estimated that 240 cubic miles of ash, rock and pryroclastic materials were released into the air at that time. The magna chamber under Yellowstone is estimated to be a single connected chamber approximately 37 miles long, 18 miles wide and 3 to 7 miles deep.

As a result of this ongoing evolution, Yellowstone National Park contains at least 10,000 thermal features-geysers, fumaroles, hot springs and mudpots. The Upper Geyer Basin contains most of the more famous geysers including Old Faithful Geyser (unquestionably the most famous geyser in the world), Castle Geyser, Beehive Geyser, Grand Geyser (the world's tallest predictable geyser), Giant Geyser (the world's most voluminous geyser) and Riverside Geyser (located along the Firehole River). Norris Geyser Basin is located approximately 30 miles north of Old Faithful Inn. Norris Geyser Basin contains many thermal features including Steamboat Geyser (the tallest active geyser in the world).

2. Nez Perce Creek is named after the Nez Perce Native American tribe which was fleeing the U.S. Cavalry and passed through Yellowstone National Park between August 20 and September 7, 1877. The tribe actually camped for a couple of days along a stream that was later named Nez Perce Creek. The creek flows into the Fountain Flats area and crosses under a bridge located about 9 or 10 miles north of the Old Faithful area on the road to Madison Junction.

3. Hayden Valley is a high-altitude plateau approximately 7 miles in length and 7 miles wide. The valley was covered in ice about 13,000 years ago which blocked the waters of the Yellowstone River. As a result of the ice blockage, the area filled with fine-grained lake sediments which included clay. When the blockage broke, the sediments left behind created a relatively impermeable layer making it difficult for water to reach far into the ground. As a result, Hayden Valley contains abundant grasses and chapparal, but trees are sparse in the valley and instead grow starting near the ridge lines of the hills on both the north and south sides of the valley.

Hayden Valley was named after Ferdinand V. Hayden. Hayden was a geologist and the leader of the 1871 Geological Survey which led to the Congressional enactment of Yellowstone National Park on March 1, 1872. In the early 1970s, Hayden Valley was known for its spectacular vistas and its abundant wildlife. The Yellowstone River flows north on the east side of the road between the Lake and Canyon Village areas of the Park; the west side of the road consists mostly of the vast treeless valley with Alum Creek flowing down the middle of the valley before its joinder with the Yellowstone River. Bison (more popularly known as buffalo), elk, pronghorn antelope and deer are frequently seen grazing- sometimes alone or in large herds. Waterfowl including ducks, Canadian geese, pelicans and trumpeter swans are common sights. But the most popular, and most feared, inhabitant of Hayden Valley is the grizzly bear.

Yellowstone has two types of bears-black bears and grizzly bears. The grizzly bear is scientifically known as "Ursus arctos horribilis." Black bears are more commonly viewed by tourists; grizzly bears are more elusive but widely feared by people. A grizzly bear has a large muscle mass on its shoulders and a concave face. A male grizzly can weigh as much as 700 pounds. The grizzly bear is often up to two times the size of a black bear. A grizzly can run up to 35 mph. Most people believe grizzlies can't climb trees, but this is a myth. Some grizzles can climb trees, but most don't because the claws on their massive paws are curved and can be as long as 5.5 inches long. Grizzlies are unpredictable and can be extremely aggressive. Without question, grizzlies are at the very top of the food chain in Yellowstone National Park.

Between 1959 and 1971, two brothers, John and Frank Craighead, spent twelve years conducting scientific studies of grizzly bears and, particularly, grizzlies in Hayden Valley. By the early 1970s, the Craigheads had concluded from their research that the most concentrated population of grizzly bears in the entire continental United States was in Hayden Valley and its immediate surrounding areas.

ACKNOWLEDGEMENTS

I want to express my appreciation and thanks to Val Agnew, Al Chambard, my brother Cliff Huffman, my cousin Dr. James Huffman, Brock Ladewig and Michael and Shauna Olds for their contributions to this book. From the bottom of my heart, thank each of you for the time, encouragement and insights that you shared with me.

I also want to thank Bill Gladstone, Josh Freel and Waterside Productions for their assistance in getting this book published. Thank you for making the book a reality.

ABOUT THE AUTHOR

David M. Huffman grew up in a loving, conservative family in Indiana. While in college and law school, he worked six summers in Yellowstone National Park; five of them as a bellman at Old Faithful Inn. If asked to describe those summers in one word, his response would be 'magical.' From the mystique of working at historic Old Faithful Inn to exploring the majestic beauty and unique natural features of Yellowstone with his fellow Savages and the lasting friendships that developed among them, he truly experienced six life changing summers while working in Yellowstone National Park.

David settled in the San Diego area when he started law school and remained to practice family law for 42 years before retiring in 2018. He currently lives in San Diego with his wife and their dachshund Poppy. He has two adult children.

In the past decade, David served as a Trustee for five and a half years on the Board of the Cabrillo National Monument Foundation. Cabrillo National Monument is the only national monument or Park administered by the National Park Service in San Diego County.

Made in the USA
Columbia, SC
26 September 2022

67902286R00157